Other Avon Books by
Johnny Quarles

FOOL'S GOLD

NO O
MAN'S
LAND

JOHNNY
QUARLES

AVON BOOKS ◆ NEW YORK

NO MAN'S LAND is an original publication of Avon Books. This work has never before appeared in book form. This work is a novel. Any similarity to actual persons or events is purely coincidental.

AVON BOOKS
A division of
The Hearst Corporation
1350 Avenue of the Americas
New York, New York 10019

Copyright © 1993 by Johnny Quarles
Published by arrangement with the author
Library of Congress Catalog Card Number: 93-90322
ISBN: 0-380-76814-3

First Avon Books Printing: October 1993

AVON TRADEMARK REG. U.S. PAT. OFF. AND IN OTHER COUNTRIES, MARCA REGISTRADA, HECHO EN U.S.A.

Printed in the U.S.A.

RA   10   9   8   7   6   5   4   3   2   1

Dedication

First, I want to thank God for any abilities I might have. Thanks also to my wife, Wendy, who is my main reason for writing. To Kay Dodrill, who came to my rescue and typed the last half of *No Man's Land*. To my editor, Tom Colgan and his honcho, Bob Mecoy, and all the rest at Avon Books who had faith in this book.

The inspiration for *No Man's Land* came from Frances White, who gave me the spark of an idea when she wrote me a letter about her late husband, Charles, who had been a friend of mine. Thank you, Frances. Another inspiration came from the fact that I live in northwest Oklahoma, in the heart of the Cherokee Strip.

In past books, I have mentioned that I enjoy recognizing people who have been kind to me along life's pathways. More of those good folks are:

Herb and Kaye Mann, Ray Schoonover, Dr. Leland Steffen, Butch Moorman, Mary Smith, J. B. Quarles and Jenny, Chet Maddox, Lonnie Killman, A. J. Shorter, Joni Smith, Carl Hendley, Blaine Reed, Ron and Sharon Lancaster, Steve Holt, Vern "Jelly" Butler, Brad Gungoll, Stan Stoner, Dick Wood, Lou Phillips, Keith Tebow, Dale Holt, Larry Rash, Herb Rash, Austin Johnson, Joe Daniel, Lester and Violet Krenz, Harold and Esther Talley, Lloyd Lanning, Jerry Riley, David Crist, Wayne and Jamie LaMunyon, Dr. Charles Ogle, Jean Harrington, H. T. and Edna Mae Holden, K. P., Rick and Larry Simpson, Jerry Hermanski, Donald Quarles, Bert Chambers, Charlie Sharpe, Odell Fair, Mark Jones, Mel Spencer, Mary Lou Mannschreck, F. L. "Drag" Thurman, Fern Johnson, Lonna Harmon, Lori Dayton, Clayton Nolan, Bill Wampler, Jim Jorden, Travis and Jackie Harris, Kenny Harrison, Jetty Crist, Don Chambers, Cecil McCurdy, Alan and Cathy Stroup, Earl Dennett, Dwight Buckles, Harold Powell, Todd Smith, Perry Hildebrandt, Bill Storm, Bruce Thomas, Leo Eastman, Barbara and Carl Dieterle, Pat Novak, Beverly Gaede, Carol Barney, Bill and Caroline Grimes, Ronnie Dow, Stan Harris, Norman and Belva Lamb, Ray Lamle, Robert DuPree, Pearl Miller, Bill Rude, Loren Avery, Jim Spencer, John Ingram, Benny

Moore, Jon Stieglitz, Robert Wentz, Court Newkirk, Hawk Quarles, Bob Isaac, Pat Maly, Tom Baker, Claudie Poole, Janice Hermanski, Ken and Wilma Clubb, Ray Miller, Tom Sworney, Nelson Perkins, Rick and Pam Steelhammer, Mike Andrews, Eddie Fischer, Bob Hoemann, Clarence Miller, Jim and Betty Goodness, Suzie Hinkle, Don Wolf, Richard Dow, Lori Kirtley, Brad George, Randall Powell, Sonny Johnson, Todd Heaps, Tom Cahill, Skip Wilson, Ray Varney, Pat Griffin, Terry Watters, Cheryl Walker, Jim Nay, Bruce Hobgood, Bob Cleland, Gary Jones, Pat Wrynn, Stan Dixon, Roy Head, Phil Kennedy, Bud McGinnis, Junior Shelton, Jim Kirkland, and a man who has given me so much pleasure with his music, Merle Haggard.

More writers that I admire: Kathryn McNutt, Jim Adair, Marvin Banta, Maxine Austin, Terry C. Johnston, Bill Edson, Pauline Omart, Mary Barnes, Celeste Meyer, Marjorie Pendleton, Candace Krebs, William Bernhardt, Vonda Ruth, Irene Scott, Ruth Scott, Mary Seitz, Don Graham, Jackie Black, Cleta Cray, Kathryn Jenson, Carol Finch, Don Coldsmith, Wilda Walker, Ruth Young, Tracye White, Ginger Hitt, Shannon Wright, Pat Warfield, Marian Collier, Deborah Camp, Earl Mabry, Diana Guilbault, Margi Springer, Judy Winchester, Debbie Waken, Terry Lewis, Donna Ita, Linda Burton, Marilyn Kennedy, Lori Taylor, George Geuder, Bobbie Cole, Peggy Morse, Nelda Jo Beebe, Sandy McKinnon, Cathy Spaulding, Pam Bickerstaff, Betty Tuohy, RosaLea Glaser, Virginia Greer, Tom Clark, Phil Brown, Roger Freeman, Betty Schultz, Areline Bolerjack, Willa Hughes, Robert Conley, Dottie Britton, Daisy Jean Suit, Shawn Tuohy, Paul Southwick, Norma Montoya, Leon and Marsha James, Jo Ann Phillips, Pat Swanner, Karen Bode, Leah Gungoll, Cameron Judd, June Park, and Jack Bickham.

When I was a boy, I dreamed of being either a truck driver or a cowboy. I admired both so much. Today, whenever I pass a horse corral or attend a rodeo or smell a barnyard, those dreams again crowd my thoughts. Driving down the highways at night, I like to hook up with the 18-wheelers. I get a sense of that youthful excitement that seems to wane in one's adulthood. I would like to dedicate *No Man's Land* to those heroes of mine, the truckers and cowboys.

1

IT WAS A BITTER, COLD DAY IN THE ARKANSAS RIVER
town of Fort Smith. Though it was still early afternoon, the sky was so gray, it seemed closer to
sundown. Snowflakes, so tiny they lacked the weight
to fall straight, swirled aimlessly through the air.

The small cabin that stood at the edge of town was
little more than a shanty, leaning to one side. A log had
been wedged against it to help hold it up. A thin column
of smoke drifted upward from the chimney. The cabin's
only luxury was the one glass-paned window. The other
window had been boarded over for years.

Inside, Alma White glanced up from her mother's
bedside at the dying embers in the fireplace. "Git some
more firewood, Toby Ray," she said to her little brother.

Toby Ray White, who at eight years was exactly half
the age of his sister, hung back next to the stairs that led
to the cabin's tiny sleeping loft. His eyes grew wide as
he shook his head. "I ain't gonna leave Mama," he said
stubbornly.

Alma White bit her bottom lip and gave her brother
a menacing look. Her instincts were to get instantly
furious over what she considered Toby Ray's insub-
ordination. But, as she returned the determined stare,
she couldn't help but notice the fright that clouded his
sky-blue eyes. Toby Ray's eyes were the window to his

1

soul; he couldn't have hidden his true feelings if he'd wanted to. Alma let out a sigh and got up from the edge of her mother's bed. "Come here, hon, and hold Mama's hand. I'll git the firewood."

The boy looked relieved but said nothing. Alma let her hand touch his shoulder briefly as he sat down on the patched coverlet on the bed and reached for the limp hand. Before she left, she took her handkerchief and gently wiped away the beads of sweat that covered their mother's forehead. The cabin was so drafty that the fireplace couldn't begin to fight off the winter cold, even when it was filled with wood. Lydia White, though, was so sick with the fever that she was sweating, anyway.

As soon as Alma was out of the way, Toby Ray eased himself up next to his mother and encased her hot hand between both of his. Lydia's eyes fluttered once, but she barely seemed to notice that he was there, and this brought an even bigger look of worry to his young face.

Alma, who was wrapping a woolen scarf around her neck, noticed and said softly, "Don't worry, now. Mama will be all right. I promise."

As cold as it was inside, the freezing air outside cut through to the bone. Alma clutched her coat and pulled it around herself like she was cradling a baby as she hurried to the wood pile. She reached for a good-sized piece of kindling, and as she did a jagged edge ripped into her finger. She cried out, dropping the wood, and stuck the finger in her mouth. Tears suddenly appeared and ran down her cheeks. Her shoulders began to shake uncontrollably as she began to bawl. She bit hard on her knuckle, letting the saliva roll from the corners of her mouth.

The finger hurt, but Alma was a tough sort—nearly as tough as any of the rowdy Fort Smith boys of her age. Still, she cried, but not because of some little finger cut. Alma was crying for her mother. Lydia had been sick for months, getting steadily worse, and now she had reached the point where she couldn't rise from her bed. The fever had set in, then the rattly cough. On top of everything else, her mind seemed to come and go. This scared Toby Ray as much as it caused him grief, never knowing when his own mama would know who he was. As for herself, Alma had, up until now, kept her fears and hurts inside. Now, it was as if some huge gush of raging waters had ripped open the walls of a dam. Her grief came spilling out, and though she tried to control it, she couldn't stop the racking sobs. In fact, the more she tried to get a hold of herself, the harder she cried. She stood there, shivering in the cold, holding her coat with one hand and slobbering on the finger of the other.

Finally, her strength gave out. Alma fell on top of the wood pile and hugged a frozen chunk of firewood next to her bosom. She tried to say "Mama," but all she could manage was a shaky breath that caught in her throat and made her gasp. The finger forgotten, she cried some more.

She would have lain there for a long time in the bitter cold, holding onto the frozen wood, if Toby Ray hadn't called out to her from the door of the cabin.

"Alma! Come quick! Please, Alma! Hurry! Mama is askin' for ya!" he called, his small voice rising to an excited yelp.

Alma rose and ran to the cabin. Stepping inside, she absently rubbed the front of her tattered dress as she turned toward her mother's bed. Her eyes opened wide as a chill ran over her body.

In the dim light, there appeared to be a white haze drifting over the bed. Lydia's eyes, which had become dull and clouded with sickness, were now open wide, searching.

"Alma, honey."

The voice came to Alma softly and full of peace. "Alma, come close. Let me see you."

Alma crossed the tiny room on trembling legs, praying they wouldn't fail her and let her fall.

"I'm here, Mama," she said, gently taking her mother's hand in her own.

Lydia's voice sounded young again. She said, "You take care of Toby Ray. See he eats right while I'm gone."

She managed a small smile and tried to squeeze Alma's hand tighter.

Alma glanced at Toby Ray. He was standing erect near the bed, barely breathing. His face was frozen in pure fear. "Don't go, Mama!" he managed to say in a hoarse whisper. "Alma, tell Mama not to go. Tell her we need her here!" His eyes fell pleading on his sister's face.

Alma wanted to tend to her own hurt, but such self-ishness had to be put away for the sake of Toby Ray. She sniffed hard and put on her bravest smile. "Everything is gonna be all right, hon," she said firmly. "Mama ain't goin' nowhere. She just wants me to take care of you while she's ailin'. That's all." She turned back to Lydia, still holding her hand and feeling completely helpless.

Toby Ray moved closer to the bed. "B-but, she said whilst she's gone!" he persisted, close to tears. "Where you goin', Mama?"

The sick woman pulled her hand away from Alma's and touched Toby Ray on the cheek. "I'm goin' on a long journey with Him," she murmured.

Toby Ray's eyes nearly bulged from their sockets. "With who, Mama?" he said, his bottom lip trembling even more.

"With Him," Lydia said. She stared up toward the ceiling, and her face lit into a dreamy smile. She looked beautiful again, just as she'd looked when she was well. "Look!" she said. "He's motioning for me! It will be a grand place I'll go!"

Both Alma and Toby Ray followed her glance up at the ceiling. The smoky haze still had not lifted. It seemed to hover right over them. Alma wondered if Toby Ray could see it, too.

"Who's him?" Toby Ray asked again in a quivery voice. He was doing his best to hold back the tears.

His mother just smiled and touched his cheek again. "Go git Papa for me," she said.

The words hit Toby Ray like a bolt of lightning. The tears would not be held back any longer as he grabbed for Alma and hugged her and wept, "D-don't say that, Mama! P-please d-don't say that!"

Alma held her brother tightly and squeezed her eyes shut. She, too, was gripped somewhere between sorrow and fear at the mention of their father. Come May thirteenth, it would be two years since their papa had drowned. He'd been seen, down by the river, a bottle of whiskey in his hands. But he had never made it back home. They'd never found his body. Now, their mama was asking for him, and Alma, too, was startled by such a strange request.

"Please, Toby Ray!" the soft voice repeated. "Go git Papa. I need to talk with him."

Alma pulled herself free of Toby Ray's grasp and kissed the top of his head. She whispered, "Go fetch Doc Thurman."

Toby Ray encased her in his arms again and buried his face into her side. He shook his head and mumbled, "No. I ain't gonna leave Mama."

Alma walked her brother to the door, pried his arms loose and took him by the shoulders. Looking straight into his eyes, she said, "Look, Toby Ray. Mama is bad sick. I—" She turned her head and saw her mother staring up at the ceiling. "—I don't think she's gonna make it much longer."

Toby Ray made a move toward the bed, but Alma held him back and shook him. "Let's don't fight! Not now! If you want to help Mama, then run and git Doc Thurman!" she urged him.

The young boy yanked hard on a strand of his white-blond hair. His unusually fair skin had turned white as a sheet. "I'm—" he began, struggling with the word that he had never allowed through his lips. He balled his hand into a fist and growled.

"I know, Toby Ray," Alma said soothingly. "I'm scared, too." She pulled him to her bosom and a single tear rolled down her right cheek. "It's okay. Now, be a good boy and go fetch the doctor. Tell him Mama's got worse."

Toby Ray gave his mother one final look before he let Alma help him with his coat. Then he stomped his foot and hurried out the cabin door.

2

OUTSIDE, TOBY RAY PAID NO MIND TO THE COLD as he willed his legs to carry him faster into the business district of town. He was so caught up with worry about his mother, he scarcely noticed the mongrel dog, Tick, at his feet. Tick was his constant companion, and under normal circumstances, Toby Ray would have been hollering encouragement to the dog to follow along.

He ran hard, the cold air blistering his face a deep red. Tick was running joyfully beside, wagging his tail and barking in delight at this wonderful treat. Several people stopped to stare at the sight of the two, but not because of any commotion they were causing. It was the horrified expression that was carried on the young boy's face.

Toby Ray ran past the sheriff's office and the Franklin Hotel, then crossed the street to Doc Thurman's office. He didn't bother to knock, but burst right on in. He stood there, panting. The office was empty, but through the window he could see the doctor, standing out back next to a big gelding. Horses were Doc Thurman's passion in life, and he owned several. Right now, he was holding the horse's reins, talking to someone who was out of the window's view.

Toby Ray rushed for the back door, knocking over a broom and nearly tripping over it. Tick followed him

6

outside, and immediately began barking furiously at the horse. The big white gelding had reddish-brown spots that looked like freckles around his shoulders. He lowered his nose to see what was causing all the commotion, but was not impressed at what he saw.

"Shut up!" Toby Ray growled, giving Tick a kick in the ribs. He turned to speak and noticed the tall Negro man who was looking the horse over. Normally, the sight of a colored man would have stirred Toby Ray's curiosity, but not today. He stepped up to Doc Thurman.

"Come quick! Mama's bad sick!" he said.

"Not now, Toby Ray!" Doc Thurman said angrily. "Can't you see I'm busy? Wait inside!" He waved his hand toward his office and turned back to the Negro. "Three hundred dollars, and that's a bargain," he said firmly.

The Negro shook his head doubtfully. "Ain't no damned horse flesh worth no three hundred," he said. "I passed by some horses in Texas that was just as good a-lookin' for a hundred."

Toby Ray's eyes shot to the tall Negro. He had never heard such insolence before. He studied the man, who was dressed like a cowboy. Sticking out from his coat, hanging low on his hip, was a Colt with a well-worn handle. The man walked, holding himself erect, around the horse. There was a hard look about him. Toby Ray stood for a second or two with his mouth open, staring disbelievingly.

The big Negro's manner also seemed to have an effect on Doc Thurman, who was pretty much an indignant sort himself. He stood there, holding the reins, while his eyes followed the Negro around the gelding.

"I'll give ya a hundred fifty," the Negro said matter-of-factly.

Doc Thurman rubbed his chin. "I'll split the difference. Two fifty."

The Negro's eyes narrowed, and there was a pause. Toby Ray's mind turned back to a more urgent matter. He broke in. "Please, Doc! Please come now! Mama's— Mama's—She's a-dyin', I tell ya!"

"I warned you, Toby Ray! Now you git inside, before I brush your britches with my boot!" Doc Thurman said impatiently.

The big Negro looked at Toby Ray without much expression. His words, however, were serious and measured when he said, "This here lad says his mama's sick. You go see about her." With that, he turned and climbed atop the saddle of his brown mare.

"Where you goin'?" Doc Thurman frowned.

"Goin' back to Texas to buy me a hundred-dollar horse."

"Doggone your hide, Toby Ray!" Doc Thurman exploded at the boy, his face crimson. "See what you done? Look here! You're mama's gonna die, whether I come now, or fifteen minutes from now!"

He started for Toby Ray, but the big Negro pulled his horse between Doc Thurman and the boy. His voice was calm and low as he said, "Look. The boy said his mama's sick. You leave him be. You understand? Now, I'll give you two hundred for that horse. Take it or leave it."

Doc Thurman stepped back out of the mare's way, still holding the reins to the gelding. He breathed in angrily. "You just bought yourself a horse, boy. But first, I wanna see the color of your money."

The big Negro pulled out a pouch and counted out ten twenty-dollar gold pieces. He tossed them at Doc Thurman's feet. "I'll be back in an hour to git my horse," he said. "That'll give you time to see about the boy's mama and write me out a bill o' sale. The name's Larkes Dixon."

Before Doc Thurman could pick up the money, Larkes Dixon reined his horse, which moved so close the doctor had to hurry to get out of its way. Larkes Dixon's dark eyes flickered briefly over them, then he rode away.

Making sure Larkes Dixon was still in earshot, Doc Thurman said in a loud voice, "I don't know what the world's comin' to, when derned niggers can go 'round actin' like white folks! And you, Toby Ray! I oughta put a boot to your backside!"

Anger welled up inside Toby Ray. He picked up a rock and bounced it hard off Doc Thurman's shoulder. "If my mama dies, I'll find a gun and kill you!" he shouted, close to tears. With that, he took off at a run for the cabin, with Tick wagging and barking beside him.

Shocked, Doc Thurman hollered, "Dern your hide, Toby Ray!" He touched his shoulder. "Dern niggers and kids! Ain't no blamed manners left in the world!" Still rubbing his shoulder, he went inside to retrieve his bag.

At the cabin, Toby Ray and Doc Thurman found the situation the same as the boy had left it. Lydia White was still mumbling and staring up at the ceiling. Doc Thurman put his hand on her head, then listened to her heart. He looked around at the sparsely furnished cabin. "Got any coffee?"

"Yes, sir," Alma said. "I'll fetch ya a cup."

"While you're at it, why don't you fetch me some money? You know, you ain't paid me a cent, since your mother got sick," the doctor said crossly.

"I know, and I'm sorry," Alma said, barely above a whisper. "We just don't have any money." She was embarrassed. Her hand shook as she handed the cup to him. Coffee spilled over the edge.

Doc Thurman looked annoyed and pulled out his handkerchief to dry his hand. "What're you young'ns gonna do? Your uncle Ted Lackey said he'd take you in, Alma, but I don't know 'bout Toby Ray. I'll write a letter to my sister in Kansas City. See if maybe she can find someone up there who might take 'im in."

"Do we have to talk about this right now?" Alma asked, her voice cracking.

Doc Thurman stuck out a scolding finger. "Don't back talk me, Alma White. You all get that foolishness from your ol' daddy. 'Sides that, you gotta think o' those things. It's clear Lydia ain't got much time. I'd say she won't make it through the day."

Toby Ray screamed. "Don't you talk 'bout my papa and mama that way!" He let loose with both fists, causing Doc Thurman to drop his coffee. He grabbed Toby

Ray by his shirt, holding him at bay, then slapped him hard across the face.

"Why, you little heathen bastard! What you need is a good strap, and I'm fixin' to give it to ya!" With his free hand, the doctor tried to undo his belt, when one of Toby Ray's small fists caught him squarely in the nose.

Doc Thurman cried out in pain. He let go of Toby Ray and cupped his hands over his face.

"Now, that's enough!" Alma said bitterly. She grabbed Toby Ray and pushed him away. "You git upstairs right now, Toby Ray. I'll deal with you later." She turned back to Doc Thurman. "I should rightfully apologize for Toby Ray," she said stiffly, "but in this case, you oughta be the one to apologize to us."

Doc Thurman shook his head and wiped the blood from his nose. "You just keep that derned heathen away from me." He picked up his cup. "Give me some more coffee," he said. "And if I'm gonna have to help wait this thing out, get me that rockin' chair to sit in."

The room fell silent. Doc Thurman rocked, while Alma sat perched on Lydia's bed, watching her mother's pale form. It wasn't long, maybe fifteen minutes, when Lydia's eyes found Alma and she smiled. "See the beautiful light, honey?" she said. "I must go with Him, you know." Her eyes closed.

Alma's breath caught, and her hand flew to her mouth. "Mama! Please, Mama!" Tears filled her eyes.

Doc Thurman stepped close and took Lydia's pulse. He shook her by the shoulder. "Lydia! Oh, Lydia!"

Suddenly, Lydia took a deep breath, then another.

Doc Thurman stepped back from the bed and said to Alma, "She's goin' through the dyin' process. Could be minutes, or she could go on like this for a day or two. But, it's my guess that she won't last long. Now, you may not believe this, but I'm sorry, Alma."

"You're right. I don't," Alma said.

Doc Thurman shrugged and reached for his bag. "Somethin's gotta be done with you young'ns. I'll write that letter to my sis. What about your Uncle Ted?"

Alma threw back her head and looked the doctor coldly in the eye. "We don't need your help," she stated. "Toby Ray and I are gonna stay together, and that's that."

"Suit yourself, but someone's surely gonna come in and take you young'n. I was just tryin' to make things easier on ya," the doctor said.

"I'm obliged to ya for your doctorin', but I must ask you to leave my house. Now," Alma said.

Once Doc Thurman was gone, Toby Ray came bounding down the steps. He ran past Alma and over to his mother's bedside. Her breathing was coming in gasps—four or five at a time, between long, breathless pauses.

Toby Ray crawled up next to his mother and stayed there through the evening, clutching her tightly. Alma tried, but couldn't budge him from the spot, even when she offered soup made of rice, a small piece of pork and corn bread for supper. Toby Ray paid her no mind. He cried silently, until he couldn't cry any more. The hurt he was feeling was more than he could understand.

In time, Toby Ray fell asleep, still holding onto his mother. Alma sat in the rocker next to the bed. She felt tired—bone-tired, but sleep would have been impossible. At least, she thought, Toby Ray was getting some rest.

Minutes before midnight, Lydia White stopped breathing. Alma had grown used to the pattern of her gasping. Alarmed at the prolonged silence, she checked for a pulse. There was none. As Alma tried frantically to think of what she could do, Lydia suddenly let out half a breath, and died.

A deep and painful emptiness tore through Alma. It was as if the whole world had fallen on her shoulders. Feeling a need for comfort, she reached over and picked up Toby Ray and cradled him in her arms. He stirred, but didn't wake as she sat down in the rocker, holding him in her lap. She hugged him tight as the tears began to pour, unchecked. They fell softly onto the boy's head.

She stayed that way through the night, slowly rocking Toby Ray. Besides the hurt and loneliness, her thoughts were crowded with a deep fear for their future.

The gray dawn was creeping over the horizon when at last Alma found the solace of sleep.

3

TOBY RAY AWOKE, STILL WRAPPED IN ALMA'S SLEEP-ing arms. THE morning sun was trying to push through the clouds, and in doing so was causing a good-sized light to fall through the small window. Toby Ray pushed himself up and rubbed his eyes a moment before he turned toward the bed and noticed his mother. She was lying much too still.

Quickly, he jumped from Alma's lap and climbed onto the bed, reaching out. Lydia's face was cold to the touch. Her flesh felt thick and hard.

An anguished cry came from deep inside Toby Ray. He threw himself down against his mother's side and cried so hard he screamed.

Alma awoke, but remained in the rocker, letting her brother have at his grief. After all, it was anyone's guess as to what lay ahead for them, especially Toby Ray. In the short span of two years, they had now lost both parents. Alma felt the hurt just as bad as Toby Ray, but being the oldest, she had to try and keep herself together for his sake. Besides that, she had cried all night, in the solace of the dark, until she felt like the tears were all used up.

A shudder came over her as she remembered Doc Thurman's words. Much as she hated to admit it, they were probably true. It was no secret that their closest living relatives were Aunt Nora, their papa's half sister, and her husband, Ted Lackey. They lived east of Fort Smith, about a mile out of town.

Alma squeezed her eyes shut. Doc Thurman was right. When their mother had taken sick, Uncle Ted had made several remarks to Lydia as to how he was more than willing to take Alma in—as a helpmate for Nora, as he put it. But when Toby Ray's name had been mentioned, Uncle Ted had shook his head and commented on the fact that he had six children of his own to raise, and that even though there really wasn't enough food to handle an extra mouth, at least Alma could work to earn her keep. Two extra mouths were out of the question.

Bunk! Alma thought. Nora might need some help, all right, but Uncle Ted had no consideration at all for what his wife needed. He wanted Alma for one reason only. It filled her with anger to think about his sharp, probing eyes and wandering hands. With her mother sick, it had become necessary for Alma to find what work she could to help out. She had regularly stopped by Uncle Ted and Aunt Nora's to help with the large brood of young'ns, ranging from one year to eleven. At first, it had been a pleasant enough job, and in exchange they would send home some cow's milk if there was any left over, along with rice and meal. The rice and milk were always a treat, but the meal tasted old and smelled musty. Alma had often thought that the corn must have been ground up, cob and all.

Alma was able to hire herself out to other homes on occasion, in return for whatever she could get: coffee, beans, bacon, or sometimes a few pennies. Times were hard, but Alma always felt grateful for whatever she received. She really didn't mind working for little or nothing. It made her feel good to see the pleased look on her mother's face when there was food on the table and her children wouldn't have to go hungry.

It was all pleasant enough for Alma, except for those times at Uncle Ted and Aunt Nora's. What started out as a pleasant job soon turned to the days most dreaded. Uncle Ted was as ugly as sin on a Saturday night—tall and gangly with a clock-stopping face. He drank often, and when he did he would sit off in a corner where he could watch Alma's every move. The intolerable thing about Uncle Ted, though, was his constant bothering of Alma's womanly parts. When no one was looking, he would always grab a breast and squeeze. At the table, he managed to take a seat next to her and reach under her dress with his dirty hand. Alma would cringe at his touch, but she let him have his way. Otherwise, he might turn her out and do something to ruin her hiring on with other folks. She just prayed he wouldn't decide to do anything more.

There was a knock at the door, and it burst open. Cold air swept inside the room, along with Doc Thurman, Uncle Ted and Aunt Nora. In Nora's arms was one-year-old Melinda, and their eleven-year-old son, Raymond, trailed in behind.

Doc Thurman marched straight to Lydia's bed, his face showing disgust at the sight of Toby Ray's crying. He leaned over the boy and looked. He didn't have to touch Lydia to know that she was dead.

"I figured as much," he said, turning to Alma. "I brought along your Uncle Ted. We got his wagon outside, so we can take her down to the funeral parlor."

Aunt Nora juggled the baby on her hip. She hugged Alma and kissed her cheek. "I'm so sorry for ya, honey," she said earnestly.

"Thank you, Aunt Nora."

Uncle Ted nudged his wife aside, leaned over and placed a wet kiss on Alma's face, just missing her mouth. He already smelled like liquor, even at this early hour. "Don't you worry, now. You got a home," he said.

Alma clenched her teeth and let the anger roll through her, her face hiding any emotion.

"Get on up now, Toby Ray," Doc Thurman said. He tried to sound sympathetic, but his words came out harsh and impatient.

Toby Ray just squeezed his mother tighter and buried his face. Doc Thurman looked at Alma, then nodded his head toward Toby Ray.

Alma didn't want to interrupt her brother's mourning, but she forced herself to get up and pried Toby Ray off their mother. "Come on, hon."

He sniffed, then whispered, "Please don't make me leave her! Please, Alma! Don't make me leave Mama!"

Alma pulled Toby Ray close and put his head on her shoulder, patting his back gently. Alma had always been fond of Toby Ray, but at this moment no mother could love a son any more than she loved her little brother.

Aunt Nora moved close and put her arm around him, too. Simultaneously, the three of them began to cry.

Doc Thurman summoned Uncle Ted and his son, Raymond, and together the three of them wrapped Lydia's body in a blanket, then carried it outside. Solemnly, the others followed.

Alma, Toby Ray and Raymond rode in the back of the wagon with the body. Before they departed, Doc Thurman took Alma aside.

"I posted a letter to my sister this morning," he said. "Ted said that Toby Ray can stay with them for a few days, until I hear back. If it takes longer—well, the boy'll have to mind his manners, but he can stay with me and the missus, I guess." He shook his head at the thought as he turned away. Again, Alma held her tongue and let the resentment pass.

At the funeral parlor, she again had her hands full with Toby Ray. He refused to leave his mother's side, crying out in a loud voice when anyone came near him. Finally, the undertaker, Vernon Skaggs, assured Alma that it would be all right for the boy to stay for a while. "Let him have his cry," he nodded sympathetically. "I lost my own mother when I was but twelve. I can certainly understand and appreciate his feelin's."

Alma offered to stay with him, but Toby Ray shook his head. She left him there, hoping a little extra time would let him do some straightening out in his mind. It might help him face the future, she thought.

It was just before supper that night when she returned for him. She found Toby Ray sitting in the foyer of the funeral parlor. He immediately stood up, but didn't speak.

"I've come for ya, Toby Ray," she said.

Toby Ray nodded and walked toward the door, rejecting the hand she held out for him. The pain in his eyes had been replaced by a hard coldness that startled her. She was standing there, staring after her brother and wondering what to do, when Vernon Skaggs entered the room.

"Alma! I'm so glad you came back," he said. "Your mother will look beautiful."

"Mister Skaggs, there's something I've been meanin' to speak with you about," Alma said. She looked nervously about, unable to meet his eyes. "We have no money. Not even a cent."

Vernon Skaggs closed his eyes and nodded gently. He put his arm around her shoulders, much like a father would a daughter, except he pulled her to him and held her frightfully tight. He bent his head, and she could feel him smelling her hair. "Alma," he said, "as I told you, I lost my own mother when I was but a lad. My only concern is for you and Toby Ray's well-bein'. Some of your neighbors have pitched in—not enough, of course, but"—He nuzzled his face deeper into her hair—"I've decided to take care of the final expenses, myself. And in return, maybe you could see your way to stop in an evenin' or two a week."

There was a smell about Vernon Skaggs that reminded Alma of Doc Thurman's office. Her nose prickled at the pungent odor. Afraid to move in his close embrace, she swallowed hard and said, "Stop by for what?"

Vernon Skaggs again pulled her tightly against him. This time, he actually kissed the top of her head. His fingers gently stroked her hair. "It'll be all right. You'll see," he said.

With that, Alma felt a shudder go through her. She pried herself free of his arms and hurried to the door, pushing her brother roughly outside. "Come on, Toby Ray," she said, barely controlling the anxiety in her voice. "Aunt Nora's got supper waitin'."

4

"**I** CAN *TOO* LICK YA, TOBY RAY," RAYMOND SAID.

"Can't."

"Can, too."

The two boys were sprawled on the ground behind the house, where a quick game of push and shove had turned more serious. Now on the underside, Toby Ray was struggling to free himself from Raymond's hold, but his efforts were fruitless. Anyone else would have admitted it, but not Toby Ray. Besides the fact that Raymond was three years older, he also weighed a good thirty pounds more. Still, Toby Ray writhed and pushed to free himself. He barely even noticed that his hands had become numb from both the cold and Raymond's tight grip.

Raymond looked down at Toby Ray with a smirk. "I'll let ya up as soon as you admit I can lick ya," he said.

Toby Ray growled and gave a furious effort to get loose. He strained so hard his face turned a beet red, but all he managed to do was get one arm off the ground. Raymond promptly pinned it back down.

"Admit it! Say I can lick ya. Then we can go for supper. Ma made beans 'n cornbread," Raymond said. He wasn't even breathing hard.

"Never! I can stay here all night if'n I have to!" Toby Ray panted.

Raymond's mouth pressed into a mean grin. "I'll just have to teach you a lesson, I reckon," he said. He eased one knee up and placed it on top of Toby Ray's arm. Pressing down hard, he let go of Toby Ray's wrist and raised himself up, pulling back his free hand into a fist. "Okay, this is your last warnin'," he said. "Come on. Say I can lick ya."

Toby Ray gritted his teeth and shook his head, his young eyes showing no fear.

Raymond's fist wavered in the air. "All right! You asked for it!" he said. The fist came down hard, catching Toby Ray smack in the middle of his nose and top lip.

Blood instantly spouted from Toby Ray's nose, and within seconds his busted lip had swollen to twice its size. Toby Ray's whole head was throbbing, but he refused to cry. Instead, when he was able to speak, he muttered, "You hit just like a girl!"

Raymond's eyes, which were blinking at the sight of so much blood, turned into angry slits at the insult. "You asked for this," he repeated, and hit Toby Ray again as hard as he could.

Blood sprayed in all directions, flying upward and covering Raymond's face with red. That seemed to make him even madder. He raised his fist again.

Toby Ray's head was swirling. There was a ringing in his ears as he closed his eyes and waited for another blow. He didn't even hear his sister's voice.

"Git off Toby Ray this instant, or I'll git Aunt Nora!" Alma hollered. She came striding up to the boys, clenching her fists and glaring at Raymond.

Raymond jumped up to his feet and sneered at Toby Ray. "Go ahead, git her," he said. "He started it, and I finished it!" He gave Alma a smirky grin and marched past her to the house.

Alma bent down over Toby Ray, taking the hem of her dress to wipe away what blood she could. She started to ask what had happened, but Toby Ray suddenly pushed her hand away and rolled painfully over onto his side. "Leave me be. I'll be all right," he said through his thick upper lip.

"I will not!" Alma said. She pulled him back around to face her and frowned. "Oh, hon! Your mouth is a mess! Why in the world are you fightin' at a time like this?" she asked sadly.

Toby Ray lay there a moment. He was hurting something awful, and the sound of Alma's sympathetic voice gave him a powerful urge to throw himself into her arms and cry. He could have done just that, if it had been his mother sitting there with him instead of his sister. As much as he loved Alma, she still wasn't his mother. So, he stifled the urge for comfort and pulled on the meanest face he could muster. Yanking roughly away from Alma, he quickly jumped up and started running toward the woods. The pain and anger were clashing inside him so hard, he was oblivious to her screams for him to stop and come back for supper.

At the edge of the woods he didn't hesitate, but ran on inside. Outside, the winter light was fading, but he could still see. Once in the woods, it became dark. Toby Ray slowed his pace, but kept running, mindless of the brittle tree limbs that slapped and cut at his bare face and hands. The tears that he'd held back from the others were now filling his eyes, blinding him even more. Angry that he was crying like a baby, even in front of himself, he blinked hard a few times and didn't see the big tree limb that knocked him flat on his back.

A whole minute passed before he could regain even a sitting position. Leaning back painfully against the very tree that had felled him, he momentarily forgot about Raymond's thunderous punches as he tried to figure out what had happened to him.

"Tick?" he called out hopefully. "Oh, Tick! Come here, boy!"

But his dog was nowhere around. He suddenly realized that it was pitch black where he was sitting and he had completely lost his bearings as well. He was cold, alone and scared, and his mouth and head were throbbing. It all came at him at once, and he tried to respond with anger, gritting his teeth and clenching his scraped hands into fists. But all the anger had been knocked out of him. There was no one left to fight but himself. He relaxed his mouth and began to whimper.

"Mama! Please, God, d-don't leave me h-here without Mama!"

Toby Ray began to pray, promising to obey every commandment until the day he died if God would bring his mother back. He prayed hard, even though he knew in the back of his mind that she was gone forever. When the praying had worn itself out, he began to think about how cold and empty he felt. What if he froze to death? What if no one ever found his body? He wondered if he would be with Mama if he died. For a while, he wished that he could freeze to death. Then, it occurred to him that folks might not get the option of who they saw in Heaven, and the idea of dying lost its appeal.

He let his mind return to more pressing matters. The pain in his mouth was becoming more intense. He ran his tongue gently over his swollen upper lip. It had a sweet taste to it. Toby Ray had had his mouth cut before, but never this bad.

"That Raymond," he said aloud. "Some day I'm gonna beat him up real good."

Maybe, he thought, he'd do it right away. Maybe he'd take a club to him. That would show Raymond he couldn't just beat him up and get away with it.

But the evening cold took over his concentration, and he couldn't hold on to any bad thoughts about Raymond or anyone else. He couldn't think about much of anything, his teeth were chattering so bad. As he sat with his arms folded around his shaking body, he tried again to pray, but he kept losing track of the words. At the same time, a kind of sleepiness was stealing over him. He let his eyes fall shut.

Suddenly, a sound jarred him wide awake. It was a dog barking. Toby Ray jerked his head up to listen. It was Uncle Ted's hound. Eventually, the barking came closer and closer, until finally it was right on top of him.

"Is that you, Toby Ray?" Uncle Ted's voice called out.

The cold had blistered Toby Ray's face so badly, he could barely open his mouth to speak. His ears were pounding from the hound's barking, and he could see the bright glow of Uncle Ted's kerosene lamp approaching. Then, a warm, rough tongue licked at his swollen face.

"You dog! Git back!" Uncle Ted hollered and kicked. The dog yelped and shrank away. Uncle Ted bent closer to look. "So it *is* you, you little runt!" There was a noticeable disgust to his tone as he sneered at Toby Ray.

Toby Ray had never liked Uncle Ted any better than Alma did, but at this exact moment he had to admit he'd never felt as glad to see anyone in his life as he did right now. Before he had time to think any more on the subject, a heavy pain streaked through his head. Uncle Ted had slapped him and was pulling him to his feet by the hair. He shook Toby Ray back and forth, like he would a rag doll.

"Stand still, you little bastard!" he growled. "Let me git a look at ya."

After studying his face for a spell, he turned and looked at Raymond, who was standing in the shadows behind him. "Boy, you busted his lip right good," he remarked. Still gripping Toby Ray by the hair, he shook the boy's head back and forth. "That'll teach ya to keep your blame mouth shut! 'Fore we git back to the house, there's a few things you need to learn, boy. That fat lip of your'n is just a samplin' of what you're gonna git if'n you don't behave yourself." Then, he pulled the hair on Toby Ray's head so hard it almost lifted his feet from the ground. "You hear me, boy?"

Toby Ray was scared. He didn't know what to say that would help matters any. Just when he had thought things couldn't get any worse, here they had. As he stood there, trying to think of something to say, each second of silence made Uncle Ted more angry. Toby Ray was sure that his hair was being pulled from the roots, as he dangled there. He looked at Raymond, who stood in the lamp's shadow with his hands stuck in his pockets, looking pleased with the goings-on. Hatred welled up inside. No sooner had the words left his lips, when he already wished he could take them back.

"I'll git you for this, Raymond!"

Uncle Ted let go of the hair, much to Toby Ray's relief. Any pleasant hopes were short-lived, however, as Uncle Ted let out the growl of a bear and slapped Toby Ray hard across the face. "You shut up, Toby Ray!"

Uncle Ted turned suddenly to Raymond. He looked so angry, Raymond took a step backward and stumbled over a dead tree. His father appeared not to notice. Instead, he muttered, "Let's git this little bastard to the house 'fore I kill 'im."

That night, Toby Ray slept in a bed with Alma. His head was ringing. It stung where Uncle Ted had hit him, and his mouth ached and burned. Every time he moved a muscle, it seemed like his swollen lip would rake against his teeth and bring on more misery. Alma had tried to soothe him, but it was no use. Right now, he felt so alone that he could die. He wasn't sure if anyone would even notice or care. Finally when Alma's breathing became deep and even, he wept. He tried to mouth his mother's name, but even that was too much of an effort.

5

LARKES DIXON TIED HIS HORSES TO A SMALL TREE
and looked over at the row of shanty houses. There were
maybe twenty of them, all made of graying, unfinished
lumber, patched with splotches of tin or old boards or
whatever else could be scavanged. Thin fingers of smoke
rose out of the roofs. Fires had to be stoked low to save
on wood.

Larkes had never set foot in this town, but he had
ridden right up to the Negro section just like he had a
map in his head. Most towns were laid out in a similar
fashion—even the big cities—with the coloreds getting
their plots somewhere on the outskirts.

The night air felt cold, bitter cold, what with the
gusting wind. Larkes pulled his hat down low over his
forehead, then tucked his hands in his pockets. He'd
slept out in colder places than this, like Colorado and
Wyoming, but somehow his bones had taken to aching
more with each passing year.

He stepped up to the first shanty and rapped on the
door. He could hear muffled voices inside, but at the
sound of his knock, all went quiet. The door was opened
a crack, and a man's nose and eye appeared.

"Who is ya and whats do ya want?"

"Name's Larkes Dixon. I'm lookin' for a place to stay
for the night. Gotta git myself outta this cold. I'm willin'
to pay."

24

The door opened a little wider, revealing the round face of an older Negro man, his hair graying at the temples. He shook his head. "I be sorry as can be, but we so full o' folks right now, can't hardly moves around. Gots me six young'ns, and de oldest gots two kids o' her own," he said.

Larkes' mind swept over the small-framed shanty, knowing what that one room would look like all filled with people. He nodded and started to turn away, but the man stopped him.

"Down yonder." He pointed. "De last house. Dat be Reasa Peters' place. She ain't gots nothin' but a little ol' three, four-year-old young'n. I'm sho she could use de money." The man stepped out and closed the door behind him, shivering at the cold. "Dat Reasa, she sho be a looker, too." He grinned at Larkes.

"You say the last house?"

"Dat right. Reasa Peters' place be de last house down yonder, on de end." His eyes smiled mischievously at Larkes. "If I's be younger, I's be slippin' off to Miss Reasa's myself."

Larkes gave him a half smile. "I surely appreciate the information. Yessir, I do," he said to the old man. He untied his horses and walked down the row of shanties. He could hear people talking in some. Others were dark and silent.

There was a cluster of trees just beyond the last house on the row. Larkes tied the two horses to the trees and approached the shanty. He knocked softly on the door and waited for what seemed like a long time.

When the door finally opened, the cold, miserable night was a thing forgotten. A tall, light-skinned Negro woman opened the door and looked him up and down. She was barefoot, wearing a cotton dress that revealed shiny, well-built legs. Larkes admired them for a second or two under the moonlit night before he spoke.

"Are you Reasa Peters?"

"I'm Reasa. What you want?"

Larkes' eyes traveled up to her face. He stood there, his mouth hanging partly open. This surely had to be the most beautiful woman he'd ever come across. Awkward as a schoolboy, he nodded with his head. "Yes'm. The man in the first house said you might be able to put me up for the night."

Reasa laughed. "Otis Bell! Why, that ol' fool! Does he think I run some sort of boardin' house? Mercy! You can just go back 'n tell him I most assuredly don't!"

"No, ma'am. He didn't say any such thing. Look, I'm cold and hungry." He looked past her, trying to see into the shanty. "Is that cracklin' bread I smell?"

She seemed amused. "You like cracklin' bread, do ya?"

"Yes, ma'am. I ain't had no good cracklin' bread in a spell," he said with a smile. "Look here, I'll pay ya for your troubles. I just need to get out of the cold, and you know there ain't no place in town I can stay."

"Lord knows I can use the money." Reasa sighed. "What can you pay? Got two bits?"

"I'll give ya four bits for some of that cracklin' bread, and a dollar for a place to lay my head," Larkes said.

Reasa opened the door wider. "Come on in, then. It's too cold to stand out here," she said. "I'll heat you up some of this cracklin' bread. Got peas to go with it." She turned around and looked up at him. Her eyes met his. "How tall are you, anyway?"

"Six foot four."

"Six foot four," she repeated.

Larkes was used to the question. He found it a bit odd, being as she was tall for a female, herself. He figured her to be five-eight or five-nine, maybe even taller. He removed his coat and noticed Reasa staring at the Colt in his holster.

"Where you from?" she asked, setting out a plate with a spoon and tin cup.

"Just rode in from Fort Smith."

"No. I mean, where you from? Where were you born and raised? You look like a white man, with that gun tied to your waist." She pointed.

Larkes took off his hat and laid it on the table. "Past few years, I've been in Texas and New Mexico. But I was born and growed up in Georgia," he said.

"You don't talk like no Georgia colored," Reasa said as she set the peas and cracklin' bread on the table.

"How's a Georgia colored 'sposed to talk?" Larkes asked. He stepped over a chair and sat down.

Reasa shrugged. "Like ol' Otis Bell, I 'spose. You know how they say 'yessuh Massah' and 'nossuh Massah.' Why, they sound to me like a bunch o' fools talkin'. I know, 'cause I'm from south Louisiana, myself. I know all about how southern coloreds talk. Makes me kinda angry sometimes that they ain't learned better."

"Well"—Larkes looked up at her hard—"I reckon people can't help what they don't know. Most of us weren't taught how to read and write. I was just lucky, is all. I made myself learn those things. You shouldn't be so critical of those who didn't have the chance."

"I'm not talkin' critical," Reasa said. "Just fact." She got up to fetch the pot from the stove and poured him a cup of weak coffee. "Well, all the same, at least you're a southern colored that talks like everybody else."

Larkes tried to smile when he said, "By everybody else, you're meanin' white folk, ain't ya?"

"Believe what you want, but ain't nothin' wrong with learnin' better," Reasa said defensively.

"Now, that's a fact, I 'spose," Larkes said agreeably. "Which one of your folks is white, your mama or your papa?"

"My daddy was mostly colored, and my mama was Creole," she said.

"I heard about Creoles," Larkes said. "Ain't that French and Negro mixed together?"

"Somethin' like that," Reasa said with a proud look.

Larkes took up his spoon and ate like a starving man. Reasa fell silent as she watched him. When his plate was clean, she refilled it. Larkes nodded his approval at the offering.

"This is as good a cracklin' bread as I ever et," he said. "What you got in these peas? They sure are good."

"Peppers 'n spices. That's the secret to cookin' in

south Louisiana. I find they work in just about anythin'
I make."

Just then, something metal dropped in the corner of
the one-room house. In the time it takes a person to
blink an eye, Larkes dropped his spoon and pulled his
Colt, jumping to his feet at the same time.

Reasa gasped. "My Lord! Put that thing away! Come
here, baby," she added softly.

A little boy stepped out of the darkness and into the
light of the coal lamp. He wiped sleep from his eyes
and ran toward Reasa. She pulled him onto her lap and
hugged him. "See there, now? You've scared him." She
frowned.

Larkes felt ashamed as he reholstered his Colt. "I'm
sorry, ma'am. Too many nights of sleepin' out in hostile
Indian country."

Reasa cradled the boy's head in her arms and talked
to him. "It's all right, baby. This here's Larkes Dixon,
and he needs him a place to stay tonight." She smiled
at Larkes. "And this is my little Noah."

Larkes reached out and rubbed the boy's head. "Noah.
Now, that's a pretty name."

"I picked that name 'cause I want him to survive, like
the Lord let Noah survive," Reasa said, her face full of
pride for the boy. "Out of the whole Bible, Noah's the
one that the Lord let live. I 'spect He'll look after my
Noah the same way."

She took the boy back to the corner to his bed, kissed
his forehead and hummed him back to sleep. Larkes
finished his coffee and was putting the dishes in the
washpan when a knock sounded at the door.

Reasa jumped up from the boy's bed and ran her
fingers over her hair. "Oh, Lord. What's tonight?" she
asked Larkes nervously.

"I believe it to be a Wednesday." Curious, Larkes
dried his hands and turned to face the door.

Reasa looked more nervous. She took in a deep breath
and straightened her dress. Another knock sounded, louder this time and with a voice attached.

"You got somebody in there? Open this damned door!"

Larkes looked expectantly at Reasa, who still stood frozen with a worried expression. He took a step forward, but she put a hand against his chest to stop him.

"No, please. I don't need no trouble. 'Sides that, it's the deputy sheriff. I better go to the door."

She opened it just wide enough to peek out, and talked in a low voice that Larkes couldn't understand.

"I don't give a damn who's in there," the voice said. "You know I come every Wednesday night!"

Suddenly, the door was pushed open, sending Reasa stumbling backwards. A big man stepped inside, barrel-chested with a potbelly. He glared at Reasa, then noticed Larkes.

"Who the hell's this nigger, Reasa?" he demanded.

Reasa glanced at Larkes, then back at the deputy. "He—he needed a place to stay—out of the cold. Please, Frank! He's payin' me."

"I don't give a damn about that. Let him go stay with one of the other nigger families." Frank stared wickedly at Larkes and laughed, his belly shaking up and down. "Aw, hell, I don't begrudge you a place outta the cold, boy. You give me an hour here with Reasa, and then you can come back."

"Don't believe I'll do that, mister," Larkes said calmly. He reached into his pocket and threw some coins on the table. "I done paid for the night. So, I guess I'll just stay right here." His dark eyes stared unflinchingly at the deputy.

"Reasa!" Deputy Frank shouted, his face bright red. "You better get this nigger outta here. Now! You know Wednesday nights are mine. That's the reason you and that little boy of your'n always has food on the table. I've been more than generous. Now, I'm gonna step outside and give you a few minutes to explain to this here nigger that he's got to get his ass outta here." With that, he turned and closed the door behind him.

Larkes picked up his money. "Look, Reasa, I don't wanna cause no problem. You've gotta live here, and I'm just passin' through."

Reasa sniffed hard. "No. Wait. I want you to stay,"

she said. Her eyes filled with tears. "I'm so ashamed that you had to see this. B-b-but, you see, I got little Noah to think about. His daddy was knifed in a card game when he was barely five weeks old. Times are hard."

Larkes held her chin up with his finger. "Don't cry," he said. "I understand. Besides, won't be the first time I slept out in the cold, and you're right. That little boy needs lookin' after. I'll just be on my way."

From outside, Deputy Frank banged on the door. "Ain't gettin' any warmer out here, Reasa!" he shouted.

Reasa grabbed hold of Larkes' arm and held on tight. "Don't go," she pleaded. "Please. I'll just tell him no." "Besides, I ain't had no decent manly company in a long time."

Her face held such a sadness that he hesitated. "Are you sure?" he asked.

"Yes."

"In that case, let me go talk to him," Larkes said.

He was starting for the door when it suddenly swung open, and Deputy Frank stepped back in. "My patience is running mighty thin, Reasa."

Larkes' eyes fixed on the big deputy. "Not tonight. I reckon you'll have to find someone else to keep you company."

"Is that so, Reasa?" Deputy Frank glared at her.

She nodded.

Deputy Frank spat on the floor. "Well, I'll be damned! This ain't gonna be good, Reasa. No good a'tall! Good as I've been to you and Noah!" His eyes darkened with anger. He turned to Larkes. "Those horses outside yours, boy?"

"They are," Larkes said.

Deputy Frank leaned against the door frame and said slowly, "Now, I've gotta wonder, where's a nigger like you get the money for a horse? 'Specially one as fine as that white gelding. You got papers on him? I think I seen that gelding before, over at the doc's in Fort Smith." His eyes narrowed. "I'll bet you stole him, boy."

"I got papers. He was the doctor's, all right. But I bought him, two days ago," Larkes said. He pulled the bill of sale from his pocket and handed it to the deputy, who glanced at it, then tossed it on the floor.

"Don't mean a thing," Deputy Frank said. "I reckon any nigger sportin' a fine horse like that gelding would have some kind of paper sayin' it was his. No, I believe you'd better come on down to the jail. We're gonna check this out properly."

"I ain't goin' nowhere with your fat ass," Larkes said in a calm voice.

Deputy Frank's face flushed. "Why, you—" He reached for his sidearm, but his hand had barely touched the handle when Larkes' right fist flew, smashing into Deputy Frank's nose so hard it sounded like a gunshot. He stumbled, then fell on the seat of his pants, cursing.

"You son of a bitch, nigger bastard! I think you broke my nose!" He wiped a handful of blood from his face, then reached again for his sidearm.

Larkes stepped forward and pinned Deputy Frank's hand to the floor with his foot. "Broken noses mend. Bullet holes don't," he said. "You just remember this, mister. You ever accuse me of horse stealin' again, and I'll send your fat ass to hell."

6

CURSING AT LARKES, DEPUTY FRANK LEFT REASA'S and rode off on his horse, holding his nose. They could still hear him squawking threats when he was well off in the distance. Reasa sighed as she shut the door. She checked briefly on Noah, then joined Larkes at the table.

They sat there in silence, both staring at the fire. Larkes couldn't tell what she was thinking. Her face was calm, her expression blank. Serene, even. Himself, he was feeling sick at what had just happened. It wasn't the fact that he had just beaten up a lawman. Deputy Frank definitely had it coming. What bothered him in the worst way was the burden he had just laid on Reasa. Once Larkes was gone, he figured Deputy Frank would most likely take his anger out on her.

He looked again at her face. He might have sat there all night until bedtime, thinking his worrisome thoughts, if there wasn't one overriding fact. Reasa Peters was a beauty of the overwhelming sort. He could barely pull his eyes away from her. She was so pretty, it could run anything serious out of a man's mind. It made him feel like an adolescent, gawking at the first beautiful female he'd ever laid eyes on. What's more, he didn't even care. It felt good, in fact. Larkes had always liked to feast his eyes on pretty women, just as much as the next man. Unfortunately, it had been years since he'd found one who could make his heart flutter in his chest. And his heart was full of flutters right now.

Reasa finally broke the silence. She had leaned against the table and propped her chin in her hand.

"Ol' Frank, when he wakes up tomorrow, he's gonna be mad as a snake that has to crawl on its belly!" she said without a trace of worry in her voice.

"I'm real sorry, ma'am," Larkes said, brought suddenly out of his pleasant thoughts. "You know, I surely didn't mean to cause you and little Noah any trouble." He frowned at the small figure sleeping in the bed.

Reasa offered him a small smile. Her eyes half-closed, she said, "Don't you worry one bit. I reckon Frank'll come around soon enough. He can lose his temper fast as any man I ever saw, but it never lasts long." She paused a moment, then sighed. "I suppose he'd give me every last cent he owned if I had a mind to be that generous back. Why, it about drives him crazy that I only let him come to see me on Wednesdays." She studied something deep within the flames of the fire. "But, that one night a week is what keeps me and little Noah from starvin' to death."

"Ain't there some other kind of work to be had?" Larkes asked.

Reasa turned on him sharply. "Yes, there is, and I do it," she said. "Got two women with big houses and I clean 'em. I do washin's for others." She glared at Larkes a moment. "Do you think I like havin' ol' jelly-belly Frank comin' to my house?"

"No, ma'am." Larkes was sorry he'd made the inquiry. "I didn't mean nothin'," he said.

"Yes, you did." Reasa looked insulted for a moment, then shrugged and added matter-of-factly, "I don't make enough off of doin' other ladies' work to keep decent food on the table. So, I supplement with Frank."

She went back to staring at the fire, and Larkes decided to let the conversation rest for a while. Maybe he could think of something more pleasant to talk about, when she was ready. He drained his coffee cup, and was wanting some more, but he didn't want to appear to be greedy. So he sat there and rolled the cup around in his hands until she had finally seen enough of the fire.

She turned toward him and, in a more gentle tone, asked, "Can I get you some more coffee?"

He was considerably cheered. "Yes. That would be nice," he said and held out his cup.

As she poured, Reasa seemed relaxed again. She said conversationally, "Where you headin' to?"

"Colorado."

"Colorado," she repeated. "Why, I hear tell it's colder there than here! Who in the world's waitin' for you in Colorado?"

"Ain't no who. It's gold. I hear they've got lots of it in Colorado."

"So." Reasa put back the pot. "You're gonna go find you some gold? Lord o' mercy, I've heard men talk about such folly before!" She gave a short laugh.

"You call it folly?" Larkes said.

"Yes. Folly." Reasa smiled. She sat down and crossed her legs, then stared at Larkes with eyes that seemed to see inside him. He leaned back a little. She went on, "You men are all alike. Always gonna find some easy way to get rich." She shook her head. "Us women? We know better."

"I didn't say I was gonna be huntin' for gold," Larkes came back. "I just said that's what's waitin'."

"Well now, if it's not gold you're after, then why are you goin' to Colorado?"

"I'm goin' after gold all right," Larkes explained. "But I mean to make it off the ones who've already found theirs."

Reasa's eyes widened. She pulled at her hair. "What? You mean you're gonna steal it off'n some other poor soul who's dug around in the ground and earned it?" she asked.

"Wasn't plannin' on stealin' it, either." Larkes smiled.

"You surely are a confusin' man," Reasa said, almost irritably. She got up to poke at the fire with a stick, making angry little jabs at the chunks of ash. She added a couple of small pieces of wood, then poked some more.

Larkes watched her with a kind of fascination. Reasa Peters, he thought to himself, was a strange one at best. For one thing, she seemed all too eager to speak her mind on things that Larkes felt sure she couldn't know that much about. Why, he doubted whether she knew the first thing about gold, and how men went about finding it. No, he figured her to be one who did a lot of listening to men's conversations, then put what they said into her own words, as if she knew things firsthand. He'd run across a few others who pretended to know a lot, but he'd always been able to turn a deaf ear to their ramblings. None of them, however, had come close to looking like Reasa Peters. Whether she was a rambler or not, she had a mesmerizing grip on him, and he couldn't help but listen to every word she said.

She turned from the fire and caught him staring at her. He pulled his eyes away, hoping she wasn't starting to wonder over his ogling.

He went on, as if their conversation hadn't been interrupted. "You see, around those gold camps, men spend their money foolishly. There's lots of ways to make some good honest money."

Reasa burst out laughing.

"What's wrong?" Larkes asked in a defensive tone.

She put her hands on her hips. "Why, you show me a white man that's gonna let a colored get ahead in life, and I'll show you snow in July." She nodded her head and laughed again.

Larkes tried to conjure up something smart to say back, but when she turned her dark eyes on him, all he could do was think about how beautiful she was. The fluttering started up in his chest again, stronger than ever. He said weakly, "Aw, you sound jus' like a silly female who don't know what she's talkin' 'bout."

"Is that so?" Reasa paused and looked him up and down. "Well, just 'cause you dress like a cowboy and hang a gun off your hip, that don't make you white. And you sound like you think you are."

"That's enough, now." Larkes shook his head. "I think you're the one who's messed up in her thinkin'. Just a while ago, you was the one talkin' about coloreds betterin' themselves. Now you say what's the use? Ol' Mister White Man's gonna keep us coloreds under his boot? Well, he can try all he wants, but I tell you a fact. I'm one colored that's just stubborn 'nough to think I can do what I want. Long as I'm legal in the law, they'll have to bury me with my boots on to stop me."

Reasa chuckled sarcastically. "Lord o' mercy! You got some quick temper, Larkes Dixon! What I meant was, it's a disgrace that coloreds don't learn better. I never said that whites were gonna help them along! Some might, but most think we're just dirt under their feet. Why, I've known so-called decent whites who really believe in their hearts that we ain't nothin' more than slave dogs, with no human feelin's of our own."

Larkes wanted in the worst way to scold Reasa for what he considered her ignorance about their people. It must be the white blood in her, he decided, that caused her intolerance. But instead of pursuing the subject, he dropped it. It had been a long day and he was tired. Besides that, he had no intentions of wasting any more time arguing, no matter how wrong he thought her to be. "Why don't you sit yourself down?" he said amiably.

She shrugged and slid back into her chair. "You ever been to Colorado before?" she asked.

"I have."

"Tell me what it's like." Reasa bent her leg and propped her foot on the chair, then rested her chin on her knee. Larkes took another moment to enjoy her startling eyes before he answered.

"Well," he began, "the eastern side is all flat. Sage brush and a few scattered trees is all. You can see for miles and miles. It's real big and open. Then when you go on west, you hit the Rockies."

"The Rocky Mountains," Reasa murmured.

"That's right. I ain't never seen anythin' like 'em. They're so big, you can't believe your eyes. And way up high, in the clouds, you can see snow scattered over the mountaintops. From far away, they look kinda blue and purple. Up close, they make you feel like a tiny little speck in this world. It's beautiful, all right, with the freshest air you ever breathed. And the game in those parts is fine. Why, if a man lived there, he'd never want for plenty of fresh meat." Larkes paused and gave Reasa a soft smile. "Colorado is a lot like a woman, you know. Full of contradictions. It's a lot like you, Reasa."

She allowed her smile to mix with his, but only for an instant. "That's pretty sassy talk, but I reckon that's the folly of a man speakin'."

"Didn't mean nothin' disrespectful."

"Now, I never thought you did. Tell me more." Her eyes sparkled. Her face took on a more youthful look.

"I tell ya, outside of the Yellowstone area, I think the Rockies might be the prettiest place on God's earth," Larkes said. "There's fresh mountain streams, meadows and valleys all through 'em. Why, it's enough to make a nonbeliever believe. Only God could make a place so beautiful."

"What part are you plannin' on goin' to?" Reasa asked, unable to hide her enthusiasm.

"In the Rockies, south of Wyoming. I was through that part of the country fifteen, maybe sixteen years ago. It's one of them places that God seems to put a special touch on. You can sit on a hilltop and see for miles. Hmmmm." Larkes made a satisfied sound in his throat, much like a man who's taken a bite of some fine vittles. "I stayed there a few months, mostly in the summer. It was green and pretty. I once spent a winter in upper Wyoming, where the snow can get waist-deep. I hear tell the Colorado Rockies are like that."

Reasa frowned at the idea of that much snow. "Why, Lord o' mercy! My feet get cold right here, and we don't get hardly any snow! How's a body keep from freezin' to death?"

Larkes said, "They manage. Cold's different there. It's of a drier nature. 'Sides, you kill you enough meat to last out the winter, then stay up in your cabin with a nice warm fire."

"Does it snow all winter long?" she asked.

"I don't know about that. Like I said, I ain't ever spent

a whole winter there. Seen some snow, but it wasn't much. Not nearly as much as I seen in Yellowstone."

Reasa pulled at her hair and thought a moment. She looked at her small son, then gazed around the small shanty at her few belongings. Her breath quickened. "Take me and Noah with ya," she blurted out.

"What? Uh . . ." Larkes' face suddenly turned serious. He coughed. "Well, ma'am, that wouldn't work a'tall. Why, just ain't no way you and that boy could make a trip like that! You'd freeze to death this time of year. 'Sides that, I ain't got no wagon or nothin' to keep you out of the weather."

"Shucks. Winter's nearly over," Reasa said. "We wouldn't be no trouble, I promise. You got an extra horse, and I can ride a horse darn near as well as a man. Wouldn't need no wagon."

Larkes' mouth hung open like it had when he'd first laid eyes on Reasa's beauty. He shook his head back and forth, his eyes open wide. And tried to think of what to say. All of his adult life had been spent in an independent manner. He'd cowboyed all across Texas and New Mexico, hired his gun out years before in Wyoming. Through all of his travels and experiences, he'd always managed to keep one thing constant: He traveled alone. What few friendships he'd made weren't much more than acquaintances. In fact, the last two or three cowboying jobs had put him working with eighteen- and nineteen-year-old boys that weren't even dry behind the ears. He'd had nothing in common with any of them, so he'd kept to himself. As far as hiring his gun out, about the only ones hiring any more were the cattlemen's associations. He'd claimed a bounty or two in recent years. In fact, he'd just collected a thousand dollars for the capture of two murderers who'd been holed up in southwest Missouri. But bountying was a lot of hard riding, and a man was just as apt to run into a series of dead ends as he was to locate his quarry. A lot of times the outlaw would either end up dead or have gotten himself captured months before Larkes caught word of it. Much like his cowboying, hiring his gun out had not led to any lasting friendships. Larkes had never decided if he liked being alone or not, but the mere fact that he had been alone so many years had finally led to his acceptance of the role. He was comfortable with it. Reasa's question scared the daylights out of him, though, so bad the hair on the back of his neck bristled.

Reasa seemed to take his silence in a positive way. "I promise," she said. "I won't be no trouble at all. I'll even cook for ya. Might slow ya down a bit, but I'll make up for that inconvenience." She smiled.

With an extra effort, Larkes pushed his chair back from the table and shook his head. "No, no! It's just not possible. I've damn near froze to death, myself. There's rowdies out there on the trails, full of no good. They'd as soon shoot ya over a dollar as look at ya. 'Sides, ain't no towns, especially in Texas, where we could even find a place to lay our heads at night. We'd be left out under the stars, for sure." He shook his head again, staring down at the table to avoid her eyes.

Reasa's face had grown serious. "If you want me to beg, I will," she said in a low voice.

Larkes held up his hands. "I surely don't want that. That's not the point at all."

Reasa got up and grabbed the coffee pot, then stood next to him and stared down. "You know what it's like, livin' here in this good-for-nothin' town? Cleanin' white ladies' houses? Washin' their dirty ol' clothes? Then for my weekly excitement, I got ol' jelly-belly Frank to look forward to." She bit her lip and forced back a tear, then took in a deep breath. "Ain't got no colored men. They're all married, or run off to somethin' better. Got a bunch o' ol' fools like Otis Bell. That's about the pickin's around here." She couldn't fight back the tears any longer. "I mean, m-m-my baby Noah ain't got a chance! If you think a little cold weather and sleepin' out under the stars is gonna dampen my travel spirits any, then you got another think comin'. If I got to beg, I'll beg. Please, take me to this place that you say was made special by God. You say you don't want to get down on your knees and dig for gold? Well, I'd be willing to do it, for my little boy." Her eyes widened.

"And I'll do your diggin', too. All we want is a chance to get out of here, and you're the only chance I'm ever likely to have."

Larkes' hands trembled. He wanted to run and hide somewhere. It would have been better, he decided, if he'd just slept out in the cold. He didn't want to add to this pretty woman's suffering. He didn't need the burden, nor the guilt. Larkes couldn't help his eyes as they looked nervously toward Noah's sleeping form. "Look, I got some money. I'll leave you some money," he offered weakly.

"That's kind," Reasa said, her face now wet with tears. "Might last me three, four months, but then what?"

He didn't answer. His gaze was locked again on the dancing flames in the fireplace. There was a miserable look on his face, and Reasa knew he was regretting his knock on her door. The walls of the shabby house seemed to close in on them.

Reasa stared hard at Larkes, then took in a shuddery breath. "You mean it, don't ya? You ain't gonna allow us to go?"

"I'm as sorry as I can be, ma'am."

"Me, too," she said, wiping her nose. "Me, too."

7

CONVERSATION SEEMED POINTLESS AFTER THAT, SO Reasa silently made Larkes a pallet beside the fire. She politely told him good night, then took herself to bed. Larkes could tell that she was still hurt, but at least she had stopped sniffling. He took a deep breath as he lay down and turned toward the warmth of the fire.

Normally, sleeping in such a luxurious style would have been a grand occasion. But not tonight. Larkes felt troubled inside. He stared wide-eyed into the flames and tried to sort it out in his mind. It would have been worlds better if he'd never knocked on the door of this little shanty. In a way, he was sorry he had. Reasa had laid a heavy load of guilt on him, a fact that made him angry as much as upset. But Larkes knew deep down that there wouldn't be any guilt or anger or anything else if it weren't for the fact that he was smitten, plain and simple. In just a few hours, she had managed to shoot one of Cupid's little arrows, and it had landed smack dab in the middle of his heart. Larkes couldn't figure how it happened, but it had. Guilt was a high mountain to cross, but he could manage that, given time. But Cupid's arrow? That was a new territory to his emotions. He had a suspicion that any feelings that included a woman had to be a lot more complicated and sticky. For one thing, just thinking about Reasa made him feel weak. The fluttering that had been confined to his chest had now spread to various other parts of his body. His hands felt tingly and wet. He wiped the sweat off his palms and held up a hand against the backdrop of the fire. It was trembling like a newborn calf. Seeing just what an effect this woman was having on him, Larkes jerked back his hand and stuck it under his armpit, trying to steady it down. It baffled him to think that a man who had collected outlaws at gunpoint could so easily be buffaloed by a woman armed with shining, inviting eyes.

He tossed the same thoughts around, over and over, until he started to blink. The fire was burning his eyeballs dry, causing them to ache. Finally, he closed his eyes to sleep, and the dreams came. They were silly, pleasant dreams, all about Reasa. They were together, doing things that Larkes would have found even more enjoyable if he were awake.

It was deep into the night when the dreams turned harsh. Larkes started to toss about, as one nightmare after another raced through his mind. His breath began to catch in his throat. He tried desperately to sit up, but some overpowering force held him. He couldn't budge an inch.

Panic grabbed at him. It was as if he was awake but still asleep, all at once. He tried hard to relax, but even then he found it harder and harder to breathe. He opened his mouth to scream at Reasa for help, but no sound would come forth from inside him. Fear like he had never experienced struck him, squeezing his chest to where he expected that it would surely explode any second. He tried again to yell out, but still there was not even as much as a moan.

Several seconds passed. Larkes' breathing was becoming more labored. He'd given up on trying to sit up or holler out for help. He lay there, sweat beading on his face.

Then, he saw a long tunnel filled with fog. Through the dense fog, there was a light—not a very bright one, but it was there all the same. Larkes could feel himself being pulled into the tunnel and the thick fog.

His body, which had been frozen to the point where he had no control, suddenly relaxed, and he let himself be pulled along. The fear that had gripped him so was now subsiding. He couldn't breathe any better, but that didn't seem to matter any more, as a serene feeling came over him.

Somewhere off in the distance, he could hear a train chugging up a steep grade. The chugging got louder, so loud in fact that the tunnel with all the fog and the pretty light started to fade away.

With a jolt, Larkes sat straight up, suddenly realizing that something was terribly wrong. He got up so violently from his nightmare, he literally threw himself into the fireplace. Quickly, he slapped away a burning cinder from his shirt sleeve. Then he heard the chugging train again, off to his side and in the direction of Reasa and Noah's bed. But, it wasn't a train at all. Someone was coughing in deep, ragged breaths. Frowning, Larkes turned around, and finally came awake when he saw the smoke that filled the room.

There were flames of orange, red and yellow whipping up the front of the shanty.

"My Lord! Git up! The place is on fire!" Larkes screamed as he jumped to his feet and ran for Reasa.

She sat straight up. Her eyes flew to the blazing flames, and her first thoughts were maternal. "My baby! Save my baby!" She grabbed Noah and handed him frantically to Larkes. "Hurry, please! Save my baby!" she yelled.

Like some uncontrollable monster, the flames were sweeping from the front to the sides of the shanty with each passing second. Larkes covered the boy's head in his blanket. He yelled at Reasa.

"Grab my belt and follow me."

Even with the light of the fire, it was almost impossible to see through the thick smoke. Larkes remembered seeing a small window in the back of the shanty, so he groped blindly in that direction. The smoke seemed to have filled his lungs now, and the heat of the fire was searing them. He tried to hold his breath, but he was getting too weak. Just as he thought he would collapse and give into the fire's will, his head rammed into the wall. His hand touched the glass of the window, just inches away.

Larkes quickly shifted Noah to one hip and grabbed his Colt. With one bash, the glass shattered and the rotting wood fell away. He slipped Noah through the small opening and let him drop, then grabbed Reasa and pulled her roughly forward. His chest was pounding for fresh air. "Jump!" he said, half pushing her through the window. In seconds, the three of them were lying out on the frozen ground, gasping as their bodies inhaled the cold, life-giving night air.

As soon as Larkes could muster up the strength to move, he grabbed Reasa and Noah and ushered them away from the heat. The shanty was quickly engulfed by the raging fire, and burning embers flew out at them. They found safety in the trees, where his horses were still tied. Reasa immediately sat down with Noah held tightly in her lap, to shield him from both the heat of the fire and the cold of the frozen earth. Larkes was just about to join them, when he caught a movement at the front of the shanty.

His eyes felt dry and singed. He squinted to look against the bright flames. At first, he thought one of the other coloreds had come to help. Then, the silhouette of Deputy Frank's sizeable belly appeared, clearly outlined in the firelit night.

Larkes realized at once what had happened. A surge of anger raced through his aching chest.

"You sorry, no-good bastard."

Deputy Frank turned and faced him. Larkes raised his Colt and aimed dead center at the middle of Deputy Frank's chest. His finger squeezed on the trigger. Deputy Frank was as mean and low-down as a snake, but something disturbing crawled through the back of Larkes' mind. He shoved it aside as his finger squeezed harder. An instant before the gun exploded with its deadly load, Larkes dropped its sight to the deputy's leg.

Suddenly, Deputy Frank hit the ground screaming. The bullet had blown away his left kneecap. He rolled on the ground in agony, hollering out in shock and pain.

But Deputy Frank's shock couldn't match the surprise Larkes was feeling, himself, for not having killed the man. He stared down at the Colt that was gripped tightly in his hand, wondering why they had both betrayed him. Not that taking a man's life was a pleasureable thing to do. Larkes had never enjoyed that kind of feeling. Each time there'd been a death—there were seven, as he vividly recalled—Larkes had nearly gotten sick over it. But the empty, sick feelings always came after the fact. He'd never had any problems, once the time came to fight. Not until now. He turned around and glanced at Reasa, who was staring at the writhing deputy in stunned silence. She clutched Noah against her bosom, holding his head so that he couldn't see.

The cold night air was mixed with the sounds of the fire's destruction and the yelps of agony from Deputy Frank. He was pleading for help, his pudgy cheeks glistening red from the heat of the fire. He had been felled too close to the burning shanty and was sounding panicky.

"Please! Somebody help me! My leg's been shot off!"

Deputy Frank was yelling so loud, Larkes was sure he could be heard all the way back to the white section, which was a good three hundred yards away. Yet, not a soul appeared. Except for Reasa's, the row of shanties remained dark and silent.

Reasa stood up, still holding Noah in her arms, and nudged Larkes roughly. "We better git, and fast. The last colored that had a run-in with the law here was found floatin' in the river," she said.

Larkes, who had gone back to staring down at his Colt and wondering what had taken possession of him, blinked hard and tried to let some calm settle in. He nodded. "All right. I'm goin'. But what about you? Where can you and the boy stay?" he asked.

Reasa's eyes widened. "Look here!" she said, her voice rising. "You just git me away from here! That's all I'm askin'! Why, there ain't a soul who'd put me up after this done happened!" She looked at the ruins of what had once been her home. "Even if they had room for Noah and me, the same thing would most likely happen to them."

Larkes tried to take in a deep breath. His lungs felt raw and full of smoke. He was tired and drained, but nothing could compare with the sick headache he had gotten over this whole mess. The pain started at the back of his neck and followed a line up the right side of the back of his head, all the way to his forehead. He let his eyes run over the fiery scene and the wounded deputy, then turned instinctively to his horses. It would be so easy to just mount up and ride away. But what would happen to Reasa and her boy? He glanced back at her and was immediately caught up again by her beauty. His teeth gritted in anger. Why? Why was he letting something so trifling as a woman's beauty send his life tumbling into ruin? It wasn't Reasa he blamed, either. It was his own fault, and since Larkes had never been in such a situation before, he had no easy idea what to do about it.

Reasa was watching him expectantly. Noah had managed to squirm loose from her protective hold, and his small face was turned toward the fire. His eyes stared, uncomprehending, at the bright light. He pulled a hand free and started sucking his thumb.

Larkes was still standing there in his indecision, when he noticed a figure had appeared next to Deputy Frank. It bent over the deputy briefly, then straightened and turned toward Larkes. "You shoot dis here lawman?" The figure gestured.

It was the old man that Larkes had first spoken to, Otis Bell. Larkes nodded silently.

Otis Bell's eyes were wide with excitement. He shook his head and started talking in a low, breathless tone. "Dat be terrible bad. You bes' be movin' on, and fas'! Yessuh, you be sho' and git on outta here. Fas', now!" He looked down at Deputy Frank and shook his head again, but there was no sign that he was the least bit upset to see the lawman lying wounded at his feet.

Larkes was feeling the trepidation growing inside him. He studied the situation around him. Otis Bell was standing over the wounded deputy with a concerned look, waiting to see what Larkes would do next. The deputy had managed to come to his senses a little bit. He had quieted down to a low moan, but he was still hurting too badly to feel angry toward Larkes. Reasa had not moved. Her eyes were glued to Larkes' with a hopeful shine to them that made him groan inwardly. He said weakly, "I ain't got a saddle for ya."

Reasa tried to suppress her smile. "I'll make do." She patted Noah's head. "Won't we, baby? We'll make do."

She quickly climbed up on the big white gelding, tucking her long, white sleeping gown around her legs and taking hold of the reins. Noah held his arms up to her and tried to stand on his tiptoes. Reasa reached down to pick him up and almost fell off the horse before she grabbed the horse's mane and pulled herself back up.

Larkes' jaw twitched. He reached down and picked the boy up. "He can ride with me," he said.

They mounted up, and as they started to leave, Otis Bell hurried over. He looked sad and worried. "Miz Reasa," he said, "I sho' wish dey be someplace you could stay." He gestured toward one of the shanties. "What about de Williams'? Mebbe dey got room."

Reasa shook her head and sat up straight. She was an odd sight, still in her nightgown and barefoot—a woman who had just lost her home and everything in it, even though it was just a shanty. Still, she looked proud. "That would never do, Otis, and you know it," she said firmly.

"Well, den." Otis Bell shook his head and shivered. "If yo' has to go, den you bes' be puttin' somethin' aroun' ya. My oldest girl, de one wit' de chile? She got somthin' you could put on your back. Ain't got no shoes, but we could wrap yo' feet in somethin'. Come on."

It didn't take long for Reasa to slip on an old burlap dress over her sleeping gown and a pair of worn-out socks.

Larkes threw one of his blankets around her shoulders. He unrolled another one and wrapped it around little Noah, then propped the boy securely in front of him. Soon, they were on their way, riding into the bitter cold night. The winter skies had cleared, and a million stars twinkled overhead. Normally, riding out under such conditions would have been to Larkes' liking. Tonight, though, his heart was pounding with worry, not only for his own future, but for that of Reasa and the little boy he held in his arms.

8

ALONE IN THE DIMLY-LIT ROOM, ALMA STARED DOWN into the simple wooden coffin. She had left her uncle's house and walked to the funeral home, just to get a moment alone with her mother.

As she stood there, the words of the undertaker, Vernon Skaggs, ran through her mind. "Your mother will look beautiful," he had said. Her eyes widened as a sudden anger mixed with the hurt inside her. Beautiful, she thought. Why, her mother didn't have the slightest look of beauty about her! Not at all, the way her skin was all drawn up to the point where she looked twenty years older than her age of thirty-five. The mouth was stretched wide, as if the corners had been pulled toward the ears. Alma almost couldn't believe it was her own mother. She had been a beautiful woman, with eyes that sparkled and a deep dimple in her cheek when she smiled. The sickness had eaten slowly away at her, until she had barely weighed eighty pounds when she died. Her skin, once so soft and clear, had turned ashen. Charcoal circles rounded her eyes.

Alma had an urge to give Vernon Skaggs a piece of her mind. Still, she knew that he really hadn't had much to work with. He must have done his best, she thought. Still, it hurt her to think that this thin, pale form would be everyone's lasting impression of her mother. Her prettiness had always been a source of pride for Alma, who secretly hoped that she would grow up to be just half as comely. Alma grabbed the handkerchief that Aunt Nora had given her from her pocket and sobbed into it.

"How could you do this?" she asked God under her breath. Then, realizing there was nobody to hear, she let her voice rise. She talked to God just like he was a mortal being, standing there beside her. "Wasn't it enough that you took our papa?" she cried. "What about me and Toby Ray? Poor Toby Ray! Oh, God, nobody wants Toby Ray. Why, God? Why doesn't anybody want poor, poor Toby Ray?"

She looked up at the dirty ceiling through her tears. Her words became shrill. "What about my brother? Your words say you're a God of love—" Her voice broke, and she fell to her knees.

She cried in deep, racking sobs, letting out all the hurt and resentment she'd let build up inside her. Then she felt someone taking her by the arms.

"Now, now. You just have your cry, honey. Lord knows you have every right," Vernon Skaggs said in a low voice. He sat down and pulled Alma into his arms, patting her back and kissing the top of her head. "You just go right ahead, now."

Alma slowly let her body sink down onto his lap. Her need to be comforted was stronger than anything else right now, and for a brief moment she felt almost secure. She closed her eyes and let his arms hold her tightly, until the deep sobs started to go away.

It didn't last long, before she felt Skaggs' hand begin to move up and down her back. Alma had never been romantic with anyone in her life, but she knew right away that there was more than just comfort in the way he was touching her. His hand lingered too much in the wrong places, and his breathing was getting louder in her ear.

She wanted to scream out at him, but she couldn't bring herself to do it. Instead, she sat there paralyzed as his hand moved down over her buttocks. "Oh, God!" she cried silently. "Have you deserted me completely?"

Vernon Skaggs was just starting to work his hand under Alma's dress, when the bell over the front door jingled. He suddenly jumped to his feet, sending Alma sprawling face-down onto the floor at the base of her mother's coffin.

She lay there a moment, stunned and relieved at the same time, before she looked up to see Uncle Ted standing inside the door. It surprised her that he would come to the funeral home. When she had last seen him, he'd been out at the edge of the woods, cutting down a dead tree for heat. Even if he was an unexpected sight, Alma had to admit that she was glad to see him. It made her shudder to think of what Vernon Skaggs might have done to her if he hadn't been interrupted.

Uncle Ted took a half step inside the room and stared at both of them, perplexed. He looked first at Alma, sprawled on the floor beside the coffin, then at Vernon Skaggs, who was doing his best to recover his artificial undertaker's demeanor while standing with his hands folded across his crotch.

"What's goin' on here?" Uncle Ted asked, his voice unsure of his own question.

Vernon Skaggs looked sadly at Alma, then closed his eyes and nodded his head, making little clicking sounds with his mouth. "Poor dear," he finally said, opening his eyes and breathing deeply. "It's always this way when they're so young and lose a parent." He made a show of bending over Alma and patting her on the shoulder. "Now, now. Have at your grief, child," he said.

Uncle Ted looked at them both for a moment, then said, "Come on home, girl. Aunt Nora's lookin' for ya."

Alma got up slowly without looking at Vernon Skaggs, who smiled at her uncle reassuringly. She was worried that her trembling legs might betray her before she made it outside to the wagon. She crawled in weakly beside Uncle Ted.

They rode in silence, and Alma was grateful. Right now, she needed to be alone, if only in her thoughts. It was her and Toby Ray's future that concerned her.

She knew that Uncle Ted's generosities and letting her live with them was for all the wrong reasons. Oh, Aunt Nora did need help. She was a frail woman to begin with, and her husband and children kept her busier than most healthy women could handle. Besides the cooking, washing and cleaning, she was up before dawn every day, milking and gathering wood to make breakfast. Still, Uncle Ted was purely more interested in satisfying his own wants than finding help for his poor wife.

Then there was Toby Ray. Alma had to swallow the lump that forced its way into her throat. It haunted her mind to think of what might happen to him. Doc Thurman was sending that letter to his sister in Kansas City. Alma tried to think exactly where Kansas City was. It had to be at least a month's ride away. For all practical purposes, she thought, it might as well be a million miles. She'd most likely never see her brother again. Suddenly, Alma felt all the love she'd had for her mother being willed over to Toby Ray. She wanted to take him in her arms and hold him, protect him. The lump came back to her throat, and she had to fight to keep from crying over her helplessness.

They were half-way home before Uncle Ted broke the silence.

"That undertaker feller, Skaggs. Was he botherin' you?" he asked.

Alma was startled. She looked nervously away and said nothing, hoping that somehow her stalling would make the question go away.

"Answer me, girl. Was he botherin' you?"

"I-I don't know what you mean," Alma said, barely aloud.

Uncle Ted pulled the wagon to a stop, right in the middle of the road. He turned so that his rotting teeth were right in Alma's face. His breath was strong with liquor.

"Now, listen here. I married your Aunt Nora when she was younger than you. So don't play stupid with me. Was he botherin' you or not?"

Alma had an urge to laugh in his face. She would have, if she didn't feel so much pain inside. Instead, she turned her face away from him. "No. In what you're talkin' about, he didn't bother me. Now, can we just go on home?" she said shortly.

Uncle Ted leaned closer and said, "Well, if he wasn't botherin' you this time, he will the next. Why, I hear tell ol' Skaggs ain't above foolin' with a dead woman, if 'n you know what I mean." He grinned.

Alma thought about her mother, and a sick feeling came over her. She turned suddenly and stared at him. "Why are you goin' on like this?" she asked, her voice trembling. "You know my own mother's lyin' in that funeral home! Are you tryin' to hurt me more than I've already been hurt?"

"Aw, just relax, girl," Uncle Ted said. "Your mother, rest her soul, was all wasted away. No, I'm a-talkin' about others. You remember Bessie Andrews? I heard—"

"That's enough, Uncle Ted!" Alma screamed at him.

They were both surprised. Alma had never raised her voice to him before. Alma had always managed to keep her temper in the past. For all of his bad ways, Uncle Ted had helped out just enough to keep them from starving to death, ever since their father had drowned. But this was too much for her to take in her time of sorrow.

Uncle Ted looked angry for a moment, then seemed to shrug it off. "Now, you just lower your voice, you hear?" he said. "I was just tryin' to warn you about that sorry no-good, that's all. Besides, you're gonna be livin' with us now, and I feel a responsibility for ya. You know, Aunt Nora is feelin' right poorly in life." Without any show of dignity, he paused and put a chew in his mouth, then worked it around to where he could spit, all the while keeping an eye on Alma. "Hell, girl. Let's be honest. It ain't cheap raisin' a family these days, and you're gonna be another mouth I gotta feed. Now, the way I see it, with your Aunt Nora bein' frail and all—" He spat and licked his lips. "She just don't feel like havin' my companionship any mores." He smiled and reached up to touch Alma's hair. "You could kinda fill in for her. You know, a man needs a female's comforts from time to time."

Alma had always felt a strong disgust for her uncle, but now the hatred that rose up inside her was stronger than any she had ever felt. She wished she were a man, so she could beat the smile off his face and pound his head to a pulp. But even that wouldn't be enough. She wished he were dead. She wished Vernon Skaggs were dead. She wished they were dead and her mother was alive and healthy.

Alma started to cry. She had to get away from this awful man and his dirty smile and filthy hands. Suddenly, she stood up and jumped from the wagon.

A sharp pain went through her leg as her ankle twisted. Alma ignored it and tried to run, but fell. She got up, and fell again.

She felt Uncle Ted standing over her. He tried to take her by the arm and pull her up, but she pulled away. "Don't touch me! Not now, not ever!"

Uncle Ted grabbed her and yanked her to her feet. "Shut your ungrateful mouth," he said, then slapped her hard across the face. "Now, you git in that wagon and behave yourself, less'n you and that 'lil bastard brother of your'n want to try and feed yourselves tonight." He flung her onto the wagon and whipped the team.

Alma let her mind go blank. She sat there with her eyes fixed on the horses ahead as they rode in silence. She didn't move a muscle when, after a few minutes, Uncle Ted reached over and ran his hand along her leg.

9

THE COLD SNAP THAT HAD SET IN FOR THE PAST THREE weeks, bringing frigid temperatures and freezing winds, finally broke on the day of Lydia White's funeral. By one o'clock, the time she was to be interred, the temperature was hovering just above the freezing mark. The sky had turned a deep gray, with clouds so thick there wasn't as much as a peek-hole to be found through them. The winter-stripped brown trees looked like drawn-up figures silhouetted against the dark sky.

The cemetery was located next to the little church, where Alma and Toby Ray had spent many a happy Sunday, back when their mother had been alive and healthy. The funeral party consisted of Alma and Toby Ray, Uncle Ted, Aunt Nora and their children, Doc Thurman and his wife, a few ladies from the church, the Reverend Silas Jones and, of course, the undertaker, Vernon Skaggs. Alma tried to pay no attention to the latter, but every time she looked his way, he would give her a little knowing smile. She had managed to be strong through this ordeal, even though she was so wrapped in pain that she often wondered how much longer she could go on. While doing her best to ignore Vernon Skaggs and his awful smile, she held on tightly to Toby Ray. She had kept him close by her side since they'd gotten up that morning. Somehow, she had the feeling that once their mother was in the ground, Uncle Ted would surely get rid of her brother. Their uncle had never had a kind word or soft look where Toby Ray was concerned, and Alma sensed that things would happen fast.

She stared at the coffin, which sat next to a pile of dirt. A light rain began to fall, bringing a chill back to the air. The tiny wet drops on the new wood held her attention. She wasn't really thinking about the raindrops, but she used them to keep her mind off other things. By the time Reverend Jones began his eulogy, there was barely any of the coffin top that hadn't turned dark from the rain.

"Lydia Mae Baxter was born October third, 1857, to Jerome and Gertrude Baxter in Richmond, Virginia. She grew up to marry Paul White of Tennessee on April twenty-first, 1875, at which time they moved to the Fort Smith area. A daughter, Alma Kay, was born on September sixteenth, 1876. A son, Toby Ray, was born June fourth, 1884. And—" The Reverend paused, looked up at the gray sky and wiped his face. He glanced at the people who were gathered around. "Lydia White was called home from this wicked world on February twenty-seventh, in the Year of our Lord, 1893."

Reverend Jones turned to Alma and Toby Ray. "You poor children." He shook his head. "I know her life seemed terribly short. And it was, by our standards. But I knew your mother to be a good, wholesome Christian woman. And I must tell you that, if I were ever to venture to say that a person was goin' to cross that river and spend eternity with our Lord and Savior, Jesus Christ, that person would be Lydia White. In her thirty-five-some-odd years, I hope she instilled enough of her undyin' righteous ways in you young'ns, so that some day, when you make your own journey, you will taste that sweet River Jordan, yourselves. Your poor mama," he went on. "Ever since the day I met her, fourteen years ago, it seemed like she always had a heavy burden to carry. She lived through your daddy's drinkin' and gamblin' ways. Why, not a soul in this community can remember seein' poor Lydia that she wasn't barefoot and threadbare, takin' in people's washin's, cookin' meals for the sick and needy when she barely had enough for her own. She lived like an angel of mercy, until she finally became sick herself." Tears filled the reverend's eyes as he clutched his King James' Bible to his breast. "Lydia!" his voice raised. "Her life may have seemed that of a pauper, but let me tell you that God loves the Lydia Whites of this earth, for she walked with Him. And though her clothes were of rags, she carried the Lord's Word with her every day. Some—no, most—carry it with them only on Sunday mornin's, or when a man of the cloth comes to visit." Tears rolled down his face and he shook his finger at the sky. "But I say unto you, Lydia White carried that Word with her every day of her life."

The rain was turning to sleet, making little spitting sounds as it hit the earth. It bounced off Reverend Jones' black hat. He threw a glance back at the sky and hurriedly leafed through his Bible. "I turn now to the Twenty-Third Psalm." He sheltered the book with his hand and read.

" 'The Lord is my shepherd, I shall not want. He maketh me to lie down in green pastures; He leadeth me beside the still waters. He restoreth my soul. He leadeth me in the paths of righteousness for His name's sake. Yea, though I walk through the valley of the shadow of death, I will fear no evil, for Thou art with me; Thy rod and Thy staff they comfort me. Thou preparest a table before me in the presence of mine enemies; Thou anointest my head with oil; my cup runneth over. Surely goodness and mercy shall follow me all the days of my life, and I will dwell in the house of the Lord forever.' "

By the time he finished the psalm and closed his Bible, sheets of ice were pelting the group unmercifully. Reverend Jones quickly stepped forward and laid a white ribbon across the coffin. His wife had stitched a cross on the ribbon, along with Lydia's name. Then he moved close to Alma and Toby Ray and put his arms around them both.

Alma caught herself stiffening at the reverend's touch. Lately, every grown male she had come into contact with had seemed to have more than comfort on his mind when he touched her. She pulled back and looked into Reverend Jones' eyes. There was a sadness about them that she had not seen in the others. Relaxing a little, she said, "I thank you kindly for your kind words. Mama sure would have appreciated it." At the mention of their mother, she felt Toby Ray press into her side, and she felt closer to her brother than she ever would have thought possible. She put her hand over his head to protect it from the stinging frozen rain, and he didn't protest.

Doc Thurman and his wife, Esther, gave Alma and Toby Ray their condolences and started to walk away, when the doctor stopped suddenly and turned to look closely at Toby Ray's face. He raised Toby Ray's chin with his finger. "Who gave you this lickin', boy?" he asked.

When Toby Ray said nothing, Doc Thurman stared for a moment at Uncle Ted, then frowned. "Well, I got my own idees." In a matter-of-fact tone, he said to Alma, "We've posted the letter to my sister in Kansas City. Hopefully it won't be too long. If you're—" He hesitated. "Well, if things get too rough for the boy, you send him over to me and the missus. Heathen though he may be, you can count on him gettin' three squares and decent treatment." Before he turned to leave, he added, "That is, of course, only until I hear from my sister."

Alma managed a weak smile. "Thank you," she said, and put her arm around Toby Ray's shoulder. Together, they left their mother's grave and climbed into the back of Uncle Ted's wagon.

They were barely settled, when Uncle Ted announced, "I thought that old Preacher Jones would talk forever. I'm hungry!"

Some of the ladies of the church had brought food to the house, and Aunt Nora had almost had to stand guard to keep Uncle Ted and the children out of it until the service was over. That food was all Uncle Ted had on his mind. Alma wanted to scratch his eyes out of his head. She looked at his ugliness and wondered if there

was one ounce of decency in the man. If so, she had
never been able to find it.

Aunt Nora looked woefully at Alma and Toby Ray.
"Now you hush up, Ted," she said. "No reason to talk
like that in front of them."

"Talk like what?" Uncle Ted said. "Everybody knows
how that Reverend Jones goes on and on. That's the
very reason why I don't darken the door of that church
of his."

"I don't recall you ever darkenin' the door of any
church," Aunt Nora said as she reached around to squeeze
Alma's hand.

"You hush your mouth, woman! Now, let's get on
home with as little talk as possible. I got chores to do."

With that, they rode the rest of the way in silence.
When they passed through the gate of Uncle Ted and
Aunt Nora's 63-acre farm, Alma again had to wonder
over life's unfairness. The farm had been handed down
to Uncle Ted by his father. On it, they kept a sizeable
garden. Roaming freely about, there were three milk
cows, seven goats, a pair of mules, a longhorn, Uncle
Ted's team of heavily muscled horses, more than a dozen
layers and a rooster. He also had boar, two sows, five
half-grown pigs, half a dozen dogs and two cats.

The two-story house was large, but had been patched
over and was badly in need of paint. The barn was new—
the townspeople had pitched in and helped him build it
two years ago when the old one had burned down. There
was a chicken coop in bad need of repair and a smoke
house. Over half the farm consisted of woods, and the
rest was pasture land for the animals and play yard for
the children. To any decent farmer, the place was an
eyesore, what with the buildings and the lack of fences
to separate the livestock.

To Alma, though, this was a majestic place, indeed.
She had often wondered how Uncle Ted managed to
keep such a fine array of food and animals, since he was
as lazy as any man she had ever known. He was always
complaining about tough times, but it was plain to see
that there was plenty, what with milk to be had from

the cows and the goats. The chickens kept them in eggs for breakfast, and the garden was plentiful with food to eat fresh in the summer and preserve for the winter. In the summer, Uncle Ted would trade garden vegetables to Old Man Winslow for young roosters, so Aunt Nora would fry one up at least twice a week. There was always a hog to kill, or a goat, and in wintertime the woods were full of squirrels, rabbits, deer and turkey.

As Alma looked around, she didn't begrudge Aunt Nora and her children any of these fine luxuries, but it still pained her to think of what she, Toby Ray and their poor mother had had to endure all those years, just to stay alive. Why, Uncle Ted could have kept them in enough food that they would never have had to go to bed hungry, and he wouldn't have missed a thing. No, Uncle Ted had never felt anything but self-pity. He just wanted to justify his laziness. He was a slickster, she thought suddenly. He slicked people into thinking what he wanted them to. She remembered back when her daddy was alive. Uncle Ted had always been afraid of his wife's half brother, but as soon as Paul had died, Ted had taken to pointing out how lazy and corrupt her father had been. Alma knew the things he said were partly true, but she also knew that her daddy was known to put in a good day's work when he wasn't taken by drink. He had told her about Uncle Ted, too—about the times he'd gotten his brother-in-law a job and Uncle Ted had barely lasted a day before he'd quit, claiming a sore back or some other ailment. Alma looked around the big farm. Her daddy had never had this kind of success in life. And poor, poor Mama, she thought. Working her fingers to the bone, going to bed hungry and never complaining. Life just didn't seem to balance out for some folks. She wished she could like Uncle Ted. This would, indeed, be a fine place to live.

Alma had been right. As soon as the team was unhitched from the wagon, Uncle Ted and Raymond headed straight for the kitchen table, which was filled with food. Neighbor ladies had brought fried chicken, green beans and winter peas. The preacher's wife had made a roast, complete with potatoes and a thick gravy. There was boiled cabbage, several apple pies and a cake. Alma nearly yelled out in protest when Toby Ray reached out for a chicken leg and Uncle Ted slapped his hand.

"You warsh first, boy," Uncle Ted said.

"Go on, Alma, honey," Aunt Nora said quickly, giving her a smile. "Get yourself a plate and eat."

Alma was seething as she watched Toby Ray walk slowly to the back porch to wash his hands, his head hanging down. She expected him to look hurt, but instead she saw anger on his face. It was the kind of anger she had seen many times in her little brother. It made her feel a little better, knowing his good Irish temper was showing through. Toby Ray desperately needed to be strong, what with the uncertain future he was facing.

"I'm not really very hungry," she said softly to Aunt Nora.

"Oh, but you must eat, honey," Aunt Nora insisted. She handed Alma a plate. "Here, sit down next to Uncle Ted."

"She's right, girl. Eat," Uncle Ted said, his mouth already full of food.

Soon they were all seated. Alma felt a resentment over the way Uncle Ted and his children kept their heads bowed over their plates, eating like heathens— just as if there had been no death or burial at all. She nearly choked over a piece of roast when she felt Uncle Ted's heavy hand grab her on the inside of her thigh. He didn't even look up, but kept shoveling food in his mouth with his other hand. She tried to lock her knees together, but Uncle Ted's thick fingers pinched her tender skin so hard it forced them open.

"Uncle Ted!" she blurted out through clenched teeth. "Please!"

Aunt Nora looked up at the urgency in Alma's voice.

"You know, I was just thinkin'," Uncle Ted said, his hand still clenching Alma's thigh. "I reckon that boy could stay a few more days with us." His cold stare turned to Alma. "You'd like that, wouldn't ya?"

Alma's heart sank. She dropped her eyes from his.

Uncle Ted said, "Was there somethin' you was wantin' to say, Alma? Wantin' more roast?"

"Maybe a biscuit," she mumbled. This wasn't happening, she thought, right there in front of Aunt Nora and their children. She kept her legs drawn as tightly together as possible. They were starting to ache, and she felt more than grateful when Reverend Jones and his wife, along with two ladies from the church, rapped on the door.

"I'll get it!" she said, jumping to her feet and nearly knocking over a pitcher of milk. She tried to smile at Aunt Nora as she straightened her skirt. Then she noticed the greasy spot where Uncle Ted's hand had been.

That evening, mindless of the rain and sleet, she went with Raymond and Toby Ray to do the chores. She was glad it was dark when they headed back to the house. She grabbed two biscuits, along with some roast, and headed for the bedroom, Toby Ray in hand.

Uncle Ted appeared outside the door. "Where you two goin'?" he asked.

"To bed. It's been a long day," Alma said simply.

Uncle Ted stood in the doorway, blocking their way. "Well," he said, "I let both of you sleep in here last night, but the room belongs to Melissa and Amy. I was pretty much figurin' on lettin' you sleep with them two, Alma, but havin' Toby Ray bed down in the barn."

When Alma's eyes widened, Uncle Ted added, "Now, surely you don't expect me to make all four of my own young'ns sleep in the same bed, whilst you two hog that one?"

"But, but, couldn't Toby Ray stay in the house? He could sleep on the floor somewhere. It—it's so cold outside," Alma begged.

"Why, shoot fire, girl! Whilst I was growin' up, I slept more in the barn than in the house! Do the boy some good to learn the hardships of life! No, sir, he'll sleep in the barn tonight. I'll have Raymond go and help him fix up a nice warm spot," Uncle Ted said. As he turned to leave, he looked back around and pointed a finger. "Don't you be settin' no fire. Hear me, boy? I done had one barn too many burn down."

Alma sat down, stunned. She tried to pull Toby Ray next to her, but he yanked free with his shoulders. He stood there with his chin jutting out stubbornly. "I'll be all right," he said stiffly.

"Honey, you'll freeze to death, out in that damp ol' barn," Alma worried.

"Will not. Papa and I used to go huntin' and we stayed in the woods when it was cold as this."

"That was different, Toby Ray. You had Papa to keep you warm."

Toby Ray looked down at his feet. "I can take care of myself. Don't you be worryin' none," he said in a low voice.

Alma brushed his blond hair off his forehead and tried without success to kiss him. "I know you can. I'll tell you what. I'll get some blankets from Aunt Nora, and I'll stay out there with you."

Toby Ray looked up at her. "You don't have to do that."

Alma knew her brother well enough to know that he didn't mean what he was saying. "Come on." She smiled. "You'll see. We'll make it an adventure. Now, let's go see Aunt Nora."

She expected a protest from Uncle Ted, but he only smiled at her in silence. Aunt Nora, however, threw up a big protest. "Why, you'll freeze to death!" she said.

"Aw, hell! They'll be all right." Uncle Ted silenced her. "Be good for 'em. 'Specially the boy."

With that, Alma and Toby Ray took what blankets Aunt Nora had to spare and crawled up into the hayloft. They rooted around until they had piled up enough dry hay to pack around them, and made themselves a bed for the night.

Sleep was hard for Alma, between Toby Ray's tossing and kicking and the damp cold that seeped through the hay and their blankets. She wanted to cry and grieve, but it somehow seemed useless. She had lost her home and both parents, and now, even her emotions had been taken away from her.

10

By THE TIME LARKES FINALLY LOCATED THE ABAN-
doned dugout, a light but steady rain had already started,
and with it came a stout wind. It was March. The February freeze that had gripped the area for so long had
given way to a warmer climate, somewhere in the upper
forties. Normally, this change of conditions would have
pleased Larkes quite well. The rain, though, was causing
him more misery than anything else. It had soaked everything, leaving the ground covered with puddles, the trees
and sage brush drooping from the weight of the water.
Even the dugout was too wet and cold to provide much
of a shelter. Larkes cussed the idiot who had designed
the thing. Why, whoever it was had simply dug a big
hole out of the side of a little knoll, with no thought as
to how durable or rain-proof the thing might be.

A few boards had been laid across the top, and the
sod roof was mostly worn away. They hadn't, Larkes
noticed, even bothered to put in a chimney. He wondered
how they'd cooked their meals. Must've had to make a
campfire outside. Inside, the room was no more than six
by eight feet.

Larkes looked around for something to start a fire
with, hoping to warm them up and dry things off. There
was nothing dry enough to burn. He cussed again. Even
if he could start a fire, he thought, they'd probably choke
to death on the smoke, what with no chimney.

He stood in the doorway, the rain blowing in his face, and looked the situation over. His wet clothes felt heavy on his body, and he was tired. He wanted in the worst way to pull himself inside, away from the relentless, wet winds and find a bit of comfort, but he couldn't. Instead, he had to force himself to disregard any of those discomforts if he wanted to get off by himself and think. He was thinking a lot lately about the predicament he'd gotten himself into.

He turned around and looked at Reasa and Noah. They were huddled together in the corner, sitting in the driest spot they could find. Reasa had wrapped herself around her son the best she could and was talking to him in a low voice as she tried to warm his little body. His chest fluttered at the sight. That was one of the worst parts of his dilemma, he thought. After two weeks of traveling with Reasa, she still caused his heart to go weak at the sight of her. It wasn't good, a woman having that kind of a hold over a man.

He bit the inside of his lip, suddenly angry with himself. What was he going to do with a woman and a young'n? Colorado, he thought, seemed like a world away, even if he hadn't shot Deputy Frank. Traveling with a female that occupied his every emotion was one thing for a man to have to deal with, but a female with a four-year-old son was just about more than he could take. He tried to rationalize his thoughts, but deep down he felt ashamed. He was glad that Reasa had Noah. He was a fine son for her, even though Larkes did find him a little bit on the sissy side, always clinging to his mama. And as far as traveling was concerned, it was a common thing these days for men to take their families across the country to start a life in new and untamed lands. He'd been witness, himself, to a huge migration west for the last dozen years or so.

Larkes was still standing there, blinking against the cold rain, when he noticed a movement. At first, he thought it was a deer in the wet gray distance, but as the figure neared, he saw that it was a rider, hunkered forward and pushing his mount southward. Larkes could see water spraying upward as the horse's hooves pounded the muddy ground. The horse was a fast one, he thought, for it moved gracefully over the soggy ground with no apparent effort.

Larkes pulled his eyes away and glanced over at his own white gelding, tied to a tree nearby. Such a fine animal—he had a sudden urge to mount up and challenge the unknown rider and his fast mount to a race.

He was pondering that thought when the rider suddenly stopped, jerking so hard on the reins, his mount's rear nearly touched the ground. The rider swung the horse eastward to face Larkes. Still a hundred yards away, he sat there, motionless, for two or three minutes. The restless horse nodded its head up and down, then shook away the coat of water from its mane.

The rider was leaned forward in his saddle, as if straining harder to see. After a while, he nudged the horse forward.

Larkes' wariness began to turn into curiosity as he watched the man come in closer. Ever since he'd shot Deputy Frank, he'd been leery of any passing horseman. It was that wariness, in fact, that had brought him to this sorry excuse for a hide-out in the first place—it being out of the way and all. Larkes figured whoever had built it, out in the middle of nowhere, had done so for just the same purpose as it was serving him now.

Soon the rider was close enough for Larkes to get a decent look. He appeared to be an Indian. This wasn't surprising to Larkes. Outside of the black families he'd run across and gotten clothes from for Reasa and Noah, Indians were about the only folks he'd seen since he'd crossed over into Oklahoma Territory.

The rider was young and average in size. Just as Larkes had suspected, he was Indian, but not full-blooded. He rode his horse to within ten feet and again stopped.

"What's your name, boy?" the rider snapped in a high-pitched voice.

Larkes purposely ignored the question. Instead, he stared at the big nostrils of the rider's fine horse, as it heaved vapors of hot breath into the damp air. Larkes had always held a fascination for good horses, and this one looked to be just as fine a specimen as his own gelding.

"That's awful good horse flesh you're runnin' to death," he said, his eyes still on the animal. "Ain't good to run a horse so hard in weather like this."

"Perhaps you didn't hear me, boy. I asked you your name," the rider repeated, ignoring Larkes' observations.

Larkes was used to the title. He'd heard it all of his life. He didn't like it, but it wasn't worth killing a man over, he figured. If that had been the case, he would have been forced to kill many men. Still, there was something unusually irritating about the tone of the young rider.

"Who's askin'?" Larkes said deliberately, his eyes boring directly into the rider's.

The rider sat up erect. His right hand edged slowly toward his revolver. Larkes, who had been leaning against the doorway of the dugout, stood up straight and let his hand hang loosely next to his Colt.

Seconds passed, as the rider seemed to contemplate whether he should go for his pistol or not. Suddenly, he burst into laughter.

"Hell, boy!" he said. "I thought maybe you was a lawman, or somethin'. No, I'd judge you to be on the other side o' the law." His dark eyes swept past Larkes to the entrance of the dugout. "What you doin', standin' out here in the rain?"

Larkes kept a serious stare, his eyes fixed on the rider's face. He'd learned years before about enthusiastic young riders like this one. Life and death held little difference in their way of thinking. "I'd say if anybody's runnin' from the law, it'd most likely be yourself," he said.

"Now ain't you the smart one?" the rider said. "What ever gave you such an idee?"

Larkes looked around, then up at the sky, all the time keeping his hand close to his Colt. "I don't reckon a body'd be out here ridin' such a fine horse so hard, and in weather like this, unless he had some kind of urgency about him," he pointed out.

"Hot damn, boy! Don't you know curiosity can get a man killed?" the rider exclaimed, then laughed. "You got any coffee?" He tried to look inside the dugout.

"I got coffee, 'cept I ain't got nothin' to heat it up with," Larkes said.

The rider reached behind him and into his saddlebag. Larkes edged his hand closer to his Colt, a move that wasn't lost on the rider. He laughed again.

"Name's Henry Starr, and you can relax your hand. If I'd wanted to kill ya, I reckon I'd already done that!" He pulled out a bottle of whiskey. "Here." He tossed the bottle to Larkes. "It ain't coffee, but I promise it'll warm your innards just the same!" He stepped down from his horse. "Go ahead"—he gestured—"and have a drink. It's good stuff."

"To be honest with ya, I could use a good drink," Larkes said, his voice softer. When he was finished, he offered the bottle back to the rider.

Henry Starr waved it away. "Keep it. I don't touch the stuff. Don't drink no tea nor coffee, either." He gave a twisted smile to Larkes. "And don't offer me no tobacca."

"What you carryin' it for, then?" Larkes inquired before he took another swig of the burning whiskey.

"Sellin' it for an old boy. Shucks, I got six more bottles, there." Starr pointed to his saddle bag. He turned around, still with a smile on his face. "Hell, boy, you gonna tell me your name, or are ya just gonna stand there and drink my whiskey?"

Before he could answer, Larkes had to catch his breath from the second drink. This whiskey may have been fine stuff in Henry Starr's opinion, he thought, but it was pure rotgut to Larkes. Still, it was warming him up just fine. He finally took in a deep breath and said, "My name's Larkes Dixon."

"Ain't heard of ya," Henry Starr said. He leaned past Larkes to peer into the dugout. "Got a wife and young'n, huh'?"

Larkes started to protest, but stopped short. It wasn't any of this Henry Starr's business, he thought, and not worth wasting a conversation over.

Henry Starr didn't seem to notice or care that Larkes hadn't answered him. Instead, he turned his attention to Larkes' horses. "By dawg," he said, "that's a fine-looking gelding you got there."

"I was thinkin' the same thing about your mare," Larkes said. "That is, if you don't run it to death in this weather."

"Why, you some kind o' veterinarian?" Henry Starr asked as he approached Larkes' gelding. At first, the horse tried to jerk away, but Henry Starr rubbed its head and soon had it calmed down. He walked around the horse, patting it here and there, a look of admiration on his face. Larkes noticed the grace in Henry Starr's walk. His body was fluid, and there was a sureness about him.

"What'll you take for the gelding?"

"It's not for sale."

"Everything's for sale, boy. Only the price matters," Henry Starr commented.

"All the same, that horse ain't for sale. Not at this time, anyway," Larkes said.

Reasa appeared at the door then, looking inquiringly at Henry Starr. He noticed, and quickly pulled his hat from his head, nodding. "Why, beggin' your pardon, ma'am," he said. "I don't reckon we been properly introduced by your husband, here. Hasn't as yet even told me your name." He glanced quickly at Larkes, then back at her. "He didn't tell me you was so pretty, neither."

A small, pleased smile appeared on Reasa's lips and worked upwards to where it soon covered her face and sparkled in her eyes. "Why, ain't you nice," she commented. "My name's Reasa, and this here is my baby, Noah." She reached around to coax Noah out from behind her. He moved reluctantly forward and peeked around her skirt, his thumb stuck in his mouth.

"Why, that's a nice name. Right out o' the Bible," Henry Starr said. Losing interest in the gelding, he moved closer to Reasa. "Larkes Dixon, I'd say you got a fine-lookin' family, here. Yessir, a fine-lookin' family," he repeated, his eyes glued to Reasa.

"They're not my family," Larkes said simply. "But we're travelin' together, just the same."

"Well, I declare! Ain't that interestin'?" Henry Starr said, giving Reasa a flirtatious smile. He looked down at Noah for a moment. "The way that boy's chewin' on his thumb, I'd say you folks must be hungry," he said, moving back to his horse. "Here, let me get you somethin' to eat. Got some ham and biscuits." He offered a sack to Reasa. She glanced at Larkes, then took it from him.

The aroma spilled out into the air when she opened the sack. Reasa pulled out a biscuit and some meat and handed them to Noah, smiling as he hungrily shoved the food into his mouth.

"Go ahead, git yourself some," Henry Starr prompted her. "There's plenty in there."

"Thank you kindly," Reasa said. She helped herself, then offered the sack to Larkes. He hesitated a moment; then, with his eyes held on Henry Starr, he reached inside. Henry Starr looked pleased as he watched them devour his fine fare.

The rain showed no signs of letting up, so they decided to stay in the damp dugout, where they could at least get some shelter. Reasa invited Henry Starr to join them. That afternoon, they huddled inside, listening to Henry Starr tell stories about how he intended to be the next Jesse James. His boastfulness held a fascination for Reasa, who thought him more charming than evil. Noah, who was shy at best, seemed to take to Starr right away, what with Starr's funny facial gestures and exciting stories. All of this was not lost on Larkes, who contented himself with sitting apart from the group and drinking Henry Starr's rotten whiskey.

He decided to let Starr have his way with the two, until it became apparent that Starr was going to great lengths to get Reasa interested in himself. Starr's stories were entertaining enough, but it disgusted Larkes the way he seemed to be carrying on just for the woman's benefit.

On top of that, it pained him that Reasa seemed to be enjoying the flirtatious behavior. The more agitated he became, the more he drank. Finally, he couldn't hold himself back any longer. He rose slowly to his feet and glared down at Starr.

"Why, I don't reckon you'd never catch Jesse James doin' such a fool thing, runnin' his horse to death in weather like this!" he said, taking another long drink of whiskey.

The suddenness of Larkes' statement brought a look of surprise from the others. Larkes looked hard at Henry Starr. "No, I'd say you ain't nothin' but a common thief. Prob'ly stole this whiskey, and the food, too," he added.

Henry Starr's face grew taut. "What you tryin' to say, boy?"

"I ain't *tryin'* to say nothin'. I said it. I think you're full o' hot air."

Henry Starr started to rise, but Reasa jumped up and grabbed his arm. "Please," she said. "He's drinkin'. 'Sides that, he'd kill ya before you even got up."

Henry Starr stared at Reasa. His eyes blinked. He gave a sarcastic laugh. "Kill me? Why, there ain't a man in this part o' the world quick enough to kill me, less'n he catches me sleepin'. Is that what you was figurin' on doin', boy? Catchin' me sleepin'?" He looked at Larkes and laughed hard.

Reasa stood there nervously between the two. She turned to Larkes. "Now, looky here, Larkes Dixon. We was near starvin' when Henry brought us somethin' to eat. And you! Drinkin' his liquor and not even feelin' grateful! Now, you stop this talk, before someone gets himself hurt." Her words sounded angry, but there was a look of pleasure in her eyes as she looked up at Larkes' drunken face.

Henry Starr was standing behind her, still angry from Larkes' accusation. "You better listen to what the pretty lady says, boy. I'll let it drop, if you will."

Larkes' head swirled. His thoughts were bitter ones, but he knew Reasa was right. Starr had brought them food, and they had been hungry. Even the whiskey, though foul in taste, had soothed his body just fine. The haziness in his mind, though, couldn't completely cloud the fact that he was jealous. More anger welled up inside him as he considered this fact. His eyes left Reasa's and settled on Henry Starr, who had a smirk on his face. Larkes had a strong urge to call Henry Starr outside. But then his eyes fell on Noah, who stood in the back of the darkened dugout, fear on his tender young face. Some of the anger drained away, and he felt disgusted.

He stepped out into the rain, mumbling, "To hell with you, then. Tell your big stories to the women and children." He took another drink of Henry Starr's whiskey.

11

WHEN LARKES WOKE UP, HE KNEW IT WAS EARLY morning, even though the rain was still coming down steadily and the overcast sky had kept everything in darkness. He could hear the drops making splashing noises in the puddles on the ground.

He'd fallen asleep sitting in the doorway of the dugout. The rain had soaked him from his thighs to his feet, while the rest of his body was considerably wet, as well. Not only was he cold, but he had a splitting headache. It wasn't just the rain that was causing his head to pound, either. He felt for the empty bottle that lay next to him and cursed softly. He rubbed his hand against his eyes and tried to focus, but it seemed like too much effort. He started shivering, but this only made his head hurt more.

Once again, Larkes had to curse his situation. Cold, wet and miserable. His breath smelled so bad he could hardly stand to be with himself. In disgust, he tried to kick the empty bottle, but he was so stiff his leg betrayed him. Instead, his foot struck only mud.

Larkes leaned back and thought about his mama. He thought about her a lot these days. They were good thoughts. He wished she were still alive. He wished he was still home on the plantation, living in the shanty. Not that he had ever appreciated working from daylight to dark while the white master's own son roamed freely, doing whatever he took a notion to do. No, what Larkes missed was his mother's soothing hands rubbing his face, her arms holding him tight. He'd give all the gold in Colorado for just one of her simple yet tasty meals of turnips, collard greens, fried fatback and cornbread. Why, if his head didn't hurt so much, he could almost smell such a fine meal, right now.

But, his head did hurt. It hurt so bad, in fact, that Larkes hadn't even remembered Reasa or Noah or Henry Starr. He didn't know why, but he continued to sit there in his miserable state, his aching eyeballs fixed on his aching legs. His legs seemed detached from his body as he watched the pounding rain fall on his boots. He let a good half hour pass, sitting in his hungover state, thinking about his mama and the pleasantries such memories brought.

He might have sat there all morning if there hadn't come a roar from somewhere behind him. He forced himself to move his detached, wet legs and looked around. There, inside the door, was Henry Starr, lying on his back and snoring.

With a start, Larkes suddenly remembered Reasa. His heart pounding, he tried to see into the darkened dugout. He stumbled around like a Saturday night drunk, his feet slipping and sliding, trying to get up. Panic tore at him, thinking that Reasa had spent the night inside, with Henry Starr in close proximity. On his second failed attempt to get to his feet, he gave up and crawled madly inside, ready to rip their bodies apart, away from each other. He would teach Starr a lesson for being so bold.

Larkes crawled into the dugout and right on top of Starr, but Reasa was nowhere in sight. He backed away from Starr and hesitated, looking for her. It wasn't until he heard her voice from somewhere in the dark that he realized his foolishness.

"What you doin', wakin' everybody up? It ain't even daylight yet! It's cold enough, without us havin' to wake up and face it!" Reasa stopped her scolding and pulled Noah close. "Go back to sleep, hon. It's all right."

Larkes felt as stupid as a jackass, perched on his hands and knees just above Henry Starr, who was still snoring away. He wished he could think of something clever to say to Reasa, to help erase the foolishness of the situation he found himself in. But his splitting headache prevented any normal retort. Of course, in Reasa's presence, he rarely found himself without his tongue twisted in knots. This fact didn't set too well with him, but there was nothing he could do to change it. Finally, he said, "And he wants to be another Jesse James! Sure wouldn't catch Jesse snorin' with people up and about!"

Sheepishly, he raised to his knees, making sloshing sounds as he walked back out into the rain. As he stood there with the rain pelting his face, Larkes became enraged at himself. How in the world had he ended up in such a fix, standing out in the rain, drunk on rotten whiskey, with his sole worry being over a sassy-talking female's feelings? He looked toward his horses. For two cents, he thought, he could mount up the white gelding and move on to Colorado. He could leave his other horse for Reasa and the boy. Under his breath, he said, "Let Mister Henry Starr, the famous outlaw, take care of ya. Sleepin' in the same room!" He spat in disgust.

He wanted to go inside and talk to Reasa, but his pride wouldn't let him. Instead, he stood out in the rain with his horses, watching the clouds carry the rain on past overhead. By the time Henry Starr did awaken, the rain had stopped and light filled the sky. He moved slowly out of the dugout and took a deep breath, then noticed Larkes.

"Hot damn, boy! What you been standin' out here in the rain for?" Starr shook his head and laughed at his comment.

Larkes paid little attention. He'd been thinking the same thing, himself. Any knot he'd like to tie in Henry Starr's tail would have to come at another time. Right now, he needed to think, and in doing so, he didn't need to be bothered by Starr, or Reasa's charm, or Noah's churning belly. He'd thought about the Colorado question all morning. The urge to leave had hit him so strong at times, he'd actually started to grab the gelding's saddle a time or two and mount up. How he hated guilt! And a woman's guilt, at that!

Larkes stood silently, his back to Starr in the hope of dissuading any conversation. Henry Starr wasn't deterred one bit, though. He went right on, boasting of his outlawing intentions. The name of Jesse James, he said, would someday be of little significance next to the name of Henry Starr.

"Listen, boy," Starr said. He walked up close to where Larkes was forced to be a part of the conversation. "I got me a girlfriend. May Morrison's her name. Lives about seventy, eighty miles from here, near Nowata. What you and me oughta do is take Reasa and Noah to her place. May's pap, J. O., wouldn't mind a bit. Why, he knows all about me and my ways. Anyways, I was thinkin' we could leave 'em there and you could join my gang. Someday, the name Larkes Dixon might mean somethin', knowin' you rode with me. Folks might sit up and take notice." He stood there, waiting for Larkes to jump at the chance.

Larkes felt like smacking Henry Starr in the mouth, much like a man would swat a bothersome fly. But he knew that would only cause a ruckus between himself and Reasa. Nonetheless, his irritated look wasn't lost on Starr.

"You think I'm kiddin', don't ya?" Starr said. He put his hands on his hips and leaned forward. "Listen," he said, "I've already had me one gang. Can't say too much about 'em, though, seein' as how they all got themselves caught or shot up. But I'm startin' again. Got me one man already, name of Kid Wilson. You could make it three."

Larkes couldn't hold back a sarcastic laugh. Disgusted, he walked past the enthusiastic Starr. Unfazed, Starr followed close behind, still talking a blue streak. Larkes just shook his head. He figured besides being young, Starr must be crazy to boot. Still, something underneath told him there was a danger about this young pup. Not that it worried Larkes for his own personal safety. Still, it was something that a man had to recognize. When he saw that he wasn't going to put an end to the conversation, he reeled around, so suddenly their chests collided.

"You talk mighty big for a man that looks to be runnin' from somethin'," he said. "You probably do have ambitions to be like Jesse James, all right, but I figure you're still too wet behind the ears to have done any robbin' of banks and trains, like you boast. So, if you don't mind, I'd like a little peace and quiet this mornin'."

Starr's face turned angry. "I reckon I do mind!" he said. "You tryin' to call me a liar?"

Larkes' eyes narrowed. "You keep that hand away from your sidearm," he warned. "I just want ya to shut up. I'd hate to have to kill ya to achieve that wish."

Starr studied Larkes for a few seconds. He began to step backwards, his hand hanging loosely next to his pistol.

Just then, Reasa stepped out from the dugout. "You men!" she said. "You plannin' on killin' each other?" She glared at both of them. "Well, to tell you the honest truth, I don't much care. All I know is, I'm hungry, and my baby's hungry."

Starr relaxed as he smiled into Reasa's eyes. "Shucks! I don't mean to kill nobody, but if you care about this boy, here"—he motioned toward Larkes—"you'll teach him a few manners when he's talkin' to me." He nodded at her. "Let me get you some more ham and biscuits."

Starr walked toward his saddlebag, then stopped and studied something in the distance. "Hey, boy, you see that tree over yonder? See that little finger branch, the bottom one?" He pointed.

Just as Larkes turned to look, Starr cleared leather, dropped to a knee and shot off a good nine inches of the tiny naked branch, at a distance of forty paces.

"Don't mean to show off," he said to Reasa. "Just tryin' to save the boy's life, here." He smiled as he holstered the pistol and turned his triumphant look toward Larkes.

For an instant, their eyes met. Then, like a bolt of unexpected lightning, Larkes pulled his pistol and fired, clearing off another few inches of the branch. Before Starr could blink twice, another shot cleaned the branch completely away.

Slowly, Larkes holstered his pistol and walked past Starr, who stood with his mouth gaping open like an envious schoolboy.

"Believe I'll have some ham and biscuits myself, if'n Mister Starr's got enough to go around," Larkes said.

When Starr spoke, his words came out in a rush. "By damn! That's the finest shootin' I ever seen in my life. Except for myself, that is. Hot damn!" He slapped his leg. "Why, I don't reckon there's a deputy marshall in the Territory—No, by golly, there ain't ten deputies in this whole dang *country* that would stand a chance against the two of us! Come on and join the Henry Starr gang!" he said.

"Like I told ya," Larkes began, "I ain't interested in robbin' no banks or trains. We're on our way to Colorado, and Colorado is where we're goin'."

Amiably enough, they huddled against the dugout, and divided up the remainder of Henry Starr's provisions. Reasa brought Noah out and gave him a generous share.

"Col-o-rado," Starr said after a moment of silence. "Now, there's a place I always wanted to see. Kid Wilson and Frank Cheney and myself has talked about goin' to Colorado Springs. We'd be goin' up there for social reasons, but I just might rob a bank or two while we're at it. I figure the money there to be just as spendable as the money in these parts."

After they had eaten breakfast, Starr held the talking ground for the next three hours, chatting about his life story and that of anybody else he could lay claim to have knowledge of.

Where Larkes had been agitated before, he now found himself amused at all the talk. Ever since the shooting display, Starr's demeanor had changed, and Larkes was actually beginning to enjoy listening to the ramblings.

It was a little past noon when Larkes stood up to
stretch his long, aching body. He had just gotten his
arms above his head, when a piece of the dugout's
doorway exploded, not more than a foot from Reasa's
head. In the instant it took for Larkes to look at her,
gunshots began slamming into the dugout all around
him. It sounded like the whole world had erupted in
gunfire. As quick as a cat, Starr dove into the dugout.
His pistol drawn, he was already returning fire as Larkes
hurried Reasa and Noah inside.

Larkes pulled his gun and joined Starr. In the tree line,
a hundred yards away, he could make out at least a dozen
or more men with smoking Winchesters. The shooting
went on for several minutes, without letting up.

"Some of your admirers, I suppose?" Larkes said as
he reloaded.

"Shoot, no! They ain't no friends of mine," Henry
Starr said. He stared out at the men, firing as he talked.
"See the two darkies out there? They're U.S. deputy
marshalls, Ike Rogers and Rufus Cannon. Those two
are lower'n snake shit. Rest are Indian policemen." He
paused and shook his head, then wiped his brow. "Them
darky son of a bitches! I shoulda killed 'em when I had
a chance, back at May's house!"

It was a fairly hopeless situation, and Larkes knew
it. The shots were coming fast and furious, ripping into
the dugout and the ground at their feet. Larkes expected
at any minute to catch a piece of hot steel, himself.
As desperate as the state of things seemed to Larkes,
however, Henry Starr didn't seem very nervous, at all.

As Larkes was thinking about the situation, a bullet
cut a hole in Starr's sleeve.

"Shit!" Starr gasped. "I could feel the heat of that
one!" He slipped back into the dugout to reload his Colt.

"My God!" Reasa cried out. "They're gonna kill all
of us!" She looked up into the darkened ceiling of the
dugout. "Please, Lord, don't let them get little Noah!"
She squeezed her son tightly.

Starr paused from his reloading and looked pityingly
at Reasa and Noah. He bit his bottom lip. "Don't worry

'bout a thing," he said. Turning to Larkes, he added, "I'm goin' for my horse. When I say 'now,' you open up with everything you got, and I'll be outta here."

"Why, they'll kill you before you go three steps," Larkes said.

Starr laughed out loud. "Ain't no lawman gonna kill me," he said. "Luck runs in my family." He started to leave, then paused. "Now, you remember, May's pap is named J. O. Morrison. Their place is north of Nowata," he said. "Everybody knows 'em. You be sure and stop in on your way to Coloradee!"

With that, Henry Starr made a mad dash for his horse. Bullets started flying so fast, Larkes was in total amazement that Starr didn't fall dead. Instead, he jumped on the back of his horse, and was soon racing away, bent down low over his mount's neck.

It was apparent that it was Starr that the posse was after, as the shooting stopped the minute he was out of sight. Some of the Indian policemen followed him, while the others mounted and rode toward the dugout. Larkes turned his attentions to Reasa, who was close to hysterics.

"It's all right. It's over," he said. "For the time bein', it looks like Henry got away. We've got nothin' to worry about."

Reasa started to sob. "B-b-but w-what about Frank? Maybe they after you for shooting Frank."

"No. It's all right. I promise," Larkes said. He rubbed a tear from her cheek. "Why, I don't reckon they'd send a big ol' posse after a man who just shot another man in the leg. No, it's Henry Starr they're after."

Outside, Larkes could hear the hoofbeats of the posse as they approached the dugout. As he started to rise to his feet, he thought about all of Starr's stories about robbing trains and banks. Mostly to himself, he muttered, "I guess ol' Henry Starr isn't so full of hot air, after all."

12

WHEN ALMA STEPPED INSIDE THE SMOKEHOUSE, SHE didn't see the dark shadow in the corner. There were no windows, and by the dim light that was allowed by the open door, she could barely make out the meat that hung from the rafters. Aunt Nora had sent her to fetch a ham for Sunday dinner, and Alma was glad to oblige. Any chore that allowed her to get away from the loud chatter of kids and Uncle Ted's sinister gaze was a welcome one.

The smokehouse was dark and stuffy, but at least it was quiet. Alma took in a deep breath. The smells of the smoked meat brought back memories of when she was little—Toby Ray's age, in fact. They were such sweet memories, back to a time when her father hadn't been drinking so heavily. He had really tried to make a better life for all of them. Alma could remember running along behind her mother to the smokehouse, laughing and telling stories. That same smell had always greeted them. They had been a real family. Life could have been good, Alma thought, fighting back a sudden tear. Now, though, everything was so disheveled for her and Toby Ray that thinking such nostalgic thoughts only made her feel worse.

Alma was staring down at the floor, deep in her thoughts, when she realized that she wasn't alone. In that moment, a hand suddenly clamped down on her

81

mouth. She tried to scream out, but Uncle Ted's large
hand cut off her airway. She struggled, but her strength
was no match for his, as he pulled her tightly against
him. His harsh breath burned her ear.

Alma had always been afraid of her uncle, and she
could barely stand the disgust she felt when he would
try to fondle her, whether it was under the table at
mealtime or alone in the kitchen as she tried to wash
the supper dishes. Now, though, an even bigger terror
washed over her. She knew his intentions were much
more serious than a poke of his fingers between her legs
or a squeezing of her breast.

With his free hand, Uncle Ted flung a quilt down
on the dirt floor at Alma's feet. Then, in one powerful
motion, he lifted her up and laid her on the blanket,
pinning her down beneath him. Still covering her mouth,
he lowered his hand so that she could breathe through
her nose.

Alma sucked the air into her lungs, but instead of the
nostalgic aroma she had just been enjoying, her nostrils
were filled with the sweaty, foul odor of Uncle Ted. She
tried to holler, but all that came out was a low moan that
only she could hear herself. A silent scream continued
to fill her body, causing her throat and lungs to ache.

Uncle Ted reached down and ripped at her underpants.
They came off in shreds. He worked his free hand, trying to remove his britches, but Alma's struggles were
making his progress too slow. With a curse, he stopped
and glared down at her.

"I'm a-gonna take my hand off'n your face, and so
help me, you better not let out so much as a peep, ya
hear?" he growled. Slowly, he peeled his hand from
Alma's mouth and reached down to work at his britches.

Alma took in a bellyful of air and intended to scream,
but Uncle Ted was ready. He pulled back his arm and
slapped her, so hard her head thumped against the floor
like a melon being smashed against a rock. Alma thought
her head might explode. Stars flashed before her eyes
and the pain was worse than she'd ever felt in her life.
Uncle Ted's voice seemed far away.

"I warned you, girl," he said as he pulled his britches down around his ankles.

Alma was afraid to try to scream again. Her head was pounding, and she could feel her lip swelling up. The taste of blood filled her mouth. Uncle Ted would only hit her harder if she called out for help, so when he moved off of her for a second, she did the only thing she could think of. She pressed her legs together and squeezed as hard as she could.

This seemed to amuse Uncle Ted. He let out a gutteral laugh that sent spittle flying from his mouth. "You females are all alike," he said. "Think you got some sorta treasure down there." He paused and spat on the floor, just inches from Alma's face. "But in the end, you all give that treasure up, easy enough."

He reached down and shoved his thick fingers between her knees, trying to push them apart. Alma squeezed harder. Uncle Ted cursed and forced his hand between her legs. Alma strained against him, so hard that she felt a vessel pop in her nose. Droplets of blood began to roll toward her mouth. She tossed her head from side to side as she fought to push him away.

His strength was too much. Alma knew it was just a matter of time before he won out. The thought of what was about to happen made her so sick, she wanted to die and be with her parents.

It seemed so long ago, but once, when she was thirteen, Alma had promised her mother that she would save herself for marriage. "Be pure of heart, soul and body," her mother had often said. "With times so hard for us, it will be worth a queen's dowry to your husband." The words echoed in Alma's mind. She had known a few girls who had given up their virginity before marriage, and none had seemed the worse for it. Still, she had made an oath, and that promise was all she had left of her mother besides the memory of a frail and sickly woman. Gritting her teeth, she fought with all she had left. She was losing ground fast, but at least she could make Uncle Ted's conquest as unenjoyable as possible.

It was only seconds before her strength gave out. With a grunt, Uncle Ted positioned himself on top of her. Alma shut her eyes and tried to lose consciousness of what was happening. Something hard began to jab painfully at the inside of her leg. She wriggled to get away, but he had her pinned to the point where she couldn't move more than an inch or two. Then, Uncle Ted moved, and she realized with horror that he had found the spot. She felt her body stiffen as she waited for the pain. Her stomach began to lurch, and she knew that she was going to vomit.

But there was no pain. Somewhere off in the distance, she heard a loud crack. Then the heavy weight of Uncle Ted's body was lifted.

He was rolling on the floor beside her. "Holy shit!" You broke my damn skull!" he hollered, holding his head. "I'll cut your gizzard out, you little bastard!"

Alma blinked and looked up at her brother. Toby Ray was holding a big piece of firewood in his hands. His face was filled with anger. "Git up and run, Alma," he said as he lifted the wood and swung it down again.

The second blow broke Uncle Ted's knuckles as he reached up to protect his head. He tried to sit up, but couldn't. Bewildered, he stared at Toby Ray.

"You're gonna kill me, boy. Please don't hit me again," he said in a trembly voice. Again, he tried to raise himself, but could only make it to an elbow. Carefully, he shook his head and wiped his brow with his busted fingers. When his hand moved away, it left a red smear across his nose and forehead. Fresh blood began to run down his face.

Toby Ray let the chunk of wood hover over his head. "You touch my sister again, and I'll kill you in your sleep," he warned.

Uncle Ted cowered, shielding his head with his hands. "Please, don't hit me with that thing again," he said.

Alma got to her feet. Just a moment ago, she'd been scared half out of her wits. Now, here she was, looking down at her uncle with both disgust and curiosity, while he sat on the dirt floor, helpless to a boy of eight. Blood was covering his face. One particular stream ran from the top of his head to his left ear. There, it divided, one half running around the front of his ear, the other following the curvature of the back. Normally, the sight of so much blood would have made her feel weak-kneed. But Alma didn't feel queasy at all.

"Come on, Toby Ray," she finally said, her gaze still locked on Uncle Ted. She tugged on her brother's coat. "Let's go, hon. He's not apt to sit there, all queer and all, for very long."

Toby Ray backed slowly away from Uncle Ted to the door. He stopped, raised the firewood high over his head, and hurled it. Uncle Ted tried to dodge, but the wood bounced off his shoulder. Uncle Ted yelped in pain. Quickly, Alma grabbed Toby Ray outside and pulled the door shut behind them.

Turning to him, she swept Toby Ray up in her arms. "Thank God!" she cried as she hugged him. "You're always there when I need you. But now, we've got to run, or Uncle Ted'll git you, and git you good." Alma wanted so badly to sit down and hold Toby Ray with the love that she felt for him right now. She wanted to hold him the same way her mother had held her when she was eight years old and needed comforting. But, as happy as she was that Toby Ray had rescued her, she also knew that it meant the end of their life with Uncle Ted and Aunt Nora. He was an evil man, to be sure, and Toby Ray's life would be in serious danger as soon as Uncle Ted came to his senses.

She bent down and took Toby Ray by the shoulders. "Now, you listen and listen good. I'm gonna go inside and distract Aunt Nora. When I do, I want you to put some supplies in a poke. Pack up somethin' we can eat on for a couple of days, 'til we find out what we're gonna do. I got some blankets hid in the barn."

Toby Ray looked surprised. Alma kissed him on the cheek before he had a chance to pull back. She felt quite pleased with herself. She had known this day would come and had planned ahead. She had no idea what the future held, but she had decided long ago that she would never be separated from Toby Ray. No one would ever split them up.

Toby Ray, who had resisted her kiss, hugged her quickly around the neck before he broke away and ran back into the smokehouse.

Alma watched him, stunned. She was so shocked, she clutched at her chest. "Toby Ray," she yelled weakly. "You get back here!"

There was a loud crash. Alma felt her legs begin to tremble. Just as she was fearing the worst, the door opened, and Toby Ray emerged with a large cured ham in his arms.

"I got him a good one, Alma! A real good one! He won't be fit for chasin' us or nobody—not for a while, anyway!" he said with a satisfied grin.

13

ALMA AWOKE LONG BEFORE DAYLIGHT. HER FACE and body ached. She was so tired, she felt like she could curl up and sleep for days, but worrisome thoughts about her and Toby Ray's future wouldn't allow it. She had dozed off and on all night.

Before they left Uncle Ted and Aunt Nora's farm, they had managed to gather up the cured ham, three biscuits from the noon meal and a few potatoes. Alma had hidden away two of Aunt Nora's hand-made quilts, and they took those as well. Though they were traveling light, it was still hard, walking through the darkness on foot. They had finally made it to their parents' cabin, where they spent the night. It was the first time Alma had been to her home since the funeral.

She got up and lit a candle, then began to look around for anything else they might be able to take with them. It was strange—she had forgotten just how poor they had been. The cabin looked like a half-empty old shed. Except for the bed, table and two chairs, there was no furniture. Alma didn't remember it being so small and bare. There was no food, just a moldy piece of bread on the table. It was hard for Alma to imagine that they had lived without even the tiniest of comforts and not felt even a little bit depressed over the fact. Not that she had been totally blind about their situation. Many times, Alma had longed to invite one of her school friends to visit or spend the night, but she'd been afraid they would make fun of her home, even her family. Instead, she'd gotten the reputation of being shy and stand-offish. It hurt, but Alma realized that this was life's judgment for them. Besides, she knew that what her family lacked in worldly comforts, they more than made up for in love. Even their father, when he was alive, had been a loving man. She had learned to turn a deaf ear to all the whispered comments about her daddy's whiskey habits and lazy ways, because when he was sober, he had seemed to genuinely care about all of them.

Tears began to roll down Alma's face as she moved slowly around the little cabin. They hadn't built a fire, for fear of alerting someone that they were there. It was cold and empty and somehow nothing at all like the home that it once had been for her and Toby Ray. It could never be a home to them again.

Crying quietly, she looked around for anything that might be useful in the long journey that lay ahead. She found a frying pan and a few eating utensils. The sheets and quilt on her mother's bed were frayed and worn. Alma lovingly touched the old quilt. Before her mother had taken sick, she had always slept in the bed with her. They had both tried to convince Toby Ray to sleep with them, but he had insisted on sleeping on a thin pallet on the floor. It had irritated their mother to no end, especially on cold nights, but since his father's death, Toby Ray had stubbornly insisted on trying to act older than his years. Now, Alma had found that she couldn't bring herself to sleep in the bed, either. Instead, she had curled up next to Toby Ray on his pallet by the fireplace.

She laid out the two blankets, then packed the food and utensils into two rolls. When everything was ready, she woke Toby Ray.

"Come on, hon. We gotta git."

They stepped out into the cold dark night and walked in total silence. Ten minutes passed before Toby Ray spoke up.

"Where we goin' to, Alma?" he asked, barely above a whisper.

"Just away from here, for the time bein'," Alma said.

"Come on, Alma," Toby Ray said, a little louder. "Tell me where we're headin'."

Alma could hear the fear in Toby Ray's voice, even though he tried to hide it, so she said sharply, "I don't rightly know yet. So hush up."

Toby Ray fell silent again and they continued. Nearly two hours passed before it was completely daylight. There was a fine sunrise, and normally Alma would have enjoyed such a sight, but her thoughts were clouded with worry. Toby Ray's question was a legitimate one. Where were they going? Alma really didn't know about any places except Texas and Kansas. Texas was out, since Uncle Ted and Aunt Nora had family there who would surely write and tell Uncle Ted that she and Toby Ray were there. Alma doubted if Uncle Ted would travel all the way to Texas for revenge, but then again, she couldn't say he wouldn't. There was a great-aunt and great-uncle living in Kansas, but Alma had only seen them once when she was a little girl. They were her daddy's kin, and she didn't remember much about them.

Knowing it was better to walk anywhere than to stay and face Uncle Ted, they continued west, hoping to find some bit of inspiration as to what to do. They took turns carrying the ham. It soon became heavy, but Alma knew that such discomforts couldn't be avoided. Traveling without money or even a single-shot rifle, getting something to eat would soon become a major undertaking.

It wasn't only food that was pressing on her mind. Alma kept a close eye on the sky above them. The weather had grown mild after a terrible December, January and February, but it was now time for the stormy season, with endless days of cold rain. The kind of rain that caused the fever and pneumonia. All the clothing they had was what they wore on their backs. Their coats were shabby, and with only two quilts between them, they would have no protection, at all.

As much as Alma tried to convince herself that things would turn out all right, she realized that their chances of surviving might not be so good.

As the day wore on, thoughts about Uncle Ted began to fade away. Alma found a new appreciation for the countryside around them. This may have seemed a small pleasure, but she enjoyed walking along beside Toby Ray with their newfound freedom. It was quiet and peaceful and the air smelled good. And best of all, there was no one around to give them cause to fear. She glanced at Toby Ray. He looked as happy as could be. Just like the old Toby Ray, she thought, talking like a magpie. His constant jabbering usually drove her crazy. Now, though, it sent a good feeling through her. She felt a new kind of love for her brother, almost maternal, and a heavy sense of responsibility.

It was late in the morning when they happened upon a deer, so close that it kicked dirt at their feet as it bounded away. Without a word, Toby Ray took off after it. Alma tried to stop him, but before she knew it, he and the white flag of the deer's tail were out of sight.

Fear gripped at Alma. It was her turn to carry the ham, and its weight slowed her down. She called out, but there was no answer. Imagining that he must have fallen off a cliff or something, she was just about to drop the ham and her blanket roll and take off running after Toby Ray, when he suddenly reappeared. He ran back to her, laughing, his eyes full of excitement.

"You stay close to me, you hear?" Alma scolded him. She felt angry, but had the urge to hug him at the same time. She tried, but Toby Ray broke loose and was off again. With a small smile, she shook her head. She was glad Toby Ray was feeling so happy, but his good fun was going to worry her to death.

That evening, they made camp under a large old cottonwood tree. The night air brought a coldness with it that cut through their clothes. Alma was afraid to try to build a fire, for fear of drawing attention. She spread one of the quilts over the damp earth, and they covered up with the other. Huddling next to Toby Ray to keep him warm, she spent a fitful night, awaking over and over again. It was so cold, she was sure they would freeze to death before morning.

But they didn't freeze; in fact, Toby Ray seemed to have slept right through the miserable night. When the faintest hint of light appeared in the far eastern sky, Alma jumped up and had to shake him hard to wake him up. She was convinced that walking, even in the darkness, was the only way to keep warm. Even if Toby Ray was handling the temperature all right, she couldn't bear to be still any longer.

Toby Ray sat up, rubbed the sleep out of his eyes, and went behind a bush to relieve himself. Alma took out the ham and cut several generous slices, then packed up the two blanket rolls. She was too impatient to sit down to a leisurely breakfast. Instead, they set out again, stumbling through the dark and eating the ham as they felt their way along.

By ten o'clock, the sun was sitting high in the sky, its beautiful rays making everything glisten around them. At the same time, Alma was beginning to realize that she'd made a mistake. They hadn't come across any water all morning, and the salted ham was making her thirsty. She scolded herself. The cottonwood tree they'd slept under had been right next to a small stream, and she'd been in too big a hurry to take a good long drink before they left. The day before, they'd run into plenty of small creeks and streams, but today, there was nothing but dry earth as far as she could see. Alma's tongue began to feel enlarged in her throat. The thirst was getting unbearable. It depressed her to think that she hadn't been any smarter than that; after all, she was responsible for Toby Ray's welfare as well as her own. She wondered if he felt as miserable as she did. If so, he didn't let on.

High noon came and went, and still no sign of water. Alma didn't mention stopping to eat. The torture of thirst was consuming her every thought. She noticed that she was sweating profusely, and that only made her mouth feel more dry. The blanket roll and ham were getting heavier with each step. It would have been nice to stop and rest, but she knew that would only keep the next water hole farther away.

Alma soon got so weak, her legs began to quiver with each step. Her tongue was sticking to the top of her mouth. To make matters worse, Toby Ray was beginning to complain about wanting a drink. Alma wanted to scream at him to shut up, but her mouth was too dry to form the words.

For months, the sun had been hidden away behind dense gray clouds, leaving a chill over the earth below. Now, its rays were freed, along with the first warmth since Mother Winter had held her iron grip on the land. Normally, the burst of sunshine and the abundance of spring-like weather would have thrilled Alma's heart. Today, though, she was thirsty and tired, and the sun burned down on her miserable face. As it sank to the west, its bright rays blinded her eyes.

Finally, Alma stopped. It wasn't that she wanted to. It just happened. Her legs suddenly became numb. She knew that if she didn't get off her feet, she would fall. Spotting a big rock that jutted out of the ground, she managed to get to it and sat down.

"I'm thirsty," Toby Ray said for the tenth time in ten minutes. His face was bright red and shiny with sweat. He wiped his forehead with his sleeve. "I gotta pee," he said and turned to relieve himself where he stood.

"Blame it, Toby Ray! Do you have to do that right next to me?" Alma moaned. Her words made smacking noises in her dry mouth. It surprised her that she still had a voice, at all. She had supposed it had dried up and blown away, along with her spirits. Hearing Toby Ray relieve himself made her angry, because the sound made her think even more about water. She looked at the ham and frowned. It made her sick just to think about it.

Toby Ray fastened his pants and sat on the rock next to her. Crossing his legs, he said, "Well, did you ever figure out where we're goin' to?"

Alma didn't answer. It was too much of an effort to talk, and besides, she didn't have any ready things to talk

about. They were just about at a dead-end, she thought.
Either they kept going and took a chance of dying in the
middle of nowhere, or they turned back, which wouldn't
be any better than dying. She looked off into the horizon,
and her thoughts froze.

There was someone riding toward them on a mule.
Alma's instinct was to run and hide, but she was too
exhausted. Whoever it was would just have to find them,
even if it was Uncle Ted—

Uncle Ted? What if it was him? Suddenly, her thirst
was forgotten. Alma's heart started to pound as she
remembered what had happened in the smokehouse and
Uncle Ted's warning words to Toby Ray. Quickly, she
pulled herself to her feet and grabbed Toby Ray by
the arm.

"What's wrong, Alma?" Toby Ray said. He followed
her gaze and squinted at the rider. "Who's that?" he
asked, without much concern.

Alma stopped and studied the man riding toward them.
She relaxed some when she realized it couldn't be Uncle
Ted. This man was a lot older. Besides, Uncle Ted would
never be caught riding a mule.

The two watched the man approach in silence, as if
they'd both been thrown into some kind of trance. The
man appeared to be studying them, too. He rode straight
in to where they stood.

He looked to be in his fifties, but Alma reckoned as
how she'd never been good at telling someone's age,
especially someone past twenty-five or thirty. The man
had a white beard that had yellowed around his mouth.
Alma could tell his hair had once been black as a crow's
back, but it was streaked with white. His legs were long
and fairly skinny. He wore overalls and a black coat
with a sweat-worn hat. He carried a shotgun in his
free hand.

They looked each other over. The man's eyes were
hard and emotionless. "You young'ns look all tuckered
out. Where you from?" he finally said.

Alma was surprised at the kindly tone in his voice.
It surely didn't match his eyes. She was thinking about

how to answer his inquiry when Toby Ray stepped forward.

"You got water in that canteen, mister?" he said, pointing.

"Why, yes. Yes, I do," the man said. "Please," he added, handing the canteen to Toby Ray, "have all you want."

Toby Ray lifted the canteen to his lips, then stopped and handed it to Alma. "Here, Alma. You should be first."

Alma smiled at him through her misery and started to drink in large gulps.

"Not so fast, girl," the man said. "You'll likely get sick, drinkin' so fast. Besides, there's plenty more where that came from."

Alma kept on drinking the wonderful water, not even listening to the man who'd come and saved them. She drank like she'd never drunk before, then handed the canteen to Toby Ray. She took in a deep gulp of air. Her body felt alive once more.

Toby Ray took a long drink, then handed the canteen back to Alma. She accepted it eagerly and drank, then, without even asking, poured some water over her face.

This seemed to strike the man as funny. He chuckled when Alma reluctantly handed back his canteen, but she noticed his eyes still had that dead expression in them. "You all never did say wheres you come from," he said.

Before Alma could open her mouth, Toby Ray volunteered, "Fort Smith."

Alma wanted to kick his backside. Even if this man was kind enough to share his much-needed water, he was still a stranger. She gave him a poke in the side with her arm. Toby Ray shrugged her away.

The man pulled at his yellow-white beard, then took off his hat and pushed the sweat back from his forehead with his arm. Under the hat, his hair was still pretty black. "Fort Smith," he said. "Ain't that far away, but I don't git there very often. Too many cussed people for me." He glanced briefly at Alma's face, then blinked and turned to Toby Ray. "Well, we've established where you came from. Where you young'ns headed?"

Toby Ray looked down at the ground. He wanted to talk to the man, but he felt Alma's warning gaze.

"Why—why, we're goin' to see some relatives," Alma said. She wanted to trust the man as much as Toby Ray did. They needed to trust someone. Right now, what they needed most was a friend, especially one with such wonderful water. But ever since her mother's passing, the only men Alma had come in contact with were the undertaker, Vernon Skaggs, and Uncle Ted. That was surely enough to make her leery of any strange men she didn't know. She took in a breath and said, "We're going to Kansas, mister. You see, we got folks up there on our daddy's side."

"Kansas, that's a pretty far piece from here," the man said. "You two tadpoles don't look like you got enough supplies to get you all that way. You best come on home with me. We'll fry up some of that good ham. I got some taters, and we'll have us a nice big supper. How does that sound?" He tried to look pleasant under his cold eyes.

Suddenly, Alma was sorry she'd said anything about Kansas. Now that her thirst was cured, she knew it was time for them to be on their way. She looked at the old man, avoiding his eyes. "I guess we'll just be headin' on to Kansas," she said.

"Won't hear of it. No, sir. I think you best stay the night. Get some good food in ya. 'Sides, it might rain tonight," the man said. "By the way, what do you two tadpoles go by?"

Alma grew angry. Whereas Uncle Ted and the undertaker had assumed too much about her womanhood, it irked her even more to think that this strange man considered her to be nothing more than a tadpole, same as Toby Ray. She'd heard the name before, and it had always been used to refer to small children. Maybe this man was just so old, she thought, he didn't know the difference any more between a young woman and a little girl. Still, it irritated her.

But, the man was apparently not going to leave them in peace. With resignation, she finally said, "I'm Alma, and this here's my brother, Toby Ray."

"Those are right nice names. Toby Ray." His lips smiled at the boy. "I surely do like that name. I'm known as George Tubbs. Now, I ain't gonna take no for an answer. You all come to the house and we'll fix us up a nice supper. Here." He stuck his hand down to Toby Ray. "You ride behind me. Your sister can follow along."

Toby Ray's eyes jumped with excitement as he gladly took the hand and climbed up behind George Tubbs.

Alma felt helpless over Toby Ray's eagerness with a stranger. But they had already headed down the road on the mule. Toby Ray turned and looked back at her. With a sigh, she picked up the ham and bedroll and followed along behind.

14

GEORGE TUBBS' HOUSE SAT AT THE FOOT OF A ROLL-
ing hill. When they crossed over the rise, Alma looked
down at the spread and took in a breath. This man must
be rich, she thought. The place was impressive and well
tended. There was a two-story house, painted white.
Across the yard was a barn, painted white to match the
house. Chickens were gathered up in a fenced-in area
beside a small building. There were no flowers or other
signs of a woman's presence. Still, everything appeared
so pristine and peaceful, Alma felt the doubt and fear
that had been gnawing at her insides began to subside
as she walked alongside George Tubbs and Toby Ray.
She began to wonder why it was always other folks who
got to live in fine houses and own chickens and horses
and sit down to a fine supper table. It was sad to think
that she and Toby Ray might never get to live such a
wonderful life.

She had always known that the world was divided into
the haves and the have-nots, and had never complained
over the fact—not out loud, at least. She had held a few
discussions with God about the subject, but always felt
a little guilty afterward to be bothering Him with such
a triviality.

At the house, George Tubbs pointed to the porch and
said to Alma, "Have a seat. Me 'n the boy'll put up my
mule."

Alma sat down on the top porch step and watched them disappear inside the barn. Then, she let her gaze sweep back up the low-rising hill. The scene was just as breathtaking from this direction, she thought. Yes, this was exactly how life would be for her and Toby Ray if she had her say in things. Her eyes suddenly filled with tears. She didn't want to cry, but she couldn't help it, any more than she could stop breathing. They were angry tears, and they were directed at God. Her lips motionless, she began to scold Him in her mind for not taking better care of her and Toby Ray. She even looked up at the sky in defiance, as if that would give God a clearer message.

The tears were still running down her face when Toby Ray and George Tubbs walked up.

"What you thinkin' 'bout, girl?" George Tubbs asked. He laid his hand on Toby Ray's shoulder and pushed the boy up the stairs before him.

Toby Ray hesitated. "Come on, Alma," he said. "Mister Tubbs said we'd fry up some of our ham for supper."

Alma didn't know if George Tubbs had noticed she was crying. She rubbed at her brow with her sleeve, wiping her eyes dry at the same time. Managing a quick smile, she nodded at Toby Ray. When he grinned back at her, she instantly felt a lot better. He seemed happy, tagging along behind George Tubbs. It was good for him. A boy needed the nurturing of a man, and since their father's death, Toby Ray had only had the company of men who were intolerant and mean. This man named George Tubbs seemed to genuinely like the boy.

She followed them inside the house and was startled to find another man, sitting in a rocking chair by the fireplace. Like George Tubbs, the man had a full beard, only his was dark and thinly streaked with gray. Tobacco juice ran from the corners of his mouth. He was grinning at her, his lips pulled back to show one yellowed tooth.

Alma tried to look away, but her eyes were drawn to the strange man. She stared dumbly as he began to rock back and forth, nodding his head and smiling at her. Once, he glanced at Toby Ray, who was watching George Tubbs slice the ham. Then he turned and nodded again at Alma. A gravelly humming sound started from his throat.

Alma walked to a chair and sat down. Trying to ignore the strange man by the fireplace, she looked slowly around the room. The house was mostly bare, with only a couple of nice pieces of furniture. A hand-carved sofa with a brocade covering stood against one wall. The table where George Tubbs stood was made of a heavy, dark wood and had four chairs that matched. There was another rocking chair besides the one the strange man was sitting in, but one of the arm rests had been broken off. There were no pictures on the walls, and the floor was bare. Still, it seemed like a palace to Alma.

The humming by the fireplace had become louder as the strange man began to rock harder back and forth. He was still grinning at her. Alma felt herself shudder and tried to be as inconspicuous as possible. She kept her eyes busy on George Tubbs, wishing he would hurry up with the ham. The humming grew even louder.

There was a loud noise, when George Tubbs suddenly raised the knife and jammed its sharp tip into the cutting board. Turning to the humming man, he said in a scolding voice, "You mind yourself, else I'll send you upstairs without no supper. You hear?"

It was almost like he was talking to a child. His tone was harsh, yet Alma noticed that his eyes had that same dead expression in them. She felt her heart pounding as she watched him, wide-eyed.

George Tubbs seemed to notice her fear. His voice turned kindly again as he said, "Don't mind him, girl. That there's my brother, Elken. He's sick in the head, but he's mostly harmless." He glanced briefly at his brother. Though his eyes were still noncommittal, Alma could read a deeply hidden rage. His face had turned a slight crimson, and the veins on his neck bulged. He pressed his lips together tightly even as he tried to smile at her. Alma thought she'd never seen such unspoken emotion in her life. She remembered her father's

ability to scold her with just a look in his eyes. Her
father, though, had been a pure amateur next to George
Tubbs.

By the time he had the ham and a plate of corn bread
ready for supper, it was nearly dark. George Tubbs
directed his brother Elken to a chair at the table, and
motioned for Alma to take her place. Then, instead
of sitting down himself, he leaned over and whispered
something in Toby Ray's ear. Toby Ray smiled and
nodded, and together they started out the back door.

Alma didn't know what to do. She stared helplessly at
the door, while Elken started rocking his chair back and
forth, letting the legs bang on the floor. Saliva ran down
his chin and he grunted loudly as he stared at Alma with
his wild eyes.

The door swung back open, and George Tubbs took
three long steps to his brother's side. He grabbed Elken
and, with a strength that belied his slender build, jerked
him to his feet, to where they stood eye to eye.

"One more time," he warned. "You just try it one
more time. You hear?"

Elken licked his lips feverishly and grunted, his eyes
rolling back in his head.

George Tubbs looked like he was going to set his
brother back down, but instead he pulled back his arm
and slapped Elken, so hard it sounded like a gunshot.
Alma hollered and jumped out of her chair. She looked
toward Toby Ray. If he was scared, he didn't show it.
In fact, he seemed only a little surprised.

George Tubbs was holding on to his brother and talking in a low, guttural voice. "Now, you sit down and
behave yourself, or it's no supper," he said.

Alma stood frozen. She could hear herself breathing,
and her heart was pounding against her chest so loud, she
hoped the noise wouldn't set George Tubbs off again.
Toby Ray, although he still didn't appear to be worried,
stood unmoving in the doorway.

The seconds ticked by. George Tubbs held on to his
brother and stared until Elken's head began to roll back
and forth. He hadn't cried out, but his eyes were half

closed. It reminded Alma of an abused animal that's gotten used to being beaten.

Slowly, George Tubbs relaxed his grip and pushed Elken back into his chair. He turned his dead eyes on Alma and Toby Ray and shook his head.

"Doggone it! He spoiled our surprise! Why"—he turned to Toby Ray—"me and the little tadpole was goin' to the spring and fetch us some good buttermilk. Well, let's git anyways."

With that, George Tubbs marched out the door with Toby Ray behind him.

At the table, Elken silently began to bob up and down in his seat. He grinned at her. Alma stood by the door and watched him for a while, then, with a dreadful feeling in her heart, she sat down at the table with him.

A few minutes later, George Tubbs and Toby Ray returned to the table. George Tubbs said grace, then he and Toby Ray dug hungrily into their food. Alma noticed they seemed to have become instant friends, in spite of the nearly half-century between their ages. They weren't saying much, but both of them appeared to be relaxed in each other's company. She picked at her food, keeping an eye on George's brother. Elken seemed to have a fascination for Toby Ray, himself. Most of the time, he kept his head almost buried in his plate, but once in a while he would sneak a peek at Toby Ray. If George Tubbs happened to look his way, Elken would let his head drop back into his plate, his eyes rolling around and around in his head, and the grin would reappear. After a while, he started humming again, so low Alma could barely hear it.

They finished with supper, and Toby Ray helped move Elken back to his rocking chair by the fireplace. George Tubbs pulled the other rocking chair close to the fire and sat down next to his brother, then motioned for Toby Ray to pull up a footstool and sit beside him. Alma was left sitting alone at the table. "I'll do the dishes," she offered.

No one paid any attention to her, so she decided to do them, anyway. As she poured water in the washbasin,

she heard Toby Ray's laughter. George Tubbs was playing a game of silhouette with his hands from the light of
the fire. She paused a moment to watch as George Tubbs
formed rabbits and dogs and an elephant and some other
animals that Alma had never seen before. The way Toby
Ray was leaned forward and studying George Tubbs'
hands, she knew he'd soon be making silhouettes himself. Beside them, Elken was either staring into the fire
or grinning at Toby Ray.

True to George Tubbs' prediction, a light shower
commenced outside. Alma felt grateful to be inside,
instead of having to bed down in the rain. Still, it was
a small solace for the fear she felt at having to sleep
under the same roof with a retarded man. There had
been a simple-minded man, once, in Fort Smith. One
day, he had up and killed his own mother with a hunting
knife, for no apparent reason. That killing had been the
talk of the town for years—ever since Alma was Toby
Ray's age, in fact. She had had many a sleepless night
over the fact, lying there, trying to sort it all out and
wondering if he was coming to get her next. Now, as
she watched Elken grin and stare, that same fear came
back like an awful nightmare.

Another thought kept working at Alma's mind.
Nowhere was there a single sign of a woman's presence, yet the house was as clean and orderly as any
she could ever remember. She wondered if George
Tubbs had ever been married. He must be a widower, she concluded. How else would he have learned
such tidy ways? Alma felt a bit sad for him, being
a widower and all and having to take care of his
brother. Even if he was a bit too mean to Elken,
it would be a terrible burden to take care of a
retarded man. She felt glad that Toby Ray was of a
sound mind.

When the dishes were done, she joined the others and
sat on the floor by the fireplace. Again, no one seemed
to take notice of her presence.

Several minutes later, George Tubbs paused and tilted
his head as he listened to the gentle patter of the rain

on the roof. "See," he said in a soft voice, "I told you tadpoles it was gonna rain."

Alma's head turned to the window. The rain was coming down a little harder all the time, a gradual thing. It was the kind of spring rain that people liked for the ground and the crops. Slow and constant, sinking into the soil. One of Alma's biggest pleasures had always been to listen to the patter of the raindrops on the roof while she slept warm and dry in her bed. The thought reminded her that if George Tubbs hadn't happened upon them, right now she and Toby Ray would most assuredly be shivering in the cold, listening to the patter of the raindrops on their heads. She tucked her knees up under her chin and was grateful to be near the comfort of the fireplace, feeling its warmth creeping up her side.

They passed the evening sitting around the fireplace, with Elken playing his child-like game, sneaking long glances at Toby Ray, grinning and humming to himself. It puzzled Alma at how George Tubbs seemed content to spend the whole evening playing silhouettes with Toby Ray. He would occasionally rub his hand over the boy's head. Nobody said much, except Toby Ray laughed out loud every once in a while at one of George Tubb's animal shapes.

The only real attempt at conversation of the evening was made when Alma timidly asked George Tubbs if he'd ever been married.

At first, George Tubbs pretended not to hear her. She had given up on getting an answer, when he slowly turned to look at her. In the shadows of the firelit room, she could still see his dead eyes. They seemed to penetrate deep into her own. He stared at her for what seemed like a full minute.

"Nope. My life's work has been in takin' care of my brother, Elken," he finally said. " 'Sides that, don't need no woman. We're confirmed bachelors. 'Course, I don't reckon Elken coulda fetched a woman if he'd tried." He turned his gaze to the fireplace and the flame made his eyeballs glisten. "Nope," he added, barely above a whisper, "ain't never needed no wife."

Alma wanted to ask him more, but he suddenly stood up, stretched and said, "Well, I reckon it's time we hit the sack. Mornin' comes early. You two tadpoles follow me upstairs and I'll show you your room." He paused and turned to Elken. "You set right there and behave yourself, you hear?"

They followed him upstairs to a long hall. There were four doors, all closed. He took them to the last door on the left. "I think you tadpoles will sleep right nice in here," he said. He opened the door to the darkened bedroom, then lit a lamp and handed it to Alma.

The place smelled bad, Alma thought. She had noticed the odor when they reached the top of the stairs. Now, it was stronger—an almost putrid smell. She looked at Toby Ray. He rubbed his nose a couple of times, but didn't look back at her.

Alma turned to George Tubbs. How could he not notice, she wondered? They surely needed to air the place out. She started to suggest they open a window, then felt guilty for thinking such an ungrateful thing.

George Tubbs nodded at them and left the room. Just as the door was closed, Toby Ray said in a loud whisper, "What's that awful smell?"

Alma hissed at him, "Be quiet! He's likely to hear you!"

Toby Ray made a face and silently mouthed, "I know, but what's that smell?"

"Shush!" she whispered. Alma couldn't blame the boy. The longer they stood there, the worse the stench became. She tried to take in small gulps of air through her mouth, for fear she might vomit. Toby Ray was holding his nose. They stayed quiet until Alma was sure George Tubbs had gone away.

She raised the lamp to look around. Its flickering flame cast shadows about the room. There was a brass bed that was covered with a multicolored quilt. Between the pillows lay an old doll.

Strange, Alma thought. This looked for all the world to be a girl's room. Raising the lamp higher, she noticed a dresser sitting against the west wall. It held a wash basin and what looked to be some fruit jars. On the other side of the room was a chest of drawers with more of the jars sitting on top of it.

Toby Ray pulled at Alma's sleeve, causing the lamp's shadows to dance around the room.

"Blame it, Toby Ray! You almost made me drop this lamp!" she scolded him.

"I can't sleep in here. I'll get sick," Toby Ray said.

"You hush up and get in bed," Alma said in the most authoritative voice she could muster. On the inside, she was wondering herself how she could make it through the night in that smell. Being raised around livestock, she wasn't usually offended much by odors. She'd been in barns before where the smell was so ripe it could make a grown man dizzy. There was something about this smell, though, that was unlike anything she'd ever experienced. It reeked of a sweet, musky death.

She knew Toby Ray was likely to stand there and complain half the night, so she briskly walked toward the bed. "I'm goin' to sleep. You can stay up if you want," she said. She wanted to appear as calm as possible for Toby Ray's sake. Besides, as bad as the smell was, the thought of being out in the rain—not to mention the risk of offending the odd mens' hospitality—left her no other alternative.

Toby Ray, whose curiosity had taken over his concern about the smell, let out a soft cry from beside the dresser.

"Yeek! Alma, bring that light over here!" he said.

"You get away from those jars, before you break somethin'," Alma said. She got up from the bed and stepped closer. "What are you doin', fiddlin' around with those things?"

"What's in here?" Toby Ray asked, picking up a jar and holding it up to her light.

"Beans or corn, I 'spect."

Toby Ray looked closer. His eyes widened. "Look at this!" He shoved it toward her face.

"Get that thing away from me!" Alma pulled back.

"But look Alma! It ain't beans or corn."

Alma took the lamp and stepped closer.

The lamp light struck the jar and Alma gasped, grabbing at her chest.

"My God! It's a kitten!" she exclaimed.

Toby Ray cried out and dropped the jar on its side on the dresser. Alma somehow caught it before it rolled off and crashed onto the floor.

"Let's git outta here!" Toby Ray said in a trembling voice.

Alma took a deep breath. She was trembling all over. Why in the world would someone want to do such a thing, she wondered? She pulled Toby Ray against her, and they looked at the rest of the jars. As awful as the kitten had been, it was even more shocking to see a dead rat floating in a clear liquid of some sort. There was another kitten. A large gallon jar in the back corner held a baby piglet.

Alma's whole body was covered with goose bumps, the hair on her neck standing on end. She felt cold. She wanted to say something comforting to Toby Ray, but no words would come out.

The lamp's light bounced around the room in her shaking hands.

"Alma, I don't wanna see no more jars," Toby Ray was begging. "Let's get outta here, please."

Alma was surprised that she was able to move and even more surprised that she had the courage to look at the top of the chest of drawers, even though she knew what she would find. The jars there held dead animals, too. Her throat constricted as she fought back the urge to throw up.

"Please, Alma," Toby Ray said. "I think I peed my pants."

Alma looked at Toby Ray's frightened face. All of a sudden, the cold rain outside was of little concern. Alma put her arm around Toby Ray's shoulder.

"You're right. Let's go."

At the door, she turned and put her finger to her lips. "Be real quiet," she whispered, "and walk softly." She turned the handle slowly. It wouldn't move.

"Hurry up, Alma!"

"It's stuck!"

She turned harder on the doorknob and pulled as her heart raced in her chest. A panic rose up inside her. There was no use. The door was locked.

15

THE PERSISTENT RAINS TOOK THEIR TOLL ON REASA and Noah. What started out as head colds soon spread to their chests. They had no choice but to bed down in the small dugout, huddled next to each other. Larkes gathered up all the dry wood he could find, but there wasn't enough to keep a fire going steady. He had to save what there was to cook the rabbits he shot for their food.

How could he have let this happen? he wondered again. He had thought he was in love a time or two before, but now he knew that hadn't been the case, at all. No woman had ever made him ache inside the way Reasa did. She only had to say a word, or just walk past him to relieve herself outside, and the blood in his chest would start swirling, so hard he thought he'd have a heart attack. But he didn't; instead his heart kept beating and the feelings kept coming more and more frequently.

It was their sixth day in the dugout. Reasa and Noah were still feeling poorly, and Larkes had just sat down to skin another rabbit, when he looked up to see a welcome sight. It was Henry Starr, riding toward him with another man Larkes didn't recognize.

His depression quickly subsided. Ever since Starr had been run off by the posse, Larkes had entertained himself by recalling Starr's stories, over and over in his head. He and Reasa had talked about what must have happened to him. Reasa believed that Starr was surely captured and hanged, the posse being so close and all. Larkes didn't agree. He insisted that Starr was too cunning to have gotten himself caught. Probably got far enough away to hide out a spell, he said. He'd enjoyed discussing the matter, until Reasa got too sick to argue.

But there he was, riding in as if nothing had happened. As Starr approached, Larkes took an instant pride in the fact that his prediction had been right. Even though he knew Reasa was sick, he couldn't help sticking his head inside the dugout and grinning at her. "Well, lookee here. It's Henry Starr."

Reasa gave a violent cough. "You don't say," she said and coughed some more. She managed to get up and slowly walked to the door to peer out.

"Yes, ma'am. Looks like he outsmarted that posse just fine," Larkes said, pleased that Reasa was taking notice, even though she wasn't mentioning it.

Henry Starr rode up with a big smile. "Well damn, boy! Did you stake this land for yerself?" he asked.

"Nope," Larkes said back. "Reasa and the boy been sick."

"Sorry to hear that," Starr said, nodding at Reasa. He raised a finger at the rider beside him. "This here's Kid Wilson."

Larkes looked at Starr's companion with an uneasy feeling. He was young, like Starr. Larkes could see a rough life ahead for him.

Starr slid down off his horse, took off his hat and pushed his hair back on his head. "Git on down, Kid," he said. "These are the folks I told you about. Larkes Dixon and Miss Reasa."

Kid Wilson swung his leg over his horse and jumped down. He ignored Larkes, but tipped his hat at Reasa, a gesture that wasn't lost on Larkes.

"What brings you back this way?" Larkes asked, his eyes challenging those of Kid Wilson.

"Well damn, boy! I just couldn't get you off my mind," Starr said and resettled his hat on his head. "When you didn't show up along the trail, I figured them low-life marshalls must've planted you six feet under."

"Not me," Larkes said. "But that ol' hoss, Ike Rogers, says that's exactly what he has in mind for you."

Starr laughed. "Shoot! That darky lowlife and his twin ain't seen the day they could handle the likes o' me!" He turned to his partner. "You hear that, Kid?"

"I hear it, all right," Kid Wilson said. He gave a short, harsh laugh, like he thought it was the most ridiculous thing he'd ever heard.

Starr motioned toward Kid Wilson and smiled. "You see? I keep with smart company."

"Yeah, I see that," Larkes said.

Starr squatted down on his haunches. He pulled off his hat again and rubbed his head. "Lookee here, boy. Like I told you the other day, I'm puttin' together a gang. Besides the Kid, here, I got Frank Cheney and Hank Watt joinin' up. How 'bout you?"

Larkes didn't mean to laugh at Starr, but he couldn't help letting out a chuckle. "Why, you don't need me, Henry," he said.

Starr's face grew hard and serious. "You makin' fun o' me?"

Larkes shook his head. "Put away that long face, Henry. I ain't makin' fun o' nobody." He stared down at Starr a moment. "You're gettin' a mite edgy, ain't ya? Maybe I shouldn't o' said anything about those deputies," he said.

"Pffft!" Starr blew. "That'll be the day when I worry 'bout the law!"

On Larkes' invitation, Henry Starr and Kid Wilson stayed the next few days. Starr was in fine form with a batch of new stories, while the Kid seldom said much more than a word or two to confirm that Starr's tales were true. The second evening, Starr rode off and came back with a doe, and for supper they had fried venison.

Meanwhile, Reasa and Noah began to get better, and by the third morning, Reasa announced that they were ready to travel.

They set out shortly after and rode along together the entire day. Larkes had his reservations about their traveling companions. He'd ridden with the likes of Henry Starr and Kid Wilson before, but what worried him was having Reasa and Noah in such close proximity to a potentially volatile situation. It would be best, he decided, if they could part company as soon as it could be done in a proper way.

He had to admit that he was starting to admire Starr. The young outlaw seemed as loose and relaxed as anyone Larkes could remember, especially in view of the fact that every lawman in the territory was on his trail. The way Starr told his stories and laughed as easy as he talked, he was entertaining to have along, too. It was too bad he'd decided to use his talents in an unlawful way.

Starr had a fine skill of communicating with strangers, too. Along the trail, they passed by several Indian farms, and Starr liked to ride on in ahead and say his hellos. Before long, he'd come riding back with an armload of food or water for the others. People took easily to his friendly ways and offered up what they had to share. That first night, he managed to get an offer to make their camp in an Indian family's barn. Not only did they get fine sleeping arrangements, but they also enjoyed a generous supper of roast venison and potatoes. Reasa and Noah were also invited to sleep in the main house. Larkes had his first decent sleep in weeks, lying in the soft warm hay and listening to Starr recalling another one of his exploits. He nestled down and had dreams about Reasa and a fine ranch in Colorado, and slept until he woke on his own.

The next morning, Reasa came to them with a basketful of food and a pot of coffee. They ate until they couldn't eat any more, while Starr's talk turned to more serious things, like his plans for the future. It was as if he sensed that Larkes was desiring to part ways with him.

Starr leaned back against a pile of hay and cradled his coffee cup against his chest. He bit into a piece of fatback and chewed a while, then looked at Larkes. "Shoot, boy," he said between chews, "there's money and fame to be had. Why, there's this store up in Kansas with a safe full of money. And there's more stores just like it in every town. It'll be like taking candy from a baby, sure enough!"

"You're gonna rob stores?" Larkes asked. "I don't reckon you woulda caught Jesse James robbin' stores. No sirree."

"Now looka here, boy. That's just what we're gonna do to sharpen our skills," Starr said. He frowned and leaned closer to Larkes. "In a month or so, we're gonna hit the People's Bank over in Bentonville, Arkansas. Not only that, there's a train or two that we've been thinkin' about." He waited for Larkes to react with a smug look.

"I haveta say I admire your spunk, and that ain't no fib," Larkes said.

"Well, then, what do ya say? You wanna join us or not?" Starr said.

Larkes shook his head. "No, Henry. I'll leave the bank robbin' to you. My destination is Colorado. I'm gonna make me a little money, then go buy me a place to live out my days."

"Shoot fire! If it's a place you're wantin', I can give you a better deal than that, and save you a trip," Starr said. "All you gotta do is come with me and rob a few banks, then you can make the land run over in the Cherokee Strip."

Reasa came next to Larkes to pour him some more coffee. Her nearness set his heart to fluttering. He hoped no one would notice. Blinking hard, he frowned as he tried to concentrate on what Starr was talking about instead of what Reasa was making him feel.

"What land run you talkin' about?" he asked. "Hell, I worked in the Cherokee Strip a time or two, myself. I thought the cattlemen already took it over."

"Well, they didn't. In fact, the President is runnin' them out. They're gonna have a land run, sure enough, like they did in '89. There's more'n six million acres over there for anyone fast enough to claim him a piece of it," Starr said.

Larkes said, just to make conversation, "Where'd you hear that?" He wasn't even remotely interested in what Henry Starr had to say about racing for any land, but it might distract anyone from noticing that Reasa was having a powerful effect on him. She had set the coffee pot down and was sitting next to him on the floor of the barn. He could reach out and touch her if he wanted. And he wanted to real bad.

Starr was going on. "Read about it in the paper, 'bout a week ago. President Cleveland is workin' on a deal with the chief of the Cherokee nation. Shoot, they been talkin' 'bout it for a long time, but now it looks like it's gonna happen. With the way that gelding of yours runs"—he pointed to Larkes' horse—"you could pick your claim."

Larkes let the comment go by. "Well," he said, "the mornin's just wastin' away. I think we best be takin' a more northwesterly direction." He hoped Starr would see the futility of trying to convince him that he needed to live a life of robbing banks and entering races and such. He thought he'd made it clear enough that Colorado was his destination of choice.

If Starr did intend to let the subject drop, he never got the chance to do it, for Reasa suddenly broke in. "This land run," she said in a thoughtful voice. "You mean a body can claim land? Free?"

"That's right." Starr smiled. "Northwest part of the Territory. A man could get him a hundred sixty acres of good grass land. Why, you could raise you a mess o' cattle. And they tell me wheat will grow there like weeds in rain."

Reasa bit her lip thoughtfully.

"I ain't much interested in growin' no wheat," Larkes said.

"Well shoot! Run you some cows, then!" Starr shot back.

Larkes offered a smile. Inside, he was starting to feel a little vexed at Starr's insistence on keeping a dead issue alive. It was true that he'd grown fond of the outlaw and even enjoyed his unending chatter. Still, there was

a sense of urgency growing inside at the deeper risk he
was taking for Reasa and Noah with each day. More and
more, he felt ready to travel and get on with things. After
all, Colorado wasn't getting any closer, and he wasn't
used to such a meandering pace in life. It seemed like
months since that night he'd shot Deputy Frank and left
with Reasa. He looked at Reasa, meaning to give her a
sign to get ready to leave, but she was staring hard at
Henry Starr.

"This land is free for the takin'?" she asked again.

"That's right," Starr said.

"I ain't never had no land of my own," she said in a
soft voice.

Before Reasa could say any more, Larkes stood up
abruptly and said, "Anyone goin' to Colorado? I'm a-
leavin' in ten minutes." He glanced at Reasa and noticed
the pain in her face. He knew she wanted to hear more
about free land in Oklahoma Territory, but his plans had
already been waylaid long enough. She'd just have to put
such silly ideas aside if she wanted to travel with him,
he thought.

Reasa flipped her head at him. "I reckon Colorado'll
be there a while longer," she said with a menacing look.
To Starr she said, "How much land did you say they're
gonna give away?"

"Like I said, over six million acres is the word. The
President's workin' out a deal with the Cherokee nation,"
Starr said. His smile faded. " 'Course, you can bet the
Cherokees'll take a beatin'. Government'll figure out a
way to keep from payin' 'em." He stared into a dark
corner of the barn as if he were in a deep trance. His
eyes widened as he kept his gaze on that unknown
fascination in the corner. "That's the way it always is
with white folks," he said. "I reckon they'd steal from
their own mamas if'n they could."

Larkes was folding his blanket. He shook his head.
"You talk as bad as Reasa," he said. "Talkin' 'bout white
folks, when both of ya got white man's blood runnin'
through ya."

"I got white blood in me, all right," Starr snapped,

"but I'll tell ya right now, if it were up to me, I wouldn't have a drop. I'd be all Indian." He looked at Larkes. "And what're you doin', defendin' the whites? You think you ain't still a slave to 'em?"

Larkes said, "I ain't defendin' nobody. Lookee here, this *is* a white man's world. But the way I see it, you got two roads to travel in this life. You can worry yourself sick over how things are, and you won't change one damn thing. Or, you can accept the fact and set about livin' your own life the best you can. You see, Mister Lincoln done freed my people, so I ain't worryin' 'bout Mister White Man. He ain't my master, and I ain't his slave."

"You really believe that, boy?"

"Boy, your ass! See there? You wanna cuss the white man, yet you talk just like one! Then you talk about bein' all Indian!" Larkes shook his head disgustedly and walked to the door of the barn.

Starr started to get up and follow, but Reasa grabbed his arm. "Please," she said. "Tell me more about this land run."

"I told you 'bout all I know. They're workin' it all out right now. If it's anything like the run of '89, they'll line people up, far as the eye can see. Then they'll fire a shot, and if you're the first person to reach a piece o' land that's staked out, that land is yours. Free 'n clear." Starr nodded his head toward Larkes. "That white gelding of his? If he's as fast as Larkes proclaims him to be, why, you all could pick out any claim you wanted. 'Course, I think you gotta be man and wife to claim it together. Less'n you could borrow the gelding and ride yourself."

Reasa sat down next to Starr. She looked forlornly toward the barn door. "You mean to tell me a body's got to be married 'fore they can claim any o' this free land?"

Starr shrugged. "Shoot, I ain't sure about that. But lookee here. You watch the papers. When they finalize it, the papers'll tell you all about the qualifications." He smiled and looked deep into her eyes. "Why don't you marry Larkes?" he said in a barely audible voice. "It's plain he loves ya."

Reasa gasped. "What? Where'd you get such a foolish idea?"

Starr chuckled. "I knew it the first day I laid eyes on you two."

"You must be crazy."

Starr grinned as Reasa's eyes turned to stare uncertainly at Larkes.

16

THEY HADN'T RIDDEN A MILE FROM THE FARM WHEN Larkes spotted the men. Henry Starr, who'd been too busy in a last-ditch effort to sway Larkes into riding on to Nowata with him and Kid Wilson, hadn't noticed.

There were five riders, shadowing them about fifty yards to the east in a thicket of trees. Larkes cussed to himself. It had been his intention to ride another mile or so out, then part company with Starr and the Kid. If only they had set out earlier, he thought.

"We got company," he said.

Starr glanced over his shoulder. "They're Indian policemen," he said. "I know a couple of 'em. Low-down, worthless apples." He shook his head. "Ain't acquainted with the other three. Dern it, if it weren't for them two apples, I could probably talk them others out o' anything foolish!"

"Apples?" Reasa said. "I thought you said this was Cherokee country."

"It is. Apples ain't no tribal name. It's what we call Indians that's like apples. You know, red on the outside and white on the inside." Starr spat at the ground and said with a bitterness, "There ain't no lower vermin on this earth than apple Indians."

They kept riding at the same pace. Larkes casually worked his gelding between Starr, Kid Wilson and Reasa, to where she was shielded by the three men. The

117

Indian policemen had pulled themselves into a group and were talking.

Kid Wilson, who in Larkes' opinion had never seemed to have an original thought of his own, stole a quick look at the riders and said in a low voice, "The way I see it, we can try and out-run 'em, or ride on over there and give 'em a breakfast of smokin' hot steel."

Starr shook his head. "No, no! Reasa and the boy might could get hurt that way. 'Sides"—he looked at Kid Wilson—"we're the ones they're after. I say you 'n me high-tail it north."

Reasa's eyes flew to Starr, then to Larkes, who nodded in agreement. She started to say something, but Larkes' look told her not to protest.

Starr said to Larkes, "You sure you ain't interested in becoming wealthly and famous?" He gave him a warm smile.

"I reckon not. You shoulda caught up with me twenty year ago. Then, you just might coulda swayed me," Larkes said.

Starr moved his horse close to Reasa and Noah. He rubbed the boy's head, then took Reasa's hand and kissed it. "You best go on and try to get ol' Larkes domesticated," he said. "He's a pretty good one, I'd say."

"Bye," was all Reasa could think of to say.

"Take care, Mister Larkes Dixon, and until our paths cross again, I'll say adios amigo."

Starr touched his hat at them. Larkes felt sad seeing him go. He'd surely miss the lively stories and generous company. He also appreciated the fact that, at the time of their parting, this was the first time Starr hadn't called him "boy." There weren't many men who'd gained Larkes' pure respect, and Starr had done just that.

Starr gave a quick nod to Kid Wilson, and they both gave spur to their mounts. As their horses raced off to the north, the policemen immediately opened fire.

Larkes watched the goings-on with more of an amusement than a fear for Starr's safety. Either those police-men were sorry shots, or Starr was one of those men who was born lucky. Larkes had seen a couple of individuals with luck like that. It was almost like they had a special guardian angel watching out for them.

He was still thinking about the luck of some, when there was a sudden dull pain in his side. At first he didn't pay that much attention to it. But then an explosion of pain hit his insides. Somewhere in the distance, he heard Reasa scream.

His head went dizzy, and all he could see were little black gnats, flying all around his head. He swatted at them, but they wouldn't go away, and all his hand felt was air. He swung harder and lost his balance. Slowly, he dropped from his saddle. It seemed to take forever before he landed on his back. But the ground was swaying under him. Again, he heard that distant voice screaming at him.

"You've been shot!"

"What?" He tried to raise his head, but he couldn't get his mind clear. Who'd been shot? Was it Starr? Larkes wanted to stand up, but his body felt too heavy to lift.

With an effort, he pushed himself up on one arm. Instantly, the gnats swarmed around him, and his head began to spin faster and faster, until all he knew was darkness.

When he awoke, he felt a soft bed underneath him. Before he thought to wonder where he was, Larkes remembered Henry Starr. He had to check on him, he thought, and started to rise from the bed.

An unbelievable pain shot though his side, causing him to holler out. He fell back onto his pillow.

"You best lay still. You'll get that wound to bleeding," a man's voice said.

Larkes turned to look at the voice. It was an elderly Indian man, dressed in a farmer's clothes. His long hair was in a braid down his back. Larkes waited a moment for the pain to subside and his head to clear some. He touched his side.

"Was I shot?"

"Yes. Yesterday morning. You must rest now," the face said.

Larkes felt shocked. He'd been lying unconscious since yesterday morning, but it seemed like just a few minutes ago that he'd fallen from his horse. He wanted to sit up and try to talk some sense with this old Indian man, but the effort made him so light-headed he nearly passed out.

"You have lost much blood. You must be still and rest now," the man repeated.

Larkes closed his eyes for a moment. "Where's Reasa?"

"I'm right here." Reasa's voice came from across the room. Larkes felt her hand take hold of his. He opened his eyes to see her staring down at him. A soothing relief went over him. She tried to smile, but he could see the fear behind her eyes.

"Who shot me?" he asked.

Reasa squeezed his hand. "One of those Indian policemen."

Larkes nodded, and the movement made his head start to swim. He felt things starting to go dark again. Reasa asked him a question, but the answer slipped away as he closed his eyes and gave in to sleep.

He drifted in and out of consciousness for the next few hours. His body was weak from the loss of blood, and his mental capacity came and went. Reasa told him that one of the Indian policemen had ridden back to question them, and was surprised to discover that Larkes had been wounded. A single warning shot had been fired in their direction, only as a warning for them to mind their own business. Larkes had just been unfortunate enough to get in the bullet's way, he said. There was no apology offered and little sympathy in the policeman's demeanor. All he really seemed concerned about was finding out all he could from Reasa about Henry Starr and Kid Wilson and where they might be heading. When he was satisfied that she knew nothing, he left and rode off north.

None of this meant anything to Larkes, for what clear thoughts he had one minute were soon faded from his memory. He was too sick to know how sick he was.

It was that evening when Larkes raised his head and, clear as a bell, asked, "Where in the hell am I at?" The Indian farmer leaned forward and introduced himself.

"I am Hawk Vann. I heard shots, and when I rode out to see what was going on, I found you and the woman and boy. You are a guest in my house."

"Much obliged," Larkes said, then drifted back into unconsciousness.

Hawk Vann had been a widower for many years. It amused Reasa to watch how Vann hovered over Larkes. He seemed to be a lonely man who was enjoying tending to the needs that she and Larkes had presented to him.

Vann tried feeding him some some chicken broth, but it made Larkes' stomach revolt. Undaunted, Vann patiently spoon-fed it to him, anyway, a little at a time. "You must try and overcome your pain," he insisted. "This will help you regain your strength."

In spite of Vann's efforts, time passed with little improvement in Larkes' condition. At times he would seem alert, but most often he lay there on his pillow, staring up at the ceiling lethargically. Reasa spent her time between taking care of Noah and sitting at Larkes' side. A worried frown was settling in on her brow as the days went by.

17

SHE CRIED A LOT. LARKES HAD REPRESENTED A BET-
ter life for her and Noah. He had taken them from
a miserable, dead-end existence and given them hope.
Now, there was no telling if he was going to pull out of
death's grip or not. Reasa knew she might soon be left on
her own again, and the thought made her cry harder.

Hawk Vann offered little in the way of encouragement. All he seemed to want to talk about was how
much blood Larkes had lost, and how weak he was.
He kept forcing the chicken broth down, refusing to
let Reasa help. She found herself resenting the way he
pushed past her to be near Larkes. It ought to be her job
to take care of him, she thought.

Still, she stayed by his side day and night, resisting
Vann's offer of his own bed for her and Noah. She
made them a pallet at the foot of Larkes' bed, fearful
that if she left him he would up and die. Maybe, she
thought, her presence was helping to ward off the grim
reaper. Anyway, she wasn't going to risk finding out
otherwise.

As their vigil grew longer, Noah began to grow
despondent. He had always enjoyed having his mother's complete attention. It wasn't enough that she
was with him in body, it was her heart that he
missed. Noah began to complain loudly, growing easily
agitated.

Reasa had little patience left to give the boy. Once, she reached out and slapped him, hard across the face.

They were both shocked. She grabbed him and held him in her arms as they wept together.

The days crept by. Larkes' sleeping periods grew longer and deeper with less time in between. The sparse diet of broth was hardly adequate, and his face began to draw up. As Reasa sat by his side and watched him grow weaker and thinner by the day, she began to wear down, herself. Her stomach was so irritated from worrying, she got to where she could barely keep a bite of food down, and she carried a constant feeling that she was going to vomit.

Reasa had always prided herself on being a survivor in life, and this newfound weakness scared her. Times had been hard, way before Larkes had come into her life. Before, she had always been able to pull herself through. She had never lost control like she was doing now.

To compound the matter, Hawk Vann had presented a new problem. It had started shortly after he had taken them in. At first, he had mostly just looked at her in a longingful way. Reasa was used to men losing themselves like little boys over her. She usually just ignored their stares. This time, though, what with Larkes being so sick and her future uncertain, she tried her best to ignore him and shrug off the uneasy feeling it gave her.

Then he got bolder in his advances. He began to talk in a soft, low voice, telling her how lonely he was and how lonely she must be, with Larkes' being laid up and all. They could help each other with their misery, he suggested. Then he licked his lips and stared at her with more longing in his old eyes.

Reasa was too afraid to tell him to forget such an awful idea, for fear he would kick them all out of his house. So, she held her tongue and refused to look at him. The mere thought of giving in to his request made her stomach revolt even more. She would get cold chills just thinking about his dried, wrinkled hands pawing at her.

Listening to Hawk Vann go on about his desires made Reasa remember Deputy Frank. Was this really any different, she wondered? Why, if Hawk Vann only knew about her former life, he'd either laugh himself silly before he took her and made her satisfy his needs, or just simply run her off.

She let her gaze fall on Larkes' sleeping face. But things were different now, she thought. The Hawk Vanns of this world didn't know about her past, and they didn't ever need to find out. Larkes Dixon had taken her from that life and given her the promise of a new one. She realized that it didn't really matter that Larkes was near death and probably didn't give one iota about her romantically. He had given her back her pride and will to live. It was important to her to be true to him, even if he had never made the slightest move in her direction.

One night, Hawk Vann had gotten particularly vulgar in his conversation. He'd been drinking for a couple of hours and his tongue was loose. He waited until Reasa had put Noah to bed, then sat down beside her and offered her a drink.

For all practical purposes, they were alone. Reasa felt uneasy, but tried not to show it. After giving the matter some thought, she decided to take him up on his offer. She accepted one glass and sipped at it conservatively, afraid to drink too much. Meanwhile, Vann emptied glass after glass, his talk turning hotter than a two-peckered billy goat.

"I know what you are thinking," Vann said. He waved a finger at her and took another drink, then had to stare ahead for a moment to recollect his thoughts. His finger still dangling in the air, he finally turned back to her. His eyes were glassy and twinkled in the light of the fireplace. "Yeah, I know what it is. You're sitting there thinking that ol' Hawk could never satisfy a long-legged young woman like you." He nodded. "All you coloreds think like that."

Reasa had felt bad enough having to sit there and sip her whiskey while he carried on. She'd felt no desire nor inclination to participate in his conversation. In fact, she had thought she was doing a pretty good job of ignoring his foul comments, until now. Something in his last statement hit her like a fast punch.

"What's that you mean about coloreds bein' 'like that'?" she asked, sitting more erect in her chair.

Vann seemed amused by her sudden defensive attitude. He smiled broadly, then chuckled. "All you coloreds think only a colored man can satisfy your needs," he said. "I know. Why, the colored men all come to the Territory and take Indian women for their wives. There is much talk about how a colored's built for such things."

Reasa had never heard such bold talk before—not even from Deputy Frank. She could hardly hide the anger in her voice. "Why, you old coot! You're crazy!" she said. "You don't know a single thing about people! Why can't you talk about something decent?"

Vann was leaning forward in his chair, grinning at her face. "I have seen your man," he said.

"What are you talkin' about now?" Reasa said.

"I changed his soiled bedding. I have seen him," Vann said, nodding at Larkes. He got up slowly from his chair and stood right in front of her. "Here," he said, "give me your hand."

"What for?" Reasa frowned.

"Give me your hand. I will not hurt you."

He stayed right there, holding his hand out to her. Reasa hesitated. He was getting drunker and crazier by the minute. For all she knew, he was expecting her to follow him to his bed. If that was the case, she thought, he'd just have to think again.

Getting no response from Reasa, Vann suddenly reached down and grabbed her hand. Before she could figure out what he had in mind, he cupped her hand over his crotch.

"There, you see? The coloreds are not the only ones built for pleasure," he said.

It shocked and pained Reasa to hear such a thing. She pulled her hand away and jumped to her feet. "You're a sick old bastard!" she yelled, her chest heaving as she gasped for air. Tears began to roll down her cheeks.

"You cry like a schoolgirl," Vann said. He reached out to wipe her tears with his hand, but she jerked her face away from him. "Because I am old, you think you can play innocent with me," he went on. "But it is no secret that you colored people spend your lives seeking pleasure."

"Is that what you think?" she said, blinking back the tears and glaring at him. She took a deep breath and held her hands in fists at her sides. "You talk like we're nothin' more than a bunch of dogs or rabbits." She threw back her head and scowled at him, her anger taking the beauty from her face. "Well, I'll tell you something. It may be hard for a drunken old fool like you to understand, but pleasure, or whatever you wanna call it, comes from what's in your heart—not what's in your britches."

She took a step closer to him and jabbed a finger in his chest. "Not that it's any of your damned business, but me 'n Larkes have been ridin' together for weeks, and I couldn't tell you from nothin' what's in his britches." She jabbed at him again, then poked her finger deep into his breastbone. Vann lost his balance and stumbled backwards into his chair. "So I'd say there's a chance you don't know a damn thing about us coloreds." She put her hands back on her hips. "I can say one thing about Larkes. He's certainly more of a gentleman than you are."

Hawk Vann tried to speak, but Reasa was still seething. She talked right over him. "I guess now I can leave here and tell everybody how you Indians are rude in your dealin's with women. How an Indian will give you the comfort of his home, just as long as he can insult you." She stood looking down at him. "Are all you Indians that disgustin', or is it just the way you are?"

Vann dropped his head and sat hunched over in his chair. He stayed that way for so long, Reasa wondered if he'd fallen asleep. Pretty soon, he raised up and took another long drink that set him to coughing. "I'm sorry if I've offended you," he said between coughs. He shook his head slowly, his eyelids half closed. "But if this here man has been riding with you for weeks and hasn't partaken in his pleasures with you, I'd say there's something wrong with him."

Reasa's eyes widened. She had half expected Vann to either throw her out for her tirade or at least show her a small bit of remorse for his behavior. But his attitude hadn't changed. His single-mindedness amazed her. Tired, she sank back into her chair. There was no use in trying to make any sense with him, in anger or otherwise.

Vann offered her a drink from his bottle, but she shook her head. "Remember," he said amiably, "I'm close by if you change your mind. Besides"—he glanced at Larkes—"your friend is likely to die."

Hearing it said out loud sent a wave of shock through Reasa. She had worried about the same possibility herself, but having someone else share the thought made it even more frightening.

"Do you think so?" she asked in a trembly voice.

Vann drank more whiskey and used his sleeve to wipe what spilled down his chin. "Maybe. He's lost so much blood, he is weak and is not responding well."

"Shouldn't we go for a doctor?"

Vann shook his head. "There are no doctors around here. Even if there were any, I doubt if they could do any more for him than I am doing."

Reasa felt her legs go limp. She wanted to fall down at Larkes' feet and cry, but she couldn't show such weakness in front of Hawk Vann.

Vann seemed to have drunk himself through the talking stage. He sat and nursed the rest of the bottle while his head bobbed up and down. It was nearly one o'clock when he downed the last drop and stumbled off to find his way to bed.

Reasa stayed in her chair, unwilling to leave Larkes' side. There was a knot in her throat so big, she could hardly swallow. She watched him, so deep in sleep, his breathing hard and labored. He's gonna die, she thought. And when he does, what in the world would she do on her own? The Lord might just as well take her, too.

Then she looked down at Noah's sleeping form, and her heart nearly broke for thinking such things. How could she be so selfish? For all her needs, there was someone more important who depended on her. A sudden prayer came to her lips.

"Please, Lord. Remove the devil's sickness from Larkes' body. We . . . me and little Noah . . . we need him, Lord."

18

"Toby Ray, you git away from that door," Alma said. "We got enough problems without you causin' us any more." She pinched his ear and tried to pull him toward her.

They were standing in the upstairs hallway, next to the door opposite of the room where they'd been forced to sleep.

"Ouch! Why'd you have to do that for?" Toby Ray said, grabbing his ear. "I was only wantin' to peek in."

"Leave that room be," Alma hissed at him. "We best git downstairs before he knows we're up."

It had been a week since the day George Tubbs and his mule had picked them up. For some unknown reason, they'd become virtual prisoners. Each night, Tubbs had accompanied them to the same foul-smelling bedroom and locked them in. The next morning, the door would be unlocked.

Toby Ray reached for the doorknob. "Maybe this room don't have any jars of dead animals in it, and maybe it don't stink so bad," he said.

Alma grabbed his arm. "Sssssh! Stay away from that door and don't talk so loud."

"Sssssh yourself. I get bad dreams sleepin' in there," Toby Ray said as he looked pleadingly at his sister.

Alma cupped his cheek in her hand, then pulled him away from the door and toward the stairs. She wished they had never even heard of the Tubbs brothers. She wished she knew how to get away.

But, get away from what, she thought? George Tubbs had never actually told her they couldn't leave. He'd just kept encouraging her to stay another day or two, and for some reason, they had stayed. Even with the idea of spending another night locked up in that eerie bedroom, they had stayed. It was a matter that seemed to be out of her control.

Meanwhile, each day George Tubbs had taken Toby Ray along to do his chores, while she stayed in the house and sat with Elken.

Elken was a strange one, all right. Besides the fact that he was obviously an imbecile, he was an excitable sort. The moment George and Toby Ray went out the door, he would pull his rocking chair to the window and strain to see their every move outside, always bobbing his head and licking his lips. Sometimes, he'd get so carried away, he'd jump out of his chair and run out into the yard to look for them. That made George so angry, he'd go into an awful fit. On at least two occasions, Alma had seen him slap Elken hard. She felt sorry for Elken, but she was too scared of them both to say anything about it.

Today, he seemed to be more agitated than usual. He rocked his chair back and forth so hard, it worked itself up against the window and started knocking against the sill. Several times, he stopped staring out the window long enough to throw back his head and salivate on himself. His eyes were rolling in their sockets. He reminded Alma of a dog that's been left behind by its master, all nervous and worrisome.

She ignored him for as long as she could, but he seemed so concerned, it finally got the best of her. Trying to keep a safe distance, she leaned over his shoulder to look out the window. Toby Ray and George Tubbs were nowhere to be seen. Curious, she leaned down closer, and as she did, she felt Elken's hair brush against her chin.

How stupid could she be, she thought, pulling back. Why, she surely would have screamed her head off if

Elken had been the one leaning over and touching her. But he didn't appear to have noticed, so she carefully leaned down again to look out, and saw them.

Down past the barn was a small pond. Toby Ray and George Tubbs were sitting on the ground, fishing poles stretched out over the water. They were talking; Alma could see Toby Ray's head turning back and forth between his pole and George Tubbs.

A feeling of bewilderment came over her. What was so disturbing to Elken about a man and a boy fishing together? Breathing a small sigh of relief, she quietly moved away from the window. Elken was even battier than she had first realized. She felt a flash of anger at him for making her worry so unnecessarily, then was instantly sorry for being angry. He couldn't help it, any more than she could help the circumstances she and Toby Ray were in.

She went into the kitchen and sat down at the table. It was a shame Elken had to be crazy, she thought. Why, this would be a good place for her and Toby Ray to settle in. It was as nice a farm as she had ever seen, and it had everything a person needed to sustain himself. There was fish from the pond, wild turkey, rabbit and deer. They had good milk cows, chickens and hogs. Toby Ray would have plenty of room to run around in, and there was lots of space for a garden. She'd always enjoyed the small garden she and her mother had tended.

But there was a crazy man in the house. Not only that, Alma was downright scared of George Tubbs. She'd been frightened of Uncle Ted, but that had been of a different variety. She could sense in George Tubbs a deep-down meanness that went to the core. There was something evil lurking behind those emotionless eyes. She knew it, even though he'd been good enough to her and Toby Ray. In fact, he was the first man she'd encountered in a long time who hadn't shown any unwanted interest in her, and she was grateful for that. Still, she had no intentions of crossing him.

Her eyes drifted toward the staircase and moved upward. Their nightly prison was another thing. That foul-smelling room with the horrible jars of preserved animals was more bizarre than anything she had ever seen. Why were they there? Were there more jars in the other bedrooms? They must have been put there by Elken, she thought. Why would a sane person like George Tubbs want to keep a bunch of dead animals? The brothers' bedrooms lay at the top of the stairs, but the fourth room was a complete mystery. She almost wished she had let Toby Ray open the door. Maybe it had dead animals in jars, too.

In the back of her mind, she could hear the sound of Elken's rocking chair, scraping against the window. He was making those sickening sounds again. Alma paid it no mind. Her eyes were deeply focused on the staircase and the rooms it led to. Her mind was filled with both curiosity and trepidation.

Almost without thinking, she reached down and untied her shoes, then slipped them off her feet. She stole a quick glance at Elken, then tiptoed gingerly toward the stairs. At the top, she waited for her eyes to adjust. Though the sun was shining brightly outside, the upstairs hall was dark. Only a tiny slit of light shone through a break in the heavily curtained window at the other end.

She wasn't sure what had made her decide to do this, but the allure of the fourth bedroom was suddenly so strong, she couldn't have turned back if she'd wanted to. Carefully placing one foot in front of the other, she crept toward the door opposite her and Toby Ray's room.

A board beneath her foot suddenly made a loud creak. She froze. Her heart nearly stopped when she noticed that Elken's rhythmic rocking had ceased. She turned and watched for his hulking form to appear at the top of the stairs. If he caught her, she thought, she would surely die.

She waited for what seemed like a long time and tried to keep her breathing even and quiet. Her heart hadn't stopped beating; instead, it was pounding so hard she could feel it in her chest. She was scared, but not so scared that she'd lost her appetite to see what was in the fourth room at the end of the hall. Maybe Toby Ray was right, she thought. Maybe there weren't any jars of animals in there at all. Maybe it didn't have the same horrible smell of old death. But if that were true, then why did George Tubbs insist on keeping them locked up in the room that did? Alma felt the hair on her arms and neck bristle up.

There was a possibility that it wasn't even a bedroom. It could just be used for storage. The thought brought a little bit of disappointment to Alma. But hadn't George Tubbs referred to the "four bedrooms upstairs" at breakfast one morning? Surely, he was a man who said exactly what he meant.

Downstairs, Elken's rocker finally began to move again. Back and forth, faster and faster. Alma waited until he'd gotten it to hitting against the windowsill again before she dared to creep further down the hall.

Sweat had begun to gather on her brow and was rolling through her scalp and down her neck. It wasn't that hot upstairs. Alma took in a deep breath and let it out slowly, trying to ease her nerves some. Then, she wiped her brow with the back of her hand and stepped up to the door.

Her hand was clammy. She wiped it on her skirt and reached for the door handle. Taking a firm grip, she turned the knob.

The door wouldn't budge a bit. Alma tried again. Still no luck. She bit hard on her bottom lip as disappointment flooded over her. How could she not have known that the door would most likely be locked? Frustrated, she grabbed and turned the handle again, ramming her shoulder hard against the door before she stomped her foot and turned away.

She didn't know what to do. The urge to look inside the room was so strong, she couldn't bring herself to go back downstairs and sit with Elken for the rest of the day without knowing what was in there.

She turned back to the door, and something caught her attention. A thin ray of light that came from the only window cut a small diagonal path across the door. She moved closer to peer at the doorknob and the frame next to it. The light was so dim, she had to run her hand along and feel it, but it was there. A split in the door frame. It had given, just a little, when she had rammed the door with her shoulder.

Slowly, she edged her shoulder against the door while turning the knob. She strained, but the door gave very little. She gritted her teeth, held her breath and pushed again, this time putting every bit of her hundred-pound frame behind it. At first, nothing happened. Then, with a swoosh, the door suddenly opened. Alma stumbled, then fell inside onto her hands and knees.

The room was dark and had a closed-in feeling. There was a different smell about it; not as bad as the other room, but peculiar and unpleasant, just the same. Alma made her way to a window and pulled back the curtains. Bright sunlight flooded into the room.

There was a dressing table next to the window. Alma frowned. There was a white lace doily, with a hairbrush, looking glass and fancy glass bottle arranged on one side. A porcelain music box lay on the other side with an identical doily.

In the corner of the room was a child's rocking chair. A doll dressed in a white dress with pink embroidered flowers was sitting on it.

There was a bed with a canopy of white eyelet lace in the corner of the room. "This looks like a little girl's room," Alma thought aloud. She squinted against the sunlight to see into the shadow under the canopy. Unsure of what she saw, she stepped closer, to where she was almost touching the white coverlet.

Suddenly, terror flowed through her like a lightning bolt, and she screamed before she could stop herself. She started trembling all over as she cupped her mouth with her hands and stared at what lay under the eyelet canopy.

It was dressed in a black dress and had long flowing white hair. A book was clutched in its hands.

It was a dead woman.

Alma jumped up and down to keep from wetting herself. The woman was so horrible, her skin was drawn up like a dried apple doll. In fact, that was what it reminded Alma of. She had an aunt who had once made dolls out of dried apples, using buttons for eyes, and the like.

When she had recovered somewhat from her initial shock, Alma got curious enough to look closer. It had been a large woman; the corpse covered one end of the bed to the other. She had been laid in repose, like Alma's mother had been at the funeral parlor. This woman's skin, though, had wrinkled a thousand times over and was drawn up tightly against her bones, like old worn leather.

Who was it, she wondered? And who had brought her here and made the room into some sort of shrine? As she stood there trembling and trying to make some sense out of it all, she suddenly heard faint voices talking. Toby Ray and George Tubbs were returning to the house.

Alma wasn't sure she could walk on her shaky legs, but she couldn't be discovered, snooping around. She quickly closed the door and ran down the stairs. She had just made it back to the table and was trying to put her shoes on when she heard George Tubbs say, "Go ahead, tadpole. Show your sister this batch o' fish we just caught."

As Toby Ray proudly held five fish up close to her face for inspection, Alma offered him her biggest smile, her eyes furtively studying George Tubbs.

19

ALMA COULDN'T CLOSE HER EYES WITHOUT THE
vision of that mummified dead woman suddenly appearing. She and Toby Ray had gone to bed at least an hour
before, and she still hadn't been able to get herself to
sleep. Their lamp had been extinguished, and the room
was coal-black. Still, she kept her eyes focused on the
darkness.

She was pretty sure Toby Ray had drifted off. His
breathing was deep and even. Carefully, she moved
closer to him—so close that they were touching from
shoulder to toes. But even the comfort of his body
against hers couldn't relieve the horror she felt, there
in that dark bedroom with the dead woman lying just
across the hall.

The night grew. Alma felt so tired, yet she couldn't
close her eyes. If she did sleep, there would surely be
nightmares, so horrible she might die of fright, and she
didn't want to die and leave Toby Ray all alone.

The next thing she knew, someone was shaking her
shoulder. She opened her eyes and saw Toby Ray's sleepy
face, watching her. Sunlight shone through the curtains,
warming the room. Funny, but she didn't remember falling asleep, and there had been no nightmares. Relieved,
she reached over and hugged Toby Ray tightly against
her. He didn't seem to mind, and they lay there for
a while.

When Toby Ray began to squirm, then tried to tussle himself out of her arms, she let him go with a sigh and threw back the quilts. They couldn't stay in bed forever, but she wished they could. When she was lying there under the covers, it seemed as if everything in life froze in place, and nothing bad could get to her. Alma watched Toby Ray jump out of bed, then reluctantly followed. They dressed quickly and without speaking—for all his chatter, Toby Ray was at his most quiet in the early mornings.

As they stepped out into the hall, Alma felt the hair raise on her arms as she faced the closed door across from them. Her legs went to shaking as she thought about what lay beyond. In her mind's eye, she looked through the closed door, across the room, to the bed where the dead woman with the flowing white hair lay. She moved closer, closer, to where she was finally face-to-face with the old woman. The eyes were sunken and shriveled in their sockets, the tiny mouth wrinkled and dry. As her mind's eye watched in fascination, the mouth began to twitch, the dead skin breaking open as the dead woman tried to smile. . . .

Alma shook herself in horror. Her breath was coming in short gasps and her hands had become sweaty. She realized that Toby Ray was staring at her with puzzlement. He followed her gaze to the closed door. "Let's go," she managed to say and pushed him away from the door and down the hall to the stairs.

She was still shaking as they descended the stairs. She hurried to the breakfast table and sat down to hide her trembling hands from George Tubbs.

Elken was in his usual position at the table, grinning like an eager child in anticipation of his breakfast. There was a fork in one hand and a knife in the other, his elbows resting on either side of his plate. A plate of biscuits sat on the table. At the cookstove, George Tubbs was stirring up a pan of gravy. Even though there were plenty of plump laying hens on the farm, breakfast always consisted of biscuits and gravy. The eggs were usually fixed at noontime. Alma found this a bit odd, but she couldn't complain much, since the biscuits and gravy made a fine and filling meal in themselves.

She tried to calm her shaky hands and knocking knees before George Tubbs noticed her nervousness, but as it went, she needn't have worried. As usual, he paid her no mind at all, but offered Toby Ray a greeting.

"Mornin', tadpole," he said to the boy. "Set yourself down here 'n eat." He plopped the pan of gravy down in the middle of the table and motioned to it.

Alma's eyes were drawn to the steaming pan of gravy, as if it could take her mind off her nervousness. The gravy was still hot and bubbling in the pan. She watched until the tiny burps finally faded away as it cooled.

George Tubbs sat down and reached for a biscuit. He pulled it apart and laid the two halves on a plate, then spread a generous amount of cow's butter over both. After repeating the process with a second biscuit, he spooned some of the hot gravy over the top of the biscuits and passed the plate over to Elken. He always served Elken first, then Toby Ray, then himself. Alma helped herself to a biscuit and was about to reach for the gravy, when George Tubbs bowed his head to pray. Hurriedly, she pulled back her hand and closed her eyes.

When George Tubbs had finished the blessing, he smiled at Toby Ray. "Dig in, tadpole," he said.

As Alma ladled some gravy onto her plate, the three males dug noisily into their food, as if eating was the most serious business of the day. She couldn't share Toby Ray's enthusiasm. She picked listlessly at her food. Her throat felt like it was closing up on her. How, she wondered, had she let their lives keep going from one mess to another? What in the world were they doing in this strange place for so many days? Why, at the first sight of those jars full of dead animals, she and Toby Ray should have hightailed it out of there. There was a wickedness about the place. She had felt it, way down deep inside, the very first day. But still, something had held them there. Her deep-rooted fear suddenly turned into anger as she looked across the table. There sat the Tubbs brothers—feeble-minded Elken, who had no more

sense than a young child tugging on his mother's dress.
And George . . . old pious George, she thought, praying
over the food like a true believing man. Why, he hardly
ever acknowledged her existence, but treated Toby Ray
like a cherished son. Toby Ray, who sat there between
the two men, eating like he'd never had a single lesson in
manners. Her hands tightened into fists under the table,
and she bit her bottom lip. She felt like jumping up and
grabbing him by the ear and shouting at him that their
mama would never have allowed him to bury his head
in his plate like some animal. No longer than they'd been
with the Tubbs, and he'd picked up their habit of eating
like stray dogs.

Yes, she thought, they had to get out of there, and fast.
Last night, it had taken all the fortitude she could muster
to go to sleep, knowing about the sinister-looking corpse
that lay across the hall. Even without all the strange
goings-on, it had been foolish to think that this situation
could ever amount to any good. No matter where they
went, they couldn't possibly run into any more bizarre
surprises than the Tubbses had given them. It was best
they go back to their original plans. Kansas, that was
where they had been headed in the first place. She
had to admit, she would love to have a place as nice
as George Tubbs' to call home, but she had a feeling
deep down inside that it would never be. Tonight, she
decided, they would leave.

She raised her head to stare defiantly at George Tubbs,
her eyes almost narrowed into slits. Her breathing deep-
ened. What kind of man was he, to keep a dead woman
in the house? Where was his wife? In her whole life,
she could only remember one older man who had never
married. But, everybody had known that old Benjy Hertz
was feeble-minded. Maybe George was feeble-minded,
too, she thought. Maybe he just didn't show it like
Elken and old Benjy Hertz did. She remembered back
years ago. Her grandmother had once told her that, after
the Big War, there had been so many more women
than menfolk, the South should have passed a law that
would allow two women for every man. The thought had

always fascinated her. Now, though, the story made her feel irritated. She caught herself staring at George Tubbs, his white beard and long hair. Her mind drifted upstairs to the face that lay on the bed, then back to George Tubbs. Suddenly, as she watched, tiny wrinkles started to appear. Then, deeper ones. He began to age, right before her eyes. His eyebrows thickened. His beard became thick and unruly, his skin pale and dry. And then, his lips cracked and curled into the dead woman's smile.

"My God!" Alma blurted out. "It's your mother!"

The three heads popped up in unison. Toby Ray looked confused. George Tubbs' eyes widened.

Elken began bobbing up and down in his chair. "Mama? Mama?" he repeated, looking back and forth between Alma and his brother.

"Whose mother?" Toby Ray asked.

George Tubbs' emotionless eyes turned hard and cold, and Alma realized she'd made a foolish mistake, letting her anger and frustration get away from her so easily. She waited for his outburst.

Instead, there was a short silence. "So," he said, "you've paid a visit to Mother, have you?" His voice was calm, but there was a storm brewing in his eyes.

"Mother? Whose mother you talkin' about?" Toby Ray said.

"Just shut up and mind yourself," Alma snapped.

"Leave the tadpole be," George Tubbs said, rubbing his hand over Toby Ray's head.

Elken had picked up a chant, calling for his mama, over and over. He swayed back and forth in his chair, smiling at something on the far wall that only he could see.

His cold eyes fixed on Alma, George Tubbs said in a scolding tone, "Now, why'd you have to go and ruin my surprise, girl? I was goin' to introduce you to Mother, in time. I swear, you females are all alike."

"Won't somebody please tell me what's goin' on?" Toby Ray said in a pleading voice, his eyes wide. He knew there was something exciting going on, and it pained him not to be involved.

"It seems, tadpole, that your sister has sneaked into Mother's room without first asking permission," George Tubbs said calmly.

"Your mama's upstairs?" Toby Ray asked George Tubbs curiously. "How's come she don't ever come down and eat with us?"

"She's dead, Toby Ray," Alma said in a flat voice, her eyes fixed on George Tubbs.

"D-d-dead? Where?"

"Why, her room is right across the hall from yours, tadpole," George Tubbs nodded.

Toby Ray looked puzzled. "You got a dead woman upstairs?"

"Oh, there's nothing strange about it." Tubbs' lips smiled. "She meant so much to Elken, and I just couldn't make myself take her from her room. That was always her room, you know. She loved it so. Come, tadpole. Now that the surprise is out"—he frowned disapprovingly at Alma—"I will take you to visit her. She would like that. Yes"—he rubbed Toby Ray's head—"she would find you to her liking, I'm quite sure."

The color drained from Toby Ray's face. His eyes widened. "No!" he said, yanking his head away from George Tubbs' touch. "I don't wanna see no dead woman!"

"Oh, come now, tadpole. You must come and visit Mother." George Tubbs smiled broadly. "You know, it's not often I allow guests. This will be a treat for all of us, I promise." He tried to take the boy's hand.

Toby Ray ran to Alma and grabbed hold of her. "Please, Alma," he begged. "I don't wanna see his mama."

George Tubbs looked almost shocked. "Why, there's nothin' to be afraid of, tadpole! I'm ashamed of you for actin' this way. You're scared! I just can't believe it."

"I'm not either scared," Toby Ray said from behind Alma. "I just don't wanna . . . I just don't wanna go, that's all."

Alma held her brother tightly against her. She stared at George Tubbs. The confusion on his face made her shiver, but it also made her angry. "Now look here," she said. "Our own mama just died. Toby Ray's been through a lot lately. If he says he don't wanna go, you shouldn't oughta force him."

"Why, that's pure nonsense." George Tubbs stepped around and took hold of Toby Ray's arm. "I'll not stand here and listen to any more of your disrespect for Mother."

Toby Ray made a desperate sound, and Alma firmly pushed George Tubbs' hand away. "You listen here," she said. "He don't wanna go, and that's that!"

With unexpected suddenness, George Tubbs pulled back his arm and smacked Alma hard across the face. She flew across the room, landing in a heap on the floor.

"I'll not have any female sassing me in my own home," he said coldly. "Now you, tadpole, get yourself up those stairs, right now."

Toby Ray's face twisted with rage. "Don't you dare hit my sister!" he hollered, letting go with his fist. He caught George Tubbs high in the stomach.

George Tubbs gasped. "You little son of a bitch! I'll teach you a lesson!"

Toby Ray tried to set to defend himself, but George Tubbs was just too big and strong for him. The punch caught Toby Ray in the jaw and sent him sprawling on top of Alma on the floor.

Elken was growing more excited by the minute, dancing back and forth in his chair while drool ran down from his mouth and off his chin. A growl came from deep down inside as he jumped to his feet.

"Mama!" he cried out. "I want Mama!"

George Tubbs turned from Alma and Toby Ray, and with the same anger he'd used on them, he lashed out at Elken. Only Elken didn't fall. This enraged George Tubbs even more. Bellowing like a mad bull, he began to hit Elken again and again, flailing his fists with an unnatural energy. Elken just kept growling and hollering for his mother. Blood and spittle sprayed from his lips. Finally, he turned and tried to start for the stairway.

George Tubbs grabbed him in a chokehold and tried to hold him back, but Elken pulled his brother along as he groped frantically for the steps.

Wrestling with Elken, George Tubbs turned a desperate eye on Alma and Toby Ray, who still sat on the floor, hugging each other. "Just look what you've done, you dirty female!" he said.

Elken broke free of his brother's grasp and started climbing the stairs on his hands and knees. George Tubbs tried in exasperation to kick at him, but Elken kept crawling.

"You sons of bitches!" George Tubbs hollered. "I'll git you for this, girl!" With murder in his eyes, he started for Alma.

Toby Ray quickly jumped to his feet with both fists swinging. George Tubbs smacked him aside with no effort.

Even in her hysteria, Alma knew that Toby Ray was much safer than she was. She decided to make a break for the front door. She made it and was just pulling the door open when George Tubbs swung down with his fist, catching her squarely on the top of the head.

Lights flashed before her eyes, then Alma's senses left her. She thought for sure her neck must have been broken. She couldn't feel anything. Her hand reached up for the door handle, but fell limp. Behind her she could hear Toby Ray again grappling with George Tubbs. Again, she tried to reach for the handle. It was no use, she thought. Maybe if she lay there, for just a minute or two, she could make it. She could run and get help and come back for Toby Ray. Then they'd be safe again. Slowly, she turned back around, to make sure Toby Ray was all right. She didn't see the fist come at her again. It struck her high on the cheekbone, knocking her cold.

When Alma came to, the first thing she noticed was that her head was a solid mass of pain. She felt around again for the door handle, but instead she got hold of a brass headboard. "How did that get here?" she thought groggily.

She tried to open her eyes, but one of them was swollen shut. Gingerly, she touched her face. Heat radiated from her mouth to above her right eye. It was swollen bad, she could tell. Her neck hurt. Finally, her good eye slowly started to focus. From outside, she heard a rooster crow and birds chirping, but it was still mostly dark. With an effort, she pushed herself up. The rush of blood to her head almost caused her to black out again.

A panic rose up inside her. Frantically, she felt around. Toby Ray was not in the bed with her. She started to cry. "Where are you, Toby Ray?" she sobbed.

Alma got up and stumbled to the door. It was locked. She started pounding on it with both fists, calling for her brother. "I want Toby Ray! Where is he? Oh, please, God in Heaven, don't let them hurt him!"

The pain in her head was nothing compared to the fear that ripped through her heart. Alma felt her legs give way as she slid to the floor, feeling totally helpless. She lay there, crumpled, and continued to cry and call out for her little brother, until long after the sunlight had found its way through the curtains.

But no one answered her.

20

LARKES' IMPROVEMENT TOOK ITS TIME, BUT AT LAST he started to show some signs of coming around. His sleeping spells grew shorter, while his wakeful moments became more alert.

Reasa felt a renewed hope. Night after night, with Hawk Vann's drinking and sick talk about his romantic prowess, she'd nearly gone crazy. She tried again and again to tell him what she thought, but her sharp words of disapproval served their purpose only when he was sober. Each evening, with the downing of the sun, Vann continued to drink himself into a deep stupor. Then, his nastiness crept forward.

The dirty talk had gotten nastier and he'd started fondling her. It made Reasa feel sick, having his gnarled old hands on her, but there wasn't a lot she could do. If he kicked her out, she and Noah would be all alone. That would be disastrous, and she knew it. Even though Larkes seemed to be getting better, she was still worried to death that he might not make it.

Some mornings, Vann would be apologetic. Others, he didn't seem to remember the goings-on of the night before. Whether he remembered or not, though, the situation was getting worse. He'd soon gone to fondling her breasts and backside and was getting even bolder by the day.

On the morning Larkes came more alert, her spirits

lifted so high, she wanted to laugh out loud. Larkes still looked to be near death. He'd lost so much weight, Reasa didn't see how anyone could be so thin and recover. The meat was mostly gone from his shoulders, and little knobs of bone poked up against his skin. His ribs dominated his upper body and his cheeks were sunken in. Reasa glanced over at Vann, who was watching Larkes' progress with as much enthusiasm as she was. Even though she couldn't stand the old man, she had to admit that he had kept Larkes alive where she'd thought it was impossible.

Even Noah seemed more perky this morning. This pleased Reasa to no end. The fact that Larkes was the first male to make Noah smile had not gone unnoticed. Before he was shot, Larkes hadn't seemed to pay the boy any mind at all. Still, she could see a bond growing between them. Not a real strong one, but it was there just the same. Maybe life would someday be good, she thought as she stared down at his body, which looked as much like a skeleton as she'd ever seen.

She was sitting with Larkes when she heard a horse ride up outside. Within moments, Henry Starr's familiar voice called out. She grew excited as she heard his boots climbing the wooden stairs.

"How's Larkes?" he said as he took off his hat and clutched it to his chest. His face was serious with concern. "I heard about you folks and what happened. I tell you right now, I ain't slept more'n two winks a night, thinkin' I caused this."

Reasa stood up, smiling. "Why, go on!" she said. "You're not to blame for this. Just one of those things in life that happens, I guess." Inside, she had been blaming Starr for Larkes' getting shot. But seeing Starr again, there was something about his endearing charm that made her forget every bad thought she had had about him.

Starr crossed the room and put his hand on Larkes' forehead. Slowly, Larkes' eyelids opened. It took him a while to recognize the sober face that stared down at him, but finally, for the first time in a long while, he spoke in a voice that was dry and crackly and painfully weak.

"What you say, Henry Starr?"

Starr's eyes were full of hurt and disbelief at Larkes' condition. "Gosh, I'm sorry," he mumbled.

"Sorry?" Larkes said, then started coughing. When he could regain himself, he tried to raise his head. He pointed to his throat. "I'm thirsty."

Reasa raced out of the room. In less than a minute, she returned with a big glass of water. Gently, she held it to Larkes' lips. She looked up at Starr, and they both grinned.

Starr stayed with them for several days. He mostly talked while Reasa nursed Larkes, who was showing improvement each day. Reasa was happier than she'd been since Larkes had been shot. For one thing, Starr's presence had stopped Vann's nightly harassments. He still drank; in fact, he got just as drunk as ever, but Reasa could see in him a deep respect for Henry Starr that cut through his drunken stupors.

Another reason she thoroughly enjoyed Starr's company was the fact that he read to her. He'd brought books by Thoreau and Longfellow and Hawthorne. She especially liked Hawthorne's *Scarlet Letter*. The words fascinated her. Listening, Reasa noticed that Starr's voice seemed to change as he read the words that thrilled her so. He became almost genteel in his manners. The brash outlaw enamored her with his attentions. He was the first man who had ever taken such patience with her. If she could, she'd have made him read to her all day and through the night. In fact, if they didn't have to stop to eat or tend to Larkes' needs, she reckoned he'd have been more than willing. Besides that, the books somehow made her feel more important, as if she was the only one who'd ever been privy to such great stories.

She wished she was a better reader herself. She was able to decipher a few songs in the hymnbook. She could even read the newspaper, but it was slow. A book, she thought, would be insurmountable to her. Starr, however, was soon encouraging her to read, too. While he'd be reading one book, she'd hold another, clutched to her chest.

Reasa had not told Starr that she wasn't a good reader. One day she commented to him, "You read so well. You must have lots of schoolin'."

Starr said solemnly, "It wasn't schoolin', Reasa. That gives you a good start. You really learn to read by repetition. The more you read, the better you get at it."

As he spoke, she buried her nose between the pages of the book she held and breathed in. Yes, Henry was right, she thought to herself. She would most definitely learn to read these books. Before, she'd always been satisfied to just hold the books close to her heart. That had been enough for her. Now, though, she wanted more. She wanted each and every word to be hers.

It wasn't just the excitement of Thoreau, Longfellow and Hawthorne that stirred her heart. There was a newspaper story that Starr had read to her on the first day he had arrived. She had kept that paper and read the story over and over until she knew every word.

The story held proof of what Starr had told her and Larkes about free land in the Cherokee Outlet. It told how President Cleveland had made an agreement with the Cherokee Nation of Indians, and the nation ceded its lands lying in the Indian Territory to the government of the United States for $8,597,736.12. Reasa had read the story so many times, she could almost say it from memory. The land, according to the article, would be separated into 160-acre allotments. No mention was made when all this was going to come about—the newspaper only speculated sometime in August, September or October. When Reasa mentioned this to Starr, he said they'd been talking about it for a couple of years. Still, she queried him about it, unable to hide her excitement. Had he been there, in the Outlet, she asked?

Starr smiled and said, "Many times."

"Please," she said, "tell me about it. Is the land beautiful?"

Starr shrugged. "Personally, I like it better around Fort Gibson, Bartlesville, Lenapah and Nowata. Land's prettier. More water, trees, good berries to eat. Where-as the Outlet's mostly cattle country. Got flat, rolling grasslands." When he noticed Reasa's face fall a bit, he added, "But that's just 'cause I'm not from the Outlet. I was born at Fort Gibson, myself. A body likes what he's used to. Now, if I was gonna raise me some cattle or wheat, then the Cherokee Outlet would be a fine place. Fact, they got cattle ranches all through it. All in all, I'd say a body couldn't find a better place to settle into."

Reasa smiled again. When she fell asleep that night, she still held the newspaper tightly in her hands. She couldn't imagine owning land of her own. Why, people back home would think she was crazy, just thinking such a thing.

These had to be the happiest thoughts of her life. She dreamed of a little house, with Noah playing in the front yard. In the distance, she could see Larkes on his big white gelding, tending to a herd of cattle—their cattle.

But that was in her sleeping dreams. In reality, there was a dampness thrown on the subject. Larkes had pure-ly shown his distaste for settling down at all, let alone in Indian Territory. Colorado was all the man had ever been able to talk about.

Well, she thought, he'd best get ready to hear about President Cleveland's free land. Just as soon as he was up to listening.

Henry Starr made his departure, but left Reasa with the newspaper story and the books he'd brought for her to read. For days she rubbed her fingers lightly over the books. She picked them up one at a time, leafing gently through the pages, opening and closing each several times. Though she wasn't quite ready to read a whole one, she did satisfy her yearning somewhat by poring over an occasional page. She found the writings to be more complicated than the news stories, but that didn't dampen her spirits. Starr had given her the audacity to believe that she could read enough to someday be able to read and understand an entire book.

As for the newspaper story, Reasa read it over and over every day. The words got so easy to decipher, she knew she must be getting better and better at her reading abilities, overlooking the fact that she had memorized the words.

Larkes continued to improve each day, to where he was now feeding himself and sitting up for hours at a stretch. At first he tried to argue with Reasa that Henry Starr's visit had only been a dream. Finally, Reasa produced the books as proof that he'd really been there. She showed him the book where Henry had inscribed, "To Reasa Peters, with friendship and fondest regards— Henry Starr, 1893."

Larkes was dumbstruck over the fact that he couldn't remember Henry Starr as anything more than a fading dream. That worry aside, he seemed quite content to let Reasa tend to his needs. He hadn't depended on anyone since his mama and he slowly came to accept Reasa's mothering.

The fact that he had regained his alertness had also kept Hawk Vann away from Reasa. Since Larkes was now awake most of the day and evening hours, Vann had taken to drinking downstairs in the front room by himself.

This both satisfied and irritated Reasa at the same time. It was just like a drunken man, she thought, to cover up his irresponsible acts with liquor. "I was crazy with drink," he would tell her. Well, she huffed to herself, he wasn't so crazy with drink that he didn't notice when Starr and Larkes were present. Reasa hated drunks, but she especially hated those who got a false bravado from it. Though Vann had not taken on much meanness from his drinking, he had nonetheless hidden behind the drink in trying to seduce her. He was just a coward, she thought, plain and simple. With Larkes growing healthier each day, she had a mind to get right in the middle of him over his drunken activities. The truth was, though, she couldn't risk losing his hospitalities just yet. Besides that, she was glad to have him out of the way. Best to let him drink all he wanted. It gave her a chance to have Larkes all to herself to talk to him about the upcoming land run.

Now, Reasa had a purpose in life. The first one she reckoned she'd ever had, aside from making sure that Noah had a decent life. Her thoughts were consumed with land. Free land. Her land.

21

ARKY SMITH STARED DOWN AT THE WATER TROUGH. The reins of his mare were gripped tightly in his left hand. He let go a little to allow the horse to drink.

He hated being in this predicament. It seemed like something always happened to spoil his best-intentioned plans. Absently, he ran his right hand deep into the pocket of his britches and felt the stickiness. They needed a washing bad. His middle and index fingers poked through the hole at the bottom and dug at his underwear. All of him needed a washing.

He squeezed his eyes shut, wishing he could somehow will his pockets to fill up with money. If only he had some way to get himself across Texas, then he wouldn't have to be here, worrying over this new dilemma that the German, Reinhart Frey, had laid upon him.

His hand came out of his pocket, still as empty as before. He sighed, pulled his mare away from the trough and walked her toward the two covered wagons. Several dirty-faced children stared out at him curiously, but he tried not to notice. Instead, he faced the man who watched him expectantly.

"You say a hundred American dollars if 'n I take you folks to Kansas?" Arky asked.

"Ja ja," Reinhart Frey said in his heavy German accent, his eyes twinkling with encouragement. "You taken us to der Kansas, and you I will give one hundred American dollars. Twenty-five now, twenty-five when we reach Oklahoma Territory, and den de fifty I give you when we reach my bruder's place in Kansas."

Arky looked off, down the street of Longview, Texas. How, he wondered, did he always manage to get himself into fixes like these?

He was on his way to southwest Texas to work cows on a huge ranch owned by a Mr. Flood. The job had been promised to him by a man name of Dudley Simms, whom he'd met in a saloon in Little Rock. Simms, who was visiting family in the area, had introduced himself as Mr. Flood's ranch manager. They'd spent a friendly evening over a bottle of rye, with Simms filling Arky's head full of dreams with stories about the huge ranch that was spread out for miles. When Simms cordially offered to take Arky on, Arky had jumped at the offer like a bear takes to honey. Since that time, he'd been working his way toward the ranch, picking up enough day work to keep himself fed until he got there.

Right now, he was hating the fact that he'd stopped at all in the town of Longview. There'd been a bad feeling about the place since he first rode in. He should've just moved right on through, he thought. But he hadn't— instead, he'd been fool enough to stop and lend a hand to Reinhart Frey and his family when he saw they'd broken a wheel. After that, it had seemed rude not to accept a meal from the missus. Then, Reinhart had complicated things even further by asking Arky to take him and his family all the way to Kansas.

Arky let his eyes wander past Reinhart and over the two wagons. They were loaded down with pots, pans and furniture of all sorts. Children hung out the back and front of both. Arky thought there must be at least a dozen of them. Suddenly his eyes were caught by those of Reinhart's wife, Helena, and he felt his own thoughts come to a momentary halt. Helena had strong, challenging eyes that matched her large frame. She was nearly six feet tall. Arky knew that, because she had offered him water while he was fixing the wheel. When he stood up to accept the drink, he noticed that she rose

up a little past his own five foot ten. Hefty, she was.
He guessed her to be well over two hundred pounds.
Her hands were big and worn thick, like a man's. For a
moment, he forgot himself and glanced back at Reinhart,
whom he guessed to be five eight or five nine and no
more than one-fifty tops. He knew at that instant that he
had no desire to tangle with Helena Frey. Even though
he hadn't noticed any such inclinations, he supposed
Reinhart had no such desires, either.

Reinhart smiled and said, "Vell, vhat do you say? One
hundred American dollars. Twenty-five now, und—"

"Okay, okay! I understand your offer," Arky said,
feeling a little bit like a trapped animal. "Lookee here,
though. Do you know how long it would take us to go all
the way to Kansas, with them two wagons and all them
young'ns? And these mules of your'n." He gestured.
"Why, they're old! Who sold 'em to ya, anyway?"

"De mules, ve buy from goot man outside of
Shreveport. De be goot mules, so far!" Reinhart said.

The weather was hot, and Arky was sweating heavily
around his neck and forehead. He pulled off his hat, dirty
and sweat-stained, and wiped himself. "Now, lookee
here, Mister Frey. You gotta quit trustin' folks so easy!
Now, whoever sold you them mules lied to ya. They's
old, I tell ya! And, what about me? Who's to say I
won't just take off with your twenty-five dollars in the
night?"

Reinhart Frey smiled. "You don't think me and de
missus is not aware of such things? Ve talk it over, und
ve can tell you be from goot parents. Ja." He nodded.
"You from goot parents. So, you take us to Kansas?"

Arky stared out at the western horizon. All his life,
he'd been looking for a job like the one that waited for
him on Mr. Flood's ranch, out in the wide open country.
Stability. That was something a job like that could offer,
and stability was something Arky had always wanted.
At twenty-four years of age, he'd put in a good ten
years, working small spreads, ever since he'd run off
from home. He'd always yearned for a job just like the
one Dudley Simms was promising. Why, Simms had

leaned back in his chair and told Arky of how a man could ride all day and not set sight on another soul— about how Mr. Flood's cook was renowned for the fine fare he set on the dinner table each evening. How he'd let a cowboy cut out a head of beef at Christmastime, if he was married. Arky wasn't married, but he figured that was another thing that this job might change for him. Dudley Simms had told him about the pretty senoritas in the small towns of west Texas.

Arky let out a sigh, as if to say good-bye momentarily to his dream. "Okay. Let's see the color of your money," he said.

"Ja! It is goot decision," Reinhart said as he smilingly walked toward the wagon seat. He spoke in German to his wife. From up under her dress, Helena pulled out a brown bag and said something in German to her husband, her eyes flashing a warning shot at Arky. When Reinhart offered up the money, Arky frowned toward Helena.

"What did she say?" he asked. "Seems like she was mad about somethin'. Now, I don't wanna be startin' out on no long trip, if'n your wife's gonna be mad at me."

"You take money. She is not mad," Reinhart said.

Arky took the money. He tried to match Helena's piercing gaze, but he couldn't. He quickly blinked and looked away, cursing himself. Why, he told himself, if he couldn't even hold his own with a woman, what kind of man was he? Angrily, he forced himself to look back into Helena's gaze. But she had lost interest and had turned her attention to the children in the wagon.

Reinhart was just starting to crawl up on the seat of the other wagon as Arky mounted his mare. Arky took a deep breath and pushed any thoughts about southwest Texas out of his mind.

"Kansas, here we come!" Arky shouted, nudging the mare northward.

22

THEY WERE TWO DAYS NORTH OF LONGVIEW, TEXAS, when the mule died. Arky wasn't an I-told-you-so type of fellow, but he did have a strong inclination to say just that to Reinhart Frey. He'd warned Reinhart about the awful condition of the mules more than once.

They'd been riding along slowly—so slowly, in fact, that Arky had gotten impatient, jumped down from his saddle and walked his mare. He felt kind of silly, walking along like that, and hoped nobody of any cowboy decency would come along and take notice. Why, a person might just see him walking his horse alongside that wagon with all the dirty children hanging out and get the awful idea that Arky belonged with Reinhart Frey and his family, like some sort of hired hand. That would surely be humiliating. Arky kept a close watch for other travelers. He got lucky—only a couple of farmers crossed their path, and Arky didn't much care what any farmer thought.

They had just pulled out of a dry, sandy creek bed when the right mule on the lead wagon began to quiver, then stumble sideways. Arky thought at first the mule was just turning stubborn, pulling away and refusing to go any further. Then the mule stopped and started wavering back and forth. By the time Arky realized the animal was in a serious state, it was too late. The old brown mule's lips slowly pulled back, revealing teeth that were rotted and worn. Its eyes began to roll, and the sound that came from deep inside the mule was nothing more than a small whine—more air than anything—instead of the usual loud hee-haw. The mule's front legs stiffened as if it were trying to resist the cross into the hereafter. Then, the mule fell dead.

Reinhart Frey jumped down from the wagon and bounded toward the mule. He grabbed hold and began to wrestle to get the dead mule's head in his arms. Pretty soon, the veins were popping out on his red face as he struggled.

A smirk appeared on Arky's lips. It looked silly, Reinhart's butt bobbing up and down as he worked so hard to hug on a dead mule's head. He wanted to shout at the German, remind him that he'd warned Reinhart about those mules. He didn't, though, because at that same moment it dawned on him what a desperate situation this put them in. Making it to Kansas with two wagons, and two mules apiece, was a monumental task that had had Arky plenty worried in the first place. Now, he thought as he stared at the lead wagon, there wasn't any way a'tall that one bone-skinny mule could pull the load all by itself.

Arky sat perched in his saddle, his arms crossed over his saddle horn, and thought. There hadn't been any sign of another human being for several hours. He tried to remember back. Was it five or ten miles since they had passed the big farm with all the livestock? They'd been traveling so slowly, Arky couldn't remember how far back it was, and he had no idea how far ahead they'd have to travel to find an animal suitable for pulling a wagon.

Resolutely, he slid down from his horse and walked to the dead mule, where Reinhart Frey was frantically blowing into its face.

"You can blow all day, but you ain't gonna revive that mule," Arky said dryly.

"Vat is wrong? Der mule act like it be having heart attack," Reinhart said, his face panicky.

"I'll tell you what's wrong, Mister Frey. That mule

died of old age. I doubt it's done any serious pullin' for the last six years."

"But, der mules, dey be goot mules," Reinhart insisted. "Mebbe skinny, but goot."

"Nope. They ain't good mules. They old, Mister Frey." Arky shook his head. "And I'm afraid it's just a matter of time before the other three come to the same endin'. Now," he said, talking slowly so the grieving Reinhart could understand, "it might not be any of my business on the one hand, but it sure could be on the other. What we need to do is go find us some good stock. Maybe some big plow horses or mules. Doesn't matter, as long as they're healthy. If you're fixin' on makin' it to Kansas with these here wagons, you ain't got no choice."

Reinhart Frey paid little attention to Arky's words. Instead, he turned back to the mule and started blowing on the animal's face again. Beads of sweat covered his head from the neck up. Arky started to say something, but he stopped when he realized that Helena Frey was standing next to him.

"Vas ist los vit der mule?" she asked.

"What?" Arky said, mindful not to look directly into her eyes.

"Der mule be dead," Reinhart said respectfully.

"Dat be crazy!" Helena Frey said. Her English was even better than her husband's. This surprised Arky, who for the last two days had assumed that she spoke no English at all.

"Vat you say, Arky Smith? Dis not be crazy?" Helena demanded.

Arky caught himself taking a step backwards.

"W-w-why, it's crazy all right, but the mule's dead. It's an old mule. Like I pointed out to your husband, I'd say they all quit their plowin' days, years ago," Arky said.

"Aw!" Helena waved her hand in Arky's face. "Vat do you know about der mules? Ist you a mule skinner?"

"Why, no ma'am. I ain't no mule skinner, but I reckon I can tell healthy stock from old and sick stock, whether it be a mule or a horse." Arky's words trailed off weakly as he realized that Helena Frey was again ignoring him. She stood there for a moment, watching her husband's futile attempts to revive the dead mule, then turned and walked back to talk to the children, whose heads poked curiously out of all ends of the wagons.

It took a while, but Reinhart finally gave up and stopped blowing in the mule's face. He sat there, still cradling its head in his arms. This irritated Arky to no end. What kind of man would sit there, worrying over a used-up old dead mule? He sincerely hoped no cowboys would come along and see such a ridiculous sight. They'd surely attach Arky as some kind of family member. The fact that he hadn't seen a single cowboy since they'd hit the trail didn't even occur in his train of thought.

Helena Frey must have agreed with him, for she soon quit fussing with the children and came to Arky's rescue. Bending over Reinhart, she said in a scolding voice, "Der mule ist gone. Get you up! You look silly, holden der mule's head!"

Arky hadn't cared much for Helena Frey to begin with. He couldn't help the fact. He did, though, feel a great sense of relief and gratitude as he watched Reinhart release the mule's head and rise slowly to his feet. Arky gave Helena a small smile and a brief nod, expecting her to smile in return. Helena paid him no mind, though. Instead, she returned his gesture with a hard stare, then turned back to the wagon.

Arky wondered if all German women were so head-strong. His own widowed mother, who lived by herself just outside of Little Rock, had German blood—at least, that's what he'd been told once. Arky believed a lot of things were true, whether he'd actually heard them said or not. Sometimes, he just thought he'd heard something, and before long it became a fact in his mind.

His mother, though, was a frail woman, yet spunky. That fact alone had given Arky a great feeling of pride back when he was a skinny little boy. Now that he was a skinny grown man, whenever anything was said about the fact that he was so thin, he'd talk about how spunky his little mama back in Arkansas was. Arky was so skinny, he could put his hands over his head and stretch to where his ribs would show through his shirt in good weather. Arky would strike his hard, flat stomach, much like a farmer would thump a ripe melon, and explain how he was built just like his mama. It was obvious that he was proud of it.

Arky's papa had claimed to be Scotch-Irish, but his mama had always told Arky that he was more English than Scotch or Irish, either one. This didn't bother Arky in the least. He hoped he was more English. Once, when he'd needed pocket money, Arky had taken up with a Shakespearean actor, ridden with him and the little acting troupe all the way from Dodge City to St. Louis. Arky had the fondest memories of that period of his life. He had sat in wonderment at the nightly stage shows, watching the performances of Hamlet, Othello, Macbeth and King Lear. Not that Arky understood very much of what the actors were saying, but the words seemed magical to him. Another fond memory was that of Sarah Bodie. Arky had been smitten by her the first day he'd laid eyes on her. What's more, Sarah had seemed to take to Arky with the same fervor. Arky thought Sarah to be a fine actress, even though the director, Horace Agater, always seemed to be impatient with her and scolded her unmercifully after each performance. The more he scolded, the deeper Arky fell in love. So much so, he knew better than to cross Horace Agater. He wanted so much to travel the world with them and hear their stories about such faraway places as Syracuse, Albany, Pittsburgh and Boston. Many nights, Arky went to sleep thinking about the allure of those cities and the beautiful Sarah Bodie.

But, like most things in Arky's life, there came an end to such happiness. Sarah Bodie decided one day that Arky would make a fine Shakespearean actor. The mere fact that he had no proper schooling whatsoever didn't dampen her plans one bit. She worked with him, day after day, making him repeat the tedious lines over and over as they rode along. Then, one day, Horace Agater had called Arky aside and told him he had agreed to give him a reading. He chose Othello for Arky's test. For all the hard work Sarah and Arky had done, Arky could just as well have chosen to read something in Greek. He was a pitiful sight, struggling with the masterful words of Shakespeare. Needless to say, Horace Agater had never summoned him back.

"Vat are ve to do? Set here in der Texas until der summer?"

Helena Frey's booming voice brought Arky out of his deep thought. If his mama was, indeed, German, he thought, she must certainly have come from a different part of the country than Helena. His own mama would never be so rude in the company of men. No, he decided, she must have just a tiny bit of German blood, if any at all. This instantly brought an ache to Arky's heart. After all the years of thinking himself to be part German, he'd become comfortable with the thought.

"Ma'am," he began, "my guess is we've got two ways to go about this. A few miles back, we passed a sizeable farm with lots o' stock. The other choice is to go on ahead. Might run into something sooner. 'Course, I don't know."

"Goot!" Helena Frey nodded. She turned her back on Arky and reached up under her skirt, then faced him again. "Forty dollars," she said, handing it to him. "You go back to der big farm and buy one goot mule, and get bill of sale."

Arky toyed with a clump of prairie grass with the toe of his boot. "Lookee, ma'am. I don't mean to be disrespectful, but you need four mules—or horses or oxen. Whatever, you need four." He held up four fingers to emphasize his point.

"Vat? Ve got three mules! Vat ve need four mules for?" Helena frowned.

"That's just the point, ma'am," Arky explained. "You got three mules, but they're gonna end up just like that dead one, if'n you try to pull them wagons on up to Kansas. In fact, I'm not sure these mules could pull *empty* wagons much farther."

"Aw! Dat ist crazy talk!"

Arky backed away from Helena Frey and decided to try to reason with Reinhart. "Lookee here, Mister Frey. I'm tellin' ya these mules aren't gonna go far, pullin' these wagons. We can sit here and jaw about it all day, but these mules ain't goin' nowheres."

"He ist right." Reinhart Frey nodded, careful not to look at his wife. "Der mules, dey be old."

"Old?" Her voice raised and her eyes opened wide. "Vat, then, do you buy der mules for?"

Reinhart Frey didn't answer. Instead, he took in a deep breath and said in a strong voice, "Arky ist right. You given him enough money to buy four."

Helena fell silent and did as her husband told her. As he took the money, Arky looked off, first to the north and then to the south, before he locked his gaze on the western horizon. He sighed. He had a notion to just head that way, leaving Reinhart and Helena Frey where they sat. Someone would surely come along and help them. Someone better suited to such things. Why, he thought, there wasn't one thing about this job that he liked. He wanted to get angry at Reinhart for letting Helena talk to him the way she did. It wasn't right, in his way of thinking. As for Helena, she made Arky downright ashamed of himself, to think that a woman could make him feel so uneasy. Oh, he'd felt uneasy around a female before, but it wasn't fear that made him that way. Arky respected his own mother, but he'd never feared her. No, it was always when a woman set his heart to stirring that he got to feeling unsure about himself. Helena Frey, though, was different.

Then, there were the children. Arky had to admit they weren't bad, for kids. But, from the moment they'd left, they'd taken to asking him questions. Not just a few questions. Those kids wanted to know about everything. One question just seemed to lead to another. Arky figured they'd only get worse as the days passed.

And the mules. When Arky was a boy, back in Arkansas, all the farmers had had mules. It was an animal that Arky associated with dirt farming, not cowboying.

He pulled his eyes from the west and squinted down at the dead mule. It gave him a sinking feeling. Instinctively, he nudged his mount toward the west. The horse took a couple of steps before Arky reined it to a stop.

Reinhart and Helena Frey were standing together, watching. Without a word to either of them, Arky pulled his horse to the south, and headed back to the farm they'd passed to buy the new stock.

23

IF HER LIFE DEPENDED ON IT, ALMA COULD NEVER explain why she and Toby Ray hadn't left the Tubbses' farm that very first day. There'd been enough signs that things weren't exactly normal, but still they had stayed, until their chances to leave had run out. Now, Alma was a prisoner.

Ever since the day she had been found snooping around in the bedroom with the petrified corpse of the Tubbses' dead mother, she had been locked in her room. She'd thought George Tubbs was going to kill her, he'd been so angry. But instead he'd shoved her into her room and slammed the door shut.

She could only guess how long she'd been locked up. Three weeks, maybe. There had been only an occasional foray out of the bedroom, under the constant supervision of George Tubbs. She wasn't even allowed to use the privy out back. A bedpan was her only source of relieving herself. It had been emptied only twice, and only after Alma had pleaded through the locked door that it had spilled over onto the floor. Already, it was full again. Alma could barely stand the smell; it was even worse than the jars of dead animals.

There was barely enough water for drinking, let alone for washing. George Tubbs had allotted her a pitcher a week. Her time of the month was particularly heavy, and Alma had never felt so dirty in her life. She thought often about how her mother had said, time and time again, "Soap is cheap." No matter what life's circumstances, she'd told the children, there was no excuse for a person not keeping himself clean.

Now, she sat in her locked room and wished she could hear her mother say it one more time. Not only were the filth and stench cause to worry. Why, those problems paled in comparison to the anxiety that she felt over what might be happening to Toby Ray. She had been allowed to see him only once, when he accompanied George Tubbs upstairs to bring her supper.

When she and Toby Ray had seen each other, Toby Ray had jumped into her arms. This had infuriated George Tubbs. In a furor, he'd slapped Toby Ray across the back of the head and issued a warning.

"Boy, I told you about females, and look what you do!" he'd said. With that, he had jerked Toby Ray away from Alma's embrace and slung him into the hall. Glaring at Alma, he'd tossed her supper onto the dirty floor.

That night, Alma had cried tears she didn't think she had left.

She sighed, getting up to look out the window. She'd spent hours peering through the dingy glass, hoping for a sign of another human being or a sudden inspiration as to how to escape.

Another day came and went. Alma's sleep was restless and interrupted, as her thoughts kept settling on Toby Ray. The next morning, she awoke with her head mashed up against the headboard, her neck twisted at an awkward angle. She got up and immediately had to sit back down again. Her head was pounding. She tried to stretch, but it hurt just to raise her arms. Every time she moved, a terrible pain shot up the back of her head. It took several minutes before she was able to get up and move around.

In spite of all her aches and pains, she felt hungry—hungrier than she'd been in a long time. The Tubbses had quit feeding her any breakfast at all, and the noontime and supper meals weren't usually anything more than a biscuit and a piece of fatback. There'd been a few times when she'd not been fed a bite until the evening hours. She figured those must be the days when George Tubbs was out fishing, since he smelled fishy when he brought up her supper.

She was in the worst state this morning. The hours had grown into days and the days stretched into weeks. She was hungry and miserable and growing more and more desperate. There was nothing she could do but walk. She paced, back and forth, back and forth, rubbing her sore neck while the hunger gnawed at her insides.

She stared at the windows. They were stuck solid. Any sound of breaking glass would bring George Tubbs up to the room in seconds. She had a terrible fear of heights; besides, she knew the jump would most likely break her legs.

Alma walked to the door, reached down and wrapped her hand gently around the knob. Her body began to shake with the rage that filled her up. Her hatred was so strong, she wished the doorknob in her hand was George Tubbs' neck. Though the Good Book said, "Thou shalt not kill," and Alma believed it with all her heart, she would, nonetheless, take great delight in choking the life out of him.

Her fantasy overwhelmed her. She took the knob in both hands and gripped it until her knuckles grew white. Clenching her teeth together, she pretended she was holding George Tubbs by the neck and squeezed as hard as she could.

The knob turned and the door suddenly swung open, striking her in the foot. She had to bite her lip to keep from crying out as it ripped back her toenail. Pain was soon forgotten, however, as she came to realize that George Tubbs had failed to lock the door the night before. She had turned that doorknob a hundred times, every day. The fact that he'd actually forgotten to lock it made her legs go weak.

She looked down at her bleeding toe to make sure she wasn't dreaming. Even with the door open, she turned the knob again and again, just to make sure.

She stood there a moment, her heart racing as fresh air from the hall swept into the room and filled her nostrils.

Her eyes grew wet at her instant good fortune. She felt like laughing, or crying, or both. She wanted to run down the stairs, snatch up Toby Ray and get as far away from there as possible. In her mind, she could see herself doing just that.

But she had to compose herself, to think clear thoughts. She had to take her time and figure out a way to get past Elken without being seen. Once outside, she could sneak around until she'd found Toby Ray. Then they'd have a chance to make a run for it and get away from this horrible place. She had an urge to smash the jars of dead animals. What a sick man, she thought, hatred welling up inside again.

She tiptoed to the bed and put on her shoes, easing the sore toe inside. When she stood up, the pain shot all the way up her leg. She started for the door, then quickly sat back down. How stupid, she thought. She pulled off her shoes, scolding herself. There she was, needing to get out of the house unheard, putting on her shoes to go stomping down the wooden hall and stairs. Poor Toby Ray, to have such a foolish sister!

With one last look around the room, she crept down the hallway, her shoes clutched in her hand. At the top of the stairway, she paused and took in a deep breath. There was no one in sight. The house seemed quiet and still. Gathering up her courage, Alma slowly started down, one step at a time. She tried to remember which board it was that creaked. Was it the seventh or eighth step down? Or maybe it was the fifth. How could she be so forgetful? She moved to the edge of each step, where the footing was more solid, touching each step lightly and easing her weight onto it. It seemed to take forever, but she finally descended without a sound.

Alma stopped at the foot of the stairs and took a few deep breaths. She wanted to peek into the kitchen area. Hopefully, Elken would be at his place in the parlor with his back to her, looking out the window.

Before she could move, a woman's voice split the air, causing Alma to clutch at her chest. Did they have company? Hope ran through her. She pressed her head against the stairway wall and listened. It must be a neighbor, she thought. She'd never known the Tubbses to have any close or sociable neighbors, and they'd never talked of having any relatives in the area. But someone was in there, sure as anything. Alma felt a euphoria flooding through her. Surely George Tubbs, in plain view of visitors, would have to let her and Toby Ray go? He was crazy, she thought, but not that crazy. After all, how could he have managed all this time? Somebody would surely have come along and noticed, sometime.

Seconds ticked by. She could hear people moving around, just feet away from her, in the kitchen. Then, she heard the voice again.

"You have such beautiful blond hair, Boy. But, it needs to be cut. I will ask Mother to cut it for you. You will like that. She is so good at cutting hair."

Toby Ray, Alma mouthed silently. They were talking about Toby Ray. She was broken free from her prison upstairs, and it was time she took back her life's responsibilities. Toby Ray was her business and her business alone, and nobody was going to cut his hair unless she said so. Without further thought, she charged into the kitchen.

Two women wearing bonnets and long, flowing dresses jerked around at the sudden intrusion. They stared, and Alma stared back. Toby Ray, his eyes wide with excitement, broke the silence.

"Alma!" He jumped from the woman's lap and ran to her, throwing his arms around her waist.

Alma stood frozen in shock. Under the bonnets were the faces of George Tubbs and his brother, Elken.

George Tubbs looked embarrassed. His face grew red under his white beard. "Why—why, you stupid female! What do you think you're doing? You get back up in that room, right now!" he said, his eyes blinking wildly.

Alma's eyes grew dark. "My God, you sick old man!" she said in a low voice. She handed Toby Ray her shoes, then shoved him as hard as she could toward the back door. "Run, Toby Ray! Run as fast as you can!" Spying a hoe that was leaning next to the doorway, Alma grabbed it and held it up while Toby Ray disappeared outside. "You make one move from that table, and I'll split your head wide open!" she said.

Elken started to rock back and forth in his chair, his eyes averted to some object on the table. Alma waited, her eyes on George Tubbs, the hoe hovering over her head.

Anger replaced George Tubbs' embarrassment. His face began to twitch as a strange sound came from his throat. "You female bitch," he said, and lunged for her.

Alma swung with all her might. The hoe bounced against the wall and lost some of its force, then whacked George Tubbs across the shoulder before glancing off the side of his head. He grabbed the end of the handle and yanked, but lost his balance and fell over the back of the chair. That was enough time for Alma to burst through the back door.

Outside, Toby Ray grabbed her hand. "Come on, Alma," he cried.

"I told you to run, doggone it!" she scolded him.

"I ain't leavin' without you."

They took off running, and were almost to the barn by the time George Tubbs burst out the door with blood running down his face. He was still wearing the dress and bonnet. He waved his arms and hollered something.

"Where we goin', Alma?" Toby Ray huffed as they ran.

"Try to make it to those woods over there," Alma said, pointing ahead about two hundred yards to the northwest.

Toby Ray was a fast runner. Back in Fort Smith, he'd always outrun all the other boys his age. It was a trait he'd inherited from his father. But Alma had inherited the same trait, and he could barely keep up with her.

Soon, they had entered the thick woods and were out of sight. Still, they ran on, their feet crunching the dead wood under them, breaking off the low-hanging branches that got in their way. They ran until they couldn't run anymore. Alma guessed they must have gone a couple of miles from the farm when they both doubled over, out of breath.

Leaning down with her hands on her knees, Alma coughed. "Toby Ray," she puffed, then coughed again. "Catch your wind. We can't take no chances."

Toby Ray grabbed his side. "I need a drink."

"Best forget about a drink right now. You just get your breath back."

"They can't catch us. We're too fast for 'em," Toby Ray panted.

"He's got horses, Toby Ray," Alma reminded him. "And we can't outrun no horses."

"I betcha I can. 'Sides that, I can go places horses can't go."

"Just shut up," Alma said. She looked down and gingerly touched her bleeding feet. The rocks and underbrush had cut them in several places, and her toenail was torn back into the quick. It throbbed mercilessly. She had to get her shoes back on, she thought. Disregarding the pain, she slipped them over her feet. Her feet had swollen. The shoes felt too tight. "Let's go," she said.

Once again, they were running through the thick growth of trees. They passed through open spaces and back into the woods, hoping but without luck to come across a stream.

Finally, they fell exhausted into some high grass in a small open field, surrounded by trees. The sun seared their faces and their mouths were dry as cotton. The temperature had risen to the mid-'90s. For the cold, wet winter they'd just been through, the last month had turned hot and dry, the sun scorching the earth and drying up many of the watering holes. The thick green grass had started to turn yellow.

Even with the blazing heat piercing through their eyelids, and the thirst that tormented them, they both fell asleep in the tall grass, free at last from the evil of George Tubbs. Alma had pleasant dreams.

24

THEY SLEPT THROUGH THE AFTERNOON. WHEN ALMA
awoke, she lay there for a moment, letting the sun shine
red through her eyelids, and did an inventory of her
body. The skin on her face felt parched. Even her eyeballs were sunburned. Inside her shoes, her feet throbbed
from the cuts she'd received running barefoot. They hurt
so bad, she momentarily forgot that she'd peeled back a
big toenail. That ache just seemed to blend in with all
the rest.

Alma tentatively opened her eyes, a little at a time.
At first, all she could see were spots. As soon as they
cleared some, she looked around, trying to get her bearings.

She sat up and felt so dizzy, she figured they must
have slept a long time under the hot sun. Why, it must
be around four o'clock in the afternoon, she thought. She
looked down at Toby Ray. She was glad he'd turned
over on his belly and thrown his arm over his head.
She touched her own face. From the burning, she knew
it was blistered real good. If only she had some lard to
put on it and soothe the burning. That and some water
to drink.

She rubbed the back of Toby Ray's head, ran her
fingers through his hair. He must have been awfully
tired, to sleep this long. What had George Tubbs done
to him while she was locked away, she wondered? It

filled her with a deep hatred for the man, and a shame for herself for letting it happen.

Alma sat there in her misery, thinking her sad thoughts. It pained her to realize that most of her thoughts had been of the dark variety during the last year or so. There had been a time once, up until just before their mother had taken sick, when all of Alma's thoughts had been happy ones. She'd once had dreams of someday getting married, having children, cooking big family meals and making all their clothes and going to church together. She had imagined lots of talking and laughter around the table with Toby Ray and, someday, his wife and children. She had even picked out names for her own: Waldo and William for the boys and Frances and Rebecca for the girls. Why, those dreams seemed so long ago and far away, she could barely remember having them.

Now, Alma could only think of surviving, with no clue as to how. They had been headed for Kansas, but their relatives there would most likely turn them away. She'd tried not to think about it, and hadn't mentioned the fact to Toby Ray for fear of breaking his spirit. Kansas was worth a try, though. If no one would help them there, then she would just have to think of something else.

Alma hated to wake Toby Ray, except for the fact that she'd like to move him out of the sun. She sat there a few more minutes, trying to think past her misery. Besides the pain, she nearly cried over the fact that she could smell herself. Why, she decided, humans surely smelled worse than animals when they didn't bathe. How she'd love to find herself a creek and sit down to soak herself clean.

After she aroused Toby Ray, they got up and moved into the woods to wait until the sun had fallen. Then, they walked until well into the night. Toby Ray was unusually quiet. Alma knew he must be hungry and unbearably thirsty, and it wasn't like him not to complain. Alma worried over the fact. What had George Tubbs done to take away his spirit, she wondered again? Or was Toby Ray just too tired from running to say much?

The next morning, she was awakened by Toby Ray blowing on her face.

"Git back, Toby Ray! Your breath stinks!" she said, waving her hand back and forth.

"Your face!" Toby Ray cried, staring down at her with wide eyes. "There's bubbles all over it!"

She wasn't surprised. Her face was stinging all over.

Where Toby Ray had been quiet the night before, he made up for it when he started to complain that he felt hungry enough to eat a bear. Alma took him by the shoulders, trying to forget her own hunger pains and the miserable way she felt.

"Now, listen here, Toby Ray. Try to forget about being hungry and thirsty. We've got to keep movin' and find some water. You've just gotta toughen up, hon."

"Toughen up?" Toby Ray spat the words like they had a nasty taste to him. "I reckon I'm tougher'n any old girl! Come on," he said as he kicked a rock. "You just try to keep up!"

They set out again, and the day wore on, their hunger growing. Along toward evening, they came upon a patch of half-ripe sand plums. The juice felt especially good on their parched tongues. They ate until they were both nearly sick, even after the half-ripe plums started to taste only half ripe. Alma tore off a piece of her dress. They picked as many as they could carry with them. Feeling a little better, they slept that night in a blackjack thicket.

They spent the next day much the same way, wandering aimlessly, the plums keeping their mouths just moistened enough to prevent them from choking on their tongues. The fruit had another effect on them, though, that wasn't so pleasant. Toby Ray developed a bellyache first, then Alma. Soon, one or the other of them would have to stop every mile or so for relief. This only added to all of Alma's other miseries. She wanted to throw up from her own stench.

Once, while she was relieving herself, she and Toby Ray both spotted an Indian family in the distance, riding in a buckboard. Before she could stop him, Toby Ray started to wave, but, fortunately they didn't notice.

George Tubbs was still too fresh on Alma's mind to trust anyone. And though they were tired, dirty and hungry, she would rather endure more of the same than take any chances.

The next day, Toby Ray killed a blue jay. He had been throwing rocks at every rabbit and bird he'd seen, and had somehow managed to knock the bird out of a tree. As hungry as she was, Alma still had reservations about eating a raw bird. Then, Toby Ray gave her a triumphant smile and pulled some matches out of his pocket.

"George Tubbs gave 'em to me," he said, full of himself.

Alma smiled and let him start the fire. The blue jay tasted as good as turkey at Thanksgiving, except they could have eaten half a dozen more. Still, it revived their spirits some to think that they had been able to feed themselves, if only a little.

Early that evening, they found a place on a small hill overlooking a farm. They hid in the grass and surveyed the scene. It was inhabited by Indians. Alma could see children playing in the yard.

"Ain't those the same Indians we saw ridin' by this mornin'?" Toby Ray asked, squinting down at them.

"I don't know."

"Well, let's go down. Maybe they'll give us something to eat and let us sleep in their barn."

Alma wanted to trust the Indian family, just as badly as Toby Ray did. It would have been wonderful to sleep in a nice soft pile of hay and enjoy a hot meal. Even more than that, she'd love to jump in the water trough and bathe herself. But it was a risk she just couldn't take.

"We can't do that, Toby Ray," Alma said firmly. "And I don't want to hear any more about it."

Toby Ray accepted her decision without comment. He looked around, then turned to her with a quizzical look.

"Which way does the sun set?" he asked suddenly.

Alma frowned. "In the west, hon. You oughta know that. Remember? The sun rises in the east and sets in the west."

"Well, which way are we headin'?"

Alma impatiently pushed her hair back from her sweaty forehead. "West. Be quiet, Toby Ray. I need to think."

"Well, how come the sun's behind us, then?"

Toby Ray's question caused a rush of blood to Alma's already hot forehead. My God, she thought. He was right. She moved away from the top of the hill and looked slowly around. There was something familiar about all the small, rolling hills that surrounded them. She had been taking them around in circles.

Fear gripped at her as she instantly thought of George Tubbs. Was she leading them right back into his grasp? Where exactly were they? She fell to her knees and started to sob uncontrollably.

"I'm sorry, Alma. I didn't mean to hurt your feelin's." Toby Ray was standing over her, his face puzzled.

She shook her head and pulled him to her. Poor Toby Ray. He had no idea how stupid his sister was, she thought. Why, he should have been leading the way, instead of her. He knew more about the sun than she did. She had let all her aches and pains and worries take over her good sense. Her legs quivered as she pulled herself to her feet.

"Come on. Let's go."

Toby Ray pulled back and shook his head. "No! I'm tired. If we can't go down and ask that family to help us, then I'm staying right here!" he declared.

"I said come on, Toby Ray," Alma said between sobs. "We've been going the wrong way, and it's all my fault."

Toby Ray looked at her. His face softened. "It's not your fault, Alma. I should have been watching the sun, too," he said. Without another word, he set off walking down the side of the hill. Surprised, Alma rubbed her eyes and followed him.

The Indian farm was soon forgotten. They continued on their way until late. The moon was nearly full, and they could have seen well enough to walk throughout the night, except Alma had never learned how to read the moon the stars. The problems she'd had reading the sun had had a sobering effect on her, to the point where she knew she couldn't trust her sense of direction.

Despite all their troubles, they both slept deep and hard. The next morning, they tried to ignore their empty stomachs as they pushed on westward. Now, Alma was watching the rising sun carefully as she eyed the landscape before them. She wished they'd picked more sand plums.

At mid-morning, their luck finally took a turn for the good. They were waist-deep in thick prairie grass, approaching a grove of trees, when Toby Ray suddenly sank to his knees in water.

"A creek!" he shouted to Alma. They both started to laugh.

It wasn't much of a creek, being small enough for the grasses to hide its banks. It was five or six feet across and barely a foot deep. To Alma and Toby Ray, though, it was as big as the Pacific Ocean.

Toby Ray instantly started to drink, lying right down in the middle of the creek. Soon, Alma herself was sitting in the water a few feet downstream, splashing about like an oversized fish in a small pond.

She let Toby Ray play for a while and get all the water he wanted to drink, then told him to walk upstream a ways to a high spot in the tall grass.

"Sit down a spell while I take a bath," she ordered.

Toby Ray protested, but Alma wouldn't hear any of his backtalk. "You can take one after I'm done," she promised.

"No thanks," Toby Ray mumbled as he disappeared from her sight.

Once he'd gone, Alma took off all her clothes and sat down in the water. At first, she just let the water lap against her as it traveled downstream. It made a soft, pleasant sound. If any euphoria was to be found in their life's situation, she thought, this was surely it. She turned toward the current and leaned way back on her arms so the water could run over her stomach, chest and shoulders. She closed her eyes and stayed that way for several minutes. There was a tranquilizing effect about the creek. Even the harsh rays of the sun weren't bothering her. She cupped handfuls of water over her blistered face and enjoyed the cooling relief.

She would have been grateful for some soap, but Alma had learned to live without wishes. Instead, she took a handful of mud and scrubbed it across her skin, over her arms, down between her legs and over her feet, until at last she felt clean again.

She hated for this wonderful feeling to end, but she knew Toby Ray would be getting restless. Finally, she left the water to retrieve her clothes. She scrubbed them as well as she could, using a few rocks that lay on the banks. Alma had learned to share her mother's compulsion to be clean. She scrubbed on the clothes for a long time and, even though she wasn't completely satisfied with the results, she still felt a lot better. Her mood became lighter. Maybe she wasn't such a terrible person after all, she decided. Maybe she could lead herself and Toby Ray to a better life.

She started to get up and put on her clothes, but the water felt so good, she decided to bathe again. Draping the clothes across the bushes to dry, she stepped back into the water. Again, she scooped up handfuls of water and poured it over her hair. She rubbed her fingers in and around her ears and between her toes. She made loud splashing noises and giggled as she peed in the water. How delicious it felt to be a little girl again.

Absently, she scooped up more water and let it fall over her breasts. Her dark nipples were hardened by the cool water. She stared at her breasts, fascinated. When had they gotten so large? She had been so preoccupied, she hadn't looked at her own body in months. A new excitement ran through her. She was only sixteen, and her breasts were larger than her mother's had been. She cupped them in her hands and pushed them gently upwards.

They had first started growing when she was twelve. Alma remembered how thrilled she had been, and how her mother had laughed and hugged her and told her that she was going to be a beautiful woman some day. Alma had felt so good about herself. She hadn't had such a strong feeling over her own identity since. Once again, she made the water trickle down her breasts. Inside, she felt a little bit of guilt over the sensations it caused. But it wasn't enough guilt to make her want to spoil this pleasant moment.

Alma closed her eyes and took in a deep breath. Just one more minute, she thought. Then she would get up and call Toby Ray.

She was having such an enjoyable time, she didn't hear the horses riding in behind her. It wasn't until she heard a man's voice that she jumped and covered herself. She turned in time to see three men riding up on horseback.

"Hot damn, Roy! I believe we've struck pay dirt!" one rider said as he punched the one named Roy in the arm.

Alma screamed.

"Now, calm down girl," Roy said. "He didn't mean nothin'. We ain't gonna harm ya." He leaned on his saddle horn. The other two sat next to him. They were now within ten feet of where she sat panic-stricken. She opened her mouth to scream again.

The first man said, "Now, you just hush, like Roy tol' you. My name's Ben Sutcliffe"—he tipped his hat, then pointed—"and this here's my brother, Roy, and this here handsome varmint on my left is our cousin, Keith Reynolds. What's your name, honey?"

Before Alma could think of what to say, Toby Ray suddenly appeared with a tree limb in his hands. He gave Ben Sutcliffe a whack across the back of the head, knocking him off his horse. That set Ben's bay stallion bucking wildly. The other two riders scattered.

"What the hell?" Ben said as he grabbed the back of his head. His hand came away smeared with blood. Before he could take a look around, Toby Ray struck him in the face with the limb, bloodying his mouth.

"You leave my sister be, you hear?" Toby Ray said, his face wild with anger.

Ben was down on his knees, his hand holding his swollen mouth. "Roy, get that little scalawag away from me!" he yelled.

By now, Roy and Keith had settled their horses and were laughing hysterically. "Why hell, Ben! That ain't nothin' but a half-pint kid, whippin' your ass with a tree limb!" Roy said.

Tentatively, Ben looked around, holding his hands protectively over his face. "Don't you hit me again, boy," he said cautiously. "I'll whip you good if you do."

"You leave my sister be, then," Toby Ray warned him, "or I'll whip you some more."

Ben started to get up, when his cousin, Keith, hollered out, "Watch out, Ben!"

Ben immediately threw himself down on the ground and pulled himself into a ball, arms over his head. Roy and Keith found this to be so funny, they laughed until they both started coughing.

Ben quickly jumped to his feet, spitting out blood. He held an eye planted firmly on Toby Ray.

Alma had retrieved her clothes and turned her back to get dressed. The wet clothes weren't cooperating. In her hurry, she was nearly falling over herself.

"I oughta burn your backside," Ben told Toby Ray as he ran his tongue around inside his mouth. "You loosed some o' my teeth!"

His threat only seemed to make Toby Ray angrier. He swung again, the tree limb catching Ben on the elbow when he reached up to block the blow.

"Better leave that half-pint alone," Roy said. "He'll tan your ass, yet!"

Ben looked irritable. "Just shut up, you hear me, Roy? It wouldn't be so damned funny if'n it was you the boy hit with that stick," he said.

Keith nudged his horse closer to Alma. He surprised Alma by looking genuinely sorry. "We didn't mean to give you such a start," he said. "We're on our way to Texas. What in the world are you two doin' out here, anyway? Ain't seen no houses close by, 'cept for a couple of families of Indians west of here. And them Tubbs brothers live back over across those hills, there. I know you don't belong to either o' them."

Alma squinted up at him. "You—you know the Tubbses?" she asked.

"Hell, everybody around here knows the Tubbses," Roy spoke up.

Alma looked frightened as she stared off in the direction of George and Elken Tubbs' farm. She rubbed her hands over her arms and felt her knees begin to shake.

This wasn't lost on Keith. He looked at Roy, then back at Alma. "You looked like you mighta seen a ghost at the mention of them Tubbs brothers. They been botherin' you two?" he asked.

"You might say that," Alma said. "But it's over now."

"That ain't so!" Toby Ray hollered. He stepped out from behind the three men and looked directly at each of them. "That George Tubbs tried to hurt my sister."

"You don't say?" Keith said with a look of compassion toward Alma. "I knew he was crazy, but I thought him to be mostly harmless."

Roy eyed Alma with a puzzled look and said, "Well, if you're so worried about them Tubbses, what in the world you doin' here, swimmin'? Why, their place is only two and a half, maybe three, miles from here."

"Put some slack in your rope there, Roy," Keith said. "I'm sure they ain't a-lyin' to us."

Alma finally stepped out of the bushes in her wet clothes. "We been gone from their place for a couple, three days," she said. "But"—she dropped her eyes—"I've been walkin' us around in circles."

Toby Ray stepped close to her side, still holding the tree limb in a defensive posture. "It wasn't all her fault," he said. "I'm just as much to blame."

Keith shrugged. "Don't make no difference who's to blame or who ain't," he said kindly. "The important thing is gettin' you two on down the trail. And in the right direction. I'll bet you're hungry." He reached into his saddlebag and grinned when he saw the looks on their faces when he pulled out some beef jerky. "Here, have somethin' to eat."

Even though Alma had become hardened when it came to trusting strangers, the meat looked so inviting, she took it from him with a smile. "Thanks," she said, and broke off half for Toby Ray.

The jerky was tastier than any she'd ever eaten. In fact, Alma had never really acquired a taste for it. Back when he was still alive, their father had made jerky, and even though it wasn't to her liking, she'd learned to eat it because that was how she'd been raised. This jerky, though, was mild and easier to chew than most. And it felt wonderful in her empty belly.

The three men turned out to be friendly, and they seemed to be concerned about Alma and Toby Ray's situation. Ben even smiled at Toby Ray a time or two as if to say that all was forgiven. Alma felt glad, not only for the food they offered but for their company in such close proximity to the Tubbs farm.

She decided they reminded her of the young men back in Fort Smith. After their boisterous arrival, their manner had taken on a certain politeness. The young men in Fort Smith had been like that—full of pranks and laughter but harmless underneath it all. Alma still wasn't sure if they could be trusted. She wanted to put her faith in somebody in the worst way, but lately there hadn't been anything to happen in her life to base any trust on.

The three men tied their horses to trees and sat down to eat with Alma and Toby Ray. They brought out sourdough bread to eat with the jerky.

"How old are you, boy?" Ben asked Toby Ray through his swollen lips. He had buckteeth to begin with, and the puffy lips only made his mouth stick out worse.

"Nine," Toby Ray said with his mouth full.

"Not yet," Alma corrected him. "Not 'til the fourth of June. Don't you remember?"

Keith said, "This here's June the sixteenth."

"Seventeenth," Ben said. He counted on his fingers. "Yessir, it's the seventeenth of June."

Alma felt a lump growing in her throat. She'd lost all track of time. Toby Ray's birthday had come and gone while George Tubbs had her locked up in that awful bedroom. Her eyes started watering. Poor Toby Ray, she thought. If their mama had been alive, she would have baked him a cake and made him feel special. Now, the responsibility was Alma's, and she had failed him. Again.

25

ALMA WAS MORE THAN JUST A LITTLE GRATEFUL
for the food they'd received. Ben, Roy and Keith had
treated her and Toby Ray with kindness, and she had a
brief chance to lessen her fears, if only a little.

Trust. That was the word that kept coming to Alma's
mind. She had to trust these three men. After consid-
erable thought, she had agreed to their suggestion that
they ride together for a piece.

More than anything else, Alma wanted to make tracks
and put distance between themselves and the Tubbses'
place. The only problem was, Keith, who seemed to be
the strongest of the three, was in no hurry to move on.
They sat for some time, chewing jerky and querying her
about George and Elken Tubbs. Keith said he'd always
known they were strange, but he hadn't believed them
to be as bad as Alma and Toby Ray suggested. Ben,
who was still nursing his swollen lips, was particularly
fascinated by the story of the dead woman.

"We grew up a few miles east of here," he said, pointing his finger. "I remember hearin' about her dyin', but,
come to think of it, I don't recall no funeral. How 'bout
you, Roy?"

Roy scratched his head and thought. "To tell you the
truth, I don't remember nothin' about her," he said.

Keith shrugged his shoulders. "I remember hearin'
that she'd died, but nobody ever said nothin' about a

funeral. 'Course, I never really kept up with such things.
There were lots of stories about the brothers bein' crazy,
but shoot, you hear all kinds of stories about people."
He shook his head sadly, looked at Alma, then quickly
looked away.

Alma could sense that Keith had taken a particular
liking to her. Every time their eyes met, he started to
blink nervously. Alma wished he was better looking, but
the fact was, he was about as homely a man as she'd ever
run across. In fact, all three of the men were ugly enough
to stop a clock. They all had buckteeth and eyes that
seemed too large for their sockets. Alma figured their
mothers must have been plain women, at best. The three
seemed to have perpetual smiles, made even more pro-
nounced by their protruding teeth. To Alma, they looked
like three squirrel heads sitting on human bodies. They
had other features in common: They all stood about five
feet eight or nine and were skinny as rails. Every bone
in their bodies seemed to stick out through their clothes.
Another thing that struck Alma as odd was that they all
carried chews of tobacco in their cheeks. The brothers,
Ben and Roy, took their chews out and laid them on the
ground while they ate. Keith ate with his chew still in his
jaw. Alma figured this accounted for their having yellow
teeth at such a young age.

As Keith nervously looked around, he commented,
"Well, I have no doubt you're tellin' us the truth, and
I'm real sorry it happened to you. You're free to travel
with us. I can promise they won't bother you as long as
you do."

When they had finished eating, Ben and Roy returned
the chew to their jaws. Roy said to Alma, "Where were
you all headin', anyway?"

"Kansas," Toby Ray said. "We got people there. You
see, our ma and pa are both dead."

Alma couldn't believe her ears. She stared hard at
Toby Ray and wondered if he'd ever learn to keep his
mouth shut. Telling them all about their business! That
was her place—she was the oldest. When she got him
alone, she decided, she'd tell him a thing or two.

"You all ever been to Kansas?" Roy said to Alma.

Alma shook her head.

"I been there three or four times. It's a whole lot like the Cherokee Outlet. Lots of grass. Pretty flat," Roy said.

"It's all flat?" Toby Ray asked, sounding disappointed.

"Shoot, boy. It's like that all the way to Coloradee. That is, 'til you get to the Rockies."

"You been to Colorado?" Toby Ray asked.

Roy nodded. "Two year ago. Ben 'n me went out with Sam Owen. Brought back a string of horses."

"I'm goin' to Colorado someday," Toby Ray said, his eyes full of excitement.

"I'll tell ya, boy, them Rockies is somethin' to see." Roy grinned at him.

Keith turned his attention to Alma. "I'm real sorry you don't have a ma and pa. I ain't had a ma since she died havin' me. And"—he blinked and looked off into the horizon—"ain't seen my pa in five or six years. Don't rightly know where he's at. That's a tough go in life, not havin' parents," he added sadly.

"Thanks," Alma said.

"So," Keith went on, "my cousins and I are headin' south. Plan to cross the Red River, then head west. We got us a job offer on the other side of Fort Worth. But I'll tell ya what. We can hold off on the Red River. We can ride west through Oklahoma Territory with ya, at least to Guthrie. How 'bout that? You wanna ride with us to Guthrie? We could put you on a train there," he offered.

Alma couldn't imagine how she would pay for train fare. But, as she chewed on the remnants of a piece of jerky and felt her sore feet in her shoes and felt the Tubbses' close proximity, she welcomed the offer. "If it wouldn't be too much trouble, we'd be glad to accept your hospitality," she said shyly.

Keith slapped his leg. "Good." He turned to Ben and Roy. "It's all right by you boys, ain't it? Goin' on to Guthrie, then down Texas way?"

"Shoot, yeah," Roy said agreeably.

Ben looked solemnly at Toby Ray. "If you promise not to hit me with any more sticks, you can ride with me," he said.

Toby Ray promised and followed him to his horse.

Keith asked Alma to ride with him, and she climbed up behind him.

"How old are you?" he asked her.

"Sixteen," she said.

"Sixteen? Why, I'da guessed you to be more like eighteen or nineteen." He lowered his voice. "You-you-you're beautiful."

Alma blushed a deep red. No one had ever told her such a thing, and it left her speechless.

They turned their horses to the west and had just started out, when Ben suddenly stopped.

"Whoa!" he said. "Look over there!" He pointed north. "Why, if it ain't that George Tubbs! And he's got a shotgun!"

Alma pinched the flesh on Keith's back and bit her lip. Fear gripped at her. She could hardly catch her breath.

Keith reach around and patted her leg. "Now, you don't worry about a thing," he said. "Shotgun or no, he ain't gonna do you no harm."

"Just relax," Ben said.

"I ain't scared of him," Toby Ray said.

"I'll attest to that," Ben said. "Just the same, you sit still and keep behind me, boy. You understand?"

Keith said grimly, "We'll talk to him. There won't be no trouble."

"He's right," Roy said. "We'll pump him full of lead if he tries anything. You can bet on that."

When they met up with George Tubbs, he smiled at them with his lips, but his eyes rested coldly on Alma, then Toby Ray. "There you are, children," he said. "I've been looking for you."

Keith spoke up. "Listen here, now, Mister Tubbs. You keep that shotgun lyin' across your saddle, there, and don't be makin' no sudden moves. We been hearin' some disturbin' things about you."

George Tubbs' eyes grew wild with anger. "It's that female bitch! She's been lyin' to you. Lyin' about things that aren't any of your business!" He eyed them a moment. "I know all three of you boys. You're no good, all of you."

"We're not lookin' for any trouble," Keith said. "Alma and her brother are travelin' with us now. I hope you'll understand and leave them alone."

"You boys are pokin' your noses in the wrong place," George Tubbs said. "They belong to me! Why, I found them, wanderin' all alone and about to starve to death. I took care of the tadpole, there. Even took in that female bitch. Took care of 'em when they needed it. Why, she even stole things from me."

Alma hollered out. "I never stole anything from you! You dirty old coot! Keepin' me locked up like that!" She reached for Keith's pistol. "I'll shoot you myself!"

Keith caught her hand just as the pistol started out of its holster. "Leave it be, Alma. Let me handle this." He said calmly to George Tubbs, "Like I said, we're not lookin' for any trouble here. Now, Mister Tubbs, we're gonna turn our horses and ride on out of here. I suggest you do the same."

George Tubbs' eyes widened. He swung his shotgun around, but before he could aim, Keith cleared leather and fired into the air.

George Tubb's horse reared, dumping him onto the ground. Roy quickly jumped from his horse. He pinned George Tubbs to the ground with his foot, then wrestled away the shotgun.

"Like my cousin said, we ain't lookin' for no trouble. Think I'll borrow this shotgun a spell, though. Just to keep you honest, let's say." Roy leaned down and spat just inches from George Tubbs' face. "Now, you ever pull down on me or my family again, I won't be as kind as Keith. You understand?" He stood up straight and moved toward his horse, taking the reins. "Now, you get your crazy old ass back where it belongs and leave these two alone."

George Tubbs lay there and watched them ride off, his

eyes burning with hatred. Alma involuntarily wrapped her arms around Keith's middle and held on like a child taking her first horse ride behind her daddy.

They rode until mid-afternoon, the only sounds coming from Ben's and Toby Ray's chatter. Ben seemed pleased by the fact that Toby Ray was so impressed with his worldly travels as a cowboy.

For the first time since her mother's death, Alma felt at peace. Though her future was uncertain as ever, there was something stabilizing about these three men. She felt sure that God had sent them to rescue her and Toby Ray, just when they had fallen at the doorstep of hell.

26

THE HEAT IN THE UPSTAIRS BEDROOM WAS STIFLING. The mid-morning sun had already accomplished its task of warming up the day. There was only one window in the room, facing east, so any chance of wind ruffling the curtains and breaking the uncomfortable stillness was nonexistent. Whenever there was an occasion for any wind, it always came from the south or west.

Larkes lay there with sweat beading up on his body, which was uncovered from the waist up. Below that was a thin sheet. He peered down at his long frame and felt helpless at what he saw. He'd lost so much weight, he looked like a skeleton. His stomach was sunken in, just below his rib cage. What was worse, under the sheet he could see the outline of his manhood. It saddened him greatly to think that he had lost his privacy in life. He was especially embarrassed over the fact that he was in full view of Reasa, who sat nearby, rereading her crumpled newspaper.

Reasa sighed and looked up at him, laying the paper in her lap. When she noticed that he was awake, she gave him a bright smile.

"You slept good. I'll fetch you some breakfast," she said. She carefully folded the paper and laid it on the bedside table before she got up to leave the room.

Larkes stared up at the cobwebs in the four corners of the bedroom ceiling. He couldn't have said why they held such a fascination for him, for at that moment he was no more thinking about cobwebs than anything. He was thinking that it was high time he got himself out of that bed.

It took him a while to sit up. Then he carefully let his feet slide over the edge.

The floor felt strange on the soles of his feet, like some foreign land. Any excitement to be gained over this fact, though, was lost as his head started to spin. Tiny black spots swirled before his eyes like a million gnats. The longer he sat there, the more light-headed he felt, but Larkes was too determined to let the dizziness stop him.

He remembered how his mother had once scolded him for not wanting to get up in the morning. "Just let yourself lay up in bed like your Uncle Lester did," she'd warned. "Then you might just as well curl up and die. Or worse yet," she'd added in an ominous tone, "You'll become an invalid."

Larkes had never known his Uncle Lester or what had become of him, but he had surely never wanted to spend the rest of his life in a sickbed. Shaking like a weak leaf, he braced himself and prepared to stand up.

Once he was on his feet, he locked his knees to keep from falling. It seemed funny that he didn't notice any pain. Instead, he felt shocked at how weak and helpless he had become. Holding onto the bedpost, he tried breathing deeply to steady himself. His eyes watered as he looked down at his bony knees and shrunken abdomen. Once, he'd been a powerfully built man, but now he'd been reduced to skin and bones.

As the moment passed, he found himself becoming more sure of himself. Sure enough, he figured, to at least walk the distance to the dresser, where his clothes lay neatly folded. Still gripping the bedpost, he took the first step. With his second, he lost control and sprawled on the floor in a heap, landing with his cheek pressed against the floor.

Larkes blinked tears from his eyes. He'd never felt so stupid and helpless in his life.

He was just pulling his face from the floor when he heard Reasa shriek.

"What in the world are you doin' out of that bed?" she said. "Tryin' to kill yourself all over again?"

She plopped his breakfast tray on the dresser and took hold of Larkes under each arm. With only a small effort, she pulled him back onto the bed. He sat there, staring down at his own nakedness.

"Woman, ain't you learned a man needs his privacy?"

"You just shut up and eat your breakfast," Reasa told him.

Larkes wiped his damp eyes. Anger crept through him. "I'm tired of bein' fussed over. If you wanna do somethin' useful, fetch me my britches, and then go on and let a man have some privacy."

She tossed her head and put her hands to her hips. "Why, you fool! Who you think's been washin' you every day whilst you been down? I reckon I know your body better'n your own mama!" she said.

Larkes locked his elbows and held as tight a grip on the mattress as he could muster. "I've been in bed too long," he said. "I feel like movin' around. Now, I'm gonna do it, and if you wanna stay and watch, I guess that's your business."

He pulled himself to his feet. Reasa took in a deep breath, but took a light hold of one of his arms to steady him as he slowly walked to the dresser.

From that moment, Larkes' improvement gained momentum with each passing day. Within a week, he was moving about at a careful pace. Getting more restless, he'd limp about outside until his legs would give out, then he'd sit down to rest until he could walk some more.

Reasa gave Larkes a week of silence to gain his strength. Then, she began to talk to him about the big land run that was coming in the Cherokee Outlet. Mentioning it occasionally at first, she was soon talking about it constantly. At first, Larkes paid her little attention. His mind was still set on regaining his health and moving on to Colorado before the snows came. By winter, he had every intention of being settled in someplace. But Reasa talked through his thoughts and intentions. She had so much to say about the land run, Larkes thought more than once that a man would have to be deaf to keep from eventually paying attention to what she was saying.

The fact that she wanted to change his well-laid plans made him angry, then resentful. But the feelings weren't directed toward Reasa, exactly. Larkes had only himself to blame, and he knew it. The truth was, it wasn't only his wants that he had to consider anymore. It surely wasn't Reasa's fault that he'd grown so used to having her around, he'd sometimes feel fear well up inside him when he'd look for her and not see her standing close by to help him.

He'd even gotten used to having Noah constantly under his feet, even though the boy didn't talk much and seemed to be a mama's boy. Larkes had often wanted to tell Reasa that she needed to smack the boy on the rear and send him on his way. He doubted if Reasa would have paid him any mind; she was so full of this Cherokee Outlet land run business.

In the next two weeks, Larkes started putting some weight back on. He was starting to feel his strength rebuild, and on noticing that Hawk Vann had let much of the farm go to ruin, he took on some much-needed chores, mending fences, cleaning the barn and shoeing the horses. If Vann appreciated it, he didn't say, but he remained friendly enough, offering his liquor to Larkes every evening. One thing that Larkes did not appreciate was Vann's propensity for watching every move that Reasa made. Not that Larkes could blame him any: She surely was the most beautiful woman in the world. Still, Larkes thought it took a certain amount of gall, or senility, to do it so openly. He entertained a thought or two of reminding Vann that Reasa was his woman, but stopped when he realized how foolish that would be, especially since he'd never made that claim. Why, he'd never as much as touched or kissed her or made his feelings known to anyone, let alone Reasa.

This final thought occurred to Larkes one evening as he was gathering eggs. It scared him. What if someone should ride in some day—someone full of himself like Henry Starr? What if Reasa took a liking to him in return? After all, Larkes had never shared his inner thoughts with her. For all she knew, he didn't care one iota for her.

That evening after supper, when she talked about the run, as she did every night, Larkes completely surprised her with his reaction.

"I reckon we got the horseflesh. We could pick out any spot we wanted in that there Cherokee Outlet," he remarked.

Instantly, Larkes regretted his words, even if he did realize the urgency of showing some kind of interest in Reasa. Like molasses, she was all over him with excitement.

She jumped from her chair and ran to his side, dropping down on one knee. Her face was glowing.

"That's exactly what I've been thinkin', Larkes!" she said. "Why, that racehorse and the mare are about the finest horses to be found. And I can ride, too. I've been takin' that mare out every mornin', and I'm really handlin' her good."

Larkes' eyes grew serious. "You been what?"

"Yes! I've been ridin' the mare every day. Oh, Larkes, there ain't nobody gonna keep me from gettin' this land. And I just knew that once you got better, the idea would appeal to you, too! Now, don't be mad at me over ridin' that blamed horse!" Reasa said, her face so close to Larkes, he could feel her breath on his cheek.

Larkes stared at her. He said softly, "I ain't mad. I'm just worried about you gettin' hurt, is all."

"Hawk helped me. He's good with horses, near as good as you are." Reasa looked around at Hawk Vann.

"She is very good atop a horse. Rides as good as a man," Vann agreed. He lit his pipe. His eyes peered down at Reasa's backside.

Larkes owed a lot to Hawk Vann for his hospitality. But he decided right then and there that Vann would be the last man to take such liberties with Reasa in front of him.

It wasn't long before Larkes felt strong enough to move on. He mentioned this fact to Hawk Vann more than once, but Vann had gotten used to Larkes' doing the chores and fixing and mending what had so long been neglected. He had no trouble guilting Larkes into staying several days past leaving time. Larkes wanted to repay Vann with money, but having to purchase the horse, food and clothing for Reasa and Noah had caused his money to deplete faster than he'd planned. He'd decided it would be wiser to keep his money and just work his way out of debt to Vann.

Besides all that, a traveling peddler of household wares by the name of Tates Datweiler had stopped at the farm. Tates and Vann were old drinking buddies, and it soon became apparent that whenever Tates came that way, he always stayed on a few days. Tates seemed like a pleasant enough fellow, but it soon pained Larkes to no end that he'd shown up at all.

Seeing Reasa's fascination with her crumpled newspaper, Tates hurried to his wagon and fetched her several papers from around the Territory. The next thing Larkes knew, Tates was adding more wood to Reasa's fire about making the land run in the Cherokee Outlet.

Drunk or sober, the man talked constantly, following one story with another. More than once, Larkes wanted to point out that he'd been to the Outlet on many occasions. In fact, he'd been up to Skeleton on the Chisholm Trail a couple of times, back when he'd ridden shotgun for a stagecoach company. The regular stage hand had suffered a heart attack, and Larkes had served as a temporary replacement. Another time, he'd camped out at Buffalo Springs while bringing in an outlaw who'd been hiding out in the Outlet after killing a deputy in Fort Worth. More than once, he'd been at Camp Supply on the business of tracking down the Negro soldiers who'd deserted. The Army had always been willing to pay traveling money to get them back.

The best Larkes could remember, the Outlet was all covered with ranches, and he couldn't imagine how they planned to go about moving all those cattle operations— not without starting a war.

He would have liked to voice his opinions, but any time he decided to break in and say something, Tates would just nod, grin and talk on. Amidst his conversation, Tates picked up his latest edition of *The Guthrie Daily News* and pointed his finger at the front page.

"This here article tells all about what a person needs to do to register," he said, then commenced to reading it out loud.

The article talked about a ten-dollar filing fee for any piece of land over eighty acres. Then, there was so much per acre to pay, depending on where you settled, that ran from a dollar-twenty-five to two-fifty a quarter acre, plus a commission fee.

Larkes watched Reasa's eyes sparkle as she listened to Tates read. Though Larkes' reading skills were limited, he'd learned to count money at a young age. This free land wasn't altogether free, he thought, wondering if she'd taken the time to ponder the situation. Just like a female, he thought, to get herself in a lather and not stop to consider all the details. Just where did she expect the money to come from? He gritted his teeth. His jaw twitched as his eyes studied her face. She was so wrapped up in Tates Datweiler and his stories, she didn't even notice.

Larkes pulled his eyes away from her to look at Hawk Vann, who sat in his own thoughts. His eyes were glazed over from both age and too much drink. Larkes wondered when Vann was going to release him from the feelings of guilt.

Not that it really mattered. Larkes knew he'd just as well stay indentured to Hawk Vann as lose his money. Whether it was Colorado or the Cherokee Outlet, Larkes' money was going to stay in his own pocket. He thought about Vann's farm. Every time he'd finished one chore, Hawk Vann would stop a moment, rub his chin and come up with something else to do. Now, there wasn't much left that needed fixing. The fences were all mended. He'd pretty near put a new roof on the chicken house. The horses were all shod and he'd even fixed the door on the outhouse.

It was nearly nine o'clock in the evening when Tates Datweiler mentioned he had to get an early start in the morning. "Got customers waitin'," he announced.

This made Larkes feel somewhat better, but there was disappointment in Reasa's face at the news. Instead of releasing him with a simple "Good night," she leaned forward and put her hand on his arm.

"Please, tell me more about the Outlet," she said.

"Why, woman, I reckon Tates here didn't leave a stone unturned," Larkes said with irritation.

"Hush yourself, Larkes," Reasa said. "Ain't often I've had such interestin' conversation. If I wanna hear about the Cherokee Outlet, and if Mister Datweiler is willin' to talk about it, then ain't nobody gonna stop me from askin'."

Tates smiled broadly and slapped Larkes on the back. "Aw! Let the woman enjoy herself. I don't mind a'tall."

"I never doubted you did," Larkes said. He stood up and went to the door to look out into the black night.

Behind him, Reasa sat while Tates Datweiler told more stories about the Cherokee Outlet. There was plenty of grass for the animals, he said, with wide open spaces, land fertile for wheat, barley and rye. He talked about how the wind blew free over the countryside. He described the chill of fall and the smell of the wildflowers in spring. The hot summers and cold winters. He told about how he'd been in a storm and seen hailstones as big as fists kill several horses. Tates talked into the night, way past bedtime. He talked through another jug of whiskey. He talked Noah asleep and left Reasa filled with desires and dreams.

Sometime during the storytelling, Larkes stepped, unnoticed, out the door. He pulled a jug of whiskey from Tates' wagon and took it with him to the barn. Leaning back in a pile of hay, he drank through his growing melancholy. In his dreams that night, visions of the majestic Colorado Rockies gave way to fields of wheat, barley and rye tossed about by the prairie winds.

27

THEY RODE STEADY, MILE AFTER MILE. ALMA SAT behind Keith Reynolds atop his spotted mare. She gripped him so hard around his waist that sweat soaked through his clothes and clung to her arms.

Her head and neck were aching. For the past three days, she had been straining to keep a look over her shoulder. She never mentioned George Tubbs' name again, but the fear of his catching up with them was never far from her thoughts, even as they put more distance between themselves and the Tubbs farm.

The cousins didn't seem to share Alma's worry. Instead, they were in a jovial mood and didn't appear to be in any hurry whatsoever. All three were natural acrobats when it came to riding. They seemed to have a genuine love for the horses, which caused them to stop often and for long stretches to give them rest. Alma didn't understand horseflesh as well as they did, but she couldn't help wondering if they didn't pamper the horses a little too much. It looked to her like the big spotted mare wasn't having any trouble at all carrying her and Keith. Both Roy's and Keith's mounts never seemed to tire, and the chestnut sorrel under Ben and Toby Ray only got to heaving when they'd ridden at a lope for a spell.

Each day's end, they would make camp early, while the sun was still high in the west. The ground was rock-hard and dusty from the need of rain, but they still managed to find an adequate number of water holes.

The cousins were excellent shots. There was never a lack of something to eat. Roy was quick to squeeze off a shot whenever a rabbit showed itself. Alma and Toby Ray hadn't eaten so much rabbit since their father had been alive.

After such a rocky start, Alma was surprised at how quickly Ben and Toby Ray became friends. They often took to wrestling and jawing with each other. Ben shook his head and remarked how strong Toby Ray was for his age and size. This brought an instant grin from Keith and Roy.

There was something about the three men—the way they smiled and laughed so easily and seemed comfortable with the antics of a boy—that made Alma appreciate them all the more. If anything, they encouraged him to be boisterous. He knocked their hats off and spooked their horses as they rode. A couple of times, he even stood up and jumped from Ben's sorrel to the back of Roy's chocolate mare. The mare had reared up, bucked a few times, and taken off running, flipping Toby Ray head over heels to the ground. Once, Roy himself had been dumped by one of the boy's tricks. But all three of the men laughed at the pranks. Toby Ray's spunk only amused them.

As much as Alma enjoyed their easygoing and relaxed manner, she held a deep respect for their toughness in dealing with George Tubbs. She saw more than once that they were three men who were not to be dallied with.

The second day, they came upon a store and stopped for supplies. Two large Indian men stood outside, sharing a jug of whiskey. They stopped Roy as he tried to enter the store and started commenting on how humorous it was seeing three grown men, a boy and a girl all riding on three horses.

The cousins took the funning as naturally as they'd taken to Toby Ray and his pranks, until the larger Indian, a wide-faced man with broad shoulders and dark, serious eyes, wanted to know which one of them Alma belonged to. He'd give a dollar, he said, for a chance to lay with her.

He'd no more gotten the offer out of his mouth, when Roy, who'd been wiping his brow, suddenly slapped the big Indian across the face with his hat, then came up with a left uppercut. It caught the Indian in the groin and dropped him to his knees.

Keith shrugged out of Alma's grasp and slid down off his horse. Before Alma knew what was happening, he pummeled the other Indian with punches that came so fast, his fists were only blurs to her eyes. Ben jumped into the fray with some well-placed kicks in the ribs of both fallen Indians.

In the few seconds following the fight, Alma noticed a hardness in the three that she'd never seen—not even when they'd confronted George Tubbs. Their easy, buck-toothed grins had been replaced by eyes that glazed over and veins that popped around their eyes and foreheads. The storekeeper, who had stepped outside to see the goings-on, watched the hasty dispatch of the two big Indians with disbelief. As the men replaced their hats and were brushing themselves off, the rotund little store-keeper pulled out a handkerchief and wiped his face.

"Well, I'll be!" he said. "I don't reckon you boys ever heard of these Indians, have you? That there big one"—he pointed excitedly—"is Joe Running Horse. Other one's his brother, Canyon. I didn't think there was a man in these parts could square off with 'em in a fist fight." He shook his head. "My Lord! Wait 'til folks hear about this!"

Keith offered him a smile first, then Ben and Roy turned back into their amiable selves. They purchased some bacon and bread and filled their canteens, then helped the storekeeper get the Running Horse brothers up on their feet. Keith offered them an apology, but the Indians only nodded vacantly. They both still had a stunned look about them.

As they rode away, Alma finally felt relaxed. She even quit looking over her shoulder. She knew these to be good men, but she also knew they were rough men, maybe as rough as could be found in the world.

There'd been toughies back in Fort Smith. Growing up, she remembered going to town with her daddy and seeing fights in the streets, but she'd never seen such quick and precise fighting as she'd seen in the cousins. No, she decided, even if George Tubbs did catch up with them, she and Toby Ray were safe. Gently, she eased her grip around Keith's waist and relaxed as the horses crossed the miles. She felt Keith pat her hand. He liked her, she knew. She wished hard that she could like him back. But even though she felt safe among the three and mighty grateful to them, she knew she could never have any special feelings for Keith. It shamed her, for she knew the only reason was because these were three of the ugliest men she'd ever laid eyes on. It was a shallow way to feel, but she couldn't help it.

After that, Alma wasn't in as big a hurry to get to Guthrie. It had been so long since she'd felt any kind of security. She quit worrying over the train fare and what she and Toby Ray were going to do next. Instead, she felt satisfied, just riding along. Toby Ray was having a fine time. They could do this forever, she thought. It was a silly idea, but it was true.

That night they found a thicket of trees with a nearly dried stream of water and made camp. Keith fried the bacon while Roy watered the horses in the tiny stream, which was no more than a foot wide. Ben and Toby Ray got into one of their wild wrestling matches.

After supper, Alma managed to get Toby Ray settled down next to her, while the cousins told them stories about their cowboying days in Texas, Kansas and the Cherokee Outlet in Oklahoma Territory. They were exciting stories for Alma, but what thrilled her even more was seeing the spark that had returned to Toby Ray's eyes as he listened to the cousins' adventures. He was clinging to every word they said.

All three of them were well-versed storytellers, but Alma decided Roy was the best. He had the gift of making each yarn even funnier than the previous one, punctuating his tales with as much humor as adventure.

She and Toby Ray laughed until their sides hurt, but Alma thought it was the best hurt she'd ever felt.

It was nearly dark, and Alma was just thinking about making up her and Toby Ray's bedrolls, when Keith suddenly started singing. Then, Ben and Roy joined in.

The only singing Alma had ever heard were the sacred hymns they sang in church. The cousins were singing songs that were new to her ears, songs about cowboys and Texas. They were stories set to song, she realized. Alma was again surprised by these men, for they had fine singing voices and sang in a pleasing harmony.

Their smooth voices soon carried her to a sleepy state. Alma was just hovering at the edge of unconsciousness when she was abruptly shaken awake by Toby Ray.

"Wake up!" he said. "They're still singing!" He made sure his announcement held true by asking them to sing some more. They good-naturedly obliged.

Sitting up again and rubbing her eyes, Alma wanted to scold Toby Ray for ruining the peace of the moment she'd been enjoying, that blissful state one encounters when crossing that imaginary line into a deep sleep. Still, it was hard for her to get angry, even a little. After all, life was looking up for them. She felt safe. Tonight, she thought, sleep would be wonderful at last, and tomorrow would again be bright and filled with laughter.

Reluctantly, she pulled herself up and made pallets for herself and Toby Ray. The cousins had lent them three blankets: one to lie on, one for cover and one to roll up as a pillow. Toby Ray still wasn't ready to lie down, but agreed readily enough when the trio promised him one more song. Alma watched her brother sprawl on the blanket and sighed when he rolled over, pulling all of the cover to his side. She'd have to wait until he was asleep to pry some of the cover away for herself. It was a warm night, but she still thought a lady should cover herself in the presence of men while she slept.

Nature made its call, so Alma left the camp circle and walked in among the horses to have her nightly relief. She kneeled down close to Keith's spotted mare, making sure to find a spot that wouldn't allow any telling sounds.

Just at that time, the spotted mare received a call from nature, too. Suddenly, the sound of making water seemed so loud, it drowned out the singing voices of the trio. Alma grimaced and squeezed her eyes shut in embarrassment. Surely, they could all hear.

The horse went for a long time. Alma waited for the steady stream to stop, then slowly opened her eyes, one at a time. The sound of the men's voices returned, and Alma felt a flood of relief. She grinned at her own foolishness.

As she was standing up, there was a rustle behind her, then a twig popped. Alma twirled around and caught a fleeting glimpse of something white, reflected against the bushes in the light of the campfire. She stood there and held her breath, waiting and straining to see into the darkness.

The hair on her body bristled when a tiny flicker of white again flashed briefly amidst the bushes. It was so tiny, Alma wondered if it was real or only her imagination. Maybe it was just a deer. Forcing herself to take in a deep, calming breath, she thought about how silly she was. Of course, it was a deer that had wandered close by, maybe curious about the campfire. Why, she'd been scared more than once in her life by the sudden appearance of a deer. They had a knack of silently showing up out of nowhere.

Alma took another breath and patted the mare's back. She was just about to turn back toward camp, when she involuntarily took one last look into the bushes.

Two eyes were peering at her. The whites glistened briefly in the light, then disappeared.

Alma blinked hard. There had been nothing but eyes. They seemed to float in the air by themselves, then vanish. Her body shuddered and she wanted to scream, but she was too scared.

Finding her feet, she bolted out from between the horses and ran back to the camp. She ran so fast, she nearly stepped into the fire. Instead, she slid to a stop and kicked up dirt, causing sparks to fly.

The cousins' voices suddenly died down, and the three men sprang to their feet.

"Say, girl! It looks like you've seen a ghost." Keith frowned, grabbing her by the shoulders.

"What's wrong?" Roy asked, peering at the horses and the darkness behind.

Alma stood there a moment, panting. Finally, she pointed to the bushes. "I-i-i-in there," she said haltingly. "In the bushes. I saw something."

Without a word, Ben and Roy dove for their weapons, while Keith whipped out his forty-four and headed for the bushes. "Bring a light from the fire," he said over his shoulder.

Ben nearly fell over Roy as they both wrestled for their guns. Roy grabbed a chunk of burning wood, and the two men followed close behind Keith.

For several minutes, they searched behind, under and around the bushes, but found nothing. They tried to reassure Alma, but nothing could stop her from shaking.

Keith put his arms around her. "You must have seen a deer."

"Wasn't no deer," Alma said, still scared. "At first, I thought it was a deer, too. But it wasn't." She shook her head.

Roy patted her back. "Keith's right," he said kindly. "Must've been some sort of animal. Like a jackrabbit. Why, I bet that's what it was. The light of the campfire just hit it in the eyes. Shoot, you can see a jackrabbit from a long ways when a campfire hits its eyes."

"Sure," Ben added. "It was a rabbit or a deer."

The boys tried everything to convince Alma that she'd seen some kind of animal. They told all sorts of animal stories from their hunting days and even tried to make her laugh.

Finally, Alma gritted her teeth and stamped her foot to make them quiet down and listen. She knew what they were trying to do, and she also knew that what she'd seen wasn't any rabbit. Possibly, it could have been a deer, she thought, but in no way was it a rabbit. She hated to think that they might consider her that juvenile.

"I know what I saw," she said, almost hollering. "You think just because I'm a girl, I don't know the difference between the eyes of a man and a rabbit?" Her bottom lip twitched in anger.

Keith tried to put his arm around her again, but Alma stiffened. "You're right, Alma," he said. "It wasn't no rabbit. But, don't get yourself all worked up. It surely had to be a deer. Come on and let me show you." He pulled on her arm. "I saw some deer tracks, myself."

Toby Ray, who'd kept silent all along, stepped up next to her. "I saw a big, fat doe right after supper, Alma. I bet they water right by here."

Alma looked into her brother's face and saw the worry in his face. "All right," she said.

Slowly, she let the cousins and Toby Ray lead her back into the bushes. The light of Roy's torch bounced off some deer tracks, plain as day. Alma looked them over hard, her lips still twitching.

"Why, those could be yesterday's tracks, or older," she said.

"You may be right," Keith said agreeably. "But, show that light a little closer, Roy. See?" He pointed. "There's no human tracks here, at all. I reckon any man, woman or child would have to leave tracks, less'n they had wings and could fly!"

"All right, then. Shine the light over there, behind us," Alma said. "Look at the ground, all around."

"Why, I don't see a thing," Keith said, puzzled.

Roy strained hard, holding the light high above his head. "He's right, Alma, I don't see nothin', either." He shrugged.

"That's right," Alma said sharply. "And all of us walked back there. Where's our tracks?"

The three men looked at each other.

"I'll be derned," Ben said. "There ain't any."

"That's right," Alma nodded. "And you know why? It's been too dry."

Still, there were no other answers and no signs of a human being. It took some convincing before Alma would relax enough to go to bed. Only with the promise that someone would stand watch all night did she finally give in. Keith volunteered to take the first watch.

Alma fought sleep. Every time she started to doze, she saw eyes. White, floating eyes, penetrating the darkness. Searching for her.

28

It was warm when Alma awoke. She opened her eyes and looked around, seeing nothing but familiar forms. The fear that had seemed so overpowering the night before had calmed itself, chased away by the day. She felt thankful to the morning for its comforting light over the landscape. The mystery was erased. The evil bush with the floating eyes now looked harmless and painfully brittle from the lack of rain.

She sat up in her bedroll and watched Keith take his turn at making breakfast. The cousins were in their usual good mood. She felt their glances and easy smiles. No mention was made of her wild imagination and phobias from the night before. She knew they were trying hard to comfort her and show her that everything was all right. She felt stupid and ashamed at the commotion she had caused.

Ben and Toby Ray mounted up on horseback with the promise of returning with fresh game. Toby Ray smiled down at Alma.

"Maybe we'll find that deer you saw in the bushes," he said.

Alma tried to smile, but she knew it was a sorry attempt. Toby Ray was trying to be kind. Sometimes her little brother could be downright ornery and mean in his teasing, but today she could see the tenderness on his face.

When they'd ridden away, Keith began to talk non-chalantly about Guthrie and the train station and how he had once eaten a mighty fine dinner at a Mrs. Burroughs' boarding house. Best venison he'd ever eaten, he said. That Mrs. Burroughs had been such a fine cook, he went on, she'd even cooked it in a way that it tasted juicier than beefsteak.

His idle chitchat fell on deaf ears. Alma felt bad over the fact that she was the cause of so much concern that everyone felt the need to reassure her. She excused herself and found a place by the water where she could bathe and sort her thoughts in private.

It was more than an hour before Toby Ray and Ben returned with nothing more than a cottontail to show for their efforts.

Roy teased Ben. "Why, I shoulda taken the boy huntin', myself," he said.

"Wouldn't of done you no good," Ben said good-naturedly. He held the rabbit up for inspection. "Why, this was the only varmint we seen, 'cept for what looked like a doe off in the distance. She was so skittish though, she was gone before we could even get in good lookin' distance. Looks like this dry spell has got all the game skittish that way."

"Well, go ahead and skin that rabbit, anyway," Keith said. "I'll fry him up in this bacon grease."

The men and Toby Ray ate with an appetite, wolfing down the bacon and fresh rabbit, while Alma chewed on a piece of bacon and sipped her coffee.

Later, as they were again riding west, Keith must have sensed that she was still worried. About an hour out of camp, he patted her leg and said to Roy, "Why don't you let Alma ride behind you a spell? Think I'll ride out a ways and look for some game, myself. Might run across a young deer or something. Saw some tracks a ways back."

"I didn't see no tracks." Ben spoke up.

"So you didn't." Keith laughed lightly. "I did." He stared hard at Ben, who shrugged.

Once Alma was up behind Roy, Keith rode up close

and gently touched her cheek. "It's all gonna be okay," he said softly.

With that, he gave spur to his mount and headed back toward the east. Alma watched him disappear. She knew that Keith was no more looking for deer than anything. He was going back to reassure her. Roy confirmed her thoughts.

"Hon, if anything's back there, man or varmint, Keith'll find him," he said. "Yessir, that boy was born fifty years too late. Why, he'd-a made one hell of a mountain man, that Keith would. He could track an owl at night."

"How in the world could he do that?" Toby Ray spoke up. "I reckon an owl would be flyin'."

"You're right, boy," Ben nodded. "Maybe he couldn't track an owl, but," he said with a toothy grin, "I reckon if it lighted a time or two, that Keith could still pick up a trail, even then."

"That's a fact," Roy said. "Old Keith'll shake the dust outta anything that might be back there. You can count on it."

The sun was sitting high in the sky by the time Keith caught back up with them. He rode in from the north. Two cottontails hung from his saddle horn, their legs tied together. One's head had been shot off, and the other was missing its right leg. He picked them up and grinned.

"Didn't find no deer, but heck, I like cottontail better, anyway."

As they ate the rabbit, Keith brought up the subject of his ride.

"I rode back to camp this mornin'," he said to Alma. "Rode east of there and made a big swath back to the north. Ain't nothin' out there, Alma. You know, we all see things at times. I swear to ya, there've been times when I've been ridin' on night herd, and I could swear I seen things in the dark. We all do that. So, you just relax yourself."

His soft manner and words were so comforting, Alma again had to feel guilty that she couldn't like him in any special way. She'd even prayed over it. Here was a man who seemed to be the sort that would settle in and be kind and devoted to his wife. Maybe, she thought, she could get used to his ugliness, after a spell. She had to admit that, when she saw his face, Keith's looks didn't come to mind quite as readily as they had before. Still, there was no denying in her mind that the three cousins were all as ugly as she'd ever encountered.

After they'd eaten, they rode at a walk. Not even once did they put the horses into a lope. The cousins sang, and Toby Ray again seemed in bliss. He'd picked up the words to some of their songs and sang along, his voice painfully out of tune. Alma felt herself enjoying the ride.

Her fears had gone when they made camp that evening under a cottonwood tree. Like magicians, the cousins managed to find water close by once again.

After supper, while the sun was still sending long shadows over the ground, Alma fell asleep in the middle of a song.

The next thing she knew, it was early morning. Not yet light, but more so than dark. A bright misty pink shot across the horizon, illuminating things just enough for Alma to make out the figure of Keith, who had arisen and was standing nearby, relieving himself. He stretched his long thin body and scratched his head vigorously, which caused him to lose his balance and stumble backward a few paces. Recovering his stance, he commenced to finish his business. With the light behind him, Alma was able to see him in perfect silhouette. He stood sideways to her, the profile of his face clearly shown. Alma studied his hawkish nose and buckteeth. There wasn't enough fat to allow for any form to his cheeks. Keith's protruding bug-eyes and long gaunt face reminded her of a half-starved animal. Alma smiled to herself. A fresh-born barn owl. That's what Keith reminded her of. She'd seen a newborn owl once at her Uncle Ted's farm. With no plummage, the baby owl's head looked more like that of a buzzard. Keith sort of reminded her of a buzzard, too. She felt sorry for him.

That fascination didn't hold for long. Her gaze drifted downward, to where he was still making a steady stream.

At first, it didn't register what she was seeing. Then, Alma's eyed widened and she tucked her head down low.

She'd seen Toby Ray naked, but she'd had no idea that a male's member grew so much when he got older. She pulled her eyes away and turned her head in embarrassment. What would people think, she told herself? Acting like some sort of peeker! She closed her eyes and tried to keep her head turned, but for all her embarrassment, her curiosity was more paramount.

She opened her eyes and peeked sideways. Slowly, her head turned back toward where Keith was just finishing up. What was wrong with her, she wondered? Why was she so fascinated? All the guilt feelings in the world weren't stopping her from this terrible invasion of Keith's privacy. Clearly, he thought everyone was still asleep. She lay there in perfect silence as he shook off the last drop. Alma had a sudden urge to laugh. She had to cup her hand over her mouth to keep silent.

Quickly, she lay back in her bedroll and closed her eyes. She could hear Keith reenter the circle of camp and start fixing a fire. She felt a desperate need to jump up, wide awake, for all the excitement of watching Keith had made her overlook the fact that her own bladder was full. She lay there, while her urgency grew stronger, until she thought a proper amount of time had transpired. Finally, she slowly sat up, careful to rub her eyes and act disoriented. She yawned loudly to let Keith know that she had just been awakened by the noise he was making with the fire.

"I'm sorry. Did I wake you up?" Keith asked.

Alma yawned again. "Oh, that's all right," she said slowly. She stood up and wrapped her blanket around her tightly. It made her feel better to know she hadn't been caught spying on him. And a little less guilty.

She found some thick bushes a safe distance away and crouched low. She couldn't help but replay what she'd seen over in her mind. It wasn't really her fault she'd peeked, she thought. After all, it hadn't been her intention to wake up. She was innocent of any wrongdoing. Still, she couldn't justify all the guilt away.

It suddenly occurred to Alma that maybe she wasn't the only one who had been doing the spying. She looked around her. How many times had someone taken liberties with her own privacy? she wondered. She remembered how the cousins had ridden up on her as she bathed in the stream. Why, they had surely done as bad or worse than she had. Somehow, this remembrance made her feel better and allowed her more leisurely recounts of her peeking.

Back at camp, she found Ben had risen and walked off into the distance. Keith was cutting slices of bacon that sizzled as he placed them in the hot skillet.

Alma blew gently in Toby Ray's face. "Time to wake up," she said softly. It took a few minutes, but as soon as Toby Ray was awake, he started a lively conversation with Keith about how Ben had promised to take him hunting after breakfast.

Alma tried to calm him down. "Shhh! Roy's still asleep!" she said.

"Don't worry about ol' Roy." Keith grinned. "Why, a feller who'd sleep through daylight ain't worth his own salt!"

Alma moved next to where Keith was cooking. "Can I do that?" she asked. "After all, I'm quite accomplished at cooking and such."

Keith gave her his familiar toothy smile. "I'm sure you are, but it's no trouble."

"You're right, but I'd still like to do something to help earn our keep. It's the least I can do," Alma said.

Disallowing any argument, she took the fork from Keith's hand and started rearranging the bacon in the pan. "You haven't started the coffee yet. Just like a man!" she said importantly. "Would you fetch some water, Toby Ray?"

Keith smiled broadly. "I'll get the coffee."

An unexpected exuberance came over Alma. The smell of the frying bacon filled her nostrils and gave her a momentary feeling of belonging. All of a sudden, standing there and cooking breakfast meant the world to her. It was these little treasures, these brief occasions, that kept her from losing her spirit. She stared at the bacon in the pan, watching it sizzle and pop and change shapes. If only she could bottle this moment up, she thought. She could drink from that bottle every time a blue mood or downturn came in life.

Beside her, Keith put the coffeepot on the fire and smiled at her. Even though he meant well, Alma wished he'd allowed her to make the coffee. Every small task held meaning for her and gave her a part in things rather than being a burden for others.

He turned to look down at Roy's sleeping form. "Git up!" he shouted.

Roy, whose head was completely covered, refused to move. Keith shook his head.

"We must've sung ol' Roy to a state of tiredness. You reckon, Toby Ray?"

"Looks like it," Toby Ray said, full of boyish laughter. He noticed Ben walking back from his morning constitutional. "Let's go huntin' now," he said.

"Boy, I told you we'd go after breakfast. Once we're movin', we'll do some huntin'," Ben said, tucking in his shirt.

"I'm hungry," Toby Ray said. He sat down for breakfast as if to hurry things along.

They ate in the fresh Oklahoma Territory air. Alma thought it surely added to a person's appetite to have the air smell so good. Alma still kept her eye on Keith. It was hard not to wonder if he knew she had been secretly watching him, but his good-natured attitude kept putting her at ease.

They finished eating, and Alma scrubbed the skillet and tin plates with clean sand, then rinsed them in the water hole.

Ben was growing irritated at the fact that Roy still hadn't gotten out of his bedroll.

"Git your lazy butt up! You already missed breakfast!" he said. When he still didn't get a response, he kicked Roy in the foot.

Keith, who had saddled up the horses, walked up with his horse in tow. His face looked to be smiling, but Alma could see that his eyes were serious as he looked down at Roy's bedroll.

"Don't mess around, Roy. You sick or somethin'?" Ben said. He looked nervously at Keith and pulled the blanket back off Roy's face.

Roy's eyes were closed. He looked to be in a deep sleep. Ben, still leaning over him, said in a louder voice, "Roy, wake up!" He patted his cheek, then touched it with the back of his hand.

Ben's face suddenly went pale. He stepped back, his eyes full of terror.

"He's cold, dang it! He's winter cold. Feel him!" he said helplessly to Keith. Alma saw his hands shaking.

Keith's own eyes took on a frightened look. He reached down and felt Roy's face, then laid his ear against Roy's chest. Frowning, he reached for Roy's wrist and felt for a pulse.

"My God!" he said slowly. "Roy's dead! Stone cold dead! He's already stiffening!"

Ben let out a sorrowful sound. "It can't be so!" he said. "It can't be!" He flung himself down on his knees and took Roy's head in his arms, cradling it as he rocked back and forth. Tenderly, he rubbed Roy's hair back from his face.

Alma didn't know what to do. She stood there, uncertainly. This couldn't be happening, she thought. Suddenly, those floating eyes were everywhere, all around them. She felt her bladder give a little and the wetness was warm on her legs.

She reached for Toby Ray and pulled him against her, and he didn't protest. They stood together helplessly as Ben began to sob openly.

Mumbling something low to Ben, Keith pulled back the blanket to examine Roy's body. There was no sign of any trauma, he told the others; in fact, it looked for all the world as if Roy had simply died in his sleep.

Careful not to take away from Ben's sorrow, Keith

gently turned the body over. Again, Roy's body was clean of any marks or injuries.

Keith stepped back and walked toward Alma. "My Lord! I reckon he must have had a heart attack," he said, almost to himself.

Alma's mouth was like cotton. She tried to fight off the thoughts of dancing eyes. The morning air was hot and dry, and her skin felt steamy. She cleared her throat.

"You reckon?"

Keith shook his head and blew out. "Their daddy, my Uncle Seth, died of a bad heart. Forty-two years old, he was."

Out of respect for Ben, Alma took Toby Ray a short distance away and told him to play quietly by himself. She whiled away her time by keeping an eye on him.

The rest of the morning passed on to high noon, then it was early afternoon. Life had seemed to come to a standstill. Ben's sobbing had turned to quiet weeping. He never once released his brother's head from his lap.

Keith walked over and sat down next to Alma. He was absently chewing on a weed. Occasionally, he would offer a comment to her—nothing more than a rambling statement.

As for Alma, she felt hollow, exhausted. It seemed to her like life had turned into nothing but ups and downs, with the downs far outnumbering the ups. How could life always be so cruel, she asked over and over? She must have done something bad, but for the life of her, she couldn't figure out what. She stared at Ben and watched as he slowly began to rise. He was finally giving up his vigil. Ever so gently, he laid Roy's head on the blanket, then stood up and wiped both of his eyes with his palm.

"Weren't no heart attack," he announced.

Keith wrinkled his nose. "What was it, then?" he asked.

"I don't know, but it weren't no heart attack."

"How can you be so sure? After all, your own pa died of a heart attack."

"Hell, Keith, he was twice as old as Roy. Besides, I don't think Pap died of a heart attack, neither."

Keith said kindly, "Ben, I was there when the doctor said it."

"Don't make no nevermind what that old sawbones said," Ben said. "Pap got throwed and kicked by his horse a couple days before that, and he complained about the worst headache in the world. I think it was that blamed horse that killed him. Always will believe it."

"I never heard that story before," Keith said. "How's come you never said?"

"Hell, I don't know why I didn't say it. Wasn't no need. Pap was dead and wasn't nothing gonna bring him back. But I was with him when he got kicked. Didn't seem like much of a kick, neither, but all that day and the next Pap complained of being dizzy and having this awful headache. Dang horse kicked him in the back of the neck at the base of his skull. I always believed that was what killed him."

Keith stood up. "Doggone it, if it wasn't a heart attack that killed Roy, I don't know what it could've been. I don't see a mark on him."

"We're takin' him to a doctor to find out just that," Ben said. "I want to know for sure."

"Where we gonna find a doctor at?" Keith said, not unagreeably.

"We'll find one."

Ben walked back toward his dead brother. He wiped his eyes again. "By golly, we'll find us one."

29

LARKES SAT ON HAWK VANN'S FRONT PORCH WITH HIS
holster belt in one hand and a knife in the other. He was
cutting a carefully measured hole in the belt. Not only
had he lost nearly two inches around his middle, but the
weight of his Colt caused the gun, holster, belt and all to
slide way down over his hips.

This embarrassed him more than he would admit,
especially since he'd tried to strap the belt on in front
of Reasa and Noah. It pained him to no end when Noah
started to giggle and Reasa, full of intentions to scold the
boy, had turned to him and burst into laughter, herself.

Larkes found nothing funny about his situation, at all.
He said as much, but all Reasa would do was grin and
touch the end of his nose with her finger.

"You just hush up your silliness and let me and
Noah enjoy ourselves," she said, still laughing. "We
ain't laughin' at you, anyways." She put her hands on
her hips and looked at him. "Even if you do look like
a scarecrow," she added, her laughter fading, "you're
a handsome scarecrow. Oh yes, a very handsome one,
indeed."

Larkes was still angry at her funning, but he couldn't
help but be drawn to her overwhelming beauty. Again,
it leaped out at him like an unexpected gust of wind and
blew away the bad feelings. A warm sensation started
swirling around in his chest. He took a deep breath and

got up to help secure the saddlebags on the horses. They were packed full; Hawk Vann had been generous enough to give them blankets and enough food to see them through several days.

When everything was ready, Larkes watched Reasa and Noah mount up, then swung himself slowly atop the white gelding. His head felt dizzy from the effort, and for a moment he was afraid he would faint. His vision went light, so he took in a few deep breaths and waited until it returned to normal. While Reasa and Hawk Vann said their good-byes, Larkes was wishing he'd taken the time to do some practice riding a few days before they set out from Vann's farm. Now it was too late, and his pride was too strong for him to admit that he might not be quite ready. He just hoped the others wouldn't notice his weakness, and that the tiny black spots that swam before his eyes would go away soon.

Beside him, Reasa and Noah rode tall and healthy looking on the brown mare, while he had to hold onto his saddle horn to keep his balance on the often-spirited gelding. He still felt weaker than a newborn calf, and that troubled Larkes greatly. It had been too long since he'd been in charge of his life. He was ready to take over again.

They weren't more than two hours out of sight of Hawk Vann's place, when they first came across other travelers. An old covered wagon was rumbling along with a man, woman and two children. They smiled and waved.

Reasa pointed excitedly to a sign on the side of the wagon.

"Look! It says 'The Cherokee Outlet. The Promised Land'," she said.

Larkes looked at Reasa.

"That's the truth," Reasa nodded. "It *is* the promised land."

More of her silly ideas. Larkes forced a smile, but inside, he had a sinking feeling.

Soon, they were meeting up with folks regularly. Nearly everyone was heading to the Outlet. Larkes had to admit that he'd never seen people so full of excitement and hope. Still, their plans were not his own, and he could feel his dreams slipping farther and farther away. He couldn't help but feel resentful. He even started to grow irritated with the other travelers. They all looked like they'd been downtrodden in life. White degradation, he named it. Many of them wanted to stop and waste his time talking, another fact that grated on Larkes' nerves. It wasn't that he begrudged them of their conversation. It was the subject that he soon grew tired of.

He had bought into Reasa's plan to settle in the Outlet, he realized. Someday, when he got the courage, he would probably even make it official and ask her to be his wife. Still, he reckoned, he didn't have to enjoy listening to a bunch of white folks moaning and going on about their hard times. That was the trouble with white folks, he decided. He'd listened to several of them talking about their great depression, some mentioning that thousands were out of work. Others said millions.

Larkes shook his head. What did they think Negroes had been going through all this time? he wondered. He surely didn't need downtrodden white folks with their dirty-faced children telling him about hard times.

Another thing that irritated him was how everybody had put President Cleveland up on some kind of mountaintop for offering up this "free land." Free to them, maybe, but hadn't it been taken from somebody else? Larkes didn't usually try to do a lot of thinking about such things, but he'd been to the Outlet. He'd known even back then that the land had belonged to the Cherokees, but it was the cattlemen from Kansas and Texas who benefited from the land.

Henry Starr had been right about white folks, Larkes thought. Here they were, these miserable, downtrodden people, praising President Cleveland like he was some kind of messiah.

Larkes grumbled to himself all day as he rode. He knew way down deep what the truth of the matter was. Putting President Cleveland and dirty-faced children and land-hungry white travelers aside, the simple fact was

that Larkes, who had never allowed anyone to railroad
him into anything, had just had his mind changed and
his heart stolen by a woman. The knowledge left him
with a bittersweet pain that wouldn't go away.

The next day started off hot. It wasn't even nine
o'clock in the morning yet when Larkes saw two wagons. There seemed to be children everywhere, running
about hollering and playing games.

It was apparent that one of the wagons had a broken
wheel. Two men were hunkered down, working, while a
big woman who had to be nearly six feet tall stood over
them, shouting instructions.

Larkes wanted to ride on by, but Reasa put a quick
change to his plans.

"Look, hon," she said to Noah. "There's some other
babies. You want to play with them?"

Larkes bit his lip. The first thing he would change,
once they were married and all, was the way Reasa
talked to the boy like he was a baby. Feeling more
and more melancholy, he turned his horse toward the
broken-down wagon and rode in close.

A scrawny cowboy sat on his haunches. He looked
up and offered Larkes a big grin. "Howdy, name's Arky
Smith," he offered. "This here's Reinhart and Helena
Frey." He pointed at the other man and the giant woman,
then turned back to the wheel. "Third time this dang
thing's broke on us," he added.

"I'm Larkes Dixon. This is Reasa. Reasa Peters. The
young'n's her son, Noah. How long you been broke
down?"

"Not long," Arky said. "I 'bout got it fixed."

The big woman stared hard at Larkes, so hard it
made him feel uneasy. He felt tempted to stare back.
Larkes had seen some big women before, but he reckoned this Helena Frey had to be the biggest he'd ever
encountered. He guessed her to be over two hundred
pounds and every bit as strong as a man. Her eyes
were direct and carried a challenge. Larkes looked at
her smallish husband. He surely didn't envy the man,
he thought.

He climbed down and went to work, helping Arky and Reinhart finish with the wagon. Reasa disappeared with Noah in amongst the children. Larkes could hear her laughing heartily. It surprised him how fast Noah had taken up with the other young'ns.

Though she didn't seem one bit friendly about it, Helena Frey offered up bacon and beans. Larkes wasn't particularly hungry, but he ate anyway while Arky kept up a steady chatter. The one thing that pleased him, however, was that he and Reinhart had not said one word about the Cherokee Outlet. It was the first group of travelers he had encountered that weren't full of free land talk.

Conversation stayed interesting enough, and Larkes was beginning to enjoy himself, until Reasa decided to join them. Right away, she brought up the thought that was heaviest on her mind.

"We're headed to the Cherokee Outlet," she proclaimed in a steady voice. "Gonna make the run and claim our own hundred-sixty acres." She looked around at the men, her chin pointed up like she was definitely proud of her statement.

"Free land? Vat ist dis dat you speak of?" Reinhart Frey asked. He had stopped eating and was watching Reasa closely so he could understand what she was saying.

Reasa ignored Larkes' warning stare and poked her chin up higher. "Just what I said," she told Reinhart. "Up in the Cherokee Outlet, the government is gonna have a run on land. Anyone with a horse fast enough can stake him a hundred-sixty-acre claim." She refused to look at Larkes.

Reinhart looked puzzled, but he was eager to learn more.

Arky said, "Ain't nothin' new. They been talkin' 'bout it for years. I worked a couple of ranches on the Salt Fork. Good grazin' land." He looked at Reasa. "So they're really gonna do it this time, huh?"

Reasa couldn't hide her excitement. She ran to the mare and retrieved the worn newspaper article. She read it out loud and then reread it more slowly for Reinhart's benefit.

Larkes wished he had some of Henry Starr's bad whiskey. If he was going to have to hear this malarky all over again, he would surely get ill. He'd just as soon get drunk as ill.

Morning wore on. Reasa read the paper a few more times, then went on for a while about her own dreams of living on her own place where Noah could run and play and she could learn how to work the land. As she talked, Reinhart and Helena Frey grew more and more enthusiastic over this newfound news. Though her eyes stayed challenging and cold as a chicken hawk's, Helena Frey was plainly almost as excited as Reasa over the Cherokee Outlet.

Larkes sat away from the group, his back propped up against a tree. He'd given up any hopes of intelligent and meaningful conversation with this group. It was a poison, it was, this promise of free land. Why, such a thing was too good to be true. And even if it was true, who was to say that every person would end up winning the race? It was a gamble, at best. He just wished he could run into somebody who had something else to talk about, even if it was the weather.

As if reading Larkes' mind, Arky joined him. He perched down on his haunches and balanced there a spell, listening to the group's conversation, then turned to Larkes.

"About a mile or so back"—Arky jerked his thumb over his shoulder—"there's an Indian man got pretty good homemade whiskey, if you'd like to ride over." He glanced over at the group. "I think this day is shot."

Larkes nodded. The two mounted up and rode away, unnoticed.

The Indian, Joe Horsehead, was an amiable sort. He sold Larkes and Arky two jars of liquor for a dollar, then helped them drink it. By late afternoon, all three were too drunk to be much good for anything. Maybe it was the liquor, but Larkes found Arky Smith much to his liking. He was an unassuming sort, but

had lots of interesting things to say that didn't deal
with anything in the future. Larkes had met other cowboys like Arky, those without much aim in life, but not
out to hurt anybody else, either. Arky was not of the
bragging nature and he didn't ask a lot of questions
that made a man have to think. Larkes enjoyed his
whiskey and the company of Joe Horsehead and Arky
Smith.

Before they left Joe Horsehead's company, Larkes
gave the Indian another dollar for more whiskey. They
bid their good-byes, and while still in sight of Horsehead's
house, their talk turned more serious.

"You don't really want any part of that Cherokee land,
do you, Larkes?" Arky said.

"Does it show?"

"Bigger'n Texas," Arky said.

"Well, you're right," Larkes said. "But, it's funny
what a man will do for a woman." He rode a spell,
thinking, before he added, "To tell you the truth, I was
headed to Colorado. Wanted to get in on some of that
gold fever. 'Sides, I always had a hankerin' to settle
down there, where the air is cool and crisp, and a man
would never get tired of all that beauty around him.
But—" he stopped and stared off forlornly. "Sometimes
a man has to choose between what his head wants and
what his heart wants."

Arky stared at him briefly, then a smile crossed his
drunken face. "Sounds to me like the wrong head is doin'
your thinkin', Larkes."

"What do you mean?"

"Aw, hell, you know what I'm talkin' about," Arky
laughed. "You're not lettin' the head under your hat do
your thinkin'. You're lettin' the one in your britches do
it. The one that don't have no brain a'tall."

Larkes thought about it a moment, smiled to himself
and took a big drink. "Your wisdom ain't lost on some
fool," he said. "I reckon you're right on that one."

When they reached camp, Reinhart stood up to call to
them. His smile was wide as a river.

"Ve not go to Kansas! Der Cherokee Outlet, dat's vere

ve go! Aww, America! Can you belief it, Herr Arky? Free land!"

Larkes and Arky stared at each other, while Reinhart raised his hands to the sky as if to praise the Maker.

"Yessir, free land!"

30

LIFE HAD CHANGED FOR LARKES. FROM THE MOMENT he'd ridden up in the shanty town and knocked on Reasa Peters' door, there'd been so many shifts and turns it would make a weaker man's head spin. Not that everyone wasn't due a few unexpected changes. But before, they had all been gradual ones. Now, here he was, seeing his life turned upside down on an almost daily basis. Larkes wasn't exactly sure how it had all come about, but in what seemed like a brief moment, he had gone from a free-wheeling loner with visions of grandeur in Colorado, to a man of family with the unlikely prospects of becoming a farmer. Sod-busters, he'd heard them called.

What's more, somewhere during his and Arky's absence, Reasa and the Freys had put together a travel schedule, whereas they would all be heading for the Cherokee Outlet and making the run together.

Larkes looked at all the faces around the campfire. He counted the children. Besides Noah, the Freys had seven, ranging from a fat little baby girl who could barely walk, to a gangly boy of about fourteen. Eight children and five adults. Larkes' head started to feel the first trace of a headache. He wasn't sure if it was the effects of too much whiskey or the thought of being in the constant company of all these people.

And Helena Frey. The woman's demeanor matched her piercing, watchful eyes. She passed out orders and insults as casually as one would fill a dipper full of water. Larkes sure didn't want any trouble with her sort. He mentioned the fact to Reasa.

She had no sympathy for his worries. "You hush your talk, Larkes," was all she would say. "Can't you see that poor woman is tryin' to raise all those kids, keep her family fed and do half the chores?" She shook her head at him. "Just like a man to find fault with a woman who speaks her mind a little bit."

Angered, Larkes climbed atop the white gelding and loped off away from Reasa and her new group. He rode for a spell, letting his anger settle before he tried to think it through. The horse seemed to understand, keeping a steady pace and offering no surprises.

By his own choice, Larkes had agreed to travel with this newly added burden. Still, he reasoned, he didn't have to stay with them all the time. He could pick his own distance. A man deserved some time alone.

He came to an area where the land was flat and dug his spurs into the gelding's flanks. The big horse half reared and raced forward, its mane flying like a flag on a windy day. Hooves thundered and pounded the earth. For all of its weight, the gelding was graceful and fast, the ride smooth and controlled. Larkes held the reins loosely in his hand. His hat blew from his head, and only the fact that it was tied around his neck kept it from getting lost in the dust that was kicked up by the powerful hooves. Larkes knew the horse was fast, faster than anything he had ever ridden. Still, it thrilled and amazed him to feel the swiftness of the ride.

He wished he were in Colorado. He could see the fat, greedy faces of the men as they bet their diggings against him and the gelding. He would have all their money. There wasn't a horse alive, nor a rider, that could match their speed.

Larkes' body, still weak, began to hurt. Still, he gave free rein to the gelding. It was only after he could hear the horse start to huff and snort that he realized the foolishness of his anger. Slowly, he pulled rein. The gelding, like a locomotive, reluctantly started to slow down. Larkes could sense the horse's pride, reluctant to end its show of power. Though he didn't really understand the thinkings of a horse, Larkes had realized years ago that there was an instinct—an understanding—between a man and his animal. He sensed the horse's indignation over Larkes' assault with his spurs.

When the gelding had finally stopped, it pranced around like some show horse in the middle of a three-ring circus. The big head bobbed up and down as the horse danced sideways, tail held high. *See?* it seemed to say. *I'm horse enough to do it again if you want.* The horse snorted angrily when Larkes climbed down off its back.

Larkes' legs were quivering from excitement as much as weakness. He rubbed the gelding's wet neck, talking softly in its ear. The horse snorted and bobbed its head. There, in the midst of the hot prairie wind and the wide open sky, the two came to an understanding and a sense of belonging to one another, both holding to his own bold temperament, but both with a new feeling of respect.

He stood there a long time with the horse's reins in his hand, gazing off into the distance and enjoying the solitude. He was still standing there when the two slow-moving wagons caught up with him. As they creaked and rumbled up beside him, he stared with disinterest. None of these new people meant a thing to him, yet there he was, saddled with the burden of more traveling companions. They were not, he assured himself, his responsibility, but he had to endure their company, all the same. He wished he could become deaf and not have to listen to any more silly meanderings about the run for free land. As far as that went, he thought, he might as well be temporarily struck blind, too. There was something about those dirty-faced youngsters and their silly grins that worked on his nerves.

The days passed slowly as the wagons lumbered along. Larkes tried to stay close by the rest of the group, but it only got him to feeling sorry for himself. When he couldn't take it any longer, he would race off ahead on the gelding and ride like a free spirit. It was a relief he needed. The horse seemed to be running faster with each passing day, and his respect for the animal grew. He knew it wasn't good, though, working the gelding so hard with their water supply starting to dwindle. With no sign of a water hole for days, he knew his forays were a luxury he'd soon have to do without.

Life became so mundane, only Reasa's company kept Larkes going. Even Arky had become less amusing. He was a pleasant enough fellow, but once the Indian whiskey ran out, Larkes didn't find the countless stories half as interesting.

Concern grew among the group as the weather turned hotter. Drought gripped the Territory. Water was becoming more scarce with each passing day. When Larkes and Reasa had first joined up with them, the Freys' water barrel had been nearly full. Now, it was over half empty, and discussions were held about the fact that they hadn't come across water for many days now. What with rationing for the work animals and enough to wet the children's mouths, the barrel was drying up fast.

One afternoon, they came to a little grove of trees. There weren't many, not even more than a dozen, but there were enough to offer a bit of shade in the piercing heat. There was room for Arky and Reinhart to pull the wagons into the middle of the grove. It was there that Larkes announced they should stay, while he took one of the horses and an empty barrel to look for water.

As he rode away from the shady grove, he thought about how foolish he had been in running the gelding so many times. The horse wasn't sweating as much as before. Larkes knew that was a bad sign.

He was barely out of sight of the trees when he heard a commotion behind him. He turned to see Arky waving his hat and hollering.

"Shoot, I think I'll ride with you," Arky said when he'd caught up with Larkes. "Need to get away from those young'ns a little bit." He smiled.

Larkes felt disappointed at the intrusion. "Ain't no use in both us goin'. Maybe you oughta stay back. Make sure everything's all right in camp. Hard tellin' when I'll find water," he said.

"Ain't nothin' gonna happen in that camp. Not with Frau Frey standin' guard." Arky laughed at his own words.

Larkes pictured Helena Frey's face and large form in his mind. He grimaced. "I s'pose you're right on that one," he conceded.

He pointed the gelding toward the west, but Arky said, "Let's go north. There should be some water about a day's ride from here, if not sooner."

Larkes had no arguments to offer, so he nodded his head and they headed north.

Arky had been right. Early the next morning, they ran across a pool of water in among some willows. The trees sat right in the middle of the pool, as if they knew where the water was and had walked right into it. Within seconds, both men were on their bellies, quenching their long-suffered thirst in the delicious water. Even the horses had taken minds of their own. They waded into the water well over their front hooves and drank deeply.

Laughing, Larkes and Arky undressed. They bathed and sloshed around like two adolescents. For the first time since he'd been shot by the Indian policeman, Larkes noticed that his body wasn't aching from sickness anymore. He lifted handfuls of mud from the bottom of the pool and rubbed them across his body, feeling alive and healthy again. He thought of Reasa. Her beautiful face and the excitement in her eyes. He wished it was Reasa instead of Arky sitting naked in the pool of water next to him. His hands moved slowly over his chest as he washed away the mud and imagined what it would feel like washing Reasa's wet body. A sensuous feeling ran through him and caused a stirring deep down. This, he knew, was why he would never see the Rockies or the faces of the greedy little miners with their hands full of money. Reasa owned him, body and soul, and like it or not, the Cherokee Outlet was to be his home. Funny, he thought, a man never knew what his destiny was, until he was in the middle of living it. Why, just a year before, he'd have called a man loco who predicted he'd be settling down in Oklahoma Territory with a ready-made family.

"What you thinkin' 'bout, Hoss?" Arky asked.

Surprised at the interruption, Larkes slowly opened his eyes. He looked through the trees and beyond at the waving prairie grass. He'd better learn to love this country, he thought. To his way of thinking, there wasn't anything handsome about it. But, as he watched the prairie grass bend northward from the southern wind, he could see Reasa standing in it, hands on her hips, the lower half of her body pushed forward. She laughed at him as she reached up and brushed away an unruly lock of hair that had blown loose. Suddenly, the prairie took on its own beauty. A beauty he hadn't noticed before, but one that was pleasing, nonetheless.

"Damn, Hoss! Whatever you're thinkin' 'bout, save some for me! You look like a man I knowed once, and if you're anythin' like him, you got a woman on your mind! Am I right?" Arky said.

Larkes looked embarrassed, but only for a second or two. He surprised himself by saying, "I s'pose you're right, but it sure is painful when it starts showin'." He laughed like a schoolboy.

"Believe me, I know the feelin'," Arky said. His face grew more serious. "You know, Hoss, with that big gelding you got, you ain't gonna have no problem pickin' out a good piece of land, and I know just the spot."

"Is that a fact?" Larkes said, his eyebrows raised.

Arky nodded. "I used to work cattle in the Outlet. Ever been to Skeleton? Well, I heard from some cowboys that they done named that place Enid. Seems like the president of the railroad didn't like the name Skeleton."

"Enid? What kind of name is that?" Larkes said with a puzzled look.

"Derned if I know. Do you know where Skeleton's at?"

Larkes thought a moment. "Seems like I been through there. Ain't that close to Buffalo Springs?"

"Right north a ways. Anyway, Skeleton, or Enid, as the railroad boss man likes to call it, got some nice land north and west of there. Fact, to the north you get into a lot of trees, which ain't real good for raisin' wheat, or cattle for that matter. For my money, though, that's what's wrong with this country. Ain't enough trees. So, I'm a-goin' for those trees north of Skeleton. You know"—Arky paused and pointed at Larkes' horse—"with that gelding, you could lead the way. I'd try to follow close on this old nag of mine. Maybe we would get a spot next to each other."

"Wait just a minute," Larkes said. "I thought you was gonna take the Freys there, then go off to Texas and work cows."

Arky laughed in that silly, harmless way he had about him. "Shoot, all this talkin' about free land got me to thinkin'. It's like your woman, Reasa, said." He paused and looked sheepishly at Larkes. "You don't mind me callin' her your woman, do ya?"

Larkes smiled. He stared back off at the waving prairie grass and shook his head.

"Good, I didn't mean no disrespect," Arky said. "Anyway, I feel just like she does. I ain't never had nothin' to call my own. 'Sides, if I should decide I didn't want to stay, I could always sell off the claim. How 'bout you, Larkes? Don't you get just a little bit excited, thinkin' you could have a place that belongs to you and nobody else? I mean, your people ain't exactly had anything they could call their own, have they? I don't recall ever hearin' any Negro cowboys talkin' about anything like that." He paused and scooped up a drink of water with his hand. "Shucks, Hoss," he laughed. "I guess the truth is, I ain't heard no cowboys talkin' about nothin' but gettin' hold of a jug of whiskey and a two-dollar whore."

The poignancy of Arky's thoughts wasn't lost on Larkes. Other men could have said the same thing, and Larkes might have been offended. There was something about the innocence in Arky, though, that Larkes found admirable. Besides, Arky was right. Negroes didn't think of such things as home ownership. Not openly, anyway. Why would they? To most, it was just an impossible dream. He'd known a few Negroes who had somehow climbed the ladder in the white man's world. But they were so far and few in between, they stuck out like a circus elephant in a cowboy town.

"Oh, I ain't got nothin' against ownin' some land," he said. "In fact, it would be right noble. It's just that, until recently, I had other plans. That's all." Once again, he took to staring off into the distance, and, like before, Reasa's form appeared, almost as clearly as if she were standing there in person. He thought about the trees Arky had mentioned. It was hard to imagine such a thing in the Outlet. "Are you sure about them trees?"

"Sure as the world. Right north of Skeleton. Got lots of good trees. In fact, I imagine some of them claims will be nothin' but trees. I don't see how anybody could plant wheat. Raise cattle maybe, but wheat? I just don't know. Man'd have a heap of clearin' to do where I want to stake my claim."

"How you gonna scratch a livin' out of trees?" Larkes laughed.

Arky snorted. "Well I ain't gonna be no wheat farmer! I'm a cowboy. If I stay, I'll clear me some trees and build me a cabin. Run a few head of cows. They's a railroad there already, so I could ship 'em and sell 'em to the Kansas City market. They tell me it's still thrivin'."

Larkes caught himself thinking about things he had never imagined himself thinking. Finally, he said, "I'd like one of the claims with a few trees on it, all right, but I'd have to have some open land for wheat or maybe hay. I guess I'd like to run a few cows, too."

Arky sat up straighter, encouraged by Larkes' words. "A little bit northwest of Skeleton, you can get both. I know just the spot. I swear I do. You keep that gelding in good shape, you hear?" He started to laugh, louder than the wind that was whipping through the treetops.

Larkes started to laugh, too. Inside, he thought about how ridiculous life could be. There he sat, in a muddy pool of water, talking about such high hopes and dreams, when he knew his chances were slim, at best.

31

THEY NEVER FOUND A REGULAR MEDICAL DOCTOR. Instead, they came upon a veterinarian in a small village.
It took some reassuring, but finally the doctor, Wally Turnbow, convinced them that he could do a good
enough examination to find out what had stricken Roy.
Reluctantly, Ben handed Dr. Turnbow the reins of Roy's
chocolate mare and watched the doctor disappear into the
barn with his fallen brother.

Alma again found herself clinging to Toby Ray. She
wanted to cry, but she held her tears in respect for Ben
and Keith. She mustn't take away from their sorrow.
Still, unanswered questions ran through her mind, questions that she wasn't likely to ask. Would the cousins
still take her and Toby Ray to Guthrie and put them on
a train? Or would they be tired of having to bother with
them? All of the uncertainties were back. She couldn't
believe how cruel life was turning once again.

Of all things to worry over, Toby Ray found this
time to talk about his dead dog, Tick. Toby Ray had
not even mentioned the dog for a long time, and Alma
had gratefully let it lie. She knew that he grieved over
the dog, but like most other times, Toby Ray had kept
his feelings to himself.

It had happened while they were staying with their
aunt and uncle. Uncle Ted and Raymond had taken the
dog hunting one morning, without asking, while Toby

Ray still slept. When they returned, Uncle Ted had told them that Raymond had accidentally shot the dog while it was chasing a rabbit. He and Raymond had both acted like it was nothing.

In Toby Ray's mind, Raymond had done it on purpose. It had been all Alma could do to keep him from getting even with Raymond. He had talked about it for days, about how he would like to take a chunk of wood and crush Raymond's skull while he was sleeping. Or hide in the barn and surprise Raymond with an axe. Alma had been terrified that Toby Ray would carry out his threats. After a few days, he had dropped the subject, but Alma hadn't stopped worrying until they fled the farm.

Now, it was all he wanted to talk about. Though he acted angry, Alma could tell that Toby Ray was choking back tears. She knew he would never allow himself to cry openly, especially in the presence of the cousins. Even when Toby Ray protested and pulled away, she rubbed his head and tried to comfort him. It occurred to her that this was Toby Ray's way of dealing with another one of life's disappointments. Misfortune seemed to follow the pair around like an ugly shadow.

"Maybe we can get you another dog, hon."

"I don't want another dog," Toby Ray said. He scowled at the ground. "I want Tick. Tick was a good ol' dog." His voice almost broke.

Alma couldn't hold back the tears any more. They ran silently down her cheeks. She said softly, "I know, hon. Tick was a good dog, a mighty good dog. But believe me, if you had another dog, maybe you wouldn't love him in the same way, but nonetheless, you'd love him."

Toby Ray gritted his teeth and shook his shoulders, knocking Alma's hand away. "I said I didn't want no new dog. I want Tick. Some day, when I'm all grown up, I'm gonna go back to Fort Smith, and I'm gonna beat the tar outta that Raymond. And if anybody tries to stop me, I'll beat the tar outta them, too."

"You say this boy killed your dog?" Keith walked over and sat down next to Toby Ray. "I know how you feel. I had a dog, once. I swear, I loved that thing like a brother. It caught some kind of sickness and died about three years ago." He paused a moment and looked at Toby Ray. His face was kind. "But, your sister's right. What you need is another dog. I bet this ol' horse doctor could fix you up with one. I ain't never run across a vet that didn't know about every stray dog in the country."

Toby Ray angrily turned his back on Alma and Keith. It sounded like a growl when he shook his head and said, "No!"

It wasn't long before Dr. Wally Turnbow walked out from the barn. He dipped his handkerchief in the water trough, wiped his face and washed his hands and arms. Without looking up, he said simply, "Broken neck."

The cousins rose to their feet.

"Broken neck?" Keith repeated. "You got to be kiddin'."

"Nope," Dr. Turnbow said without emotion. "Wouldn't kid about such a thing. Somethin' or someone snapped that boy's neck real good. From the looks of the body, I'd say it happened while he was sleepin'. He never knew what happened to him." He finally looked at Ben and Keith. "You boys need to get a holt of the law on this one. There's a policeman over in Shady Run. Name of Bertram. He'll be along this mornin'. Always stops in for coffee while makin' his rounds. I 'spect you boys ought to wait around for him. He may have a question or two for ya."

Ben shook his head angrily. "You wait around," he said to Dr. Wally Turnbow. "I'm fixin' to find out who kilt my brother."

Keith said, "The doc's right, Ben. We oughta talk to that lawman about this."

"Well, by God, you stay and talk to him, Keith. Me, I'm gonna go back and find out who kilt him. As sure as the sky, I'll hunt the sumbitch down and kill him."

"Now hold on there, young feller," Dr. Turnbow said as he finished with his washing. "You don't need to be goin' off half-cocked and causin' more trouble."

"You just shut your mouth, you hear? I reckon I'll go where I want and do what I want," Ben said challengingly.

Dr. Turnbow looked at the others and shrugged. "That'll be two dollars." When nobody said anything, he added, "I usually get five."

Angrily, Ben flung the money at the veterinarian. "You comin'?" He looked at Keith.

Keith looked at Alma and Toby Ray, then back at Ben. "Why sure, Ben. I'm comin', but what about Alma and Toby Ray?"

Ben turned to Dr. Turnbow. "Can you put them up 'til we get back?"

Dr. Turnbow scratched his head. "Aw shucks, a dollar a head a day, and I'll keep 'em and feed 'em 'til you get back."

"I see you're one of them bastards who lives by the almighty dollar," Ben said. He reached in his pocket for more money.

"No, please," Alma said. "We'll just go on our way." Her words didn't match her true feelings. Instead, she felt an overwhelming sinking feeling. She didn't want to be a burden, and the uncertainty of traveling alone once again sent fear through her. But, even though her statement of independence was unfounded and untrue, she stood by it. She waited for Ben and Keith to eagerly accept her offer.

"Aw, hell, Ben!" Keith spoke up. "Two wrongs don't make a right. Listen here. Let's take Alma and Toby Ray to Guthrie. Then, I swear, we'll go back and find the rotten bastard that did this." He turned his attention to Dr. Wally Turnbow. "Are you positive about this broken neck business? I mean, there ain't no chance that you could be misreadin' it? You sure somebody kilt 'im?"

"Now hold on there, young fella," Dr. Turnbow said. "I didn't exactly say somebody *killed* 'im. I'm of the opinion he got his neck broken while *sleepin'*. You draw your own conclusions. I still say it's a matter for the police."

"Well, *we* sure as hell didn't kill 'im," Ben said bitterly. "That leaves only one conclusion. Now looka here, Keith. I'm goin' back for whoever kilt my brother. With or without you." He motioned toward Alma and Toby Ray, avoiding their eyes. "If they don't want to stay here, I reckon they can come along. I care about Alma and Toby Ray myself. . . ." His words trailed off.

By the haggard look on Keith's face, it was clear that he had no ready answers to their dilemma. He stole glances at Alma and Toby Ray. "Lookee here, I know he was your brother, but I loved Roy near as much. We took on these two, and it just ain't like us— it ain't like *you* to not finish a job. Besides that, ain't nothin' gonna bring Roy back." He stopped and looked pitifully at Ben.

"What kind of talk is this? You think whoever kilt Roy is gonna go free?" Veins popped up alongside Ben's neck and rolled up his face as his anger reached new heights. He looked ghoulish, like some kind of monster with his buck teeth and pointed nose. He kicked the ground hard and turned from the others. Hands on his hips, he stared off toward the east.

Alma felt as lost as she had ever been. No matter what new hardship came her way, each one sent her head into a tizzy. Desperation was never something that she would become used to. She thought about her situation. She surely didn't want to be left here with Dr. Wally Turnbow, the veterinarian. Something about the man brought back fearful memories of Uncle Ted and Vernon Skaggs. The fact was, with the exception of the cousins, she had decided that men were not to be trusted. The euphoria of being with Ben, Keith and Roy had been short-lived.

As much as staying with Dr. Turnbow sickened her, the thought of going east with the cousins filled her with fears of running into George Tubbs. She remembered once when she was younger, going to fetch her daddy from a dice game. She'd been fascinated by the players. Men, like her father, with little means of support, yet wagering all their money on the roll of the dice, like some rich Little Rock banker. That's what her life had become, she thought. Just a roll of the dice, and no matter which way they came out, it was snake eyes for her and Toby Ray.

She was tempted to get angry with God again. *Why have you forsaken us*? she wondered. Why couldn't she and Toby Ray have just the tiniest bit of smooth sailing in life? She clutched Toby Ray's hand, holding it with both of her own to keep him from pulling away. She knew that he didn't mind, deep down. He just didn't want the cousins seeing any signs of weakness.

"I sure don't want to upset things," she said softly. "Toby Ray and I like travelin' with you, but I understand." She looked away, trying to hide any emotion that might be showing on her face. If there was anyone that had her personal gratitude now, it was the cousins.

Keith walked over to her and almost hugged her. Instead he patted her back. "Lookee here, Alma. I'll pay for you to stay here a spell, and I'll give you enough money to catch that train in Guthrie. Surely there's someone who'd take you and Toby Ray as far as Guthrie," he said and looked at Dr. Turnbow.

Without missing a beat, Dr. Turnbow's cherub face turned into a wide grin. "Why, I reckon I could find someone to take them to Guthrie without too much trouble. Would do it myself, but business don't allow me such pleasures as travelin'. I 'spect five dollars would cover any travelin' expenses." He paused and added, his eyes widening, "You do understand, of course, what a bargain that is. If I do, indeed, find the right person. I'm sure you would want me to be very particular." He gave Alma a knowing look and wrinkled his forehead.

Ben turned around and spoke up suddenly. "Naw, they're goin' with us! Keith can watch 'em, and I'll take care of whoever kilt Roy."

Keith's expression showed he wasn't quite convinced. With his hand still on Alma's back, he studied his boot tips as they scraped the dry ground. He looked up and chose his words carefully. "We're gonna get whoever done this, Ben. I swear to ya, we're gonna get 'im. But let's talk about it first. I didn't hear a thing that night. I know you're a light sleeper, so I presume you didn't hear anything, either. Now, I just don't see how some bastard coulda snuck in on us and kilt Roy that way. Why, I've seen Roy fight men twice his size, giving up a hundred pounds or more." He shook his head quizzically. "None of this makes any sense."

Ben's jaw started twitching. "It don't have to make any sense," he said. "Why, do you think some man just fell offa the moon? Come on down like a big black spider out of his web and got 'im? I'm tellin' ya right now, somebody did this to Roy. He sure didn't break his neck sleepin'." Frowning, he walked over to the water trough and palmed water over his face. He rubbed his eyes. "I've given thought to the strangeness of his death, myself. I keep coming to one conclusion. There's a sumbitch out there that kilt my brother, and he's gonna die for it. And none too soon." His face twisted into a grimace as he looked at the greedy veterinarian. "We'll keep our dollar a day and five-dollar travelin' fee," he said. "Alma and Toby Ray's goin' with us." His face softened somewhat as he looked at Keith. "You're right. They're with us. Alma"—he walked over and touched her head—"I'm sorry if I made it seem otherwise." To Toby Ray he said, "You reckon you can handle Roy's mount?"

Toby Ray, who had nearly stared a hole in the ground through all the talk, suddenly jumped up, full of excitement. "You bet I can. You just bet I can!"

Ben nodded to the corral next to the barn. "What'll you take for that scroungy-looking bay?" he asked.

Dr. Turnbow gave a slight smile. "Why, that horse ain't for sale. In fact, it belongs to a man who owes me some money."

"I didn't ask you that. I asked you how much. What's the man owe on the horse?"

"Seventeen dollars. At least, that's what I recollect. I'll have to check my records to be sure."

Ben started digging in his pocket, but before he pulled out any money, Dr. Turnbow held up his hand. "Now, hold on a minute. I ain't sellin' that horse for seventeen dollars. Why, that horse is worth forty. Maybe even fifty."

Ben said, "I'll tell you what. I'll pay you what the man owes you and take the horse. When I catch the sumbitch that kilt Roy, we'll bring it back. Then you'll have the horse and some money, too. Can't lose on a deal like that."

Dr. Turnbow's eyes circled about. He licked his lips nervously. "Why, that could be construed as horse stealin'. There's some parts that still consider it a hangin' offense."

"You got any other horses for sale, then?" Ben's voice was laced with impatience.

"Hold on a minute. Just hold on," Turnbow said. "I didn't say we couldn't work out some sort of deal here." He thought a moment, then said, "All right. I'd say that bay is worth, like I said, forty, maybe fifty dollars. All depends on who's wantin' to buy. I'll split the difference. Forty-five and the horse is yours." He smiled broadly. Sweat was popping out on his forehead.

"I thought you said that horse wasn't yours to sell," Ben commented. "I'll give you thirty."

"Thirty? You must be loco. Make it forty."

Ben opened Dr. Turnbow's hand and slapped forty dollars onto his palm. "I'll take a bill of sale with that, if you don't mind." He looked around. "Toby Ray, I reckon Alma needs that saddle more'n you. Can you ride bareback?"

Dr. Turnbow pulled on Ben's sleeve and leaned close to him. He turned his back to the others. "Gimme another ten, I'll throw in the fella's saddle."

"Why, you're a weasel sumbitch, aren't you?"

Keith stepped in between the two. "Get that damned saddle," he said. He handed ten dollars to Turnbow.

"Don't forget that bill of sale," Ben added.

32

ALMA HADN'T DONE A LOT OF RIDING. CERTAINLY NOT as much as the cousins had. She had ridden enough to know, though, that the bay under her had the worst gait imaginable. They hadn't been gone more than three hours, and already her back hurt, her head ached, her stomach was upset and her bottom was nearly blistered. She hoped above all else that they wouldn't get into some kind of situation where she was forced to put the bay into a run. He would surely bounce her from the saddle. She gripped the reins tightly. She knew now why Dr. Wally Turnbow had had the horse in his possession. Clearly, whoever owed him the seventeen dollars had some kind of revenge in mind.

Not that she wasn't grateful to be in the company of the cousins again, even under such adverse conditions. And, as they followed their own trail back to where Roy had been killed, she had to admit that the rough ride of the bay made it easy to keep her mind off of George Tubbs.

They rode silently. Even Toby Ray was unusually quiet. At first, she thought he seemed a bit subdued, until she looked over at him and saw him riding tall in the chocolate mare's saddle. His chin was pointed upward like a statue. It occurred to her that Toby Ray was surely enjoying himself, riding alone on Roy's horse.

In the afternoon, lightning started flashing to the north.

Occasionally, a faint sound of thunder came from that
direction. Alma noticed that everyone's spirits picked up
a little. It wasn't anything noticeable to an outsider, but
it was there, just the same, to her. There had been no
rain for so long, all of Oklahoma Territory seemed like
a desert. Still, as the lightning flickered in the north, the
sun still shone brightly above them. Was this some sort
of mirage, she wondered? She had read about such things
before, but never thought them possible. Until now.

Soon the lightning diminished, and it seemed to Alma
that everyone's mood turned somber as the promise of
rain slipped away. Only Toby Ray was unaffected. His
demeanor hadn't changed. He was still riding as tall as
he could stretch himself in the saddle.

Shortly after the false storm disappeared, they came
upon a wagon with a man, woman and two nearly grown
children setting up for supper. Although Ben was still
tight-jawed and dead set on catching up with the mur-
derer, he nonetheless agreed with Keith in accepting the
invitation for supper. They gratefully sat down with the
wagon people.

They were a family from Alabama, the man told them,
heading for the Cherokee Outlet to make the big land
run, which was coming up in the next month or two.
Speculation had it that the President was about to set
the date.

As they ate, the man, whose name was Abe Pennywell,
told them about how he'd uprooted his family and they
had left Alabama, not knowing exactly when this run
was going to take place, or if it was indeed going to
take place at all. But things had worked out splendidly,
Pennywell exclaimed, and he and his family were going
to get a new start in life.

Alma paid little attention to Abe Pennywell's talk
about this land run business. She was eager for the
fellowship with Pennywell's wife, Ann, and, especially,
their daughter, Margaret. Like Alma, Margaret was sixteen. Right away, the two girls were friends. Meanwhile,
Toby Ray had sided up next to the boy, Alvin, who was
twelve.

"Lands, I hate this place," Margaret said when she and Alma had excused themselves and walked off away from the others.

"You mean Oklahoma?"

"Yes, and every other place between here and Alabama, for that matter," Margaret said. "You got a beau?"

Alma's face flushed red. "If you mean a special fella, no, I don't."

Margaret's eyes slid toward Alma. She looked at her through her lashes and smiled. "Well, I got one, back home in Alabama. Nathan Reese. He's as handsome as a knight in shining armor. I do believe he'd die for me."

Alma didn't know what to say, so she just nodded.

Margaret looked back toward the camp and laughed suddenly. "I gotta be honest with you," she said. "At first I thought one of those men you rode in with was your beau. They've got to be the ugliest two men I've ever seen!" She made a face and giggled.

Alma smiled softly, although she felt a tinge of protective anger. The cousins had been a godsend, it was true; still, she couldn't find fault with what Margaret said. The cousins' ugliness stood out so much, one couldn't help but notice.

"I tell you right now, as soon as my Daddy stakes his claim and gets busy with things, I'm gonna run back to Alabama. Back to Nathan," Margaret declared.

"What is this run you keep talkin' about?" Alma asked.

Margaret waved her hand in the air. "Oh, they're gonna run for free land. Kinda like a race, I guess. The President has opened up part of the Oklahoma Territory for settlement." She looked around her. "Why would anybody want to run for this land?" she asked. "Back home, it's so pretty! Right now, everything is so green. We were happy there, all of us except Daddy." Her eyes flashed. "Said he was tired of sharecroppin'. Wanted a place of his own. So here we are. Can you believe such a thing?" She sighed.

Alma touched her arm. "This land you're talkin' about. Where's it at?"

Margaret shrugged. "I don't know. Daddy says we'll be there shortly. Personally, I can't wait to get it over with."

Alma's mind started racing. Free land! Could this be the answer to some kind of prayer? She briefly closed her eyes and apologized for all the doubt she had laid on God. "Can anyone make this run?" she blurted out.

"Who knows?" Margaret said, staring at Alma like she was touched. "Surely you're not interested! I mean"— she paused—"you're not actually *from* here, are you? Didn't you say you were from Arkansas?"

"I was just curious," Alma said quickly, letting the subject drop.

Margaret nodded. She leaned close to Alma and lowered her voice. "Have you ever done it?"

"Done what?" Alma asked absently, her mind still on the free land.

"You know, done it with a boy?"

"Done what?" Alma frowned.

Margaret gave her a teasing look. "Don't you give me that innocent look, girl! Why, people in Arkansas surely are't *that* far behind Alabama! Have you ever been to bed with a boy?" she said, more bluntly.

Once again, Alma could feel her face flushing. Some of her girlfriends back home had often talked about such things, but it had all been more like wonderment. Nobody had ever asked her such a thing. Alma had always figured that it was something you found out about when you were married.

She looked into Margaret's face. She could tell that Margaret wasn't one to let a question go unanswered. Alma twisted her hands nervously. She wanted to be angry with Margaret, but she also needed a friend to talk to. It had been so long since she'd been around anyone else her own age. Added to that fact, Alma found that there was something very likable about Margaret, in spite of her bold talk. "No, I haven't," she said honestly.

Margaret's mouth opened. "You mean to tell me, you've been out here travelin' with those men, even

if they are ugly ducklings, and you haven't been with
a boy yet?" Laughing, she grabbed Alma's arm and
started running, pulling her along. They ran hard, until
they were both nearly breathless. Finally, they stopped
and sat down in the tall prairie grass, silent until they
had caught their wind.

Margaret pulled up a piece of grass and stuck it between
her teeth. "Me and Nathan been doin' it for two years,"
she said.

"Two years?" Alma said. An involuntary snicker followed.

"That's right. We're in love, and I'm not one bit
ashamed, if that's what you're thinkin'."

Alma quickly hid her smile. "I didn't think you were,"
she said, "or that you should be."

"It feels real good," Margaret said matter-of-factly.

"What does?"

"Doin' it, for cryin' out loud! Girl, you truly *are* from
the sticks!" Margaret cried. "Didn't your mama never
tell you 'bout such things?"

Alma bit her lip and thought hard. She wasn't from
the sticks, as Margaret put it, at all. On the contrary, her
mother had told her plenty about the ways of men, including how to avoid such things. *Keep yourself pure*, she had
said. *Watch out for men and be aware of their ways*. Alma
could still hear her mother's soft voice. *A woman loves
with her heart, Alma, while a man loves with his eyes. Be
careful in who you select for a husband. You'll have him
to deal with for the rest of your life*. Lydia had explained
that most men, given a chance, frolick around on
their women. Some even beat them at times.

Lydia's talks had confused Alma about men. How
was a girl supposed to know who to choose? Why would
a man want to frolick around when he had a wife?
She thought of her father. She couldn't ever remember
him beating her mother, but he had drunk too much. She
wondered if he had ever frolicked around when he
was off on one of his drunks. If so, had her mother
known? Surely, *something* had caused Lydia to be so
leery about men.

Margaret's voice broke into her pondering. "What are you thinkin' about? You look a million miles away," she said.

"Nothin', really," Alma said quickly. She decided it was a good idea to change the subject. "Are you and Nathan gonna get married?"

"As soon as I get back to him, or he comes and gets me," Margaret said. There was a flicker of doubt in her voice.

They sat there until dark, talking. They would have stayed even longer, if Toby Ray and Alvin hadn't come looking for them. That night, after the others had gone to sleep, Margaret shook Alma awake, just as she was falling asleep, and they talked until the wee hours of the morning.

Alma was sad to part company with the Pennywells the next day. She would miss Margaret's easy laughter and constant chatter. Such companionship was something that Alma sorely needed in her life. Now, she realized, she would once again be without it.

Not long after they left the Pennywells, they found their original campsite, where Roy had died. There was an eeriness about the place that haunted Alma. The stillness was disturbing. Without fanfare, the cousins immediately went to the task of searching the ground for any clues. They hadn't paid much attention the day they'd found Roy dead, assuming he had died of a heart attack. Now, they were serious and thorough as an eagle hunting for prey.

They hadn't been there long when Keith hollered out.

"Over here! In this sand! These footprints don't belong to any of us." He pointed to the ground. "They're too big for Alma and Toby Ray and too small for us."

Alma's heart raced. On one hand, she felt glad that they had found some kind of evidence. On the other hand, though, it scared her to death to think that someone had sneaked right up on them and broken Roy's neck without so much as a sound. Goosebumps covered her entire body. She tried to make a mental picture of how it could have happened. How could anyone do it? Pop a man's neck the way one would wring a chicken's? She remembered how her mother had grabbed up a chicken for supper and quickly wrung its neck with one motion. But the chicken had flopped about wildly. Roy had lain there peacefully in his bedroll, like he was just asleep. How could this be?

She remembered those dancing eyes in the bush, and her body started to tremble. She wrapped her arms tightly around herself, trying to hide the shaking from the others. Ben and Keith certainly didn't need any of her silly female foolishness, she thought. She musn't be a burden. Guilt swept over her as she thought of the money they had paid for the horse and saddle and how they had virtually taken her and Toby Ray under their wings when they so desperately needed help. Now she must appear strong and not cause them any additional worry.

Once the cousins had decided they had found the killer's footprints, they began the rough task of picking up some kind of trail. They moved at a snail's pace, with Ben out front and Keith off to the side. Sometimes they would lose the trail and have to backtrack. Although Alma knew nothing about such things, she couldn't help wondering if there was a trail at all. As hard as she tried, she never honestly picked out anything more than a few horse prints in the dry, hard ground.

The slow pace made the bay's ride a little less uncomfortable and gave Alma lots of time to think. She tried hard to push her fears out of her mind. She thought about Margaret Pennywell and her stories about Nathan. She thought about the land run business that they had been talking about. She thought about anything she could. But try as she might, the fear was still there.

All day, they searched and followed the sketchy trail. By evening, they didn't seem to be more than five or six miles from the original camp. As they settled in their bedrolls that night, Ben assured Alma not to worry, that either he or Keith would be awake all night long. Keith nodded in agreement. It pained Alma that they had noticed how worried she was. She tried hard to reassure them that everything was fine.

Mercifully, sleep came quickly that night. Alma dreamed about a better life and a better time. About free land and horses with smooth gaits. She slept hard.

33

ALMA WAS SURPRISED THAT SHE HAD SLEPT SO SOUND-
ly, given the situation. She awoke feeling rested and
a lot stronger. Yesterday's fears seemed like a lifetime
ago.

There wasn't much fanfare as they hurried through
breakfast, then picked up the hunt. Earlier, Alma had
admired the jovial demeanor of the cousins. She didn't
reckon she'd ever run across a family that grinned as
quickly and easily before. The event of Roy's death had
changed that demeanor, however. Particularly in Ben.
In the last twenty-four hours, he hadn't mumbled more
than a word or two about anything except his intended
vengeance against Roy's killer. Keith, on the other hand,
was much more subdued than before, but the kindness
had reappeared in his eyes. Alma could tell he would be
back to his old self in no time at all.

One thing that hadn't changed, and probably wouldn't,
was Alma's sore backside. She had saddle sores on top
of saddle sores. Blisters had formed from riding the
very first day. She cursed the bay under her breath
as she rode atop its bony spine. Each awkward bump
stung worse than the one before. Within an hour, her
jaw muscles ached from gritting her teeth so as not to
show her discomfort. She was bound and determined
to not be a burden—whether mentally or physically—
to the cousins. She considered dismounting and walking

for a while. They were moving at a snail's pace, what with Ben's constantly stepping down to study the ground for tracks. Surely, nobody would think anything if she just slid down to the ground and walked quietly. But, as much as her body pained her, Alma didn't have the courage to do it. In light of their generosity in buying her the horse and saddle, she couldn't risk offending the cousins' feelings.

Alma grew annoyed as she looked over at Toby Ray, who had that same pleased look about him, his back arched straight. He was so proud of himself. Even as spirited as Roy's horse was, Toby Ray might not be feeling so smart, she thought, if he had to ride the lop-gaited bay. All of a sudden, she wished she could pull a switch on him and just see how well he did.

Alma had never wished anything bad on Toby Ray before. A small pang of guilt crept into her thoughts, but only for a moment. Her backside was burning like fire. Besides that, in all likelihood, Toby Ray's body was so lithe, he would probably handle the bay's gait just fine—better than she could.

Well, she decided, it was time they found out. Alma made up her mind that this would be her last day on the crooked bay. She would talk Toby Ray into switching horses. The minute they made camp.

The sun was high in the sky when they spotted two women, sitting on a blanket on the ground in cotton dresses, each with a bonnet. Alma blew a droplet of sweat from the end of her nose. The day was a hot one, and there the women sat, right beneath the scorching sun in such uncomfortable clothes, without even bothering to take a spot under a tree. Alma felt irritated. They looked like some of the German people she remembered back in Fort Smith. At least, she *thought* they'd been German. Her mother had told her they were some sort of religious group. They had always dressed in long dresses and bonnets that were just alike. Alma had watched the strange and mysterious people on their visits to town to shop in their little groups. Alma had always felt an urge to talk to them, to find out more about them. She had pestered her mother with endless questions, but was unsatisfied with her mother's comments, like "that's just their way." Still, it piqued her interest how people could all dress alike and never look into another person's eyes. Alma found this all to be very curious.

A religious group was what these two women belonged to, Alma decided. That being the case, they would offer her no female camaraderie, whatsoever.

As the riders drew closer, the two women remained sitting with their backs to them, facing the remnants of a small campfire. They paid no attention whatsoever. Ben, who was in the lead, pulled his sorrel up close, not more than five yards behind the pair.

"Excuse me," he said, clearing his throat. "Are you ladies lost?"

The backs of the women remained motionless. Their faces were hidden by the bonnets. A small chill ran through Alma. It started on her arms and swept up into her scalp. She was puzzled as to why, but there was something eerie about these women and their odd behavior, religious sect or no.

Ben said in a loud voice, "You ladies deaf, or what? We just want to ask you a couple of questions. Ain't nothin' to be afraid of." Still no answer. "Somethin' happen to your menfolks?"

Keith climbed down from his horse. "You got any extra coffee there? We'd be glad to pay you for it."

One of the women moved slightly. She was fiddling with something on her lap. Alma couldn't see what it was. The other woman sat still, her head bobbing ever so slightly.

Bobbing her head. Something caught in the back of Alma's mind. Again, cold chills swept over her. This time they engulfed her entire body. She shuddered.

Ben and Keith hesitated, unsure of what to do next. Suddenly, the woman on the left stood erect and wheeled around to face them. In her arms was a sawed-off shotgun.

Alma screamed when she saw the cold, piercing eyes that stared out from under the bonnet. Eyes that had

gone crazy. A long, flowing white beard framed the
face. George Tubbs was wearing the same sinister grin
that Alma had seen so many times before when his anger
flashed beyond reason.

George Tubbs gave a short, barking laugh. He stared
first at Keith, then Ben. "Now I've got you, you heathen
sons of bitches! You'll not be harmin' these children,
ever again!" His wild eyes widened. He thumb-cocked
the shotgun.

"Why, you crazy bastard! It was *you* who kilt Roy,"
Ben said as he pulled leather.

The shotgun in George Tubbs' hands exploded, catching Ben squarely in the chest. The impact of the blast
blew him backwards. He landed at the feet of Alma's
bay. The startled horse let out a whinny and spun into
a wild bucking frenzy.

Alma screamed. Her hands grabbed for the saddle
horn. Her feet had slipped from the stirrups, so she tried
to tighten her legs around the horse's back and hang on.
Terror filled her like nothing before as the horse bolted
and ran, bucking and kicking like something out of hell.
She knew she was most assuredly going to end up on
the ground, trampled to death.

George Tubbs paid no attention to Alma and the wild
bay. Calmly, he turned and trained the shotgun on Keith.
Keith stood frozen beside his horse, gripping its reins
and staring intently at the crazy man.

Elken, his head now bobbing freely up and down, got
up and stood next to his brother. Saliva ran from his
mouth and down off his chin. The prairie wind whipped
his skirt ludicrously between his huge legs. Underneath,
he wore heavy man's boots.

"It-it-it's Toby Ray!" Elken cried, running toward the
boy. "W-w-w-we can go f-f-fishin'!" He reached Toby
Ray and rubbed his hand over Toby Ray's leg, lovingly
and admiringly, like he would rub a newborn calf.

"You get back over here, Elken, before I whack you
one," George Tubbs warned, never taking his eyes from
Keith. When Elken didn't move fast enough, he repeated, "I said get over here, right now. I still got a heathen

son of a bitch here to deal with." He grimaced, and his
white beard parted to reveal his yellow teeth.

Alma had managed to stay on the bay's back. Finally,
she got the horse slowed down as she held the reins in
her left hand and had a fistful of the bay's mane in her
right. The horse slowly stopped its bucking and turned a
few circles, still prancing nervously. Alma's mind raced
aimlessly. She had an urge to kick the horse's flanks and
flee. But, although her instincts were to run from this
nightmare, she knew there was no way she could leave
Toby Ray. Suddenly, she started bawling uncontrollably.
A moan came from way down deep inside. She couldn't
help it. This was more than she could deal with and she
knew it.

There was no sanity left in her life. None at all. She
wished she could die. In fact, if there was any way at all
she could arrange it and still leave Toby Ray protected,
she would surely do it.

But there wasn't any way. She was stuck in an impossible, hopeless situation, and Toby Ray was stuck right
with her.

All Alma could do was continue to cry. There was
nothing left to think about, no more decisions to be
made. Life's picture had become a total blur with only
her instinctive feelings about Toby Ray left intact. Keith
was nothing more than a statue, standing there, his life
in a perilous state. Alma looked at her life through her
tear-blurred eyes and bawled.

George Tubbs had to shout a few more times to convince Elken to move away from Toby Ray. Reluctantly,
Elken looked longingly at Toby Ray, then shuffled back
to stand behind his brother.

George Tubbs stared like a wild man at Keith. He
was breathing in low, wheezy gasps. It almost sounded
like the first winds of a storm when they work their way
through the cracks of the windows.

It was almost surreal. Everyone was stock-still. Alma's
crying had quieted down to a low moan. She was staring
blankly at George Tubbs, the tears continuing to roll down
her cheeks. Even the horses took on a sense of what was

happening. The bay settled down. It now stood with its head lowered, sniffing the ground as if it couldn't decide whether to eat the prairie grass or start kicking again. Keith waited beside his horse. Only his eyes showed any movement as he looked the situation over.

Finally, George Tubbs broke the silence. His cold eyes narrowed at Keith.

"Killin' is almost too good for you. I could squeeze this trigger and end your sinful ways, quick as the bat of an eye. I want you to think about it. Think about stealin' these children." He nodded his head. "Think about *all* your sins, before I send you to hell."

Keith's eyes bored into George Tubbs'. Keith stood rigid, never flinching a muscle. If there was an ounce of fear in him, it wasn't visible to the human eye. Instead of a man who was surely expecting to die any second, he looked more like a man who was sizing up his adversary just before a fistfight. Fearsome situations affect all men differently. For Keith, it was measured hatred.

Behind George Tubbs, Elken rubbed his thumb in his palm. He was salivating heavily. His head bobbed up and down, and his eyes were rolling backward in their sockets.

It was Toby Ray who surprised everyone when he shouted, "Why don't you just leave us alone! Can't you see no one wants to be with you?"

George Tubbs was taken aback. His eyes blinked as he stared disbelievingly at Toby Ray's angry face. "What? What are you sayin', boy? Why, we've come to take you back home with us!"

"Back home!" Toby Ray said. "You must be crazy! We don't want to go with you! Please, just leave us alone!"

George Tubbs looked quickly back and forth between Keith and Toby Ray. His face was more bewildered than before. He shook his head and frowned at Toby Ray. "Now—now, you hush up, you hear? You don't know what you're a-sayin'. Git on over here by me and Elken."

"I'll not do it!" Toby Ray yelled back. More anger laced his words. "Like I told you, we don't want to go with you! You're crazy men, dressed like women!"

George Tubbs' face grew red. The whites of his eyes glistened as they turned mean and serious. "You better hush that mouth, boy, and git over here. Right now."

"I ain't gonna do it. You can't make me!" Toby Ray sat stiffly on Roy's horse, his jaw jutting out stubbornly. He stared right at George Tubbs without flinching.

George Tubbs' knuckles grew white as he gripped the shotgun. The end of the barrel began to quiver as his body shook with anger. "Boy, I'll kill this heathen son a bitch right now, if you don't climb down off that horse and git your little ass over here with Elken."

When Toby Ray didn't move immediately, George Tubbs gritted his teeth and stuck the shotgun out closer to Keith's face. "By damn! I swear I'll blow his head right off. Now, move over here. Ya hear me, boy?"

Keith took in a sudden breath at the threat, but his expression didn't change a bit. He still stood there, frozen. His fears, if he had any, were locked away inside himself, and it was impossible to tell what he might be thinking.

Alma's crying and moaning had fixed a sound into the air that had become as much a part of the world as the blowing prairie wind. It was the sound of her crying that first alerted the two men who came riding in on the group.

"What's goin' on here?" the first one said. He was a big Negro man, sitting majestically atop a beautiful white horse. Beside him rode a thin white cowboy whose eyes flashed with excitement.

At first, George Tubbs looked confused. He pulled his angry eyes slowly from Toby Ray and stared a moment. Then the hardness reappeared. "Nigger," he said, "this ain't none o' your business. I'm here to git my family back. Now git."

Toby Ray cried out. "No! We ain't his family! This man's crazy! He done killed Ben and Roy, and now he wants to kill Keith, too!" He stared at the Negro. "Please help us, mister! Help me and my sister and Keith. Please!"

Alma was still crying helplessly atop the bay. She looked curiously through her red eyes at the two riders. They didn't really register in her thinking. Where had they come from, she wondered vaguely? She couldn't see them as any kind of saviors for their situation, anyway. Fact was, her life was doomed. She had suspected it might be, all along, but now she was sure.

"He ain't gonna kill all of us." Keith finally broke his silence. "He ain't got but one shell left. Ya hear that, George Tubbs? Your killin' times are just about over."

George Tubbs nearly exploded in anger as he moved closer, to where the shotgun shook just inches from Keith's nose. "Why, you heathen son of a bitch! You'll not be alive to see what happens!" But angry as he was, his words were a little less sure than before.

Keith's face was grim, but he was calm. "Go ahead," he said in a confident voice. "Pull that trigger. I'm ready, but like I said, your killin' times are over."

"Put the shotgun down, mister," the Negro man said.

George Tubbs growled out of the side of his mouth. "I told you to shut up and mind your manners, nigger! This is white man's business. 'Sides that, you got no idea what's goin' on. I'm here to help these kids."

"Don't listen to him!" Toby Ray said. "This man's crazy, I tell ya! So's his brother. He tried to hurt my sister before, and he'll try to do it again!"

"I don't know who's tellin' the truth," the big Negro admitted. He looked doubtfully at George and Elken Tubbs and the clothes they wore. "Why don't you just put that shotgun down, and we'll work this out."

"No! I'll work it out! I'll just kill *you*!" George Tubbs swung the shotgun toward the big Negro, but the barrel hadn't moved more than a foot when the Negro's forty-four exploded, catching George Tubbs in the right temple.

Elken made a sudden move, but not a split second passed before Keith had pulled leather and buried a round into his chest. Both men died instantly.

The gunfire set Alma's bay to kicking again. As the horse ran off, Alma slid sideways, barely catching the saddle horn in her fingertips. The bay hadn't gone far, when the white cowboy rode up alongside and grabbed her around the waist. He pulled her from the bay's back, then gently eased her to the ground.

Alma's eyes met the cowboy's. She had no idea who he was, but she didn't care. She didn't know that the Tubbs brothers lay dead on the ground, just a few yards away. She couldn't remember anything that had happened. She only knew that her head was swirling. Suddenly, everything went black, and she fainted.

34

WHEN ALMA CAME TO, SHE GAZED UP INTO A WORLD
that was blue. It was a clear, brilliant sky with not a cloud
in it. A white blur moved into her field of vision. It took
more than a minute for her eyes to focus on the face that
hovered above her, framed by the Oklahoma sky.

Who was the man that was staring down at her? She
had never seen him before. She had an urge to push him
away, but instead she let her body relax. Alma had done
about all the fighting in life she cared to do. If this man
was there to do her any harm, or even kill her, then
so be it.

Then, from the depths of her mind she thought of
Toby Ray. Her eyes popped open wide. "My brother!
Where's Toby Ray?" she asked.

"Whoa there, just relax," the face said. "Your brother
is just fine. He's over there with Keith and Larkes."

"Keith and who?" Alma tried to raise herself up,
but the sudden movement made her light-headed. She
fell back, resigned. Whoever this was, it really didn't
matter. It was useless for her to do anything more than
just lie there.

Strangely, though, the man's touch was soft and gentle
as he rubbed a damp cloth over her cheeks and laid it
across her forehead.

Alma slowly felt her composure coming back as her
mind cleared. She felt silly over her behavior. She man-

aged to sit up. The cowboy smiled at her. He surely had
a handsome face, she thought. In fact, this might just be
the most handsome man she had ever looked at.

Was she dreaming? she thought suddenly. Was he
from Heaven? Had she crossed that river her mother
had told her about so many times? But Heaven surely
didn't smell like sweat and grime, and the fact was, the
handsome face she stared at had a terrible smell to it.
It was right repugnant. She turned her head away and
pushed herself to her knees.

The cowboy with the handsome face helped Alma to
her feet. She looked around for her brother.

"Toby Ray! Come here!" she called.

When Toby Ray came to her, she latched onto him
like a mother with a newborn child. Toby Ray's body
stiffened and he tried to pull away, but Alma would have
none of it. Most times, she protected his silly boyish
pride, but right now she didn't care how he felt or how
embarrassed he might be. Toby Ray was the only person
on the face of this earth that belonged to her, and having
him close made her feel less alone.

Toby Ray sounded excited as he tried to free himself from her clutches. "They killed 'em both, Alma!
You shoulda seen it! It was somethin'. And Larkes! I
mean, his hand flashed like lightnin'!" He worked to
pry Alma's hands from his arm, but kept on talking.
"And oh, Alma, you shoulda seen Keith! He's fast,
Alma. Fast on the draw! I knew he was good, but he
was even faster'n I thought he would be!"

Alma looked at Toby Ray, then at the handsome
cowboy. "The Tubbses are dead?" she asked, puzzled.
"What happened?"

"Like I told you, Alma! They're dead! Larkes and
Keith done killed 'em both!" Toby Ray exclaimed. He
looked proud.

Pieces of what Toby Ray was saying began to register
in Alma's confused mind. The Tubbses had been shot
dead. Where had she been? She remembered seeing a
colored man. He had fired a pistol. Think, she told
herself.

Then, it started to come back, like some terrible nightmare. That's how it felt to her, like a dream, when events seem so distant and unreal. Still, you know they happened.

Toby Ray broke into her thoughts. "It was somethin', Alma," he was saying over again. "Larkes and Arky here rode up just in the nick of time."

"Who's Larkes and Arky?" Alma asked. She was angry with herself for not being able to remember.

Toby Ray pointed a finger at the handsome cowboy. "This here's Arky," he said, grinning.

"Yes, ma'am, I'm Arky Smith." Arky pulled off his hat and nodded at her. "And you're Alma White. Your brother told me your name. I'm real sorry for everythin' that's happened," he offered politely.

Just then, Keith walked up with a big Negro. Alma remembered him as the man with the pistol.

"Alma," Keith began, "Larkes and Arky are travelin' with a family that's headin' for the Cherokee Outlet. They've offered to take you and Toby Ray with 'em. They'll see you get on that train in Guthrie." He smiled kindly down at her.

Alma's eyes blinked fast. Besides the cousins, every man she'd come in contact with had been evil mean. She knew Keith, trusted him, and now she was expected to let him go. Even if these two strange men had come along to save the day, that was still no guarantee they wouldn't turn out to be any different from all the rest. Her heart sank. *Please, God*, she thought, *don't make me have to beg. Don't let this happen to us again.* She wanted to grab Keith and hold on for dear life, but instead she looked down at her feet and said, "B-but, we were travelin' with you."

"It'll be all right." Larkes spoke up. "Your brother and Keith here have told us about your situation. You'll be fine with us. Arky 'n I are travelin' with a man and his wife, and how many young'n's they got, Arky? Six or seven. There's plenty o' kids for the boy to play with. Plus, there's Reasa and little Noah. They're with me. So, you don't worry yourself none, you hear?"

Toby Ray had been watching Larkes with a peculiar look. Suddenly a light dawned on his face. "I know you," he said. "You bought that horse from Doc Thurman in Fort Smith. I saw you."

Larkes' eyes turned to slits. He crooked his head and studied what the boy had said. "That's a fact," he said slowly. "I did buy 'im from that ol' cuss." He pointed his finger at Toby Ray. "You aren't . . . you couldn't be! But you are! You're the boy with the sick mama. Had a dog with ya."

Toby Ray's smile faded some. "Mama died. Tick's dead, too."

A look of sympathy crossed Larkes' face. "I'm real sorry to hear that, son. I really am."

Alma studied the man's face. She had to lean her head way back to look up at him. It struck her how tall he was. She didn't recall ever seeing a man that tall before. His words sounded sincere, and he looked as if he meant every word. There was a kindness in his eyes, too. Even though the eyes were set in the face of a hard-looking man.

Keith touched her shoulder. "Alma, I got to take my cousins back home for a proper burial. They'll take good care of ya. You know, if I thought for one moment that they wouldn't, I'd never let you and Toby Ray outta my sight. We've worked things out, and Larkes here assures me that once they get their group to the Outlet, there's trains that run through there, too."

Alma knew there was nothing else she could say. She had already caused Keith too much grief, and she couldn't ask any more of him. Sadly, she closed her eyes and nodded, trying not to let herself cry. Keith gave her a light hug, and said that, maybe someday, he'd see her again.

"You take care, you hear?" was the last thing he said before he rode away, with Ben's body draped over the bay horse. He left Ben's sorrel for Alma to ride.

And minutes later, there she was, in another unlikely situation. Larkes, the colored man, rode up in front. Alma could tell he was a man who preferred his own

company to that of others. Following Larkes were Toby
Ray and Arky, who rode side by side, talking nonstop.
One would no more stop to catch a breath when the
other would break in and continue the conversation.
Alma knew she should have grown used to having new
scenarios appearing so often in her life, but she hadn't.
She felt like a rubber ball that'd been bounced from one
hand to another, back and forth. Her only solace in this
situation was the fact that Toby Ray had made a quick
friendship with Arky. Alma felt a queer attraction for
the young man, herself.

She noticed that he kept turning around and stealing
quick glances back at her. It was unnerving, at first. Each
time his eyes fell upon her, Alma's breath caught in her
throat. It puzzled her. She'd been stared at before, but
no man had ever had such an effect on her. As the day
wore on, she came to expect his stolen glances. She even
started looking forward to feeling his eyes on her.

That evening, they rode on without stopping to make
camp. Arky explained that the packhorse they'd brought
along was loaded with a barrelful of water. They had to
try to reach their group tonight.

"Our folks need this water pretty bad. But don't worry," he assured Alma. "Won't be more'n a couple hours
ride. Won't get dark 'til after nine o'clock, anyways."

Alma was surprised at his concern over her feelings.
She started to tell him that it was all right, not to worry
over her. She was doing fine, ever since Keith had
offered her Ben's horse. Her bottom still ached and
burned from the ride on the terrible bay, but Ben's
sorrel was a luxury indeed, for its gait was pleasingly
smooth.

True to Arky's word, it wasn't long before they rode
up to a camp. There were two wagons pulled up in a
V-shape, and a large campfire with a bunch of children
seated around. A tall woman rose from amidst them and
walked toward the riders. She stiffened when she saw
Alma and Toby Ray. Her mouth turned down at the
corners.

"Vhat ist dis?" Helena Frey glared. She put her hands

on her hips and shook her head. "Ve don't need no more mouths to feed. Der's only so much food to go 'round."

Larkes stepped down from the big gelding. Ignoring Helena's scathing look, he walked past her to where Reasa stood. "This here's Alma and her brother, Toby Ray," he said. "They're on their way to Kansas. Got themselves into a bit of a bind, so we thought they could ride with us a spell. We can get them on their way right proper."

Helena followed close behind Larkes, glancing back at the two newcomers and frowning. "Vat's dat you say?" she said. Her voice rose. "Ve can't just bring anyvon along!"

Larkes stared at her. "You want your water, or you want to argue?" he said coldly. He turned to Reinhart. "Now listen here, Mister Frey," he said. "My group don't have to ride along with you folks, at all. Fact is, for my money, it's too slow travelin'." Larkes' eyes turned hard as he looked at Reasa. "You want to travel with me, woman? If'n you do, you best come along, 'cause Alma and Toby Ray here are right welcome, far as I'm concerned, and I totally intend to see 'em all the way to the train station."

Reinhart Frey stepped forward. He rubbed the white gelding's nose and shrugged sheepishly. "Ach, of course you are velcome to bring along Alma and Toby Ray." He motioned toward Helena. "She don't mean nothin'. Dat's just her vay."

Still carrying his ill mood, Larkes muttered, "Let her speak for herself." His eyes bore into Helena's.

Her cheeks were red by nature, but suddenly Helena's whole face flushed. She reached up with her arm and wiped the sweat from her forehead. She stared for a moment at Larkes, then Arky, then Alma and Toby Ray. Finally, she threw an accusing look at her husband, then raised her head proudly. "Ach, yes. Dey are velcome, too." With that, she pressed her lips tightly together and stomped off to the wagon.

Larkes couldn't believe this woman. Silently, he shook

his head and looked hopelessly out at the horizon.

Reinhart Frey gave everyone a weak smile. "It vill be fine. Come," he said to Alma, "you look so tired. Und hungry, too, I'll bet. Come get something to eat. And you come, too, Toby Ray." He hurried to help them from their horses and ushered them to the campfire. The other children moved aside and stared until their curiosity got the better of them. Then they slowly moved closer to Alma and Toby Ray.

It was plain that Larkes' anger hadn't yet subsided. He climbed on his horse and quickly disappeared.

After that, the travel was slow, and the heat was nearly suffocating, but none of this mattered to Alma. She found the company of the group to be a pleasant surprise. She especially liked Reasa and hung close to her, helping her care for Noah. She liked the boy, even if she did think he was a bit old to act like such a baby.

Toby Ray lost himself among the Frey children, having a high time. Larkes kept mostly to himself, usually riding away from the group. He would mount up and ride off right after breakfast, and they wouldn't see him until after the midday meal. Then he'd disappear again through the afternoon.

Helena was not friendly in even the slightest way, but she didn't voice any displeasure. In fact, she paid no attention to Alma at all, busying herself with her children and passing out orders to her husband. Alma didn't care. Everyone else made her feel welcome.

Arky seemed to be everywhere at once. He could be playing games with the children one minute, then riding off the next, maybe to bring back a couple of jackrabbits for supper. Or he might be talking to Reinhart and managing to steal his glances at Alma. Alma had never met anyone like him before. His eyes were constantly searching for hers, and she would let her gaze lock into his eyes, while that strange sensation would engulf her each time. She got to where she was constantly looking for him. When he'd ride off, her spirits would sink while he was away, only to rise to a euphoric high upon his return. This was all strange indeed, for they

had barely spoken a word to each other. She noticed that
Arky always seemed to lose his tongue when he'd go to
speak to her. That was unusual for a man who seemed
to be able to carry a conversation on any subject.

The second evening, they were setting up camp, when
Arky rode in with a young doe over his saddle. "Fresh
meat!" He grinned at everyone.

"Ach, a deer!" Reinhart said as he inspected the dead
animal. "Dat is goot!"

Arky's face held a look of pride, until Helena walked
up. She nudged past her husband and grabbed hold of
the deer like it was no more than a jackrabbit, hoisting
it on her shoulder. Without so much as a word to Arky,
she marched off with it.

Toby Ray, who had been watching the goings-on,
moved close to Alma and sat down beside her. "I think
Arky should get to clean the deer," he said under his
breath. "After all, he shot it all by himself." He stared
after Helena Frey for a moment. "I don't think I like
her, Alma."

Alma sighed and said softly, "Hush your mouth. We
don't need any trouble, Toby Ray."

"Well, do you like her?" Toby Ray asked.

"That's beside the point. 'Sides, it don't matter what
we think of her. We just don't need to make any more
trouble for ourselves. So keep that mouth shut, you
hear?"

"Well, it ain't right," Toby Ray said stubbornly. "He
killed the deer. He should get to clean it."

Arky walked toward them just then. "Hello there,
Toby Ray. Mind if I sit down?" he asked with his eyes
set on Alma.

Toby Ray scooted over to offer Arky a spot on the
dead log that he and Alma were sharing. Alma felt her
heart start to beat harder. She felt all nervous inside. She
hoped she wouldn't do or say anything silly.

"How long a shot was it?" Toby Ray asked.

"The deer?" Arky said. His face flushed as he stole
a glance at Alma. "Oh, not a long one, I guess. Maybe
seventy-five yards." He looked back at Alma. As if to

apologize, he added, "One time in Kansas, I got one from over three hundred yards away. Big buck. Ten pointer."

"Really?" Toby Ray said, impressed. "Will you take me huntin' with you sometime?"

"You bet I will. In fact, you can go with me tomorrow, if it's all right with Alma, here."

Alma relaxed and gave Arky a smile. She hadn't felt this happy to be with a person in a long time. Not only did she, herself, feel sweet on Arky, she felt mighty grateful to him for being so kind to Toby Ray. "I 'spect you two would scare off any deer within a mile," she said. "You'd be too busy talkin'." Heat swirled from her body and rose up around her face. She couldn't understand why this fellow's presence had such an effect on her. She'd liked a few boys before, but not so much that any of them excited her like this. Maybe it was the fact that he and Larkes had come to her rescue. Maybe he was just a hero to her. She tried hard to think of some logical reason for her feelings, but if the truth be known, there wasn't any. Alma could no more understand what was happening than the man in the moon.

Something else was apparent to her. If this was, indeed, what she thought it might be, she was positive that Arky had similar feelings for her. Not that other men hadn't looked at her before. Many had, but it had seemed like their eyes were full of evil. They had made her feel uncomfortable, like they were doing some kind of sizing up in their minds. Most of them hadn't said anything, but she had known their intentions. Arky was different. He stared at her a lot, but he seemed as nervous as she was. Besides that, he was more polite about the interest he showed.

"We won't be scarin' the deer away, Alma! What's wrong with you? Why, a deer hunter knows not to talk while he's huntin'," Toby Ray said, looking to Arky for agreement.

"Oh, we'll do fine, I 'spose." Arky grinned. "Tell you what. We got deer meat now. Maybe we'll go rabbit huntin' tomorrow. Of course, with all them kids, that little ol' doe won't be good for more'n a day or two. The Freys are out of salt, too." He rubbed Toby Ray's head. "You just might get you a rabbit or two, if'n we see any."

He got up then to leave. As he walked away, Alma studied his back. She didn't want him to leave. She had to fight the urge to follow him, just so she could be in his company. She couldn't understand her feelings. Once Arky was out of sight, she grabbed Toby Ray's arm. "What do you think of Arky?" she asked.

Toby Ray's eyes flashed with excitement. "Oh, I think he's great. He's really nice, Alma."

Alma wanted so much to believe that, but how could she let herself completely trust any man? Even though Arky had rescued her, and seemed kind, how could she know that he wouldn't turn out like all the rest? After all, except for the cousins, she'd encountered nothing but deceitful men in the last year of her life.

35

ONE MORNING, ARKY TOOK A RIDE OUT EARLY. HE came back in time for breakfast and announced that there was a railroad station just a few miles ahead. As he sat down to eat and lowered his head over his plate, Alma stared at him.

Suddenly, she wasn't hungry any more. Her stomach felt like it carried a load of lead. She had let herself forget all about Kansas during the last few days. Now, remembering gave her a feeling of dread. What was there for them in Kansas? Some relatives they hadn't heard from in years. She couldn't even recall what they looked like. How could she and Toby Ray just suddenly appear on their doorstep? What kind of story could she tell them? Would they send them away? Worse yet, what if they decided to get ahold of Uncle Ted and Aunt Nora? Alma looked slowly around at everyone, seated amiably around the breakfast camp, eating one of Helena Frey's plentiful meals. She felt comfortable here. Why did it have to end? And, when it did, what new problems waited ahead for them?

Alma surprised herself when she moved over to sit next to Arky. "Tell me about this run for free land," she urged him. "Can anyone make the run?"

Arky shrugged his shoulders. "Shucks, Alma. I don't

know," he said honestly. "They got certain rules, but I don't know what they are."

Reasa got up and disappeared inside one of the wagons. She quickly returned with a folded-up newspaper. Sitting down beside Alma, she unfolded it and started to scan the front-page story. "Seems I read in here that you gotta be eighteen years old and married," she said slowly, "but, let me see. . . ." Her lips moved as she read to herself.

Arky sipped his coffee. "Well, if that's the case, what're you'n Larkes gonna do?" He caught himself and added, "I mean, you-all ain't married yet, are ya?"

"That's right," Larkes said from across the campfire. He was standing behind the children, holding his plate while he finished eating. "We ain't. Shoot, I can tell ya right now what's gonna happen. We're gonna get up there and find out it's all been just another white man's folly." Glaring at Reasa, he tossed down his plate, mounted up on the gelding and rode away.

Reasa sat there, watching Larkes until he was plumb out of sight. Her mouth hung open in surprise.

Arky stood up and said matter-of-factly, "Aw, it was all just a crazy dream, anyway."

Reasa's face was still full of surprise. She turned her wide eyes on Arky. "What do you mean?" she cried. "This is no dream! I plan on gettin' me some of that free land, sure as I'm sittin' here!"

Arky didn't appear comfortable with the conversation. He glanced at Alma to see if she was watching him. She was. "I didn't mean nothin'," he said. " 'Cept, I bet that's right. A man has to be married."

"What would you know about it? Did you read it yourself, or were you just listenin' to Larkes?" Reasa asked, her demeanor growing more serious.

Arky tried to smile. "Now, hold on a minute there, Reasa. I think it was *you* who said it. Better look at the paper there and see."

Reasa angrily folded the paper shut and sat on it. "I'll read it later, if you don't mind."

"I'm sorry if I riled you," Arky said.

"You didn't rile me."

"Well, anyway"—Arky sighed—"any time the government's got their hands in somethin', you can expect to find some things that don't meet the eye, that's all." He looked at Alma. "Maybe you-all *can* make the run. I don't know. Is that what you got in mind?"

"I was just askin', that's all," Alma said. She bit slowly into a biscuit. She thought about how she and Toby Ray had struggled ever since their mother had died. She thought about what lay ahead for them in Kansas. Her stomach started to revolt. "No," she said firmly. "I wasn't just askin'. I guess Toby Ray and me *would* like to make that run."

"Maybe you can," Arky said, staring openly at her.

They rode up on the train station that Arky had talked about, not more than an hour and a half after they left camp. At first, Alma thought something must have happened. There were people everywhere, milling around the depot. Far off to the west, Alma could see a smattering of houses. She wondered why there were no people over there. As they grew nearer, she saw all of the familiar signs that she'd become accustomed to seeing out on the trail. Signs proclaiming intentions of staking a claim in the Cherokee Outlet. Some signs were colorful and elaborate in detail, while others were simple ones. There were big families, small families. Some looked rich, while most seemed like plain poor folks. Like her and Toby Ray. There were some who carried a mean look in their eyes. Some seemed on the verge of desperation. There were men and women on horseback. In fact, Alma noticed one entire family, four kids and three adults, all walking aside their one horse, which was loaded with their belongings. She remembered seeing them the day before and wondering about the hardships of such travel, but here they were. They had beaten them to the depot.

There were folks sitting on horseback, in buggies and fringed-top surries. Alma noticed some bicycles amongst the crowd, as well. Some folks had no means of transportation, at all. Alma wondered if they planned to make the race on foot.

She grabbed Toby Ray. "You stay with Arky," she told him. "I'll be back in a minute." She headed toward the crowd.

"Where you goin', Alma?"

"You just mind what I say," she hollered back.

Alma intended to find out more about this run. Reasa had told her that it was a few weeks away, but it was time she found out a few things for herself. She asked questions of anyone who showed even a halfway friendly face, gathering a piece of information here, a piece there. One man from Missouri went to great lengths to help her, explaining how he had lost his own mother when he was fifteen years old. He appreciated her hardship, he said. As she grew more and more familiar with the details and rules of the race, Alma's heart began to sink farther and farther. It was becoming clear that she and Toby Ray would once again end up on the short end of the stick.

A person had to be twenty-one years old or the head of a family. Surely, Alma thought out loud, she would be considered the head of herself and Toby Ray, but the nice man from Missouri said with great sympathy that he doubted very much that they would accept her, a sixteen-year-old, as the head of her brother. But that wasn't all. Another person told her she had to have money to make the run. Even though it was advertised as free land, there was a filing fee to be paid.

By the time Alma returned to the group, she was crestfallen.

The first person she saw was Reasa, who stood holding a brand new copy of the *Hennessey Clipper*. She smiled broadly at Alma.

"It says right here, 'head of a family.' You hear me, girl? I'm head of a family. I reckon little Noah and me constitutes a family, don't you? Yessir, I'm gonna get me some of that free land! That's all there is to it." Reasa laid the paper down a moment. "The Bible talks about the promised land, and this surely is it. The promised land. Ain't it just beautiful?" She turned her head and stared off. "It's out there, honey. North of here." She reached down and kissed Noah on top of the head. "See there, baby? Way out there. That's our free land."

Alma tried to smile, but her face felt stiff. She knew she should be happy for Reasa, but her actions were only artificial. All Alma could think about was more disappointment. For herself and for Toby Ray. She tried to remember what her relatives in Kansas looked like, but even her faint recollections of them had taken on a frightening change. Suddenly, they didn't look at all like her relatives. All she could see were the faces of Uncle Ted, George Tubbs and Vernon Scaggs.

Alma wanted to run off by herself and cry.

There were no trains leaving that day, so the group made camp there by the depot. Alma was grateful for the one-day delay. One more day in safe company, she thought. One more day away from whatever fate waited for them in Kansas.

At supper that night, she chewed absently as she listened to Reasa read from the *Hennessey Clipper*. All the details were there. Reasa said each word in her soft voice, almost in a loving way. Her face took on such a look of pleasure, Alma suddenly realized she *was* happy for Reasa. She could picture Noah, growing up on his own place, playing in his own yard.

She looked at Toby Ray, who sat next to Arky, grinning from ear to ear. Poor Toby Ray, with nothing but a hard life ahead for him. There would be no big yards and tree swings for him.

She wished she could stop herself from having such thoughts, but life was turning that way. And it didn't look like there was anything she could do to stop it.

That night, Alma went to sleep listening to the background of the noises of the myriad of people who had gathered at the train depot. People with high hopes and dreams and a better life to look forward to.

She cupped her hands over her ears. Suddenly, all her

thoughts about free land had now turned into thoughts of despair. A resentful feeling ripped through her and when she finally drifted off to sleep, her dreams were bitter ones.

36

LARKES AND ARKY WERE ON THEIR WAY TO GETTING drunk. They had bought a bottle of whiskey from the man at the depot, then found a quiet spot about a mile away from where they'd camped, and started up a small fire to sit around.

Larkes had never drunk that much. He was more of a period drinker. There'd been periods in his life when he would get drunk every night for a week. Other times, he could go for months without so much as a taste. Tonight, though, he was determined to get good and drunk. For added courage? He didn't know. More than likely, it was to keep from having to think about what he was getting ready to do—something that was so unlike his nature, even he couldn't comprehend it, himself.

They had downed nearly half a quart, and Arky was loosened up considerably. He was talking in his usual nonstop fashion about things in general, when Larkes suddenly broke in.

"You ever been married?"

Arky was startled by the question. "Are you kiddin'?" he said. "I ain't even been *close*. Have you?"

Larkes wasn't surprised Arky returned his question with a question. He'd grown used to Arky's ways. Much as he liked to talk, he also liked to ask information of others.

"Well, I guess I'm a-fixin' to be," Larkes said. He took a long, deep drink of whiskey, then gasped and blew out slowly, trying to catch his breath. "That is, if she'll have me."

"Well, congratulations, Hoss." Arky extended his hand.

Larkes ignored the hand. "Shoot, ain't nothin' to congratulate a man about. It's just somethin' that comes along in life and happens to a man," he said.

Arky was puzzled by Larkes' attitude. "You sound like a man with a heavy heart. Don't you want to get married?"

The words hovered like a rain cloud over Larkes' head. He thought a moment, then said, "Oh, if you'd of asked me 'bout gettin' married a year ago, I'd of said you was loco. Hell, it might be the whiskey talkin' for me right now, for all I know. But, the truth of the matter is, even though I'm not too fond of the idea of gettin' hitched, I don't reckon I wanna live my life without her." He stared into the campfire. The flames burned his eyes, but he couldn't pull them away, even after he started seeing spots. He took another long drink of whiskey.

"Aw, married life's okay for some, I guess," Arky said matter-of-factly. "I've known a lot of ol' boys who got married and seemed the better for it. But"—he paused and took the bottle from Larkes—"I've known a few fellers who was so blamed henpecked, it's dang near scared me plumb away from ever wantin' to walk down that church aisle." He put the bottle to his lips. Whereas Larkes took big swallows, Arky just sipped at the liquor. Even so, he was getting just as drunk as Larkes.

"I sure ain't intendin' to be henpecked," Larkes said. "No, sir. That woman's got another think a-comin', if she thinks I'm gonna be henpecked."

Arky grinned and decided to chide him a little. "I don't know, Hoss. That Reasa acts like she's got a mind of her own. Shoot, I bet if I see you a year from now, you'll be walkin' a narrow line in life."

Larkes snatched the bottle of whiskey and wiped the mouth with his hand. He held it up where he could see the flames of the fire through the amber liquid. "You're talkin' nonsense now. She's got a mind of her own with that young'n of hers, I 'spose, but she'll not be tellin' this ol' boy what to do. You can count on that."

"We'll see," Arky said. His words were getting slurred. "I think I'll just look you up in a year or so. I'll bet she'll have an apron around your waist by then." He giggled like a little boy.

"Shee—iit! You *are* crazy."

They drank in silence for a while, each man in his own world, deep in his own thoughts. When the bottle was nearly empty, Larkes handed the rest of it to Arky and stretched out, resting back on his elbows. He watched Arky down the last of the liquor and thought about how odd Arky's behavior turned whenever he was in Alma's presence. "Why don't you marry Alma?" he said. "It's plain you two are sweet on each other."

Arky's eyes glistened against the fire. He was plenty drunk, for sure, but he wasn't so drunk that he didn't take in what Larkes had just said. He grinned sheepishly. "Man, howdy. She sure is a pretty thing, ain't she?" he said, sounding almost wistful. Then another boyish giggle erupted. "But she ain't so pretty that I'm gonna get myself tangled up in marriage. No, sir! I'm gonna stick to my plans. Head on down to Texas and work on that ranch."

"What's that? I thought you was gonna make that run, yourself. In fact"—Larkes bent his head sideways—"it was you got everybody stirred up about this run business."

"Weren't me," Arky said, shaking his head. "It was Reasa who done all the talkin'."

"Nah, she just started it, but *you* got everybody all in a tizzy over it."

Arky shook his head. A grin covered his face. He was in too good a mood to argue. "Ah, heck. Maybe you're right. It *was* fun talkin' about it, though, wasn't it?" he said. "Shoot, Hoss. Sometimes I talk a little too much. I don't guess I was ever plannin' on makin' that run. Just a cowboy's daydream, was all."

Larkes thought about what an understatement Arky had just made. Not only was Arky the biggest talker he'd ever run across, he also brought up more new ideas for discussion than Larkes cared to think about. "Well, I hope you've come up with a plan for Alma and Toby Ray. Just what are they gonna do now?" he asked. "I'm tellin' ya, Arky, you can't take your eyes off her, and it's plain she's got the same feelin's for you. The noble thing to do is make an honest woman out of her. She'd do you proud as a wife."

Arky shook his head and tossed away the empty bottle, aiming for a large rock that jutted out of the earth nearby. He listened until he heard the sound of breaking glass. Leaning back on his elbows like Larkes, he said, "Look, Hoss, you're the one fixin' to get married. Don't be passin' your matrimonial talk on to me. I ain't interested. I might not ever be interested. 'Sides, I've only known her a few days."

Larkes' face grew serious. "Just tell me the truth, then. You got a fancy for Alma or not?"

Arky thought about Alma. The way she lowered her eyes and blushed when he looked at her, and how excited she seemed when they spoke to each other.

"I'll admit, I think she might be the most beautiful female I ever laid eyes on. But if I was to run out and ask every pretty female I ever seen to get married, why, I 'spose I coulda been married a dozen times."

Larkes said nothing. Several minutes passed.

"I bet she wouldn't marry me, anyway."

"Well, there's one sure way of findin' out," Larkes said. "You'd be good for that gal. Fact is, you two would be good for each other."

It wasn't usually Larkes' way to give advice on such private matters. He attributed it to the whiskey. Or, he thought, maybe he was just trying to distract his thoughts away from what he was about to do. At least, he still *planned* on doing it. He hadn't even given Reasa a hint.

Whatever his reasons, Larkes was sure as anything about the hurt and fear that showed on Alma's face whenever she talked about getting on that train to Kansas. For her sake, he felt obliged to make his thoughts known to Arky.

Arky was still tossing the issue back and forth in his mind. He said thoughtfully, "I know how concerned Alma's been for herself and Toby Ray. I just ain't sure if I'm the answer to their problems. That's some responsibility. And I'm not sure I'm ready to settle down yet." He sighed. "Still, I gotta admit that a man could do a lot worse than Alma. You noticed how pretty she is?"

"You already said that before, and it only goes to prove my point," Larkes said. He stood up and stretched, a move that caused him to lose his balance and stumble.

"You're drunk, Hoss. I knew you was when you went to talkin' 'bout all that marriage business."

They kicked out the campfire and spread the ashes, then made their way back to camp. Everyone else had already gone to sleep. Larkes and Arky crawled into their bedrolls, and Arky was soon snoring loudly.

Larkes lay there a long time, awake. Over and over, he rehearsed what he would say to Reasa. It was the middle of the night before he fell asleep. Then, only a couple of hours later, he woke up with a headache. He got up and stirred Reasa from her sleep.

"Reasa! Wake up. I gotta talk to ya," he said, shaking her by the shoulder.

Reasa sat up and rubbed her face. "Why, you're drunk." She grimaced, waving her hand in front of her face. "You smell like a bottle of cheap liquor. What time is it, anyways?" She squinted at him.

"About six in the mornin'. Reasa, we need to talk," Larkes said seriously.

"It couldn't have waited?" Reasa moaned. "All right. You go on over there and make some coffee. I'll get around."

Larkes relit the burned-out campfire. He was just getting the coffee on when Reasa sat down next to him. She had draped a shawl over her shoulders. Her eyes still looked heavy.

"So what in the world is so important, you have to talk about it right now?" she said.

Larkes fiddled with the coffee pot. Words that he had rehearsed all evening and halfway into the night were now suddenly distant. He'd reshifted his position so many times, he couldn't remember what he had decided to say. It didn't help matters that his head felt like a hammer was pounding away inside. He wished he could think more clearly. He reached up and massaged his eyes and forehead.

Reasa sat through his silence for several minutes before she lost her patience. "Well, I'm waitin'," she said.

"Just relax a minute," Larkes said in a nervous tone.

Reasa scowled at him. "What's wrong with you? Wake me up out of a sound sleep with somethin' big and important to talk about, and then you just set there?" She started to get up. "If you ain't got nothin' to talk about, I'm goin' back to bed," she said, clearly irritated.

He was losing his chance. Suddenly, Larkes turned and blurted out, "You know, a body's 'sposed to be married, if they figure on makin' this here run."

"Unless they're head of a household," Reasa said, still looking irritated.

Larkes raised his voice and cut her off. "A body is 'sposed to be married," he went on. " 'Sides that, there's a filing fee, *which* you don't have. Also, you gotta raise a crop, *which* I doubt you'd be able to handle by yourself. And, you gotta build you a house, *which*—"

"Hold on a minute!" Reasa stopped him. Her eyes narrowed angrily. "What's this all about? Are you tryin' to make me feel bad this early in the mornin' with all your negative talk? Well, it ain't gonna work! There's free land out there. It's promised land, and you ain't gonna foul it up by tellin' me a bunch of nonsense this mornin'. Don't you think I know what you're tryin' to do?"

Larkes' voice rose. "Woman, will you hush up for just a second? I'm tryin' to propose to ya," he said, his eyes wide and serious, his jaws set.

"You're what? Did my ears hear clearly?" Reasa said. Where Larkes had imagined her to be all happy and grateful, Reasa just looked angrier. She grabbed up a piece of wood and hurled it into the fire, sending sparks flying up around the coffee pot.

"I guess I'm 'sposed to be flattered," she said. "Well, if it's flattery you're lookin' for, you done wasted your time! Wakin' me up out of a sleep, proposin' to me, just like that! Do you think I'm one of your horses?"

Larkes shook with anger. He stood up. "Just forget I bothered you. I apologize."

"Larkes," she said.

"What?"

"I accept."

"What did you say?"

Reasa nodded. "I accept your proposal of marriage."

Larkes looked perplexed. Reasa did crazy things to him. She made his body ache. She stirred his manhood, just being close to him. She made his heart flutter so badly, it turned him weak-kneed. Sometimes, she made him angrier than he thought anyone possibly could. But the anger never lasted. He shook his head.

"You enjoy doin' this? You enjoy makin' me look like some kind of fool?"

"You can only make yourself look like a fool," Reasa corrected him. Her demeanor changed, grew softer. She shrugged slightly. "I reckon a woman likes to be proposed to right proper, that's all. Not like some animal at a sale. Lookee here, Larkes. We could have a good life together. We can make that run and get somethin' that would be all ours. Somethin' to be proud of. A place that Noah would be proud to show off to his friends. I don't want Noah to ever have to accept anything less." Alma got up and walked over to Larkes. She reached up and brushed his cheek, then took his hands in hers. "You see, I want you to want me. To *want* to spend your life with me and Noah. I'm not an animal at a sale, Larkes.

You got to understand that. I'll be a good wife. I'll love you properly. I'll take care of you. I'll mend your clothes and cook your meals and never deny ya in bed. But in exchange, you got to treat me with affection and respect. I'll not be some sale animal." She pulled his head close to hers, kissed him gently on the lips, his cheek, his forehead.

Their lips met again. This time, he kissed her, too.

37

"**H**ELP ME! OH, PLEASE, SOMEBODY, HELP!" ALMA
cried out. She was crouched on the blanket next to Toby
Ray with her hand on his forehead.

She had no more uttered the words when Larkes was
on his knees beside her. "What's the matter?" he asked,
his voice raspy with the heaviness of sleep.

The early morning sky was still dark overhead, with
the first hint of pink starting to appear in the eastern
horizon. The rest of the camp was still asleep. Alma
turned to Larkes. In the pale light, he could tell that her
eyes were wide with concern.

"It's Toby Ray," Alma said. "He's terribly sick. He's
in awful pain."

Toby Ray suddenly screamed out and grabbed his
stomach, rolling himself onto his side. "Ooooh, it hurts,"
he groaned. "Please, Alma. I can't stand it."

Alma wrung her hands. She grabbed his shoulder and
tried to pull him onto his back. "What's wrong, hon?"
she asked gently. "Tell me where it hurts."

Toby Ray's voice sounded like a whimper. "It's my
belly. It's hurtin' bad," he said.

Alma turned to Larkes. "He woke me up sayin' he
was hurtin'. He says it's gettin' worse."

Larkes bent over to where he could see Toby Ray's
face. "You got a bellyache, boy?"

"It hurts awful!" Toby Ray bellowed out. He pointed

283

to his belly button. "Right here, and all around." He reached for Alma's hand and squeezed it. "Please, you gotta help me."

Larkes was as puzzled as Alma. "Could be somethin' he et," he suggested. "Maybe if he lays here a while, he'll start feelin' better."

But he didn't. As the light of dawn crept slowly overhead, Toby Ray's pain only seemed to grow. Soon, his goings-on had everyone awake. When Reinhart and Helena climbed out of their wagon, Helena studied Toby Ray for a moment and put her hand to his forehead. "Dis ist not goot," she said solemnly and shook her head. Her eyes met Alma's and softened a little. "He needs doctor." She turned away and began barking instructions for her curious children to stop crowding around Toby Ray and to commence with their chores.

Reasa and Arky joined Alma and Larkes at Toby Ray's side.

"What do you think it is?" Alma asked Reasa.

Reasa shook her head. "I don't know. He don't have much of a fever." There was deep concern in Reasa's eyes. She took Alma by the shoulders and hugged her. "This is frightenin', child. Helena's right. It's more than we can handle. We need a doctor."

"I'll go," Arky volunteered, his eyes glued on Alma. He got up to saddle his horse.

Larkes followed Arky and helped him with his saddle. "Any idea where you're goin'?" he asked.

Arky shook his head. "None a'tall."

"Well, then, you best go to that railroad man and ask him where a sawbones is at."

Arky climbed atop the horse and looked down at Larkes. "It's serious, ain't it?" he asked.

"Serious enough."

Arky nodded. "Well," he said, "Hennessey's not too far north of here. I bet they've got a doctor. I'll ask the man at the depot."

"Right."

Larkes watched Arky ride away, then he sat down next to Reasa. Alma was holding Toby Ray's hand in both of her own. She looked upset enough to cry.

"Where's Arky?" Alma asked, suddenly looking around.

"Gone to see if he can find a doctor," Larkes said softly.

"A doctor? There's a doctor?"

"Maybe north of here. In Hennessey," Larkes said.

"Hear that, hon? Arky's gonna get you a doctor. He'll fix you right up," Alma said to Toby Ray.

Larkes and Reasa looked at each other.

"Maybe Toby Ray just et somethin' that disagrees with 'im," Larkes said, wanting to make Alma feel better. "Man, I've had some awful bellyaches before. Maybe he just needs to go." He looked down at Toby Ray. "Do you need to relieve yourself?"

Toby Ray gritted his teeth. His face was red from straining against the pain. "I don't know. I just hurt so bad," he gasped.

Willing to try anything, Larkes picked up Toby Ray and carried him to a secluded spot where he could try to move his bowels. It did no good.

They tried everything else they could think of. They shifted him onto a thick pile of blankets to make him more comfortable. Reasa kept up a vigil of wiping down his face with a cool cloth. Even Helena Frey offered a cup of weak tea, but Toby Ray could only feebly push it away.

Nothing seemed to work. Toby Ray was soon rolled into a tight ball on his side, his knees almost up to his stomach. The pain, which had started around his belly button and radiated in a circle, started moving down his lower right side.

Alma felt terribly guilty. All this time, she thought, she'd been worrying about her own selfishness—thinking life had turned so sour that she couldn't go on. Now, all of that was trifle. What really mattered was Toby Ray's well-being. Was this God's way of punishing her? she wondered. She wished she could take back all the times she had questioned Him. Lately, she'd been so caught up in asking for help, she'd lost sight of thanking

Him for all the blessings she did have.

Please God, she prayed silently, *please let Toby Ray be all right, I'm sorry for being angry. And, if you have to make someone be sick, let it be me. Toby Ray doesn't deserve this. He wouldn't hurt anyone.*

Larkes saw how worried Alma was. He knelt down next to her and Toby Ray. "Arky's gonna come ridin' back in with a doctor, any minute. We'll get your brother fixed up in no time," he assured her.

Alma nodded. She barely heard the words. Toby Ray still had a hold of her hand. It seemed like each time his heart beat she could feel it, because his hand would squeeze a little harder on hers. He was sharing his pain with her, so as not to let the others see. Alma felt so insignificant. She wished their mother was there to help him with his pain. She wished that Toby Ray would just cry—wail if he wanted to—and let all his boyish pride go.

It occurred to her suddenly that Toby Ray might die. At first, she had thought it was just a bellyache. But this was worse—much worse. She stared at the faces around her. Larkes and Reasa were both seated next to her, their faces worried. She barely knew them; yet they were sharing her pain and grief. Even the Freys were showing their concern. Helena cooked breakfast and made everyone eat. Then, she cleaned up by herself and, with Noah under her wing, she supervised the curious young'ns, and kept them occupied, making sure none of them got in the way. Reinhart, who didn't know what to say, kept smiling at Alma and nodding his head sympathetically.

Finally, one of the children shouted that someone was coming. There were two riders. One was Arky. The other was a fat little man with a round hat on his head.

"This here's Doc Castleberry," Arky said. "From Indiana. He's come here to make the run. I found a doctor's office over in Hennessey, but he was gone on some emergency. Then when I came back, I run into Doc Castleberry, here, standin' over by the depot." He motioned with his head. "That's his wagon, over yonder."

The little man hopped down from his horse and immediately went to where Toby Ray lay. He pulled Toby Ray's hand away from his stomach.

Alma stared. This was one of the most repulsive men she had ever encountered. For one thing, he was filthy dirty, with a three- or four-day stubble. His eyes were yellowed and blood-shot, and he reeked of alcohol. His shirt, which had once been white, was a dusty gray with dark stains under the armpits. He wore long pants that had frayed at the ankles, held up by suspenders. Most curious of all, he was barefoot. His feet were black and calloused.

"Appendix," he said.

"You're a doctor?" Alma asked.

The doctor looked matter-of-factly at Alma. "You must be his sister, Alma. Am I right?" He looked at Arky.

"Y-yes, I'm Alma," she said. Alma knew she should be grateful, and she was. Still, she couldn't help but think of Doc Thurman, who, besides being arrogant and foul-mouthed, was impeccable in all other ways. Even Wally Turnbow, the animal doctor, had looked professional. This man had to be an imposter, she thought. Surely, no self-respecting man of medicine would look like this.

Dr. Castleberry stood up and pulled half a cigar out of his pocket, stuck it in the corner of his jaw and chewed. "We got two choices here," he said. "Either I take out the boy's appendix, or it's gonna bust, and not too far in the future, either. And," he added, "we don't want that, do we?"

Appendix? Alma repeated the word to herself as fear struck her. One of Aunt Nora's and Uncle Ted's children, Bud, had died when he came down with an attack of appendicitis. She thought of another boy, a schoolmate of hers, who had died of the same malady. Her legs weakened. "What can you do?" she asked.

Dr. Castleberry chewed vigorously on his cigar. "Operate. Immediately. Unless," he added, "you want that boy's appendix to rupture. That's bad." He shook his head. "The poison goes all through the body and consumes 'im."

"Are you sure?" Larkes asked, uncertainly. He couldn't help looking down at the man's feet.

"Find it curious that I don't wear shoes?" The doctor shrugged. "Never did like shoes, to be honest with you. A few years ago I just shucked them."

Nobody answered. They all stared at him in wonder.

He turned to Arky. "Boy, I want you to go back to my wagon. Tell my wife, Nora, to fetch my bag. Be sure 'n tell her to pack my chloroform and the things I'll need for surgery." To Reinhart, he said, "I need you to pull those two wagons up side by side and stretch a cover between 'em. Some kind of canvas'll do. Get me a table underneath for the boy to lie on while I operate. Then, I need me about six lanterns, hung all around the table, high enough so there won't be any shadows fallin' over the operatin' table. Now." He turned to Helena. "Get me the smallest, sharpest knife you have. Sharpen it some more, then boil it for thirty minutes. Hurry."

He paused and saw Larkes standing there, waiting for his orders. "Know where there's any thin-mesh wire?" he asked.

"I think Reinhart may have some chicken wire," Larkes offered.

"Okay, then. Make me a mask that'll fit over the boy's face. Cover it with some cloth. A clean sock'll do."

Without a word, Larkes was gone.

Standing alone, Dr. Castleberry looked down at his pudgy hands. The nails were caked underneath with black grime. Sighing, he hurried off to wash up.

Soon, the "operating room" was all ready. Toby Ray lay on the table. Nearby on a clean cloth lay a small knife and four or five of the doctor's other instruments. Alma, Larkes, Reasa, Arky, Helena and Reinhart all stood by, ready to help.

Dr. Castleberry held up the face mask that Larkes had made, along with a can of chloroform. "This is gonna put the boy to sleep," he said. "Now, I need someone to hold this mask over his face, and let the chloroform fall on it, one drip at a time. You," he said to Alma. "That way, you can talk to him at first and keep him calm." He turned to Larkes, Arky and Reinhart. "You men need to hold him down while we're puttin' him to sleep. He's gonna fight it, 'cause at first he'll think he's chokin'. You other women," he said to Reasa and Helena, "can assist me."

He stopped suddenly and reached inside his bag for a bottle. He took a long swallow.

"Should you be drinkin' that whiskey while you're fixin' to operate on Toby Ray?" Alma looked alarmed.

Dr. Castleberry held the whiskey out in front of him and stared at it thoughtfully. "Nothin' better to settle the nerves." He took another drink, then handed the bottle to Helena. "Take the rest of this," he said. "Use it to make up some sugar whiskey nipples for the boy to suck on afterwards. It'll help with the pain.

"Now," he went on, "before you apply that mask, Alma, I need to ask the boy some questions."

Gently, he touched Toby Ray on the belly. "Okay, son, I want you to tell me where it feels the most tender. Do you understand'?"

Toby Ray nodded.

Dr. Castleberry began to poke Toby Ray's lower right side.

"There!" Toby Ray hollered, grimacing with pain.

"Fine, fine," the doctor said soothingly. He nodded at Alma. "All right, administer the chloroform."

Her hands shaking, Alma put the mask on Toby Ray's face. She tilted the can of chloroform slightly, so that only a couple of drops fell on the cloth.

"Breathe in, son," the doctor said. "Long, deep breaths."

Toby Ray took in a breath and started to cough. Instantly, the men grabbed his arms and legs to keep him steady. Before long, Toby Ray's body relaxed and he was asleep.

"Just keep letting the chloroform fall on the mask, Alma, one drip at a time. Not too fast," Dr. Castleberry said. He looked around at the group. "So, are you all planning on making the run?" he asked.

"Some of us," Larkes said.

"Hmmm," the doctor said. "Didn't know they allowed coloreds to make the run. No disrespect intended."

"None taken," Larkes replied. He avoided Reasa's eyes.

Dr. Castleberry nodded. "All right, then, we're ready. Knife." He nodded to Reasa, who picked up the small knife and handed it to him.

As the doctor took the knife, Alma noticed his hands. They were pink from being scrubbed. His fingernails were suddenly clean. She glanced curiously at the strange man.

Dr. Castleberry put the knife to the spot that Toby Ray had shown him. He said to Reasa and Helena, "There's gonna be a lot of bleedin'. Keep those clean cloths right up next to where I'm workin'. Close as you can." That said, he made a quick incision through the skin. A second cut was made through a top layer of muscle, followed by a third cut, which revealed a hard, orange-shaped abscess.

Larkes took in a deep breath and glanced at Arky and Reinhart. Both men were looking away, their faces suddenly pale. Reasa and Helena were watching the proceedings with interest. Alma looked frightened, but she was concentrating hard on her job of dripping the chloroform.

Dr. Castleberry kept up a constant chatter as he performed the appendectomy. He talked about Indiana, and how the folks there had never come to appreciate his services. It seemed they thought him a bit eccentric, as he put it.

He made yet another cut into the large mass and stuck a finger inside to fish around. Moments later, he came out with a funny-looking mass of tissue. "This is the appendix," he stated. "See this? See how diseased it is? And this here's the colon it's attached to." His eyes gleamed at the others. He was sure they were impressed. He looked back down. "Now, what I'm gonna do is clamp it off at that attachment. Clamp, please," he said to Reasa. That done, he ordered some thread to tie it off. "Next," he said, "we move the clamp down here to the base of the appendix, then tie it off. This boy's appendix is so rotten, I'd venture a guess that it might just drop right off." He grinned. "Like so!"

He drew in a breath and looked quickly up at Reasa. "Get the sweat offa my face. My biggest worry right now is infection."

Reasa patted his forehead and nose with the wet rag, noticing the dirt that came away with it. He'd done a better job of cleaning his hands than his face.

"Yeah," he was going on, "folks back home lost a good doctor, but the Outlet's gainin' one. I'm gonna make that run and start me another practice out here. Folks here'll be needin' a doctor, too, you know. Business should be boomin'. Why, just yesterday I rode up to Hennessey and on north to where the startin' line is. They got government troops keepin' people out. Looks like a circus up there, so many people! Yeah," he repeated, "business should be a-boomin'!"

No one in the group said a word, fearful of distracting the doctor even further.

Dr. Castleberry smiled at everyone. "So far, so good!" he said. "The next thing we do is pack the wound with some carbolized gauze. Three or four feet'll do." He nodded as Reasa handed him the gauze. "We'll leave a little bit of the gauze stickin' out, and stitch up most of the incision, leavin' a hole for the gauze to come out."

"You mean, you're gonna leave that stuff inside 'im?" Arky was surprised enough to forget about getting sick.

"Not forever," the doctor replied. "In a couple of days, you're gonna pull out about six inches of gauze. Then, every day after that, you pull out another six inches, 'til it's all out. That way, the wound can heal from the inside."

"Well, I swear! Ain't that gonna leave a hole in Toby Ray's belly?" Arky asked.

"Well, there'll be a scar, but it'll heal itself, too."

Several minutes later, Dr. Castleberry looked up and smiled at everyone. He picked up a cloth and wiped his hands. "Done." He looked at Helena. "Might I have just one more drink?" he asked.

"Ja." Helena smiled, and handed him the bottle.

"Alma, you can give the boy a few more drips of the chloroform, then take the mask away. He'll wake up shortly." To Helena, he said, "Just have those sugar whiskey nipples ready. He'll need 'em."

"How long will it take before Toby Ray's all better?" Alma asked.

"Well, now we just have to wait and see. If he don't get any infection, he should be all right. He'll need to rest here for a spell. I wouldn't move him much. Make sure he drinks plenty of water. Try to feed him a little bit of soup when he's hungry."

"What do we owe ya?" Larkes said, digging around in his britches.

"Ah, yes. My fee. Let's see." Dr. Castleberry thought a moment, then surprised everyone when he said, "Bein' as this is my first physician's call in Oklahoma Territory, this one's on me. But," he said as he stuck the stogie back in his jaw, "the next one will cost ya."

Suddenly Reasa ran up and gave him a big hug. "We're forever grateful," she said, then stepped back. "And Toby Ray—you say he's gonna be all right?"

"He'll come around in just a few minutes. Just keep him comfortable. Like I said, a little water, a little soup. Pull out that gauze, a few inches a day. You might watch for any swellin', and make sure no infection sets in. Main thing is, you don't wanna be jostlin' him about. I'd suggest you folks stay right here for a few days."

Euphoria swept over Alma. She thanked God. She thanked everyone around her.

Suddenly she felt someone's eyes on her. Then she looked up, deep into Arky's eyes. Sometime during the ordeal, she had felt his hand rest on her shoulder. She hadn't acknowledged it, but she'd known it was there. She had an urge to run and throw her arms around him, but she knew she couldn't. What would he do?

Everyone was in a talkative mood, happy and relieved that the operation was over. Helena even let the children join the adults, and soon it was a noisy camp.

Amidst it all, Alma and Arky held their gaze. Their

eyes stayed locked on each other for what seemed like forever. As far as Alma was concerned, the only thing happening in the world was happening between her and Arky. The others could have been a million miles away.

38

HELENA FREY'S ANNOUNCEMENT CAUGHT ALMA totally by surprise. Alma was standing off by herself, gazing out at the rolling plains and trying to figure out just what she and Toby Ray were going to do once they got to Kansas, when Helena walked up and stood next to her.

"Ve stay right here 'til Toby Ray ist better. Ve not go to der Kansas. Dat right?" Helena nodded and smiled. "Ja, ve are going to make der run. Der Cherokee Outlet run."

Alma was overcome with joy. All of a sudden, good fortune had come into her life. It was too much for her to contain herself. Her face lit into a huge smile, and before she knew it, she was in Helena Frey's arms. Helena's strength surrounded her. It felt strange to Alma; Helena Frey was bigger than most men. Still, there was a womanly feel about her, too. "Thank you so much," Alma cried.

Helena chuckled. "For vat? Because ve make der run?"

"For allowing Toby Ray to stay here and get better," Alma said sincerely.

"Ach, you go on vit your thinkin'. Ve vould not leave Toby Ray," Helena said. She wiped sweat from her forehead and turned to watch her children, who were playing close by. "Reinhart and I love der children. Ve could not leave Toby Ray. It could just as vell be one of our own dat is sick. You come and get something to eat. I vatch your brudder."

Toby Ray was sleeping, a sugar nipple stuck to the corner of his mouth. He'd had a frightful amount of pain, but hadn't cried once. Alma had done his crying for him, wishing she could take his pain on herself.

Now, more than anything, she longed for him to hear Helena's good news. After all he'd been through, he deserved a little of life's good fortune. Poor Toby Ray. She thought about all their fights and silly hollering back and forth—the many times their mother had begged them to get along, pointing out what the Bible said about loving one another.

Alma had always loved Toby Ray, but the world had come and gone since those days. It occurred to her that she surely could not love her own child any more than she loved Toby Ray at this moment. Now, it seemed like her entire life, all her emotions and feelings, centered around him. She wondered if their mother was looking down at them. Was she proud of how Alma had cared for him, her mother's baby? Her eyes still watered, but she couldn't help smiling at the thought. Toby Ray had always been mama's baby. It was a tag that he scoffed at, stomped his feet and denied when the fact was mentioned, but still Alma had known that he enjoyed the status. In spite of all of Toby Ray's rough and tumble ways, he still had a warm, soft heart. Alma had seen it those few times when he would crawl up in his mama's lap and hug her with so much love. Now Alma wished Toby Ray would crawl up in *her* lap and let her put her arms around him.

She went over to where he lay and bent down to kiss his forehead. She looked back at Helena, who nodded cheerfully.

"Go. He vill be all right. His sleep ist goot."

Before she filled her plate, Alma looked around for Arky. She had seen him eating a short while ago. Her heart missed a beat as she realized that the others might all have left without her. She felt a little panicky, until she saw Noah, playing in amongst the Frey children.

It scared her to think that Arky might have pulled up and left without so much as saying good-bye. Surely, she thought, he wouldn't do such a thing.

While Alma was eating, Reasa returned from the direction of the depot. She walked proudly, almost strutting. She held out a newspaper, like it was some trophy.

"Lookee here, child!" She showed Alma the Guthrie newspaper. "It says here that President Grover Cleveland has made it official!"

Just then, Arky rode up. "Climb on down," Reasa told him. "I got news for everybody."

Arky dismounted and looked questioningly at Alma, but she only shrugged.

Reasa waited until everyone had gathered. They all sat around the campfire, while she walked around them in a circle. Her face wore a funny smile, kind of like a permanent fixture that she couldn't have erased if she'd wanted to.

Reinhart grew tired of waiting. "Vat is it?" he finally asked impatiently.

"It's all right here," Reasa said, unable to contain her excitement any longer. "It says right here that President Cleveland has set the time and date! September sixteenth at noon, the Cherokee Outlet will be opened for settlement. Says there's gonna be nine counties. They're callin' 'em K, L, M, N, O, P and Q. And the man at the depot told me that north of Hennessey is gonna be O county." She paused and turned to Arky. "Go get Noah," she said. "Bring my baby to me. He's gotta hear this, too!" The smile on her face remained fixed, but it was genuine.

When Arky returned with her son, the other children came along. They, too, wanted to be in on what was so important.

Reasa grabbed Noah up in her arms and pointed north. "See the sky out there, honey? Here, take your finger outta your mouth. Now, you see that land and sky way up to the north o' here? That's gonna be your new home."

Noah stared at her with his wide eyes. Reasa smiled and spoke to him gently. "That's right, baby. You gonna live in 'O' county in Oklahoma Territory. That's what the man at the depot said."

Noah stuck his thumb back in his mouth and nodded his head.

"Read some more, Reasa," Reinhart said.

"All right, but here, Larkes." Reasa held her son out to him. "Take Noah."

"Just put that boy *down*," Larkes said firmly. "He's too big to be holdin' 'im all the time."

Usually, such a remark would bring a strong retort from Reasa, but not today. Still with her frozen grin, she set the boy down.

"All right, listen up, everyone! We haveta git everything straight." Reasa held up the paper and read. "There'll be nine booths openin' up on September eighth. Says here there'll be one in Stillwater in Payne County, one in Orlando in Logan County, and one north o' Hennessey in Kingfisher County." She paused and looked around at the others. "*That's* the one we're interested in. Gonna be other booths up in Kansas, but the man at the depot done told me that Kansas is at the other end o' the Outlet. We got to be there Monday morning, September eleventh, at seven o'clock. Everybody has to go to the booth and declare in writin' that he plans to make the run. Says if you don't get your certificate with your intentions written on it, it makes no difference. You can't have any land, less'n you register at one of these booths."

There was a lot more, and Reasa read it all to them. About how towns and cities would be established, how the government had set land aside for schools, parks, courthouses, county seats and the like. She read about how settlers had to make improvements and establish residency in a certain time period. She read about the fees. She read it all, but the only thing that meant anything to her was the fact that it was finally happening.

"What about the Indians?" Arky asked. "Didn't this land used to belong to them?"

Reasa nodded. "Used to. They sold it to the government. But it says here that they've reserved some land for several tribes in the east, west and middle sections of the Outlet."

"Tell me again how much it's gonna cost," Larkes said.

Reasa couldn't look at him when she said, "Says you gotta have an entry fee of ten dollars, and then you pay a commission fee of a dollar-twenty-five an acre."

Larkes nodded his head and looked down at the ground. He didn't say a word or look anybody's way.

Reinhart and Helena gathered up their children and went off to have a "family meeting," as they put it. Reasa grabbed Noah's hand and asked Larkes if he'd like to walk a spell.

When they had all disbursed, Alma found herself alone with Arky. Toby Ray was sleeping.

She motioned toward the fire. "There's a little bacon left, and the coffee's gotten kinda strong. Could I get you some, anyway?" she offered.

"Alma." Arky stopped her. His face was serious. He motioned for her to sit down. "Just what are you and Toby Ray gonna do in Kansas?" he asked. "Maybe I ain't very smart, but you sure don't act like someone who's lookin' forward to gettin' somewhere."

He's smarter than he thinks, Alma thought. She gave a little sigh.

"Well, we have relatives there," she said. "At least, I *hope* they're still there. . . ." Her voice trailed off. She tried to smile.

"What about this run? Does it excite you, Alma?"

Alma shrugged. "I don't know. I guess it interests me. No reason to get excited, though. Toby Ray and I couldn't make it if we wanted to." She turned the subject around, boldly looking him in the eye. "And what about you? Are you gonna make the run or head on down to Texas?"

"My mind's jumped back and forth on it so much, I don't know. I contracted with the Freys to take 'em to Kansas, but now they're talkin' about making the run, too." Arky laughed briefly, and their eyes held for a couple of seconds. "I guess I'm as mixed up as you are."

"I guess we're all a little mixed up these days," Alma said wistfully, as she turned and gazed out toward the direction of the Cherokee Strip.

39

TRUE TO DR. CASTLEBERRY'S WORD, TOBY RAY WAS getting along just fine. Alma could tell the pain bothered him quite a bit, but Toby Ray did everything he could to hide it, especially when anyone but Alma was around. Within a matter of days, it was all she could do to keep him settled down. Every time she looked around, he was up and about. She didn't feel much anguish over his obstinacy though, for Toby Ray's color was returning to normal, and he looked healthy again. He even joked about having gauze sticking out of his side.

The days of waiting for the would-be settlers were becoming monotonous, so new avenues of entertainment were created around the depot. Soon, a regular morning occurrence started taking place. Horse racing. Larkes found himself accepting the challenges to race the big white gelding. He became so busy, Arky took over as his promoter and bookmaker. One morning, they won fifty dollars from a banker from Tennessee. The banker raised seven kinds of hell, agonizing over the fact that Larkes' gelding had easily beaten his Kentucky racehorse. Arky found it all amusing. He'd heard the banker bragging about the fact that his racehorse was gonna put him at the head of the other runners to claim the first stake. Now, it looked like he'd have to settle for the second claim.

Each morning brought a new race and along with it, another victory and more money. It surprised Larkes and

Arky how, after the big white gelding had outrun all takers, there'd be fresh new money the very next morning. *Fresh ignorance* was how Reasa put it. She couldn't understand why folks would risk their hard-earned money against a horse that was a proven winner. She shook her head over it more than once.

As for Arky, he was growing closer to Toby Ray with each passing day. They almost acted like brothers, teasing and joking with each other. After each morning race, Arky would come back with stories. When Toby Ray finally got healthy enough, he started going along.

Something else was happening, too. Arky and Alma were falling in love. Maybe they had been in love since the first day they'd met. Maybe it had happened somewhere along the ride. Larkes could have been the catalyst; he'd pushed ideas about Alma into Arky's thoughts, because he'd felt sorry for Alma and Toby Ray. Alma, herself, had realized the need for some miracle in her life to make a change for her.

But, no matter what her needs or wishes might be, or Larkes' attempts at playing Cupid, she and Arky reached the point where they couldn't stay apart very long at a time. Reasa told Alma that it was inevitable that it would happen. Alma wasn't sure. She wished that she could have saved Toby Ray's appendix—put it in a little box to keep like some kind of treasure. After all, it had been the appendicitis attack that had given their love time to develop.

Not that Alma was out of the woods yet, she realized. Nothing had been said. No words spoken of love or even affection. Alma could see that it wasn't in Arky's nature to say such things. As kind and gentle and talkative as he was, he wasn't a man who could easily talk about love. Still, she knew he felt the same as she did. And she knew that *he knew* that he felt that way. She could see it in Arky's eyes and in the way he acted around her.

But Arky wasn't the only one who was smitten. Alma noticed the same glow on Larkes' face when he was in Reasa's presence. Oh, he tried like everything to hide it, but not with any success. That glow was in Reasa's eyes, too.

Even though no words had been spoken, no embraces or kisses exchanged, Alma knew that to be in Arky's arms would feel as natural as two lovebirds building a nest.

September the ninth was a mirror of the day before, and the day before that. It was hot and dry. It was on that day, though, that Larkes and Reinhart announced that they were going to move on up to the booth north of Hennessey to look things over. Though it hadn't been part of Larkes' announcement, Reasa jumped up to say that they were also going to find someone to marry them.

The camp erupted in cheers of congratulations. They all crowded around Larkes and Reasa. Reasa beamed and accepted their well-wishing with an ecstatic look. Larkes simply bowed his head, returned handshakes and exited the group as soon as he could.

Alma hugged Reasa and told her how happy she was for them.

Reasa thanked her, then whispered, "Has Arky got around to askin' you, hon?"

Alma gave Reasa a sly, questioning grin.

Reasa squeezed Alma's hands and said, "You may have to prod him some, you know. But it won't take much. The boy's definitely smitten. You are too, ain't ya?"

Alma stared for a moment. She glanced at Arky and nodded her head. *If you only knew*, she thought. She was consumed by Arky. She felt as if she were floating in his presence. The sight of him could cause her heart to jump and a fluttery sensation would run through her chest.

"You really think he likes me?"

Reasa rolled her eyes and laughed. "Oh, child! He does more'n like ya! Why, that boy is smitten, I tell ya! Listen." She leaned close. "We could have a double weddin'. Wouldn't that be fun?"

Alma had to think. Reasa was right. Still, it didn't change the fact that Arky had never spoken a word to her about his feelings, and didn't appear inclined to do so in the future, either. And time was running out.

Maybe she should prod him a little, as Reasa suggested. But how in the world was she supposed to do that? What if he said no? What if he thought she was crazy? Maybe Arky had no intentions of ever marrying *anybody*, even if he did love her.

Why, she thought, was life so complicated?

40

LARKES AND REINHART HAD NO MORE REACHED THE registration booth on Saturday, the ninth of September, when Larkes saw him. In fact, they saw each other in the same instant, there amongst the thousands who had gathered to wait for the booth to open.

Deputy Frank started to walk toward Larkes. His eyes were aimed directly at him, a sneer on his lips. He walked with a sizeable limp. There were five other men with him, all with menacing looks on their faces.

"Why, if it ain't the sorry nigger that ruin't my leg," Deputy Frank sneered. "What do ya think you're doin' here'?"

Larkes' eyes bore into his. "I sure didn't come here to look for no trouble, Frank," he said.

"Well now, ya might not be lookin' for any, but you're fixin' to git ya some."

"What happened between us was unfortunate, but it's over," Larkes said. He tried to step away and put distance between them.

Deputy Frank grabbed Larkes' arm. "You listen here, nigger boy. I'll say when it's over. You see this here leg o' mine?" He slapped it. "I damn near lost it. Doctor says I'm gonna walk like this the rest of my life." He pushed his face up close to Larkes. "Ever since that day, nigger boy, every time I take a step, I think of you and that whore, Reasa."

Anger flashed in Larkes' eyes. "It won't be your knee next time, Frank. You mind yourself. Like I told you, I ain't lookin' for no trouble, but that don't mean you won't get yourself a chest full of it."

"You fixin' to kill all six of us?" Deputy Frank grinned, tilting his head toward his friends. "I'd pay to see that, nigger boy."

A crowd had gathered around. Catcalls came from them. Someone said, "We don't need any niggers in the Outlet." Another said, "Shoot the nigger." Then, "Free the bastards, and they gonna come in here and try to live amongst us."

Then another man spoke up. "Leave the man alone. He's got a right to be here, just like the rest of us," he said.

Others agreed with him.

Larkes just stared back at Deputy Frank like he hadn't heard a word. Deputy Frank, feeling even more sure of himself, waved his arms around him.

"You hear what they said, boy? This crowd'll chew you up alive and spit you out."

Larkes' jaw twitched. "Is that what you need, Frank? A crowd?"

He glanced at the faces around them, just as Deputy Frank swung his fist.

The punch caught high on Larkes' forehead, causing stars to momentarily cloud his vision. Instantly, Deputy Frank grabbed Larkes in a bear hug and wrestled him to the ground. On the bottom, Larkes fought with all he had and managed to flip Deputy Frank over. Now on top, Larkes drew back his fist. He was just aiming for Deputy Frank's nose, when a hot stabbing pain jolted the back of his head and started moving forward. He dropped his fist.

Reinhart, who had stood watching in dumbfounded silence, suddenly went into action. He tore into the man who had just kicked Larkes in the head, and knocked the man to the ground.

Deputy Frank's other four companions converged. Soon, Larkes and Reinhart were both on the ground, surrounded by pummeling fists and kicks.

No one in the crowd volunteered any help on either side. Some started chanting encouragement, enjoying the unexpected entertainment.

Soldiers who had been stationed at the booth to keep peace and prevent sooners from sneaking into the Outlet early heard the commotion and rode into the crowd.

"Break it up!" a young lieutenant said. "Break it up or we'll shoot ya. I mean it!" He fired his pistol into the air to prove his point, and the fighting suddenly stopped.

Heaving for air, Deputy Frank pointed a finger at Larkes. His head was drenched in sweat, and the large belly shook with his anger. "You ain't seen the last of me, nigger boy," he said.

Larkes turned his back on him and said to Reinhart, "You all right?"

"Ja!" Reinhart nodded his head. He was breathing hard but his eyes had an excited look.

They mounted their horses and started back for camp. "I'm beholdin' to ya," Larkes said.

Reinhart glanced back at Deputy Frank and his companions. "Dey vill make more trouble for you, ja?"

Larkes looked at Reinhart and shrugged. "Ja," he said.

They both grinned.

Back at camp, Larkes had to tell Reasa everything that had happened. Reasa grabbed a rag and kept wiping the trickle of blood that ran from the cut over Larkes' left eye. "You shoulda killed him in the first place," she said bitterly. "He's evil. Evil to the core."

Reasa looked up to see a stranger riding into their camp. He seemed to be looking for someone. When he noticed Reasa, with Larkes lying beside her, he steered his horse to where she sat.

"I'm lookin' for the man who owns that white gelding," he said.

Reasa held her hand over her face to shield the sun. "Who are you?" she asked.

The man tipped his hat. "Name's Rocky Schoonover. I've heard about that white gelding. I think my roan can beat that horse."

Larkes' head was pounding. He slowly raised up to see who was making such boastful talk. At first, all he could see was the roan. The man's head and shoulders were a dark silhouette against the sun. He tried to stand up. His head throbbed, but he passed through the pain and made it to his feet.

"Hot damn, mister! Looks like you done fell and been trampled on." There was concern in Rocky Schoonover's voice.

"Ain't nothin'," Larkes said weakly. He moved to a better position, where he wasn't looking into the sun. The roan looked like a good horse. It had the same sculptured body as the gelding. "The geldin' belongs to me," he said.

"Then you're the man I'm lookin' for! Run into an ol' boy down in Guthrie a couple of days ago. He told me about a big colored man who owned a white gelding that was unbeatable." Schoonover smiled. He was a large, handsome man with broad shoulders and big hands. Underneath his Stetson, his hair was a deceptive white, as his face looked to be that of a much younger man who had prematurely grayed. His smile was easy with a warm look behind it. Sitting erect with confidence in the saddle, he was an impressive sight. "Mind if I step down?" he said.

"Not at all," Larkes answered.

"Like I said, my name's Rocky Schoonover, and I come to race that gelding." He extended his hand. "Any coffee in that pot?"

"I'll get you some," Reasa offered. She eyed his horse. "Those newspapers you got stickin' out of your bags?"

Schoonover turned to his roan and smiled. "Why, yes ma'am. I was takin' them back to Ness City. My brother's wife, Elaine, fancies readin' newspapers. I travel around a lot, so I always try to find her some papers to take back. You're welcome to read 'em. Lot of 'em are old ones, though. Some from back in May."

Larkes stared at Rocky Schoonover. There was a familiar look about him, but he couldn't recall where he'd seen him before. He was sure they'd met on good terms.

There'd been other men like that—men he couldn't quite place. Oftentimes there had been an uneasiness about the recollection. But this man was different. . . .

Suddenly, it came to him. Fort Worth. That's right, he thought. It was Fort Worth.

"What'd you say your name was?" Schoonover asked.

"It's Larkes Dixon."

Schoonover rubbed his chin. "Larkes Dixon," he repeated. "Do we know each other?" He laughed. "It's hard to tell with your head swollen up like a melon."

"Fort Worth," Larkes said. "We met at a horse sale back in '87."

"By damn, that's right," Schoonover said. "Well, fancy seein' you again. You're here to make the run, I suspect."

"That's our intention," Larkes said.

"Mine, too." Schoonover nodded his thanks as Reasa offered him a cup of coffee.

Larkes said, "I thought you lived in Kansas."

Schoonover sipped at his coffee. "That I do. Came there from West Virginia with my family. My folks, three brothers and a sister. We settled up there in '78. But hell! I'm full of the wanderlust, I'm afraid. I'm never home. Like to buy and sell horses. This land run, though, was too good an opportunity to pass up."

"How big a place you got in Kansas?" Larkes asked.

"Got a hundred sixty acres a couple miles outside of Ness City. We've all got quarter sections up there."

Reasa had sat down between them. She frowned. "Well, if you got all that land, what are you needin' this land for?"

Larkes gave Reasa a hard stare. He didn't like her meddling into other folks' business. She paid no attention to his look, however, and that only irritated him further.

Schoonover didn't seem to mind. He grinned. "Just sounds like a good idea, is all. Ain't nothin' wrong with a man acquirin' more land, is there, Larkes? Shoot, I'll throw me together a sod house, move the wife and young'ns down here and live in it a spell. Or maybe I'll sell it and move back to Ness City." He shrugged and laughed, then his face turned serious. He looked hard at Larkes' swollen face. "One thing's for certain though, compadre. I sure was wettin' my mouth about racin' that gelding of yours. But I'll be derned if you look up to the task right now."

Schoonover's remark irritated Larkes somewhat. He stole a glance at the roan. "You think that horse of yours is fast, do ya? Well, don't let my appearance hold ya back. How much ante you talkin' about?"

Reasa's eyes turned like an eagle's and lit on Larkes'. "Mister Schoonover's right," she said. "You sure ain't up to any horse racin'." She leaned close to him and talked out the side of her mouth. " 'Sides that, you don't need to be bettin' him a whole bunch of money. What if you lose? We need money for filin'. Or have you forgotten already?"

Larkes looked past her. Reasa's words often irritated him, and he found it better to disregard them than to worry over them. Besides, she didn't much know one end of a horse from another. She had a lot of gall, he thought.

Schoonover was watching Larkes closely. He stuck a hand in his pocket. "Well, I'll tell you what, compadre. I got a hundred says my roan can beat your white gelding."

Larkes tried not to look at Reasa, but it had become too much of a habit. Her eyes were now more like stabbing daggers.

"I thought you wanted to bet some real money," he said, watching Reasa's mouth drop open.

"Well then, what do you say to two hundred?"

"I'd say that sounds right nice," Larkes said. "Tomorrow mornin', we're gonna be movin' the wagons on up to the filin' booth. We can race 'em before we head out. Right after breakfast. What do you say?"

"Sounds like a fine idea," Schoonover said. He grimaced a little as he studied Larkes' condition. He glanced then at Arky, who was sitting next to

Alma. "Say," he said, "are all these folks travelin' with ya?"

"Everybody right down to the young'ns," Larkes offered.

"Tell you what," Schoonover said with a hint of sarcasm, "You don't look like you're in such great shape for ridin'. Why don't you let someone like that feller over there do your ridin' for ya? I wouldn't want to take your money and then feel guilty about it." He laughed.

"I do my own ridin'," Larkes said simply.

"Fair 'nough, compadre."

Rocky Schoonover made friends with everyone, including Helena Frey. He had an easy manner and quick smile. He told them stories about how he had come west with his family to stake claims in Ness County in western Kansas. About the hardships they had endured. There was wind and dry heat in Kansas, he told them, but Mother Nature sent unexpected rainfalls to bring relief.

The subject of farming came up, which brought particular interest from Reasa and Reinhart. Reinhart wanted to know if Kansas land was similar to land in the Outlet.

"Oh, I think it's flatter up there than it is here," Schoonover said. "More wind, too. But you still oughta be able to raise the same kind of crops."

"You mean wheat?" Reasa asked.

"Yeah, wheat. Both winter and spring. Gosh," Schoonover said, "we tried everythin' up there, one time or another! Rye, barley, corn, oats, millet, peanuts, Irish potatoes, sorghum. Now there's a crop—sorghum. You want a crop that ain't gonna fail ya, it's sorghum. But"—he nodded his head thoughtfully—"I'd say it's been mostly wheat and corn. When we first got started, we raised forty-one bushels of corn an acre on about sixty acres. Had corn runnin' out of my ears!" He grinned widely. "But it was tough back then. We only got two crops the first seven to eight years."

"Two?" Reinhart held up his fingers. "Only two crops?"

"That's right, compadre," Schoonover said. "But things have gotten better. For one thing, we didn't know how to contain our water back then. You see, bein' from West Virginia, I was used to lots of water. If you like lots of water, you're in the wrong part of the country here! But, you'll get enough out here for crops. Shucks, back in '78, '79 and through the early '80s, we didn't have no way to contain what rain we got. The cattlemen all overran the place with their herds. Wasn't very many people had wells back then, either. But that's all changed. Last year was a great year for wheat. In fact, it was so good we had to lay it on the ground everywhere. Most folks only got about thirty-five cents a bushel."

"So, you're sayin' we can raise about anythin' out here?" Reasa asked. She smiled and turned her gaze to Larkes.

"Anything you've a mind to," Schoonover said. "Only thing that might cause you any trouble is the drought we're in. And after that good year we had last year! If you don't get some kind of rain, ain't gonna make much difference what you raise. Still, I'd say you all ought to be all right. Another thing you need is proper farmin' equipment. I remember when we first came to Kansas. Lord, there were a lot of people didn't bring equipment with 'em! Don't know how they expected to raise any crops without equipment!" He chuckled. "But that first year, we got the breaking plow down off the wagon, hooked up the oxen and went to work. Like I said, had a pretty good corn crop that year. A couple of my brothers and my folks planted wheat. Seems like they got around thirty bushels per acre. One brother tried broom corn for a while, and it did fair. So, the land, you see, is good for about anythin'. I'd say this soil is better than some I've seen in other parts of this area."

The group was quiet, taking in all that Schoonover had said. Schoonover leaned back and smiled at each of them, his face beaming.

"Let me set your worries at ease," he went on. "West Virginia was a great place, but us Schoonovers have always liked to look on the other side of the fence, so to speak. I've found that people out in this part of the country are great. I used to miss the mountains and the good huntin', is all. But, there's somethin' about those folks in Ness County, Kansas. The ones that stayed and made it work. Why, they're the salt of the earth. Come from everywhere, Germans, Swiss, even had some Amish settle there. Lot of folks settled from Iowa, Illinois, Wisconsin—just about anywhere there's people. They're in Ness County now."

A thought occurred to Reasa. When Schoonover paused a moment, she crooked her head at him. "I can't help askin'," she said, "but the Guthrie paper done said if you own land, you can't make the run. How is it they're gonna let you?"

Rocky Schoonover's face flushed red. He looked at her sheepishly, turning away. After a moment, he sighed and said, "Well, truth of the matter is, the land ain't really mine. Shucks, my three brothers staked land, but I never did. Soon as we got there, I decided I wasn't going to settle down just yet. I wanted to explore the country first. Be an adventurer. But, this pretty little woman I'd known back in West Virginia and her family had moved there a year ahead of me. I got so caught up by that little woman, I let myself get married. Moved in on my wife's father's land." He stopped for a moment and hung his head. When he again raised up, his face was sad. "Well, it seems things just kinda went sour. The wife and I got divorce papers seven to eight years ago. Land's all hers now." A mist appeared in his eyes. "I guess you might say I wasn't much of a farmer, or much of a family man, far as that's concerned. I been dealin' in horses and such for a spell. . . ." His voice trailed off. "Seems like I only get back home two or three times a year now, to see the young'ns."

Reasa touched his arm. "I'm sorry," she said. "I shouldn't have been so personal."

Schoonover said, "Naw, it's all right. Why shouldn't a person be able to ask what's on his mind?"

He stayed a spell longer, then said he knew the station master and was going to sleep inside the depot. When Reasa offered back the newspapers, he smiled and told her to keep them. "I got an idee that you might enjoy 'em more than my sister-in-law," he said.

As he mounted up on the roan, he tipped his hat to the ladies and then looked down at Larkes. "Tomorrow?"

"I'll be there," Larkes said.

That night, the group was buzzing over everything that Rocky Schoonover had told them. Helena Frey was worried about the drought situation. Reinhart, on the other hand, was busy trying to decide what kind of seed he should buy.

Reasa settled into reading the newspapers. Her heart beat excitedly in her chest. It had been a wonderful day, and the run was getting closer. She had no reservations and no doubts. She had her and little Noah a future, a good future, and nothing was going to get in their way.

Alma and Arky took off walking by themselves. Though they each knew what feelings they carried inside for the other, neither was able to say the words that were needed to solidify their own part in the run.

As for Larkes, he couldn't help thinking about Rocky Schoonover. He seemed like a fine man. But he had a wife and children, and he had left them. He thought about Reasa and Noah. Would he, too, get the wanderlust? Would he some day up and leave on the pretense of going off to buy a horse? Would his passion to roam keep him away, to the point where he'd only get home two or three times a year? After all, he thought, Schoonover was a man after his own heart.

Wanderlust had a way of playing tricks on a man. Larkes had seen it happen to other men, as well. He remembered all the plans he had made for Colorado. Suppose those dreams came back to haunt him someday and overpowered his feelings for Reasa? Would there be other gold booms that stirred his emotions?

His swollen head ached and his ribs were sore from being kicked. It was his mind, though—his thinking self that most anguished him. Somehow, Rocky Schoonover had put it all into perspective. Whatever decision he made, Larkes knew he best not make it lightly.

41

THE MORNING OF SUNDAY, SEPTEMBER TENTH, WAS a clone of the day before and the day before that. Hot, dry and windless. Dust was in the air, so thick you could smell and taste it. It became as much a part of the food on the dinner plate as salt and pepper. The crowd of would-be settlers had traveled countless miles to make the long wait. In spite of the excitement that was about to take place, boredom from sitting idle had easily set in. Children complained and tempers flared.

Water was in great demand, more so than money. People fought over it. Some had died from thirst and exposure. Those who had a good supply, like Larkes' group, were given the same reverence as would befit a banker. Water was sold at ten cents a cup. A few took advantage of the situation, asking the desperate settlers to pay as much as a dollar. Often the water had become rancid and dirty.

The biggest source of amusement had become the morning horse races. Larkes and his gelding had whetted the appetites of others, and soon many other men were pitting their horses against each other. It had become a fever among some. The makeshift racetrack south of the depot had become clearly marked with ruts from the horses' pounding hooves, the deepest of which were caused by the big white gelding.

Larkes couldn't get Rocky Schoonover's words out of

his mind. He'd mulled them over until deep in the night. He had known only a couple of men like Schoonover, delightful men with easy manners and interesting conversation. Men who had very few ties in life. Although Larkes didn't fancy himself as exactly the same sort as Schoonover, he did admit that they shared many of the same habits.

The crowd was especially large this morning. A good number of new arrivals were betting on Schoonover's roan, while the die-hard bystanders who had witnessed the gelding's thunder and power and become believers were putting their money on the white horse. Arky had both hands full of money, accepting all bets he could handle. He was elated. Larkes and the white gelding had been a godsend to him. He now had more money in his pockets than he'd ever had in his life.

The roan and gelding pranced about as they stood close to the starting line. Larkes' left eye was swollen shut, and the right had a mouse on the outside eyelid. His head was still pounding, and each breath made his sides ache. None of these discomforts disturbed him, though, as much as the thoughts of Reasa that stirred in his mind. He tried to shake the guilt she'd put there with her disapproval over this race. The fact was, though, he couldn't.

Schoonover sat atop the prancing roan and grimaced at the sight of Larkes' condition. "Are you still sure you wanna do this, compadre?" he asked. "Like I said, I'd feel awful takin' your money when you're not up to snuff. We could wait a few days, or get that Arky fella to ride for ya."

Larkes forced a stiff smile. "You just git you a good grip on your saddle. Don't be feelin' sorry for me."

Schoonover shrugged. "Well then, I'll just say I hope the best horse wins," he said.

It was times like these when Larkes wished he wasn't so stubborn. Hell, he thought, Rocky Schoonover was right. Besides hurting all over, he surely couldn't see very well, especially on his left side where the eye was swollen shut. Underneath him, the gelding snorted and pawed the earth, ready for action. Larkes knew he was putting an unfair share of responsibility on the animal.

Normally, the race crowds were loud, with constant milling about. This morning, they were just as enthusiastic, but acted as if some long-awaited event was about to happen. The enthusiasm was of a quiet nature. Not much was being said as the crowd lined up from start to finish line.

There was something about the similarity in the two animals that made this race different. Both were magnificent animals. The sense of the moment was there, and everyone felt it.

Larkes and Schoonover guided their horses to the starting line, holding the spirited animals in check. Finally, Arky stepped forward, pulled his Colt and aimed it skyward. A hush fell over the crowd. All eyes were fixed on the two horses and their riders.

"On your mark, get set. . . ."

Slowly, his finger tightened on the trigger and squeezed.

Bang! The Colt jumped in Arky's hand and the big roan leaped forward ahead of the gelding.

Fine dust sprayed up into Larkes' face. His good eye, the right one, stung and burned. What vision he had turned blurry. Through the swirling dust, he could barely make out the roan's tail, like a flag flying in battle. He gave spur to the gelding, but the roan kept its distance.

At the quarter mark, the roan had put a length and a half on the gelding. Larkes was spitting dirt. He had given up trying to see. Every once in a while, he could make out a blur of the horse and rider ahead. He focused in on the sounds of the horses' hooves digging into the earth. He dug in harder with his spurs and gave the gelding its rein.

At the halfway mark, the lead had stretched to two lengths. Larkes envisioned Reasa's scolding face. She had warned him. Her words pierced through his heart, just like those of his mother, so many years ago when he'd gone against her warnings. He felt a familiar old guilt. Two hundred dollars was a lot of money, and he'd been foolish. He'd let his pride override his clear thinking. It wasn't that the big gelding wasn't a match for the roan. Larkes felt like he'd let the gelding down, too.

Feeling an almost hopeless desperation, he leaned down farther in the saddle, so close he could feel the horse's mane flying back and stinging him in the face. "Come on, boy," he said.

Then, at the three-quarter mark, something happened. Larkes heard a small rumbling noise escape from the gelding's mouth, then a tremendous surge of power rippled through the animal's body beneath him.

Ahead, the form of the roan appeared and took shape. In Larkes' mind, it was almost like the roan was being pulled backwards, toward him and the gelding. Then, he could see the roan's hindquarters, off to the left of the gelding's head. The roan was breathing hard. Larkes could hear it as they inched up alongside.

He had to turn his head completely sideways for his good right eye to see, but now the roan was leading by only a nose. Underneath him, the gelding's nostrils flared with indignity at the challenge the roan was offering.

Larkes blinked wildly, trying to see. The finish line was just feet away. Again, something happened to the gelding. Larkes couldn't understand, but he could feel a rifling of energy move through the horse, up through the saddle and into his own body. The thundering hooves pounded the earth and ate up the distance. In seconds, the gelding crossed the finish line, with the roan's head a half-length behind.

The crowd burst into life. Even the losers cheered the heroic efforts of the handsome white gelding. Arky jumped in the air and hollered like a schoolboy.

The gelding slowed to a trot and pranced sideways like a stallion would, its head bobbing up and down like some Austrian show horse. Larkes' body trembled from the excitement. Emotion swept through him. The gelding was surely the most magnificent horse he'd ever encountered, and Larkes felt grateful. He blinked a tear from his eye.

The gelding snorted to blow away the dust. Larkes grinned through his swollen face and reached down to rub the magnificent neck. He was in awe of the horse. His words were measured, but loving.

"Easy now. Good boy. Good horse."

Gently, he turned the gelding northward. "You see over yonder?" he said softly. "That there's the Cherokee Strip. Every man and every horse in it's gonna know about you. I'm gonna see to it that you get the finest care. We're gonna race all these new sodbusters, and we're gonna beat 'em. You 'n me."

Rocky Schoonover rode over, looking like he'd had the finest time. "Woooweee, compadre! That sumbitchin' gelding is some kinda horseflesh! I woulda never believed it!" he exclaimed. "Hot damn!" He shook his head and grinned. "And I thought this here roan was unbeatable."

Larkes grinned and nodded. "Your roan is fast, all right."

As they rode slowly back, Schoonover rolled a cigarette and offered it to Larkes. "Here, have a smoke."

Larkes wasn't a smoker, but he took one anyway out of friendship.

"Compadre, we oughta make that run together," Schoonover said. "What kinda horse has that Arky feller got?"

"Got a mare with a little speed, but she's mostly a cow horse," Larkes said.

Schoonover finished rolling another smoke. He lit up and shook his head again. "I still can't get over it. Damn, compadre! You wanna sell me that horse? I'll give you your two hundred and throw in an extra hundred and this here roan."

Larkes took a pull on the smoke and had to suppress a cough. His eye was watering again. "You may have big pockets," he said, "but there ain't enough money in the Outlet to touch this here horse. No, sir. I guess I've looked most of my life for such a horse. He ain't for sale."

"Didn't really reckon he would be." Schoonover smiled good-naturedly.

Larkes was still feeling the euphoria of the horse race as the group headed to the filing booth north of Hennessey. Rocky Schoonover rode with them.

There were even more people than Larkes remembered seeing the day before. As far as the naked eye could see, there was humanity everywhere. Some folks kept to themselves. Others sat around in groups. Some played cards. Others were trying to trade up for a better mode of transportation. Lots of folks were still in need of water, but by now the supplies had decreased and the cost had inflated out of reason. Soldiers milled about, stopping several fist fights as patience began to wear.

The group made camp off by themselves. Excitement ran through everyone.

That night at supper, Helena Frey overlooked the unrelenting heat and made a campfire. She made cornbread to go with the salt pork and fried potatoes. They all ate heartily.

They had no more than finished their last bite, when Reasa, who sat with her nose inside one of her newspapers, called out.

"My Lord, Larkes!" she exclaimed. "Listen here! Says in this July Guthrie newspaper that Henry Starr was arrested in Colorado Springs, Colorado."

"You don't say?" Larkes said, shaking his head sadly.

"My, my," Reasa mumbled as she read on. "Says they arrested Henry and his girlfriend, May Morrision, along with another man name of John Wilson. My, my," she repeated. "Says here that Henry's only nineteen. I thought he was older."

"What'd he do?" Larkes asked.

"Says they charged him with murderin' some man named Floyd Wilson."

"Why are you all so concerned? Do you know Starr?" Schoonover asked.

"We run across 'im a ways back, over in the eastern part of the Territory," Larkes said. "Seemed like a likeable sort."

"Oh, Starr's liked, all right." Schoonover smiled. "Everybody but the law likes 'im. But, that there's old news, Reasa. That's the July paper." He went on. "Why, I've heard ol' Judge Parker sentenced 'im to hang.

But shucks"—he looked at Larkes—"anybody that knows about Henry Starr can tell ya they'll never get a rope around his neck. That boy's slick as a greased pig."

Reasa seemed shaken by the news. She got up and took Noah to the rear of one of the wagons and sat down quietly.

Back at the campfire, Schoonover told stories he'd heard about Henry Starr. Even at nineteen, Starr had a sizeable reputation. Enough of one, Schoonover said, that he was the main talk of any saloon in the Territory.

It was nearly dark when Larkes got up in the middle of one of Schoonover's stories and walked toward the crowd of people near the filing booth.

"Where's Larkes off to?" Arky asked no one in particular.

Reasa, who had rejoined the group, stared off. "Oh, I reckon he's gotta be off by himself, even if it's amongst all them folks." There was a sadness to her voice and a deep look of worry. The others noticed, but didn't say anything.

About an hour later, Larkes returned with a man in a suit carrying a Bible.

He introduced the man. "This here's Pastor Schaeffer. He's a Lutheran minister from Missouri. Said he'll perform the weddin' ceremony."

Reasa's eyes lit up. A smile stretched from ear to ear, taking over her entire face. She flung her arms around Larkes' neck. His body stiffened, and he made a face.

"You just stop," she scolded. "Allow me to be happy just once." She let go of Larkes and held out her hand to the pastor. "I'm Reasa Peters," she said. "You say you're a Lutheran? I was raised a Baptist, but I guess it don't matter."

"I can assure you that God is nondenominational," Pastor Schaeffer said.

"Oh, I wasn't sayin' otherwise," Reasa said. She motioned toward the campfire. "Please, have a seat. Could I get you some coffee?"

"No, thank you. It's a bit too warm for coffee," the pastor said. "But I would prefer to sit down while we discuss the wedding arrangements."

"Of course." Reasa took Pastor Schaeffer by the arm and, talking excitedly, led him to a blanket. She sat down next to him and motioned for Larkes to join them.

The rest of the group politely moved away to give them privacy.

Alma was thinking about asking Toby Ray to take a walk with her, when Arky appeared and grabbed her by the wrist. "We need to talk," he said solemnly. Curious, Alma let him pull her to the rear of a wagon.

"Look here, I need to know," Arky said, peering down at her intently. There was an urgency in his voice. "What are you and Toby Ray gonna do?"

Alma studied Arky's face. Shadows from the fire bounced across his handsome features. His eyes glistened and searched her face nervously. Alma let her fingers slide down his arm, past his wrist, to where she was holding his hand. She shrugged, "I guess we're takin' that train to Kansas."

"Kansas?" Arky said, his voice rising. "And then where? To some relatives you haven't seen in years? Now, I don't mean to be nosy, Alma, but Toby Ray told me he can't even remember these people. Why, you don't even know for sure if they're alive!"

The truth of his words wasn't lost on Alma. She'd had the same troublesome thoughts eating away at her insides for weeks. But there really wasn't any other choice to be made. "Well, I reckon you're right about that, but I don't guess we have any choice in the matter. We'll just have to make do," she said simply. She frowned at his worried expression. "What about yourself? Still plannin' on goin' down to Texas, or are you gonna make the run? Seems to me like you got two pretty good options."

Arky didn't seem to see it that way. He said, "Shucks, Alma. This whole thing is all kinda queer. Why, I never welched on a job in my life, and I told that man I'd be there to work for him. But now this dang run has got me all excited." He paused a moment. "I guess if I did make the run, I'd have a place to bring my ma out here to live."

The idea wasn't quite the one that Alma had been hoping to hear, but she had to admire him for it, nonetheless. "Your ma? Well that's sweet," she said.

"I don't know about sweet, but sometimes I miss her. I'd sure like to give her a better life. I was thinkin' that maybe this here Cherokee Outlet would be a good place for ma to live out the rest of her life. She's a fine woman, Alma. A lot like you. I bet you'd like her. I know she'd like you."

Alma stood there, watching his fine features. She knew he was struggling to make his speech. Patiently, she waited for him to go on, but he just stood there instead, like some big puppy dog, with his head crooked to one side, biting his lip.

After a lengthy bit of silence, she finally said, "Well, I'm sure I'd like your mother just fine, Arky. I bet Toby Ray would, too."

He nodded weakly and bit his lip some more. He was breathing heavily, and Alma noticed his hand was starting to sweat. After another bout of silence, she looked up at him hopefully.

"Is that all you wanted to tell me, Arky?"

He opened his mouth to speak, but she turned her head away and looked toward the camp. "Isn't it wonderful about Reasa and Larkes?" she said. "You realize, they're as different as night and day. But they'll be good for each other. It'll be wonderful for Noah to have a daddy. Don't you think?"

"Huh? Yeah . . . that'd be great," Arky said. He stepped between Alma and the camp to stop her from walking away. "Alma," he blurted out, "there's no use in your beatin' around the bush. We've all sort of become like family here. Why, even ol' Frau Frey has warmed up!"

"What are you gettin' at?" Alma asked. She tilted her face up to give him an innocent look.

Arky's eyes widened. "What I'm sayin' is you need to stay right here in the Cherokee Outlet. You 'n Toby

Ray need to be a part of this thing. It's only natural and right."

"I 'spect you're right," Alma agreed. She sighed. "But, Reasa told me she don't reckon they'd allow me to be the head of a family. So, I've had to stop even thinkin' about the possibility. I don't qualify, and that's that." She shrugged. "We better go back to the others, before they wonder what we're doin'."

Disappointment was heavy in Alma's heart. She dropped Arky's hand and turned away to leave him.

But Arky's words stopped her. "Hang the others," he said sharply. "Let 'em think what they wanna think. Look, Alma," he said, his face shiny with sweat. He took in a deep breath. "I'm askin' you to marry me."

Alma was stunned. She had suspected that Arky might be leading up to a proposal, but it still came as a surprise to hear him say the words. "Y-you don't have to feel sorry for me 'n Toby Ray, Arky," she said in a weak voice. "I do appreciate your thinkin' of us, but please don't feel like you have to be responsible for what happens to us. You go on and make the run. Move your mother out here. You've got enough to take care of already, without me 'n Toby Ray."

"But, I wouldn't want to move ma out here without you, Alma."

Alma reached down and took both of Arky's hands. She pulled them to her chest and held them tight. "I understand what you're doin'," she said, "and I think it's the most noble thing I ever heard. But, you shouldn't get married for the wrong reasons."

Alma was breaking her heart with her own words. But she knew she was doing the right thing. She'd put Toby Ray through enough hurt to last his entire life. An ill-fated marriage wouldn't be fair to him any more than to her and Arky. It was better, she decided, to let Arky know right away that she didn't expect anything from him. Gazing up at Arky, she waited for the look of relief to cross his face.

Instead of relieved, though, Arky seemed almost irritated. His voice jumped up an octave. "Why shucks!" he said. "I wasn't askin' you out of anything noble! I was askin' you 'cause . . . I want you to be my wife, 'cause . . . Lookee here, Alma! I love you!"

Alma's legs turned weak. Her face flushed as a funny sensation ran through her, tickling her insides. "You do?"

Arky had that puppy-dog look on his face again. "What about you, Alma?" he asked. "Do you like me?"

Alma was nearly as surprised as Arky when she suddenly stretched up on her tiptoes and gave him a peck on the lips.

"I reckon I've loved you since the first day I saw you," she said breathlessly. "In fact, I reckon I love you so much I couldn't bear to see you sacrifice your life and happiness for me. If it'd been anybody else askin', I might have said yes right away, just to have a home for Toby Ray. But I couldn't do that to you. I couldn't stand to make you feel tied down or obligated unless you really wanted to get married."

"Obligated and tied down?" Arky shook his head. "Look, Alma. Even if there was no land run or anything— even if we was out in the middle of the ocean—I'd want to marry you. Anywhere."

Alma threw her arms around his neck and they kissed. Alma felt her nerves tingle on her arms and neck. She'd never kissed a man before, but kissing Arky felt as natural as taking a drink of water when one was thirsty.

They were both like two starving people who had found a bountiful feast in each other. They clung to one another, both finding the answer to a long-awaited dream.

All of the past year—the Uncle Teds, the George Tubbs, the miles of walking, the hunger and desperation—became a distant fading dream. From somewhere in the depths of her memory, Alma recalled the story of Romeo and Juliet. As a young girl, she had always longed for such a wonderful story to be true. She had played a little game with herself, in which she was Juliet, romancing a dashing but faceless Romeo. Now, her childhood dream had come true. She did, indeed, have a true Romeo. His name was Arky.

42

ON THE EVENING OF SUNDAY, SEPTEMBER 10, 1893, Pastor Schaeffer performed a double wedding ceremony. Larkes Dixon and Reasa Peters, Arky Smith and Alma White were joined in the bonds of holy matrimony. The couples stood before the minister in the soft light of the campfire, with lanterns hung from posts on either side. Rocky Schoonover served as Larkes' best man while Reinhart Frey stood up for Arky. Helena Frey served as bridesmaid to both Alma and Reasa. To everyone's surprise, the large, mannish woman broke down and cried like a baby when the couple repeated their vows and said their "I dos."

Helena had pulled out her trunk and offered Reasa the use of her own wedding veil. For Alma, she gathered up wildflowers and fashioned a sort of crown for her hair.

Reinhart walked up to Arky and extended his hand. He was holding one hundred dollars.

"Please," he said. "You take."

Arky protested. "But, I didn't earn it. We only agreed on that money if'n I took you all the way to Kansas."

Reinhart pushed the money into Arky's hand.

"Well, at least take half the money back," Arky said.

Reinhart refused. "Is gift, then," he said. He looked at Arky with the same affection that a father would show a son.

Alma stepped up to the men and said, "If you'll not take back half the money, then take the sorrel Keith gave me. Toby Ray's still got Roy's horse, Chocolate."

Reinhart looked overwhelmed. "Vat do I need vith new horse?" he asked, smiling broadly.

"Alma's right," Arky said. "You'll need it to make the run. It's got a smooth gait, and it's faster'n a jackrabbit. Wagons are too slow, and there ain't a horse among that team of yours that could go much distance at a run."

"I have seen many people vith mules," Reinhart said, "und others vith no horse at all."

"You're missin' the point," Arky said. "To git the land you want, you gotta beat everyone else to it. That takes a good, fast horse."

Helena, who was still teary-eyed, wiped her face on her sleeve. "Ach, they are right, Reinhart." She sniffed. "Take der horse." She smiled warmly at Alma and Arky.

Nodding, Reinhart said, "Ve trade, then." He handed Arky the two hundred dollars and received possession of Alma's horse.

"Now that you got good horse flesh, how are you at ridin'?" Arky asked.

Reinhart shrugged. "Goot, I guess."

"Good, you guess? Tomorrow, I'd better take you out and show you how to ride a horse properly," Arky offered.

Reinhart and Helena both nodded and smiled at each other.

The rest of that night was spent making plans. The men decided they would all get up before daylight and take their places in line. That day it had been announced that the clerks would pass out numbers to everyone. That way, they wouldn't have to stand there all day to wait their turns to register. It was estimated that nearly ten thousand people had gathered at booth number three, north of Hennessey.

As they sat around and listened to more of Rocky Schoonover's stories, Helena slipped away from the group for a moment. When she returned, she firmly announced that the two wagons had been cleared for the newlyweds. The children, she stated, would sleep on the ground along with herself and Reinhart. Larkes and Reasa would share one wagon, while Arky and Alma would take the other. Everyone looked at Reinhart, wondering what his reaction would be to such a development. Reinhart only smiled and vigorously nodded his head.

Reasa ran to Helena and threw her arms around her. "That's so sweet and kind of you," she said.

Helena laughed happily. "Und ve vatch Noah, too." She gave a knowing nod to Reasa.

Larkes took the news without so much as a change in expression. Arky, however, had turned crimson. Embarrassed, he avoided looking anyone in the eye.

Alma was just as uncomfortable. She was sure everyone was looking at her.

In a jovial mood, Helena ushered everyone to their places. Soon, all the children were bedded down with Noah nestled among them. Beside his wife, Reinhart good-naturedly rolled himself up in a blanket and ordered the children to quiet down and get to sleep. Reasa gave a nod to Larkes and they disappeared inside their wagon.

Arky and Alma were left, sitting there by the fire. They may have sat there all night, too nervous to move, if Helena hadn't gotten up and tossed a rock at them.

"I vill chase you like scared mouse, if you don't get into vagon," she called out. She and Reinhart talked and laughed softly between themselves.

Quickly, Arky grabbed Alma's hand, and they climbed into the wagon.

That night, for the first time in months, the wind turned and started blowing from the north. The hot night was quickly turned chilly. By four o'clock in the morning, Alma was so cold she shook herself awake.

Her eyes opened and she had to remember where she was. Arky's face was just above hers. She was lying with her head on his shoulder, with her arm thrown across his chest. Her naked shoulders were cold, but the part of her that touched his body felt warm. She must be dreaming, she thought. Arky felt like a treasure, a gift she had inherited, lying there next to her, loving her.

But where had this cold come from? she wondered. The weather had been hot for so long. Things were all out of place.

"We need blankets," she mumbled. "It's cold."

Arky didn't respond. Sighing, Alma huddled closer to his warmth and closed her eyes.

They both awoke just as the sky was turning an orange hue in the east. Outside the wagon, a big fire burned, its flames whipping high in the wind. Helena Frey, bundled up in a blanket, already had breakfast going. Rocky Schoonover was the first to greet Alma and Arky.

"Don't you just love it?" he said, grimacing at them over his coffee cup. "Hot one day and cold the next. Took me a couple of years to get used to the weather out here on the plains."

Arky hugged Alma and sat her down close to the fire. He whispered in her ear, "I'm gonna buy you the finest coat money can buy. I don't ever want you to be cold or unhappy again."

Alma kissed him on the lips. Tears formed in her eyes. Before she could answer, he jumped up to fetch her a cup of coffee.

The entire group was up early that day, wakened easily by the sudden frigid temperature. The line at the booth stretched as far as the eye could see. Accustomed to the severe heat, most found it hard to acclimate to the cold. People were bundled into anything they could find. Those who had ridden on horseback had brought very few personal items, and some were nearly freezing.

The commodity in demand was no longer water. Now, the bill of fare was any kind of clothing or blankets. There was complaining and ill-tempered bickering all throughout the crowd. Fights broke out up and down the long line. The soldiers would no sooner break up one skirmish, then have to race to another.

The men had been standing in line for nearly three hours. Conversation had thinned. Even Rocky Schoonover had tired of his enthusiasm and was quiet in his own thoughts, when a familiar voice called out from behind.

"Hey, nigger boy! I thought we run your ass out of this country."

Larkes turned. His jawbone twitched. Deputy Frank stood not ten feet away. Besides the original five companions, two other men had joined him. They stood in a row, each with his hand poised by his sidearm.

Arky said, "These the sumbitches you and Reinhart ran into Saturday?"

One of the men with Deputy Frank snarled at Arky. "Nobody calls me a son of a bitch and lives," he said.

Anger welled up on Arky's face. "I reckon I just did," he said, his eyes fixed on the menacing man.

Rocky Schoonover quickly looked over the situation. Careful not to make any sudden moves, he said to Deputy Frank, "Only two of us is armed. There's eight of you. Why don't you all go on? Git out of here 'n leave us alone."

"You can go on, yourself. It's the nigger boy we want." Deputy Frank smiled out the side of his mouth. "Step on out here, nigger boy."

Schoonover stepped in front of Larkes. His deep voice had a concerned edge to it. "Let it lie, compadre," he said to Larkes. "The numbers ain't with us. Why, we can take care of this fat ol' sumbitch at a later time."

But Larkes had had enough of Deputy Frank. There was no longer any reasoning to be done. "Move out of the way, Rocky," he said. "If trouble is what he's wantin', then trouble's what he's gettin'."

Schoonover held his ground. "Now listen, compadre! There's eight of 'em. You don't have a chance. Not even a hope!" He leaned closer to Larkes. "Now I'll admit, I like a good fight as well as anybody. But I'm tellin' you, this is no good." Turning to Deputy Frank, he said, "Lookee here, mister. I don't know what this is all about, but there's surely gonna be a better time and place. If you're lookin' for trouble, I guarantee we'll oblige ya, but not now." He held up his hands.

Deputy Frank pulled his pistol and thumb-cocked it. "Just get your ass outta the way," he said. "I'm dealin' with the nigger boy. Move, I tell ya." His jaw shook with anger. "Or I'll put a bullet in you and then kill the nigger boy."

Larkes unlatched his Colt. He felt sure he could pull leather and put a bullet in Deputy Frank, but then his gaze fell on the other men. He tried to figure who'd be second and who'd be third. To his left, Arky had stepped out to face the eight men. Schoonover and Reinhart moved off to stand on the right.

A hush had fallen over the crowd as they backed away and formed a large circle around the men who faced one another. Whisperings could be heard, along with the sounds of guns being readied.

Just then, a voice called out from the circle of humanity that surrounded them.

"You! You there, fat man!"

It was the banker from Tennessee who had challenged Larkes and the gelding back at the depot. He had moved to not twenty feet away from Deputy Frank.

Deputy Frank turned and eyed the double-barreled shotgun that lay in the banker's hands. It was trained directly on his big stomach.

"See here, now. This ain't your fight, neither. This is between me 'n the nigger boy," Deputy Frank spat out. He was clearly growing agitated.

The banker was unmoved. In a firm voice, he said with authority, "We don't want your kind around here." He glanced at Deputy Frank's drawn pistol. "Now, holster that sidearm before I splatter you all over the Strip."

Encouraged by the banker's stand, the crowd came to life. Off to the left, another man hollered, "Get on outta here, right now! We didn't come out here to settle this land amongst the likes of you!"

Another man dressed in overalls stepped forward, holding a single-shot squirrel rifle. He said, "I brought my family three hundred miles from Missouri. We're gonna have good schools and churches here, not gunfights and killin's."

More men stepped forward. The crowd became a murmur of voices, all directed at Deputy Frank and his men.

Deputy Frank stood there with a look of disbelief. His mouth dropped open. He held out a hand to the crowd. "B-b-but you all don't understand!" he said. "This nigger boy shot up my leg! I'm just aimin' to get even, is all! Besides"—he looked pleadingly—"do you realize what's gonna happen if ya let *niggers* settle in here?"

The banker's eyes turned steely and cold. "I don't know nothin' about your leg, fat man. I wasn't there to see it. But I'd be right proud to have Larkes Dixon as a neighbor." He raised his shotgun higher. "Now, I'm through talkin'. I'm tellin' you one last time to mount up and take your other trash with you. Get out of here."

The members of the crowd repeated the threat. Several stepped toward Deputy Frank and his men, holding shotguns and pistols. A few had picked up wooden clubs and were waving them in the air.

Schoonover said, "Looks to me like we've done taken a vote, and you lost, compadre."

Deputy Frank stared at Schoonover, then at Larkes. Slowly, he holstered his Colt. He motioned for his companions to do the same. Before he turned to leave, his eyes found Larkes'.

"You ain't heard the last of me, nigger boy."

The crowd opened up to let him through. Deputy Frank and his companions left.

As Larkes watched them depart, his seething anger gave way to amazement at what he had just witnessed from the crowd. He surveyed the throng of people around him. It was more than he could fathom. There they all were, all together. Farmers, bankers, destitutes, rough-looking men, soft men, men whose hands were more adept at dealing cards than plowing land, old men, young men, men in the middle. The most astonishing thing, though, was that they were all white. Every last one of them. Somehow, without any prewarning, they had all come together. For him. A knot welled up in Larkes' throat.

The banker, who had watched until the last sign of Deputy Frank slipped out of sight, stepped up to Larkes. "I'm real sorry this happened to you," he said. "I just couldn't stand by and watch that feller harassin' you like that. Even if you did take my money with that gelding of yours. At least you took it by honest means."

Larkes nodded, and they shook hands. "I'm sorry, but I don't recall your name."

"J. B. Jennings, from Tennessee. And you're Larkes Dixon," the banker said. "It's a pleasure to meet ya. I don't know what gets into men like that fat man, but we'll not have his sort living in the Strip, I can promise ya. I've seen enough of his kind. Why, when I was a young man, growin' up, it was a constant, day-to-day struggle to rid our town of the like. No, sir." He shook his head. "We'll stop the poison before it starts seeping into our lives, takin' advantage of the opportunity that's offered here."

Larkes didn't know how to answer such a speech. "Well, I'm much obliged to ya, just the same," he said.

Jennings slapped him heartily on the back and said he reckoned Larkes would've done the same for him.

Others in the crowd came up and spoke their support to Larkes. Some carried a genuine warmth in their eyes, while a few just shook his hand without looking at him. Larkes had seen that reaction before. There were folks who believed in right and wrong on the outside, but still held to a feeling of betterment on the inside, because of their unchosen skin color. This morning, he shook off the sad feeling it usually gave him. These were his new neighbors. He felt grateful to them, and that was that.

By mid-morning, the unexpected cold snap was taking its toll. Some folks were already showing signs of sickness from it. The soldiers did their best to keep order and issued a few blankets in their supply to families with smaller children.

The clerks at the registration booth offered relief by handing out numbers. Instead of having to stand in line, the settlers could wait their turn in a more comfortable situation.

When Larkes reached out and took his number, something changed inside him. For the first time, he caught the sense of excitement that flowed through the other men and women whose futures depended on the upcoming race. He was a little puzzled by the feeling. In his life, success had been found by doing business and making lots of money. To settle down and live in one place for any length of time had never occurred to him. He supposed he hadn't ever really intended to stay on his claim, if he got one. Until now.

He thought about Colorado. He would have been happy there, he knew. He thought about a lot of things he was giving up in life. He tried to remember how much they had meant to him. Nothing, though, could change the simple fact that something was stirring up inside him. This was a new challenge, and he'd always enjoyed a challenge.

Before he turned back to the wagons, he stopped and took a long look northward, toward the Cherokee Outlet. Maybe Reasa was right, he thought. Maybe she'd been right all along. He looked down at the little numbered tag. He squeezed it tightly in his hand as his gaze lifted again to the north.

Maybe this *was* the promised land.

43

ALMA AND ARKY WERE HAVING A DISCUSSION ABOUT Reinhart's ill attempts at learning to ride a horse, when Toby Ray ran up and jumped between them. He was wide-eyed and trying to catch his breath.

"Quick," he said, "tell me. What day is the run?"

"Toby Ray, quit that runnin'! Remember what the doctor said about takin' it easy," Alma said, ignoring his question.

Toby Ray shook impatiently. "I'm okay. Just tell me what day's the run?"

"You been asleep, boy?" Arky laughed. "It's Saturday. Everybody knows that."

"No, no! I mean what *date* is it? What day of the month?"

Reasa, who had become the group's expert and main spokesman on the run, said, "Why, baby, it's on the sixteenth, September the sixteenth, 1893, at twelve noon. You should always remember that," she added.

"That's what I thought!" Toby Ray said. "It's the same day as Alma's birthday!" He hopped up and ran off to share the news with the Frey children.

Arky looked wounded that Alma hadn't shared such a personal fact with her new husband. "Why didn't you tell me?" he said.

Alma shrugged. "Nothin' to get excited about, I guess. After all, everybody has a birthday."

"Well, maybe it ain't excitin' for you," Reasa said. She moved close to Alma and draped her arms around Alma's shoulders. "Let me hug you, child. Why, this is a wonderful omen! My Lord, do you all know what this means?" She looked around at everyone. "We're all gonna be prosperous in this new promised land! Mercy sakes, the Lord sent us an omen." She looked skyward. "Thankee, Jesus."

The rest of the group didn't know whether they should thank the Lord for the omen, too, or if they should just ignore Reasa's ravings. They looked at Larkes, who appeared cross.

He said, "Why don't you sit down and stop all this nonsense about omens and such?"

"You mind yourself, you hear?" Reasa said. "Don't be talkin' sassy talk when the Lord done sent us an omen! Be thankful."

"Omen, my foot! Sometimes, woman, I just don't understand where you get your idees." Larkes turned and left her sitting there in an uncomfortable silence. Love surely did bring a lot of baggage with it, he thought to himself. But he might just as well get used to carrying it.

That evening at a couple hours before sundown, Arky and Schoonover saddled up their horses. Without saying a word to anyone, they rode off toward the south.

Larkes watched them go. Whiskey, he thought. They were going back to Hennessey to buy more whiskey. But, as he continued to watch, he noticed they changed their course. About three hundred yards from camp, they turned their horses to the west. Larkes tried to guess what they were up to. It was curious, but he figured it wasn't any of his business.

That night, he and Reasa made up their bedroll as far away from the group as they could. Reasa commented more than once that Helena was a lucky woman, to have a nice wagon to sleep in each night. They waited until the rest of the group was asleep before they turned in, themselves.

Larkes had no more crawled inside the bedroll, when Reasa reached over and took him by the arm. Holding it tightly against her chest, she whispered in his ear. "Do you love me?"

"W-what kind of question is that?"

"What do you mean, what kind of question is that? I just asked if you love me!"

"I married ya."

Reasa tugged on his arm. "That ain't what I asked. Do you love me?"

Larkes thought about trying to turn over and feign sleep, but he knew that would be a lost cause. He sighed. "I reckon I do."

Reasa's voice sounded hurt. "Is that all you can say?" she said. "You just *reckon* you do? Can't you even form the words on your lips? I love you?"

"I reckon I could."

"Well?"

"I love you, woman." Larkes suddenly reached out and pulled her body close to his. His hand grasped hold of her buttocks.

Reasa squirmed away. "For cryin' out loud! I'm bein' serious here. Is that all you can think about?"

Larkes couldn't make any sense of this conversation. To him, his feelings for Reasa were obvious. "You're losin' your mind. That's it, ain't it?"

"Can't I ask ya a simple question without stirrin' up your manhood?" Reasa said.

Larkes let out a sigh. He released her buttocks and started to turn away, but Reasa put her hand on his face and turned it back, close to hers. She kissed his lips and whispered, "Be patient; there'll be time for that in a little bit."

Marriage was going to take getting used to, Larkes thought to himself. He had never pretended to understand women. Even if he *had* ever mastered the task, he doubted if he could understand Reasa. She was altogether a different sort of female. One minute she could make him angrier than any human being on earth, and the next she'd be flashing those eyes or putting a little wiggle in her walk and driving him crazy.

Her finger found his lips and rubbed them ever so gently. Larkes felt the familiar sensation growing down below.

"Baby," she murmured, "sometimes we fuss a lot, but I want you to know how much I love you. And though you don't say it, I think you love me, too. Larkes, honey, I want to have another baby." She paused a minute, but when Larkes didn't answer, she hurried on. "It's not good for Noah to be raised all by himself. I know you're of the opinion I spoil him rotten. Well, that's because he's all I've ever had. Until you. So, when we get settled in, I think it's important to have a baby." She kissed him gently to punctuate her point.

Larkes didn't know what to say. He wasn't displeased with the idea of another baby, but it came as a surprise to him. He'd never thought about the subject. Suddenly, the idea of making babies sounded very appealing. Larkes felt his manhood stirring again. He reached for her. Their kisses turned to passion, and this time she didn't deny him.

Later, Larkes was just about to drift into a nice, relaxed sleep, when he heard Arky calling him in a loud whisper.

"Are you awake, Hoss?"

Larkes groaned as he sat up and squinted at Arky. He and Reasa were so far from the campfire, he couldn't see much more than Arky's form. "Barely. What's the problem?"

"Shoot, ain't no problem. Rocky and I done been over in the Strip."

"That's a good way to get your butt shot off," Larkes commented. "Heard they shot a man yesterday. Did anybody see ya?"

"You know, that's funny, compadre," Schoonover said. "Couple of men started followin' us, but we lost 'em. I thought I saw 'em again later over by Skeleton station, but they weren't soldier boys. That much I know."

"The Strip?" Reasa sat up. "You been to the Strip? Tell me about it."

Arky and Schoonover sat down. Arky said, "We rode all the way to that place I was tellin' you about. The one west of Skeleton station. It's just like I remember it, Hoss. Good rollin' land, with trees."

"Trees?" Reasa exclaimed loudly. "Ain't no trees around here! You sure you went in the right direction?"

"Woman, would you mind yourself?" Larkes said. It embarrassed him that Reasa would be so insulting to Arky. "What do you think you're doin', callin' the man a liar?"

Reasa disregarded Larkes' scolding. "Are you sure there's trees?" she said. "Why, we wouldn't want trees anyway. We'd have to clear them out if we're gonna raise wheat."

"Who said anything about wheat?" Larkes said, hoping Reasa could hear the warning tone in his voice. "Listen here, now. You best get used to this idea right now. The three of us, Rocky, Arky and me, done decided to go into business together. We're gonna raise racehorses. Gonna run a few cows, too."

"What do you know about raisin' horses? Just because you fell into that gelding, you think you know somethin' about 'em?"

"I didn't fall into 'im," Larkes said through clenched teeth. "I bought 'im." He turned away from her, hoping to avoid a full-scale fight in front of witnesses. "So, you two done seen the land?"

"That's right, Hoss. Found a whole section that'd be perfect. Looks like it's about four or five miles northwest of the Skeleton station," Arky said.

"My Lord! What kind of name is Skeleton station?" Reasa grimaced.

"Aw, shoot," Arky said. "That's what it used to be called. Some railroad man didn't like it, so he changed the name to 'Enid'. It's gonna be hard for me to get used to. It's always been Skeleton to me."

"Well, I can't blame that railroad man," Reasa said. "Skeleton ain't a decent name to be raisin' babies in."

Larkes was getting worried that Reasa was going to start discussing having babies again, so he asked Arky to go on about the land.

"Anyways," Arky went on, "the two south quarters have lots of trees on 'em. On the northeast quarter, the trees thin out somewhat. Then the northwest quarter doesn't have any trees at all. Now, the way I was figurin', Reinhart is a farmer. That's all he talks about. The northwest quarter would be perfect for him to raise wheat on. If you ain't so fond of trees," he said, glancing at Reasa, "you two could maybe take the northeast quarter. That way, there'd be a few trees for Larkes and, well, maybe you could grow somethin', too, if you've a mind to. . . ." His voice trailed off. "Then, me and Rocky could take the other two quarters. But, it's whatever you want, Hoss." He looked at Larkes. "After all, you got the fastest horse."

"I don't know. I'd have to do some thinkin'. How far you reckon it is?" Larkes asked.

Schoonover said, "We guessed a little over twenty miles. Give or take a mile or two. We got so busy, we stopped countin' sections."

"That's a long ways. You never know what a horse is gonna do. Not that I doubt the gelding's ability any. But, what's the likelihood of all four of us makin' it?" Larkes grimaced. "I admit it sounds good, but I just don't know if we can do it."

"Shoot, you're just worryin' about Reinhart. Fact is, I'm worried about 'im, too," Arky said. "What in the world are we gonna do about him?"

"Yeah, compadre," Schoonover agreed. "It'll take some kinda miracle for Reinhart to cover that distance and stay out in front of everybody. I'm afraid he's gonna have to settle for some place close by, and that's might iffy."

Reasa spoke up again. "Well, the Freys have been mighty kind to all of us. Shared their food and friendship. Took little Noah in like one o' their own. Personally, I ain't about to leave 'em out in the cold."

"Ain't nobody said nothin' about leavin' 'em out in the cold!" Larkes snapped. "Rocky's right, is all. Reinhart may have to take the first claim he comes to. My Lord! We're talkin' about free land, and *all* this land looks good 'n fertile."

"I don't care," Reasa said. "I've got a mind to get a claim right next to them. You all are sittin' here discussin' a bunch o' trees! I'd rather Noah have play-mates! Neighbors to stop in for coffee and such."

Larkes stared hard at her. He knew he stood a chance of regretting the conversation, but he couldn't stop himself from at least trying to put Reasa in her place. "Lookee here now, woman. I hope as much as you do that the Freys get a claim. But if we go foolin' around about it, we could *all* end up without any land, at all. I've heard rumors that there's close to a hundred thousand people scattered about, ready to make a run on less'n half that number of claims. Instead of worryin' about such trivial things as who your neighbor's gonna be, we best be worryin' about gettin' any land at all."

Through the dark, they glared at one another. Reasa jerked on her blanket and lay back down. "If you all don't mind, I need to get some sleep," she announced. She turned her back on them.

Trying to hide the anger that was gnawing at his insides, Larkes stood up. "Come on, we can talk over yonder," he said to the men. "Best leave the women to their womanly things, like sleepin' and raisin' babies," he said sarcastically, aiming his words at Reasa's back.

44

THE MORNING OF FRIDAY THE FIFTEENTH WAS WINDY and hot. Monday's little cold spell had been short-lived and only served the purpose of making the miserable even more miserable. The wind still blew so hard, any attempts at building a fire would result in sparks flying. Grass fires were commonplace. But, with the long-awaited day just about to arrive, it was hard to dampen the spirits of the group.

Reasa was nearly hysterical with excitement. The days were too slow in passing, to her. She literally counted the hours until the race would begin.

Reinhart was spending nearly every waking moment practicing on the sorrel horse Alma had traded him. When he wasn't on the horse's back, he was asking advice from Arky and Schoonover. They obliged him, but worried to each other that it was a mostly futile endeavor. The man just wasn't capable of holding a good ride in the saddle. It was a wonder he hadn't broken a bone or two, as many times as he got dumped. Though he wasn't a large man, Reinhart was nonetheless sturdily built. He'd take a spill, then get up with a smile, brush off the dust and remount.

This morning, Alma and Arky headed off by themselves to Hennessey three miles to the south to pick up some supplies. The group had finalized their plans for the race and figured they had it all down to a science. It

would take all day, they figured, before the riders could
stake their claims and find the others. They would pick
up crackers and bologna for the men to take with them
to eat. By the time the wagons could roll into the town,
and the riders returned, they could all rendezvous at the
Government Springs Well that evening.

Hennessey was crowded with people. This was amaz-
ing to Alma, since she'd already seen more people at
the registration booth than she had ever seen in her life
at one time. Where did so many folks come from? she
wondered.

It was obvious they were all there for the same reason.
There were long lines of people, waiting to pick up last-
minute supplies. The lines stretched out the doors of the
stores as folks waited their turn to get inside. Outside,
there were vendors hawking sandwiches, drinking water,
seed, breakout plows, lemonade, melons, horses, blankets
and trinkets for the children. It reminded Alma of the
circus that had come to Fort Smith once. She and Toby
Ray had talked their papa into taking them. The crowd
had been loud and full of laughter. This crowd was loud
and full of excited chatter.

It was a couple of hours before they made all their
purchases. They bought coffee, bacon, potatoes, bologna,
turnips, crackers and two melons. Then Arky excused
himself from Alma and disappeared. Alma sat on her
horse and waited for so long, she started to wonder
if he'd gotten himself into some kind of trouble. She
was just about to dismount and go looking for him,
when he reappeared, carrying a package wrapped in
brown paper.

"Here." He grinned, handing it to her.

"What's this?"

"Open it."

Alma untied the string and parted the paper. Inside
was a blue dress with ivory white lace. There was a
bonnet that matched.

"Oh, Arky!" Alma breathed.

Arky nervously pawed the ground with his foot. "It's
your weddin' present," he said. "And here's somethin'

for Toby Ray." He pulled a slingshot from his pocket and handed it to her. "Man sold it to me for twenty-five cents. I coulda made him a good one, myself, if I had a good piece of wood."

Alma wanted to cry, but she knew that would embarrass Arky even worse. Her heart filled with passion for him. She noticed the pride on Arky's face. He was really happy. She had worried with the lingering thought that he'd married her just to get her out of a bad situation. There was nothing in the world she wanted more than for him to be pleased with their marriage. Now, from the look on his face, she knew for the first time that he truly was. Letting her passion have its way, she slid down off her horse and kissed him on the lips.

"It's so beautiful," she said. "Thank you. I love you, Arky."

"Me, too." Arky nodded, his face red. He looked around at the crowd to see if anyone had noticed Alma's display.

They hurried back to camp, where the excitement and expectations were almost as thick as the flies that had blown in with the awful wind. The insects were persistent, relighting as soon as they were batted away. Larkes and the oldest Frey boy kept busy trying to brush them off the horses.

Other members of the group were passing the time the best they could. Helena looked after the impatient children and broke up their squabbles. The wind and heat had been miserable enough without the pesky flies, and the children, who were too young to care about land runs and such, had gotten especially cross.

Schoonover gave a last-ditch effort to hone Reinhart's riding skills. Reinhart had managed to stop taking spills off the sorrel's back, but Schoonover worried to Larkes that he still wasn't sure the German could hold his own in the race.

They had made camp well away from the throng of people that had grouped next to the starting line, but during the last few hours, folks had started to gather around them. Soon, they were surrounded by a crowd that had swelled to over ten thousand.

A vendor wove his way through the people, singing, "Lemonade! Nice and sweet and hard to beat! Two glasses for five cents!"

The children followed the vendor around like he was the Pied Piper, begging for lemonade in spite of Helena's scolding to leave the poor man alone. Finally, Arky put an end to the fuss and, ignoring Helena's disapproval, bought each child a cup.

The afternoon finally wore into evening, though most members of the group could have sworn the day had had a few extra hours thrown into it. The wind was whipping up harder, to where it felt like a giant furnace was blowing heat against the weary people. By now, everyone looked grimy and miserable. The children complained that their mouths tasted dirty, so Helena cut a rag into pieces and dipped them in the water for the children to suck on.

As the evening began to turn dark, Reasa took over for Helena. She sat the children in a circle and told them a story. Then, to everyone's surprise, she began to sing. Everyone stopped what they were doing and listened. She had a fine singing voice, strong and throaty. She sang several songs, her voice rising over the hum of the wind. Larkes sat in amongst the children to listen, enamored with her beauty and this newly discovered talent.

One by one, they went to bed. Alma and Arky stayed up past the others. They talked about their future together. Arky told her about the plans he had made to go into the horse business with Larkes and Schoonover. This suited Alma just fine. She wouldn't have cared if Arky had said he was going into pig farming or butterfly ranching. The fact that there was a prospect of owning her own home, with land, was almost more than she could fathom. She held onto Arky's hand and looked lovingly at his handsome face.

"When we build our house," she said, "I want a nice big room for Toby Ray."

"Sure enough," Arky said. He played with her fingers and went on thoughtfully. "The way I see it, I'll dig us a dugout right away. There's this man I talked to in Hennessey this morning who said he'd sell me some nice wood for a house. He'll even haul it up to the claim for me. You know, Alma, what with the money Reinhart gave me—" He stopped. "—I mean, *us,* and with the winnin's from bettin' on Larkes' horse, we've got us enough money to open up an account. I wanna do business with that banker from Tennessee, that Jennings feller."

Alma nodded, so Arky went on. "The three of us— Larkes, Rocky and me—are goin' to Kingfisher to start with. Rocky says there's a man down there with good horse flesh to sell. We'll start out with a few horses and buy us some cows, too. Get a good herd goin'. We've got enough money to do that, Alma." He smiled as he waited for her reaction. "And maybe enough to build us a nice house right away."

"That's so wonderful!" Alma said. She put her head against his shoulder. She didn't want this night to end. She was afraid that if she went to sleep, she'd wake up to find this was all just a dream.

But Arky wasn't finished with his plans. "You know, Alma," he went on, "I ain't never been worth a dern with money. When we git settled in and open up that account, I want you to run it. The money, that is."

"I couldn't do that!" Alma said. "It's your money!"

"Listen, Alma. It's *our* money. The way I see it, everything is fifty-fifty. In fact, if it's all right with you, I'd like to put five dollars in an account for Toby Ray. We could add to it every month. That way, he'll have something to start out with when he gets grown."

Alma couldn't believe what she was hearing. As much as she loved Arky, there was a feeling for Toby Ray that went too deep to understand or explain. Just to think that her brand new husband felt a love for her brother was overwhelming. She didn't know what to say.

"Arky—"

"Aw, it ain't nothin'," he said casually. "I just think a boy deserves help gettin' started, if a person's able. I want you to see to it that Toby Ray has a good nest egg to build on. Like I said, Alma, I ain't never been able to keep a dern cent, and I want that to change."

Alma nodded. She'd never had money to manage before, and the thought of so much responsibility was a bit unnerving to her. But, she reassured herself, she'd always been a quick learner.

"So," Arky was saying, "I was thinkin' we'd go ahead and buy the stock, then build us a house. I'd like a big front room with a fireplace and a nice kitchen and dinin' room and a little sewin' room for you. I saw this house once in Little Rock. The way it was made, it had a bedroom downstairs and three more upstairs. We could build our house like that. You 'n I could take the room downstairs. Then, there'd be one upstairs for Toby Ray and one for Ma. And, you know, we might have a young'n sometime. That last bedroom would be for him."

There was silence. Concerned that he might have said something wrong, Arky asked, "You would like a young'n, wouldn't you? Someday? It don't have to be right away."

Alma couldn't hold back any more. Tears welled up in her eyes. "Oh, Arky! Yes, I want children. Whatever pleases you is what I want." She thought about the large Frey brood and how happy they always seemed. "Isn't it wonderful watching Helena with her family?" she said. "But, I don't ever want us to get so taken by our children that Toby Ray is left out."

"Why, we wouldn't do that!" Arky said, surprised. "I like the boy."

"I know you do, and that's more than I could ever hope for," Alma said. "But you gotta understand. We've been through so much, Toby Ray and me. Why, he just lost his mama, and his papa drowned before that. I lost 'em, too, but now I've got you. Arky, I love that boy so much, I couldn't stand to see him come second."

"He won't, Alma. I promise. In fact, as soon as he's old enough, we'll git him right in the business with us.

'Sides that, he's a tough one. I don't reckon I've ever seen a boy as tough. He's pretty good at watchin' over himself. We'll give 'im a good life, and by the time he's old enough to set out on his own, he'll be more'n ready."

They went to sleep then, wrapped in each other's arms.

That night, a peace fell over the land as the hopeful slept. The wind swept over the prairie, carrying its own song.

Tomorrow was a new beginning for life's dreamers. Not since Moses had led the Israelites had so many gathered in search of their promised land.

45

LARKES AWOKE, JUST AS THE FIRST LIGHT OF THE DAY was sneaking over the horizon. A cool northerly wind blew against his face. He took in a deep breath and tasted the dust in the air. He wished the weather would stay just as it was right now. But he knew it would again turn hot as the day wore on.

He stretched his long legs and reached down to rub Reasa's thigh. There were a lot of aspects to marriage that weren't so pleasant and took some getting used to, but waking up next to Reasa wasn't one of them. He fought off the urge to touch her even more and climbed out of the bedroll.

By the time he had finished pulling on his boots, he could hear Helena stirring in the wagon, tending to one of her little ones. From the north, where most of the people were camped, he could smell coffee blowing his way. Larkes felt hungry. Soon, Helena would have their campfire going.

While the others in his group were starting to wake up, Larkes gave the horses a good watering and feeding, knowing they weren't likely to eat again before evening. Then, he saddled up the gelding and rode out south toward Hennessey. He talked to the horse as he took it through its morning exercise.

"You wanna loosen up those muscles, boy," he said. "This is your day, big one. We're gonna get Reasa her piece of the promised land." They loped along at a leisurely pace for a mile, then turned back toward camp.

He rode in as Reasa was combing her hair. A surge of pride ran through him when he saw her. For the first time, he smiled at her first. It seemed to take Reasa by surprise. She blinked a time or two, then smiled back and waved to him like he was some long-lost relative.

Helena had cooked up a big breakfast. "Eat hearty," she said to everyone. "Who knows vhen ve eat goot meal again." She served up bacon and eggs and hot coffee.

Larkes was ravenous this morning. He ate fast, catching a whispered warning from Reasa to slow down.

Around the camp, everyone was nervous. Very little was said. Small talk seemed unnecessary. Arky and Alma talked in low voices between themselves. Rocky Schoonover, who usually enjoyed riding in for morning conversation over his coffee, sat off by himself. All eyes kept a watch to the north. Up ahead, the crowd was growing as people jockeyed to get a good position near the cottonwood tree, where the race was designated to begin.

Finally, Arky broke the group's silence. He sipped the last of his coffee and slapped at his leg. His voice was a little quavery. "Well, Hoss, think we need to get in line? It's already gettin' several rows deep over there."

Larkes peered at the people who swarmed around the starting line. "I reckon it'd be best to wait 'til just a little before the race. That way we'll keep the horses rested and not get 'em all hot 'n nervous. The way I see it, we'll quickly distance ourselves from all the folks that ain't on horseback."

"That's a good idea, compadre," Schoonover agreed. "Ain't no use in standin' there in this heat and gettin' ourselves and the horses all worn out."

While the men were having their discussion, Helena got up and stood their with her hands on her hips, waiting for them to finish. When she had their attention, she made her announcement.

"I vill make der run."

"What was that?" Arky said, unable to hide the shock on his face.

Helena went on. "Vehn I vas little girl, my papa had two horses. Very fast. I ride since I am dis tall." She held her hand at knee length. "Reinhart cannot handle der horse. His people not goot at riding. I vill ride in his place. He can bring vagon vith Reasa und Alma."

Arky looked at Larkes. Larkes shrugged.

"Whatever," he said. "If she can ride like she says she can, they'll be miles ahead. No disrespect, Reinhart."

Reinhart nodded. "She ist goot vith der horse."

Arky still sat with his mouth open. He finally managed to say, "Well, I'll be derned."

Schoonover seemed almost relieved that Reinhart wasn't going to ride. Helena couldn't do any worse. He nodded to her. "That sorrel horse is a good one," he said. "He'll give you good speed. Now, what we're gonna do is try to separate ourselves. The four of us."

Helena nodded her understanding.

"Are you sure you can keep up?" Arky said, staring at her uncertainly.

Helena snorted. "Ach! Keep up?" she said. "Don't be vorry about me. You vorry about getting land for Alma."

Everyone in the group laughed.

At eleven-fifteen, the four of them saddled up. Reasa brought bologna, crackers and canteens of water for each and packed them on the horses' backs. Alma handed them each a three-foot-long wooden stake with their names printed on the side. One end of each stake had been sharpened to a point so that it could be driven into the ground. At each site, there would be a flag with the legal description of that claim. The flag was to be replaced by the wooden stake when the claim was made.

By eleven-thirty, they had joined the mass of people. Vendors were still trying to sell their wares up to the last minute. A hog train with forty stock cars sat waiting to roll. It was covered with all kinds of humanity. People were hanging from the train anywhere a hold could be found. Wagons, surreys, bicycles were everywhere. People stood on foot, and there was even a strange-looking bicycle with only one wheel.

All around, Larkes noticed the boisterous behavior of the crowd had turned subdued. The faces of the people had turned cold. Gone was the smiling consideration of one's neighbor. It was every person for himself. Larkes could see in all of them a desperation, as they considered their futures, dangling out in front of them.

Desperation was color-blind, Larkes realized as he gazed at the sea of white faces around him. He knew how they felt. After all, Negroes had faced desperation all their lives. He felt a pang of compassion for those who had gambled everything to come here. One of the federal soldiers had told him that one hundred thousand people were encircling the Outlet, vying for only a little over thirty-seven thousand claims. Not only that, but there were the lawless to contend with. The same soldier had told of how, in the big run of '89, the sooners had sneaked across the line early and lain in hiding at their chosen claim sites. There had been shootings over land that was claimed by more than one.

Today, too, many would leave this land, heartbroken. Some might even lose their lives. Larkes wondered if there would be sooners sitting on their claims when they reached them.

"What are you thinkin' about, Hoss?" Arky said.

Larkes gave him a weak smile. "I was just thinkin' there's gonna be one hell of a lot of confusion here in a little bit."

"Boy, howdy," Arky agreed. He looked as fidgety as a cat. "What do you think we oughta do?"

"I think we oughta stay together, just like we planned. Try to outdistance the others." Larkes smiled. "Then, we'll ride right up to our claims and stake our new land."

Arky gave him a nervous grin. "Right."

At ten minutes until noon, as the ten thousand waited to hear the single pistol shot that would cata- pult them forward, something happened. There was no distinguishable sound or movement, but suddenly the crowd started moving. Early or not, the race had begun.

A great roar went up as men whooped and hollered and whipped their horses into motion. Families yelled encouragement. Moving with the flow, Larkes let the gelding have its way amongst the crowd.

The noise was deafening. Right away, wagons overturned. Bicycle riders were thrown, horses stumbled and fell, breaking their legs. Those who were on foot had to dodge wheels and pounding hooves. Mayhem was everywhere around him. Larkes heard people cry out in desperation, some in pain as they were trampled. Looters quickly moved in to pick up items that fell from the broken wagons. A huge cloud of dust swirled through the air.

Some stopped to make claims immediately, taking the first flag they came to. Land was being gobbled up like a fire spreading through a field of hay.

The riders on horseback quickly pulled away from the others. At first, they ran neck and neck. The riders leaned down low and encouraged their horses. The animals seemed to know what was expected of them.

Within a mile, the gelding was out in front with Rocky Schoonover's roan right behind. Arky and Helena rode at the head of the next wave of about fifty riders, some fifteen yards behind.

After three miles, Larkes and Schoonover had pulled so far ahead, they were barely visible to Helena and Arky, who along with five other riders had managed to move a good ways ahead of the rest. Arky looked sideways at Helena and the sorrel. She was matching him stride for stride. She nodded at him and shouted, "Dis ist goot!"

"It's good!" he yelled back.

Up ahead, the big gelding had already worked up a good lather. Larkes slowed the pace a little.

"These horses seem to like the excitement," he hollered to Schoonover. "I believe they could run all day like this."

"I believe you're right, compadre."

They'd been running for half an hour when Larkes pulled the gelding to a stop and turned around. Behind them, there wasn't a rider in sight. Off in the distance, a cloud of dust drifted up into the sky.

"What do you say we unsaddle and rest 'em while we wait on Arky and Helena?" he said.

"Sounds fine," Schoonover said, dismounting.

They didn't have long to wait before they spotted four riders approaching. Larkes felt a relief when he recognized Arky and Helena out front.

"Looks like them," he said.

"By damn, I believe you're right. That Helena wasn't lyin' about her ridin' ability," Schoonover commented.

They quickly resaddled their horses and mounted up, just as Arky and Helena rode up. Arky carried a wide grin that stretched from ear to ear.

"What do you say we head in a more westerly direction?" he said.

Schoonover said, "That's fine, but first let's lose those other two."

They didn't have to worry, because the other two riders stayed on course to the north, heading toward the Enid townsite.

"Well, I'd say that was right accommodatin' of 'em," Schoonover said.

They pulled up to let Arky and Helena's horses catch a short rest. After five minutes, they were on their way again.

The four animals ran a magnificent race, with the gelding maintaining its lead. They rode across land that was vast, rolling and beautiful, just as Arky had described it.

Up ahead, they saw a ravine. On the other side, a growth of trees stretched across a large area.

"That's our claim!" Schoonover shouted. He pointed. "Right up there in those trees!"

They slowed to a lope, staring at the fresh land that lay before them with a kind of awe.

"Listen, Hoss," Arky said, "are we still in agreement on the land?"

Larkes looked at the others, and they nodded.

"Well, then, me and Rocky'll take the land right on the other side of that ravine," Arky said. He pointed. "See that little rise on further north?" he said to Larkes. "With the two big trees? That's your claim."

My claim, Larkes repeated to himself. The words rang in his ears. It sounded like a fairy tale. His eyes moistened, and he turned his face away so as not to show his emotion to the others. He'd never felt so overwhelmed in his life.

He'd always felt Reasa was foolish, but it was he who had been the foolish one, he thought. He'd let himself be whipped by the idea that Reasa had manipulated his life. But it wasn't manipulation, he realized. It was opportunity.

In that moment, all the anguish over the changes he'd been forced to make in his life was gone. He felt a peace and a happiness settle over him that could only have been made better by Reasa's presence. He blinked away a sudden tear and mouthed the words silently.

"Thank you, dear Father in Heaven."

Without looking at the others, he took in a deep breath and said, "Well, what are we waitin' for?" and gave spur to the gelding. Behind him, the others laughed and followed.

They were within forty yards of the ravine when the sound of a rifle shot split the air. Larkes started to pull rein, when underneath him the gelding made a terrifying sound and fell to its front knees, throwing Larkes over its neck. As Larkes hit the ground, he heard popping sounds all around as bullets cut through the prairie grass.

He rolled behind his horse and pulled his Winchester from its holster. He jacked a round into the chamber. Up ahead in the ravine, he could see the tops of several hats, even a couple of faces. Then, he spotted Deputy Frank crouched low, with his Winchester issuing smoke.

Helena Frey screamed as her sorrel was shot out from under her. She lay flat on the ground, hugging the earth.

"The son of a bitches are killin' our horses!" Schoonover shouted. He jumped from the back of his roan and smacked its rump. "Git!" He fell to his knee and started firing his Winchester.

Arky's mare kicked, throwing him from the saddle. Quickly, he ran over to where Helena lay and tried his best to shield her large form with his own.

The shooting stopped. Deputy Frank's voice called out.

"You sumbitches are 'bout to trespass on my land. Now, git, 'cause the next shots won't be for the horses."

Schoonover dived in beside Larkes behind the gelding.

"Son of a bitch," he mumbled. "Any man that would shoot a man's horse ain't worth livin'. I didn't come here to die for no land," he went on. "Land don't mean that much to me. But I'll be damned if some son of a bitch is gonna make me turn tail and run."

His words were lost on Larkes. He was staring at his horse. Its nostrils flared as it tried to suck in more air. Blood was streaming from its neck, forming a dark pool in the dust.

"You got sixty seconds, nigger boy, to gather up your nigger lovers and hightail it outta here, before we get serious."

Larkes looked up. Deputy Frank's face had appeared over the edge of the ravine. Larkes stared at the smirk that he wore. Then he looked back down at his dying gelding.

A rage crept over him, consuming him. All thoughts were blocked from his mind. In one quick motion, he had the rifle to his cheek. He squeezed the trigger.

His aim was dead center. The bullet caught Deputy Frank high in the forehead, blowing out the back of his brain.

One of the deputy's companions suddenly raised up and stared down at the body.

"Why, the nigger sumbitch done killed him!" he said.

No sooner had the companion spoken, when Schoonover shot him dead.

The silence filled the air. Larkes and Schoonover waited for another challenge from the ravine, but no one moved. Then, a voice called out.

"Hey there! We don't want no more trouble. This was Frank's fight and now he's dead. Let us go."

Just then, the gelding let out a shuddery breath and died.

"No," Larkes said.

Schoonover touched Larkes' arm. "Gosh, compadre, I'm sorry," he said sadly. "But much as we'd like to, we can't kill all of the sorry bastards."

Slowly, Larkes turned his head and looked Schoonover in the eye. He nodded.

Schoonover hollered out, "Throw out your guns and come on out and don't try nothin' silly." He paused. "That is, if any of ya hopes to see the light of another day."

He looked at Arky, who had managed to take Helena into the shelter of a clump of trees and was standing with his pistol cocked. "Get in and cover 'em from behind, compadre. If any one of the sorry bastards even blinks wrong, shoot 'im."

As the men came out of the ravine, Schoonover ordered them to sit in a circle with their hands behind their heads. Then he instructed them each to empty their pockets and lay out their gunbelts, one at a time.

Arky counted the men, including the two who were dead. He said, "If I recall, there was eight of ya before. One's missin'." He trained his pistol on a man sitting closest. "Where's he at?"

"What other one?" the man said in a scared voice.

"Back there at the registration booth. There was eight of ya. Where's the eighth man?"

Another man said, "That was Bob. He went back home to Arkansas."

"Is that where all you boys are from?" Schoonover asked.

"No, sir," one said. He was barely out of his teens. "I'm from Missouri. Joe there"—he nodded his head—"is from Texas."

"It's a shame you boys rode all the way from Missouri and Texas to take up with the likes of a scum like Frank," Schoonover said. "Do you know what the sentence is for killin' a horse in Oklahoma Territory? It's hangin'. Sure enough." He turned to Larkes. "Let's hang their asses."

"Please, mister," the young one begged. "We don't have nothin' against you folks. It was all Frank's doin'."

Schoonover considered his statement a moment. "Well, then, if you all want to leave your money and horses here with us, then I guess we might consider alterin' your sentence somewhat."

"Yessir, mister," the young one said. "Take the horses. Ain't got but about three dollars, but you're welcome to it." He pointed to the pile of change that lay on the ground.

Another man that looked to be mostly Indian, sat there looking angry. He spat. "You expect us to walk in this heat? Do you know how far it is to anywhere?"

Before anyone could blink an eye, Larkes shot the man in the foot. The man started to scream. Arky, who stood not more than five feet away, jumped back and hollered, himself.

Larkes' words were measured. His eyes had filled with hatred. "You fellers gonna argue, or walk?"

There was silence among the men. The young one started crying.

"P-please, mister. Don't shoot no more of us!" he said. "We're sorry. Sorry as can be."

Arky kicked him in the shoulder. It bothered him to see a grown man cry. He said, "Ain't no call to be cryin'. What would your mama think? You heard what the man said. Git yer asses on outta here while ya still can!"

The men jumped to their feet and started to leave, but Schoonover said, "Not so fast, boys. Take your friend, here, with ya." He pointed at the man that Larkes had shot in the foot.

As they watched them leave, Arky shook his head. There was a tinge of sadness in his voice. He said, "Derned if I can stand to see a grown man cry." He turned to the others. "Reckon they'll come back?"

Schoonover shook his head. "No, compadre. Some men would, but not these ol' boys. Sorry bastards like them only understand one thing." He looked at Larkes. "And they just got a bellyful of it."

46

IN THE DISTANCE, RIDERS WERE STARTING TO FILL THE landscape. Larkes pulled the white flag out of the ground and drove his stake in its place. He took out a pencil and scribbled the legal description on the stake, copying the information from the flag.

Suddenly, he was overcome with a weariness that both weakened and pleased him. He sat down on the little rise. He could see a long ways off. Wagons and horses dotted the land below. He reached down and picked up a handful of dirt. It could have been a handful of gold, he thought, and it wouldn't have felt as good as that hot, dry Oklahoma dirt felt. Promised land, he whispered to himself.

He opened his hand and let the wind carry away the dirt, then he scooped up some more.

He'd been sitting there for a couple of hours, when Helena and Arky rode up. Arky was towing a saddle horse behind him. "This is the best of the lot," he said. "I know it can't replace the gelding, but I believe this mare'll make you a good horse."

Wordlessly, Larkes climbed atop the horse. He and Helena set out for the Government Springs Well, while Arky and Schoonover stayed behind to keep anyone from stealing their claims.

Larkes choked back a lump in his throat as he rode past the gelding's body. A coyote had already found the carcass and was ripping at its belly.

In the ravine, buzzards circled around the bodies of Deputy Frank and his companion. Helena watched the scavaging birds and made a satisfied grunt.

"Dat ist goot," she said with a bitterness. "Let der buzzards have at their rotten flesh."

When they reached the town of Enid, they were shocked at the sudden transformation. Canvas tents had been erected everywhere. Buildings were already being hammered together. People milled about. Some were arguing and fighting over the fact that many claims had more than one contester. Others were eagerly getting to know their new neighbors. City plots were being plowed, and the vendors still shouted their wares.

Helena seemed awed by the scene around her. "Ach, dis Enid vill be big town!" she murmured. "Dat ist goot!"

At the Government Springs Well, they searched until they found the two wagons. Helena jumped off her horse and ran to Reinhart and her children. Alma was with them, clutching Toby Ray by the shoulders.

"Is Arky all right?" she asked anxiously.

Helena laughed. "Arky ist goot. He is on your land. You and der little Toby Ray's land." She rubbed the boy's head. "Ja, Arky and der Rocky stay and vatch over der claims." She took Alma's hand. "Ach, der land is so beautiful, Alma!"

"Arky got land, too?" Toby Ray said. He looked up at Alma and smiled happily.

"Ve *all* get land. Goot, fertile land," Helena said. "Ve vill be neighbors. Ja, is goot." She turned to her husband and smiled. "Ve must go now. Git everyvon loaded on der wagons," she ordered him.

Reasa was standing off by herself, waiting. Larkes was touched by her beauty. She seemed breathless, almost afraid. Her eyes were serious and questioning as they swept over him, down to the horse and back to his face.

"Where's the gelding?" she asked.

Larkes rode up close to her and dismounted. To her surprise, he took her by the shoulders and pulled her close, hugging her tight. "It's dead," he said.

"What?" she gasped as she tried to pull away.

He pulled her tight again.

"Oh, Larkes, I'm so sorry. What happened?" she asked.

He let his arms rest on her shoulders and buried his face in her hair. He didn't feel like talking about his horse or Deputy Frank or anything else that had happened. All he wanted to do was stand there and hold Reasa close, letting her love soothe and comfort him and take away the pain. He took in a deep breath. "Where's Noah?"

"Over yonder," she said, "with the other babies."

Larkes pulled back from her and smiled. "Well, then, go and fetch our baby," he whispered. "I wanna take you to your promised land."

47

THAT EVENING, AS THE SUN DRIFTED WEST, AND THE prairie wind blew, Toby Ray ran freely in the tall grass with Jacob, one of the Frey boys. Arky sat against a tree, with Alma in front of him, her head pressed against his chest. She held onto his hands.

"Right here's where I wanna build our house," Arky said. "Facing west. That way, the north wind won't be so harsh. I'll put your kitchen on this side, so the eastern sun can brighten your mornin's." He pulled his hand free, picked up a rock and tossed it. "Right there. That'll be our bedroom. What do you think about that, Alma?"

But Alma didn't answer him. Her eyes were closed and her thoughts had drifted to her mother. She and Toby Ray had been born in a home that was dirt-poor, but enriched with love. Even their papa, the gambler that he was, had been a loving man. But fate had pulled them from that small happiness in the drafty, weatherworn cabin and crossed them through a hellish time of uncertainty and terror. Now, as they relaxed on their own peaceful land, under the hot Oklahoma sky, she gave thanks to the Lord. She no longer had any argument with Him.

Slowly, contentedly, she pulled Arky's arms around her shoulders. "This here's Arky, Mama," she whispered softly. "He's my husband. He's gonna take good care of us. All this beautiful land is ours." She started to weep silently.

"Oh, and just look at Toby Ray, Mama! Look at your baby boy. He's happy! Everything's gonna be all right."